W9-CML-432

PASSION'S PROXY

Dorothy had experienced the dream in a hundred variations. Each time, the shadow-figure that came to her was Paul Ely. In the shadow-play, his clothing and his man-scent were the main clues to his presence. And his hands. His large, sensitive hands caressing and searching out every curve and recess of her body, until it was tingling with a million tiny needle-pricks of anticipation.

Now, fighting against the rising sensations, trying to awake and yet secretly desiring it never to stop, she was rising to a whole new plane of feeling. She knew that the pain would come any moment, and the dream would end as it always had, in frustration and unfulfilled need.

But . . . something was different. This time, she felt a coming-together without pain, felt herself moving toward a glorious, explosive crescendo.

And then, abruptly, she reached out and simultaneously awoke. This was no dream, and the man who was assaulting her senses was not Paul Ely.

It was Dunraven, who had despoiled the land and who now was despoiling her deep passion. She let out a sharp, piercing cry. . . .

The Making of America Series

The Wilderness Seekers
The Mountain Breed
The Conestoga People
The Forty-Niners
Hearts Divided
The Builders
The Land Rushers
The Wild and the Wayward
The Texans
The Alaskans
The Golden Staters
The River People
The Landgrabbers

THE LAND-GRABBERS

Lee Davis Willoughby

A DELL/BRYANS BOOK

Published by
Dell Publishing Co., Inc.
1 Dag Hammarskjold Plaza
New York, New York 10017

Copyright © 1981 by Barry Myers

All rights reserved. No part of this book
may be reproduced or transmitted in any form
or by any means, electronic or mechanical, including
photocopying, recording or by any information storage
and retrieval system without the written permission
of the Publisher, except where permitted by law.

Dell ® TM 681510, Dell Publishing Co., Inc.

ISBN: 0-440-04762-5

Printed in the United States of America
First printing—February 1981

1

THE WINDJAMMER *Shannon* was twelve days out of Dublin with sixteen passengers and a cargo of peat moss.

The barometer had been falling steadily all day, much to the Captain's concern. The weather had been unremittingly gloomy since the ship had left the Irish Sea, and the Atlantic had behaved itself as badly as could be expected in mid-October. But, it was not until the barometer had begun its startling plummet that the Captain had become truly concerned. The *Shannon* was off the Newfoundland banks, an area of the voyage the Captain had never completely overcome his fear and mistrust of, knowing as he did that crashing onto the rocky reefs of this barren wasteland would mean certain death to all aboard.

At tea time the steam engines had finally spluttered into activity, and he was able to order the reefing of the enormous sails. The storm was still clawing its way over the snowfields of Labrador, but forewarning its approach was a rising gale which lifted the already menacing waves to mountainous heights.

The passengers took their tea in the plush, ornately gilded salon. All hatches had been battened down, and the decks put off limits. The lamps, fastened in their sconces on the walls, flickered and flared with the lurching of the ship. For the majority of the passengers this was a first sea voyage, a frightening experience even in the best of weather. Almost to a man the faces were pale and worried as they huddled on little gilt chairs in small, segregated groups. The *Shannon* had no designated class breakdown on its passenger list, but clothing, speech and positioning at the Captain's table created its own divisions.

One young woman was always on the Captain's right, although she never indulged in conversation with the Captain or other passengers. By tacit agreement she was left quite alone. The only person who dared approach her was a plump, middle-aged woman that the others automatically assumed was her chaperone.

The young woman was always attired in richly colored fabrics that high-lighted the burnished copper tones of her lush, flowing hair. Obviously high-born, her face seemed frozen in a haughty mask that was ever-unsmiling. Her ancestors had blessed her with a high, noble forehead which accented a pair of commanding brown eyes and a perfect nose that ended in a delicate upward tilt.

Many of the women thought her aristocratic nose represented perfectly her open disdain of their lowly position. As women will do, they all speculated on who she might be and why she was aboard the *Shannon* in the first place.

And as men will do, they speculated on other aspects of the young woman. Always excellently coiffured, her wardrobe suggested the exquisite body they were draped upon, but never hinted at sexuality in the least. At times, when talking with the older woman companion, her brown eyes would become flecked with a sparkling green dust and, when aroused in anger, the creamy smoothness and tone of her complexion would flush in a betrayal of what must have been a youthful showering of freckles.

But it was the full-lipped sensuous mouth that drew the men's fullest attention. It was a measure of all her moods. It could pout with pique and grow taut with irritation, it could be more Cheshire than the cat himself; and being pure Celtic it could quirk with wit. And then, it could expand to expose impossibly perfect teeth that seemed to sparkle with her levity. And when she was thus, no man could help but stare in awe at her natural beauty.

But, at twenty, these moods were fleeting and could pass in the batting of an eye. Mainly, she remained haughty and unapproachable.

Now she sat alone and apart, her brown eyes gazing out a porthole with an expression of yearning and despair. The plump matron approached slowly, too shy to impose upon the preoccupation of the young woman's thought. But she heard the rustle of crinoline, and giving a slight start turned. Seeing the older woman, staring with admiration, she smiled, and made a gentle gesture of welcome. "I thought you were going to stay abed, Mabel."

Mabel Allgood smiled too, and curtsied. "Aye, it was me intent, your ladyship. But this large belly of mine seemed to want to match the frothin' waves."

"Then sit and take some tea."

Mabel sighed and totally covered the gilt chair as she sat.

"The sittin' I'm thankful for, mi'lady, but I'll be thankin' you no for the tea. I'm sloushin' about enough as 'tis."

Lady Dorothy Goold laughed lightly. "It won't

last long, Mabel. Yesterday the Captain said we should have a fourteen day crossing."

The flinty blue eyes grew skeptical. "That was before this awful storm brewed up. Are you sure yer not a little frightened?"

"Frightened?" asked the lady in some surprise. "Whatever is there to be frightened of, Mabel?"

"Just a feeling," said Mabel gently. "I'd be sellin' me soul to Lucifer himself to be back home in Adare."

Lady Dorothy grew very quiet. The words echoed her own thoughts. The woman is as homesick as I, thought Dorothy sympathetically. It had almost taken an edict from the Holy See to get Mabel to accompany her on the journey. Dorothy's personal feelings had been much the same. She had no desire to see America. Because of the potato famines of the early 1800s, she felt America would be composed only of Irish farmers who had deserted their homeland. She was an Irishwoman born and bred and thought it the only place for a true Irishman.

Her family was one of the few of the Irish peerage that could boast of a purely Celtic origin and could trace its lineage directly to historic Ollioll Olum, monarch of Ireland at the beginning of the third Century. Adare, County Limerick, was the castle in which her mother's family had resided since 1634.

She couldn't help but resent her fellow passengers, fugitives as she saw it, escaping from a great religious and historical heritage, racing to an unknown place where evil must certainly await them.

Mabel examined the quiet young face she had known from early childhood, saw that the brown eyes were fearless and as clear as a still brook, and smiled again.

"Still, I'll be longin' to put these old legs on solid ground again. I'm just prayin' that your wee uncle has put aside his black and heathen ways."

Lady Dorothy laughed again. "I doubt that Uncle Walter is any longer 'wee', Mabel. You must remember that it is thirty years since he left home."

Mabel scowled deeply. "And our gracious Lord didn't tell me I'd be lookin' upon his godless face again, I'm telling you honestly. It makes me old heart weep to think of the dastardly things he did to your dear dead father."

Dorothy nodded and sighed, but refrained from comment. Until six weeks before she had been unaware of her late father's brother. Out of the blue he had sent a representative from his London offices to the Castle Adare. His eldest daughter was to be married in early November and it was his fondest wish for his sister-in-law to honor them with her attendance.

Lady Jane Whyham-Quin Goold was at first skeptical. Her mother, Lady Margaret, was livid with rage. She accurately recalled an image of a handsome, impetuous youth of sixteen, eager for adventure, but well knowing how to find trouble at every bend in the road. To her way of thinking he would always be a stain upon the good name of her son-in-law. It had cost Sir Thomas Goold a small fortune to buy the lad out of trouble and exile him to the colonies. Now she thought her daughter quite insane to even acknowledge the man.

Lady Jane, for ten years the voice of authority

in family matters, had ideas of her own. She feared that this might be Walter's opening gambit to claim something from his dead brother's estate. Cool, resourceful and meticulous in all things, she quietly had Walter Goold thoroughly investigated.

She was not surprised to learn that he had changed his name to Gould upon arriving in America. She was, however, very surprised to learn that his International Insurance Company of New York did indeed have offices in London and assets in England and America that made her late husband's estate look insignificant in comparison.

What then was he after? There were no grounds on which he could claim his brother's title—he had signed away that right thirty years earlier. Lady Jane did not like mysteries and knew that to refuse the invitation would be to leave certain questions hanging, unanswered, in her mind. Nothing was allowed to hang in limbo around Lady Jane. Over the strong objections of Lady Margaret she began to make plans to attend the wedding in New York.

Lady Dorothy was given no opportunity to object or comment. It was automatically assumed that the young lady would accompany her mother.

A week before they were due to sail from Dublin on the *Shannon*, Lady Jane's favorite mount threw her and she sustained a broken leg. Although Lady Margaret thought that the trip must, of course, be canceled, it was inconsistent with Lady Jane's character to allow plans to be changed over such a minor matter. Her daughter would simply have to represent the family alone.

Lady Jane had all the faith in the world in Dorothy. As an only child she had made certain that Dorothy had received the finest education available, which included tutors and the best private schools. Both Ladies Jane and Margaret had enlightened the young lady on all aspects of the family estates, farms and business enterprises. Her coterie was expertly selected with an eye toward her future. She was a well-rounded product of her mother's exacting standards. In two-hundred-fifty years no Whyham-Quin or Goold had married for love. That was considered a foolish passion practised only by commoners.

Although the constant assertion of her superiority made Dorothy appear shallow, sophisticated and snobbish, she was ill-aware of it. A spoiled and arrogant child cannot know her level of insufferableness without examples to mirror against.

The demonic howl of the gale brought Lady Dorothy out of her reverie. The anxiety on Mabel Allgood's face was now acute and Dorothy thought she might have missed something.

"What ails you?"

Mabel looked down, her eyes mooned. "The deck . . ." she gasped.

"I know," Lady Dorothy soothed her, "it is only the roll . . ." Her words trailed off. This wasn't the normal pitch and roll of the deck in a storm. Through the leather soles of her shoes she could feel a violent, spasmodic jerking of the deckboards. She looked at the walls and saw that the sconces were barely sufficient to keep the flickering lamps in place.

Someone had prevailed upon one of the lady passengers to regale them with a simple and sentimental old Irish ballad, with the obvious intent being to keep spirits up in the face of the storm.

The heat and stench from the oil lamps was becoming intolerable. Dorothy rose calmly and motioned Mabel to follow her. She couldn't be sure if the vibrations were normal, but sensed that she would feel safer in her own cabin.

But before the older woman could rise to her feet they were taken out from under her as an explosion from below deck shook the salon violently.

For a moment, reeling in the impact of the quake, Dorothy wondered if she had acted too slowly. She grabbed for a post to keep from being pitched about. Far below she could hear other muffled reports, followed by additional vibrations of the salon floor.

Then, suddenly, it was still, the only motion being the normal pitch and roll of the ship. The engines were quiet and Lady Dorothy sensed that the ship had been mortally wounded. The dancing lamplight revealed that the other passengers had drawn the same conclusion. Naked fear had molded their faces into grotesque masks. The woman who had been singing stood wide-eyed, silent, but with her mouth still open. Dorothy adjusted her grip on the post, and allowed herself to lurch easily with the pitching of the vessel. She could hear the baleful groaning of every timber as the ship swayed in the ocean's grip.

Two robust young sailors crashed through the salon on their way to the forward compartment. A stout man of middle age called after them, but they continued ahead without response.

"Saints preserve us," he gasped, crossing himself. "They're afraid to tell us we're sinking!"

It was obvious that he had put into words the

dread of all. Old women in widow's black fell to their knees and brought out rosary beads from the folds of their shawls. Younger women gathered their children about them and began to wail. The men stood in silence, unsure of what action to take.

A strange, wild excitement filled Dorothy. There was nothing in her physical body to suggest strength, but there was in her soul something that rallied against foolhardiness. She was used to standing up to the illiterate farmers on the estate during times of crisis. She knew that in an instant this fear could turn to panic.

Trembling, she braced herself against the post and shouted: "It's to your cabins you should be getting. Put on the jackets the steward showed us the first day out!"

It was the first time they had heard her speak and it was almost as much of a shock as what was going on about them. They stood and blinked back at her foolishly.

The portholes on either side of the salon were lit with a rosy glow as distress flares were lit on the decks above. A young man left his family for a moment to peer out. He spun back, coming within a foot of Dorothy.

"We're doomed!" he bellowed. "She's sinking!"

Without thinking, Dorothy reached out and slapped him soundly on the cheek. She was filled with her own panic, but would not show it.

"Shut up, you fool!" she said. "If the Captain felt we were sinking he'd have men here to escort us to the life-boats."

There was no reaction from the man. But Dorothy felt all eyes upon her. There was not an adult among them that was not her elder, but they were like children in a situation that was new and frightening. It was the six children among them that seemed the least concerned.

"We should all be calm," said Dorothy. Her confident tone was no mean accomplishment in the face of her own doubts. The fog horn was beginning to emit long, mournful blasts. Dorothy turned to face a group of the male passengers who had gathered, as if for direction, at her side.

"If you five gentlemen would go gather up the jackets for your families we'd be better prepared."

There was a silence. But Dorothy knew she had an intent audience.

"I'll be getting ours!" Mabel said soundly and began waddling toward the companionway arch.

After a moment's hesitation, the men, not at all eager to let an old servant woman make them look cowardly, followed in her wake.

Dorothy turned to address the others. "It will only take the men a few minutes, in the meantime we should get ourselves over near the outer deck door and be ready for the Captain's instructions."

She heard a sudden shout on the deck and the next instant the deck hatch was unbattened and came swinging open. "The Captain orders all forward," the sailor shouted against the wind.

There was a gruff sound from the women, a rebellious sound. They were not moving without their menfolk.

It was no time for amenities. Dorothy marched across the salon and took an old woman, still muttering in prayers, under the arm and brought her to her feet.

"I'll not be knowing if it's an old wives tale, mother, but I've heard tell they'll be taking we women and children along first. Would you be coming with me?"

The ship shuddered under their feet and they clung together to hold themselves up, the look in the woman's eyes leaving no doubt that she'd follow Dorothy unquestioningly.

Before a quarter of them were on deck, the men had returned with the jackets—nothing more than cork-filled strips of canvas. Dorothy was quiet and attentive as the sailors quickly instructed them on the use of the jackets. Mabel's was much too small and had to be tied at the front with a sailor's shoelace.

Dorothy cautiously made her way forward. The distress flares continued to burst high overhead, a red shower of sparks drifting back down to meet the ocean. By the light of the deck lanterns the stark and oily swells of the Atlantic made an awesome sight. As Dorothy watched the crewmen readying the lifeboats, she could not help but wonder how such flimsy craft could be expected to stay afloat in the face of such waves. The icy gale, laden with salt, roared by her ears. She began to think it would be safer to stay aboard. The sky was black, not a star visible.

"Ahoy!" came a voice on the wind, curt and surly.

From high above the lookout's call was returned. More flares were shot into the sky, now added to those of a nearby ship, answering their distress signals. The lights of the approaching ship could be seen, and seemed to glisten and dance on the billowing waves. Racing directly toward them under a full head of steam, the oncoming vessel began to veer sharply and pulled abreast of the foundering windjammer at what seemed the last possible moment.

Captain Bagby, megaphone to mouth, made short work of informing the rescuing Captain of his plight. The boiler had cracked a seam, scalding half the engine crew and leaving them powerless. Fearing a drift onto the banks, Captain Bagby's primary concern was the safety of his passengers.

The *Plymouth Rock* was a privately owned steamer out of New York. The owner would honor the code of the sea and take aboard the passengers, but feared for their lives in being transported across by long boat.

Mabel Allgood nestled close to Dorothy. "Are we rescued or aren't we?" she sniffed. "I knew we should never have left the castle."

Dorothy shrugged, her only feeling that of intense inward relief, as her eyes surveyed the rescuing ship gratefully. "They will figure a way to get us across."

But the way they decided to effect the crossing sent Mabel into new fits of rebellion. Lines were shot back and forth from ship to ship, securing them together. One at a time the passengers were to be strapped into a bos'un's chair and pulled hand over hand above the dancing waves. Some of the younger children would have to be strapped to their fathers' waists for the journey.

But at first it looked like even this plan was going to be doomed to failure.

"It's safe!" shouted Captain Bagby. "You men get your womenfolk up here so that we can start them across!"

"You're mistaken—Captain," said a hard voice. "I'm a fool once for takin' your unsafe vessel, but

I won't be a fool twice and let you throw me wife into the sea!"

A fool? The astute Captain knew that once a man confessed himself to be a fool there was no end to the fools who would follow him.

Dorothy chuckled. She twined her arm affectionately around Mabel.

"Let us show them that women are lesser fools than men. I'll let them send me first and you follow."

A convulsive movement of real fear shook Mabel's stout frame. "I'll not be goin' on that rig and I'll not be lettin' you go, for that matter!"

"Stop it!" Dorothy scolded. "Are you going to be acting like these other damn fools? Now stand back and let them harness me into this contraption. I'm going to cross!"

The first drop made Dorothy wish she had not behaved with such bravery. Her stomach seemed to jump suddenly into her chest as her feet came within inches of the frothing black waves. The howling of the wind between the two bouncing ships pounded savagely in her ears, as the icy spray stung her delicate skin and brought tears into her eyes. Before she was halfway across she was soaked to the skin and shivering uncontrollably.

It seemed to her that this torture would never end. For what seemed an eternity she hung suspended, barely moving except for the lurching and spinning of the canvas seat.

Then the pain gave way to numbness and the sea began to mesmerize her with its rocking, rolling swells. She felt violently ill. She wildly contemplated tearing away the restraining harness and throwing herself down into the sea. Anything would be better than this nightmare journey that would not end. Suddenly, something seemed to snap and she felt an urge to howl with the wind, to throw up her arms in animalistic imprecation and devilish joy.

Then, just as suddenly, the tone of her laughter changed completely. It was no longer the laughter of madness. She was laughing at the wisdom of a Captain who must have made the same journey many times himself. She could not possibly throw herself into the sea, because her arms and hands had been very quietly, and very securely, strapped down to her sides.

Then hands were reaching out and hauling her in upon a steel deck. Warm blankets were placed about her shoulders and a mug of hot tea pressed into her shaking fingers. A tall young officer in sparkling whites tried to persuade her to get in out of the weather, but she felt it her duty to be on hand for Mabel's arrival.

She had to stand and wait for over two hours, her anger mounting with each new arrival. Report after report was given to her of the difficult time the Captain and crew of the *Shannon* were having with the stubborn old woman. Not only was she flatly refusing to be loaded into the bos'un's chair rig, but demanding that she be rowed across or she wasn't going at all.

Then the fourteenth passenger was across and time stood still as they waited the return of the rig again.

Captain Hartog was Dutch and an impatient man. He had planned on steaming well ahead of the storm and making New York harbor by dawn. The owner of the ship was also an impatient man and Hartog did not like being on the bad side of a man like Jim Fisk, Jr. It had already taken every ounce of his persuasion to convince the man to let his ship answer the distress signal.

He paced the deck near the rigging, scowling.

"If she is the same as the rest of this lot," he said to no one in particular, "then leave her be. Queer lot these Irish."

He had not taken a very thorough look at the young woman huddled under the blankets, but now, as he did so, he felt momentary consternation after his remark about the Irish. For this was a Celt face of incredible beauty. Now, Captain Hartog had daily dealings with a man of Irish descent, but James Fisk was a race unto himself. It was the "baser" Irish Captain Hartog had trouble dealing with—the longshoremen, the stewards, the stokers and firemen in his engine room—stubborn men who had to be hit over the head before one could expect their attention. And now he saw that their women could be just as stubborn and as wasteful of his precious time.

"I'll go back for her," Dorothy said doggedly, although it was the last thing in the world she wished to do.

Hartog was struck by the soft, lilting cadence of her voice. It was not guttural and harsh like that of the other women who had been hauled onto his deck. Her statement housed more raw courage than he thought he himself possessed. But even before he could find words to dissuade her of the idea, the lookout called down with relief.

"She's on her way!"

Because of the weight in the chair it dipped precariously close to the waves. Then it swayed and danced as though Mabel was trying to free herself and cast her lot with the sea. The strain on the haulers was immense and Captain Hartog signaled for a change of hands three times. It seemed that every three inches of forward progress they would make, Mabel would jerk the rigging back half a foot.

Then the lines went suddenly limp. The haulers were working with a dead weight and Hartog's anxiety grew. He had heard that the final passenger was an older lady and he feared that she had put too much stress and strain upon her heart in her fight across. He peered into the inky blackness, but could only barely make out a large motionless bulk being inched along.

From his vantage point the lookout couldn't believe what he was seeing. Not wishing to be made a goat, he refrained from calling down his report until he was absolutely certain that his eyes were not deceiving him.

"It be two comin' 'cross, Cap'n," he finally called down and braced himself for a sound retort.

There would be no retort, for Captain Hartog was starting to see the unusual arrangement for himself. Straddling the woman like a baby Koala bear in the arms of its mother was a sailor of goodly size. His legs were wrapped so securely around her that it looked like they were welded together. Around Mabel's ample breasts he had thrown his arms to grasp at the canvas straps at the back of the rig and his head was nestled in the folds of her heavy coat to protect his face from the whipping wind.

It took six burly sailors to haul the two of them to the deck and several minutes for the *Shannon* sailor to unravel himself. The moment they were aboard Dorothy came rushing forward and, ready to scold Mabel for her reluctance to cross, was shocked to see a face that was pale and motionless, as if in death. She feared that the woman's dire omens for the voyage were rapidly bearing fruit.

"Sorry, mi'lady," the robust sailor stammered. "Cap'n thought she'd ride better with an escort. Weren't true. I feared so that she was going to buck me right down into the briney that I . . . well . . . I had to cold-cock her, ma'am."

Hartog hid a wry grin behind his hand as Dorothy stared in disbelief.

"Cap'n sir," the sailor said with a smart salute, "I've a packet from my master to you. And if it's all the same, sir, I'd like to be hauled back before this one comes around."

Hartog granted the request immediately, ordered some sailors to get Mabel onto a stretcher and then broke the seal on the waterproof pouch.

His weather-bleached eyebrows raised as he read Captain Bagby's request to show special courtesy to one Lady Dorothy Whyham-Quin Goold and her servant woman. He tried to restructure in his mind the faces of the women he had seen hauled aboard in an effort to remember one that gave some indication of nobility. The information would be of great interest to Jim Fisk, he was quite sure, but first he had to see to the batting down of the lines between the ships. He knew he would run into great peril with Jim Fisk, but he had already determined that he would have to stand by throughout the night in the event that the *Plymouth Rock* would be needed to rescue the crew of the *Shannon*.

They placed Mabel on a carved plush sofa in an alcove of the grand salon. Dorothy discarded her own blankets and wrapped the woman warmly. Her concern now was for dry clothing, but everything was back aboard the *Shannon.*

"It's all right love," she soothed as Mabel started to come around. "You just had a wee fainting spell."

Mabel's eyes grew flinty. "Faintin' spell me arse! Me jaw feels like the blighter broke it."

A hearty laugh erupted behind them. "And I hear tell you gave him quite a fight before losing."

Dorothy rose and turned. The speaker was a striking figure, tall, ruddy and portly. His light-brown hair was pomaded and carefully waved, his mustache waxed to fine points, and huge diamonds blazed on his frilled shirt front and pudgy fingers.

"Allow me to welcome you aboard," continued Jim Fisk, proudly waving his plump arms about as though to draw attention to the palatial decor of the room. "My men are seeing to quarters for you, Lady Goold."

"You know who I am?" Dorothy asked in some surprise.

"Captain Bagby was gentleman enough to forewarn me. I am Jim Fisk, ma'am. What can I do to be of service to you?"

Dorothy looked about, a little bewildered. She had paid no attention to her surroundings upon entering and was now stunned. The opulence of this floating hotel was overpowering, even to one of Dorothy's privileged background. For the other Irish passengers it was almost as frightening as the ride in the bos'un's chair. They sat huddled together in a corner of the salon afraid to move as much as a muscle. At the far end of the magnificently gilded room sat a dozen elegantly dressed men and women awaiting their host. They stared back at the new arrivals with unmasked wonderment.

"The others," Dorothy stammered, "please see to them. It's been a most unusual experience for them."

Fisk felt a rush of warm delight. Here was real class. Any of his other guests would certainly have thought of themselves first. With a flourish, he waved over a steward. "Have the crew double up to make room for these folks. The galley should be warned of the extra mouths to feed and tell Miss Farrar to come here."

Jim Fisk had a passion for notoriety. He could already see the headlines his "daring" rescue operation would create. He was not aware of how important the young lady might be, but anyone with a title made New York buzz. Polite New York looked askance at Jim Fisk. To them he was vulgar, gross and often ridiculous. As much as possible they tried to ignore him. They would not be able to ignore him after this little exploit.

Ada Farrar was buxom, blowsy and bleached. Under heavy facepaint her expression was warm, rosy and sympathetic. She took the two women under her wing as though they were old school friends. Mabel reacted as though she had been put in the hands of a harlot; Dorothy was just too tired to think.

The *Plymouth Rock* did not possess mere cabins. What would be cabins were suites of luxurious private apartments.

"Ain't these something?" Ada giggled on a

brassy note. "And there are thirty-one more just like it. Of course, only about half of them are being used on this trip. Jimmy doesn't like to be crowded in upon."

Dorothy couldn't help but wonder why the crew was being forced to double up with so many empty suites.

"Now, you ducks get out of those wet things," Ada bubbled on, "And I'll go round up some dry togs so we can all go up to dinner."

"Well!" Mabel exclaimed in her hoarse and toneless voice after the woman's departure, "I'll not be seen in fit company if I must flounce around dressed like that one."

Dorothy's tensions were easing and she couldn't help but giggle over the thought. Ada Farrar's hourglass figure would rule out the possibility of Mabel being able to wear any of the woman's clothing. Dorothy had her own doubts when she saw the armload of garments that was casually tossed over the back of a chair.

"Sorry, ducks," Ada said, in her theatrical voice. "The only woman aboard of her . . . ah . . . *stature* is Jimmy's chambermaid. There's undergarments, a robe and what little else she could offer up."

"That's most generous," Dorothy said quickly, before Mabel could make a rude comment. "Besides, Mabel has decided to retire immediately. Mabel, you may have that bedroom on the right."

Mabel was quite willing to immediately oblige and promptly left Dorothy sifting through the pile of gowns and undergarments with some apprehension. She, too, would have loved nothing more than to bathe away the sticky salt that covered her from head to toe and crawl between warm sheets. But, all else considered, she was famished and quite a bit too curious for sleep.

"I don't think I've ever known a man who owned his own ship," she said, sorting through the gowns.

"Well, Jimmy isn't just any other man, ducks. He's unique. Three years ago he saw me doing me stint in London and pops me back to Ameriky pretty as a picture. Weren't a bloke on Broadway who'd give Ada Farrar a chance though, so Jimmy ups and buys Ada her own theater and show."

Dorothy didn't dare speculate on what manner of show that it might be; she had never been inside a theatre of any sort. Unable to find any garment she felt was suitable, she decided to bathe first. To Dorothy's chagrin and embarrassment, Ada followed right along in her wake, a fountain of bubbling information on Jim Fisk.

"He ain't much liked by the snobs of New York. They call him a vulgarian, whatever that means. He sure got back at those goodies last summer. He took a bunch of us up to that exclusive Continental Hotel in fashionable Long Branch. Well, if you ask me, ducks, it may be fashionable but can't hold a candle to this tub. Well, you should have seen those lard-arses pack up and skidaddle! You would have thought we had arrived with the plague. Stupid cows didn't know that Jimmy was going to get the last laugh. Without knowing who this steamer belonged to, many of them chartered it to take them back to New York."

Dorothy failed to see any levity in the story. She too thought it a little vulgar for the man to impose himself where he wasn't wanted.

Ada Farrar's career had begun as a dresser in

London's West end. She expertly removed the feathers and lace on a beige silk gown, and tucked and folded until it was a perfect fit on Dorothy's lovely frame.

The others were waiting for them in the white marble and mirrored bar. It was an odd assortment of individuals who were introduced to Dorothy. Most of them seemed to be American business associates of Fisk's, with the exception of a lecherous old English general of questionable background.

"Whyham-Quin Goold, did you say, my dear?" he squinted through drink-reddened eyes. "Had an Irish lad in my regiment once by the name of Whyham-Quin. Any relation?"

Dorothy saw no reason to deny the fact. "That would be my mother's cousin, sir. He is the present Earl of Dunraven."

"Jolly good on him!" the old man cackled. "Always glad to see my chaps get along."

Dorothy was glad the subject could be dropped at that point. Windham Thomas Whyham-Quin was another of her mother's pet peeves. Since becoming the fourth earl of his line, he had gone out of his way to snub the Goold side of the family. No one from the Adare Castle had even been invited to the man's wedding the previous April. As it was an internal family matter, she saw no reason to have to say anything more about the man than she already had.

It was a kernel of news that pleased Jim Fisk, however. Now, beaming, he sat himself carefully on the edge of a little plush chair, and held his wine glass to the full extent of his chubby arm. Lounging at ease was not normal for one of his architecture, and so he always sat in an attitude of tenseness, his long plump thighs barely touching the edge of the seat.

"And what brings you to America, Lady Goold?" he asked with casual indifference.

"The wedding of my cousin, sir. Miss Caroline Gould."

"Would that be the daughter of your business partner?" Ada inquired.

"Hardly," he chuckled. "Jay Gould is too busy making money for us to worry about marrying off his children. But, I am aware of this wedding. It's the daughter of the 'tontine king' Walter Gould. Correct?"

Dorothy was surprised that he would be aware of the wedding and puzzled over his terminology. "You are quite correct, Mr. Fisk, but I am in doubt as to the meaning of 'tontine king.' "

Fisk commenced his rich chuckling, delighted to have an audience to educate on a new subject. "It is the most lucrative insurance scheme to ever come along. It stresses living rather than dying. A tontine policy pays no dividends for a stated period of years. If a policy-holder dies, his heirs receive only the face value but no dividends. As the insurance is bought in groups, at the end of a tontine period, survivors collect not only their own dividends but those of the unfortunate who have died or permitted their policies to lapse. Men like Walter Gould have become exceedingly wealthy just investing the insurance money of thousands of little people who'll gamble that they will outlive their contemporaries."

Dorothy was utterly fascinated. When Jim Fisk talked thusly he was quiet and informative, almost like a schoolteacher instructing students. The bourbon seemed to be loosening his tongue on other subjects as they adjourned to the gilded dining room for a twelve-course meal. Finally, when he had consumed the wine offered with each course, he launched into his favorite subject—himself.

"I am the most hated man in America," he proudly boasted, "because I am so damn smart and everyone else is so damn stupid. Have any of you ever seen eleven million dollars? Bet your fat asses you haven't, but I made that much in a single day. They all call it Black Friday because they lost their britches in the gold market. Damn fools didn't know when to sell and Jim Fisk did."

Fisk put a plump finger against his nose. "I was born poorer than a church mouse, but with a nose for survival. Got into the railroad game and quickly learned a fireman was always going to be a fireman, but an owner was something else. Jim Fisk swore early on that he would lick no man's boots and he hasn't yet. Men of my breed are assumed to be utterly without principles, but sooner or later they have to admit that they have some. Jim Fisk has none, and is proud to let everyone know it!"

Dorothy was aware that the man was now quite drunk. She was also suddenly aware, by the bored expressions on the faces of the other passengers, that they had heard this story many times before. She made her excuses, but the man was so absorbed in his own speech that he didn't even hear her.

"He is unique," Dorothy said, wishing the actress a goodnight.

"And also a little boy," Ada said sadly. "He is the best and the worst of our times and will never be accepted."

"Ada," Dorothy asked quietly, impressed suddenly by the depth of her insight, "being English, what is your impression of America?"

The actress blinked her purple-lidded eyes. "Ain't thought much on it, ducks. I guess it's a land where everyone is out to grab what they can, while they can, before some other sucker grabs it up first."

Dorothy didn't sleep for some time. It was all so strange and new to her. That a man could openly boast about swindling others out of a railroad was utterly inconceivable to her. She could not help but wonder what manner of man her uncle Walter Gould would turn out to be. She found herself fearing for the worst.

It was a different manner of man who greeted Dorothy for breakfast. No matter how inebriated Fisk might become on any given night, he was still the first to be up and about at dawn.

The ocean was like polished glass, the storm long gone. The *Shannon* lay quietly a quarter of a mile off the *Plymouth Rock*'s bow. Longboats made a steady run back and forth between the ships.

"I'm having the luggage brought over," he said, in way of explanation. "The *Shannon* can make it into port now under sail power, but the *Plymouth Rock* can have you in New York by this evening."

"You are being very considerate, Mr. Fisk."

"That has nothing to do with it," he said quite honestly. "You will make good copy for the newspapers. I'm considered a right fine judge of feminine flesh, Lady Goold, and a dazzler like you will take New York by storm. Ain't going to hurt Jim Fisk none to have his picture taken with you."

Dorothy blushed, but was flattered. "Then you won't mind if I correct you on a minor point of protocol? It is proper to address me as Lady Dorothy or Mistress Goold."

Fisk beamed. "I prefer the Lady Dorothy. Now, how about some chow?"

It was a day of carefree sailing and anecdotes from Fisk's past, and Dorothy began to notice a rough-hewn quality about him that she found magnetic.

Dressed in her own attire, Dorothy was particularly stunning in a quiet way, and it made Ada Farrar fume. Ada knew that she was a plaything for this one voyage and she resented being pushed aside like a bag of onions. Had she been able to get Dorothy alone, she would have loved to have filled her ears with the fact that Fisk was not only a married man who kept his wife at the convenient distance of Boston, but that he had no guilt feelings about keeping a mistress in a fine brownstone residence back of the Grand Opera House, and she could hardly wait to fill Josie Mansfield's ears with the news of Fisk's latest conquest.

Ada was, however, quite mistaken about Jim Fisk's true motives. Granted, he was quite smitten by Dorothy's beauty and grace, and admired her arrogance which he thought might even match his own. But she frightened the hell out of him. She was too much the "Dresden Doll" for him; he could get more pleasure out of looking than touching.

Dorothy sensed that there was something of

great importance pressing on his mind that he wished to bring out into the open, but he seemed uncommonly shy in broaching the subject.

The other Irish passengers were put ashore on Ellis Island, but the name "Jim Fisk" was enough to keep Dorothy and Mabel from having to step off the ship. The *Plymouth Rock* proceeded on to a private wharf on South Street. Like any other gracious host, Fisk saw his passengers ashore and away in hansom cabs, but held Dorothy and Mabel back. Ada Farrar raced directly to the mansion of Josie Mansfield.

"I've sent word to Walter Gould that you are safe, Lady Dorothy. My drag will be here shortly to take you to his residence."

It soon became evident that the drag would be long-delayed. It was the night of October 27, 1870. Rain began to fall hard and steadily. But that did not daunt thousands of loyal Democrats. They assembled outside their district political clubs and were each handed torches. By chance, the most magnificent parade in the city's history serpentined down South Street. Fisk pointed out the troops of stone-faced soldiers that lined the streets along the entire parade route.

"What does it all mean?" Dorothy gasped, standing with Fisk high on the bridge of the *Plymouth Rock* and gazing down at the torch-bearing paraders.

"First," Fisk said sourly, "it means that we have an old Civil War general in the White House who presumes to think that he can deal with New York as if it were part of the conquered South. That's the reason for the soldiers and it is complete foolishness. Secondly, these storm-defying citizens are all wearing red shirts to honor the boss of this town, William Marcy Tweed. It may be hard for you to understand our political situation, Lady Dorothy, but the President is called a Republican. He's out to break the Democrats and Bill Tweed's control over what is called Tammany Hall."

"You're right," Dorothy admitted, "I don't quite understand. Which of the two are you, Mr. Fisk?"

Fisk roared with laughter. "Lady Dorothy, they claim Jim Fisk has a foot in each camp, depending upon how the slice of bread is buttered." Then he scowled. "Grant scraped most of the butter off my bread with this Black Friday thing, so I'm not too much Republican at the moment."

The marchers increased until fifty thousand red-shirted citizens had carried their torches by the wharf.

"They are all so peaceful," Dorothy murmured.

"Just like ants," he scoffed. "They've been ordered to show the drunk in the White House that they will go to the polls on Election day, cast their ballots and return home without disturbance of any kind. Oh, there is my drag. I'll send someone down for Mrs. Allgood and the luggage."

Like the steamer, the drag was overpowering in its luxury. Not content with a four-in-hand, Jim Fisk had to drive six-in-hand, using three pairs of white and black horses with gold harnesses, two Negro postilions in white livery mounted on the leaders, and two white footmen in black livery on the back of the drag. Dorothy and Mabel were positively enthroned.

As though they had done some great misdeed, a hansom cab shadowed them for the whole journey through town. Jim Fisk ignored it as though it wasn't even there, although he was well aware of who it was peeking from behind the closed curtains. It rather delighted him that Josie Mansfield was showing a touch of jealousy. It would do her good to note that he could be accepted by real quality.

After the palatial *Plymouth Rock*, New York was somewhat of a disappointment. It was a filthy giant of bewildering contrasts. It was a cramped horizontal gridiron without towers, porticoes or fountains. Its buildings were a row of uniform eye-sores. It was the smell of a hundred nations rolled into an aroma that was unnameable. It was alive with greed, gaiety, richness and rapacity. Its very dirtiness was worn like a cloak of honor, with everyone doing their share to add to the questionable glory.

Fifth Avenue didn't strike Dorothy as being any different from what she had already seen. Lined on both sides with the fine brownstone homes of the wealthy, it presented an effect of somber costliness, of almost funereal magnificence. The homes were much like the row houses of Dublin, though on a larger scale, she could not help but think.

Where were the trees, the gardens, the rolling grass lawns of Adare? She felt cramped, closed in upon, confined. She could not imagine how human beings could live in such dank, soot-filled air.

Had Dorothy been expected to find the Gould brownstone an hour later, she would have gotten totally lost. Its four stories were as tall and severe as those to either side, with long narrow slits of windows fully eight feet in length.

Jim Fisk led them up the steps with a stately but benevolent air, and lifted the glittering knocker. The door, after an interval, was opened by a kitchen girl in cap and white apron, her stout Irish face flushed from the stove, her black hair falling about her neck in little tendrils. When she saw Jim Fisk, she curtseyed briefly, and seemed a little ruffled. The "missus", she informed them, was at mass, but the "master" awaited them in his study. She walked them to a closed door, down a dark and ugly hallway, and took charge of Mabel.

A gruff command bade them enter on their first rapping.

Walter Gould, austere and elegant in black broadcloth, turned to greet them, moving with accustomed grace and calm. His pale hair looked as though it had been painted on his narrow skull with a brush dipped in liquid silver, and reflected the light from his study lamp. His lake-blue eyes gleamed and flickered in his long, keen face with its ridged and slender nose. His subtle mouth, so cruel, so delicate, curved slightly in a ghost of a smile.

He was not what Dorothy had expected at all. The handsomeness of youth had long since vanished, although he was still a man of but forty-six. She extended her hand to him. He took it into his own, which was no less cold and impassive. Gallantly, he raised it to his cool lips, then held it firmly. His smile brightened, yet did not warm.

"I had almost given up hope for your arrival this evening," he said tonelessly, releasing her hand as he continued to appraise her with his piercing eyes. He seemed to want to ignore the presence of Fisk altogether.

"The political parade delayed us, Uncle Walter."

"Quite some show, Gould," Fisk said boisterously. "Boss Tweed certainly turned his forces out to the fullest tonight, wouldn't you say?"

The two men had never met, but were well aware of each other by reputation. Gould was still a little abashed at the news of his niece's "rescuer."

"I wouldn't be aware, Fisk," he said coolly. "For the moment, I find it discreet to stay above the political fray."

"Bad for business?" Fisk chuckled.

Gould glanced at him with cold contempt and reproof.

"It is more of a personal family matter, sir. My son-in-law-to-be is a nephew of Mrs. Grant. As the young man looks forward to having his family attend the inauguration, I am not involving myself in the forthcoming election. But let me not detain you with family talk. How can we be of service to you for your kindness to my niece?"

"Ah," murmured Fisk, to cover the awkwardness of such a pointed question. He looked at Dorothy. She had seated herself on the sofa after Gould had turned his full attention to Fisk, and it was evident that she felt totally out-of-place.

"I have found that the pleasure was all mine," said Fisk, his voice hearty and rich in the chill silence. "Out of consideration for Lady Dorothy, I've even asked the newspapers not to make an issue over the matter."

Dorothy looked up, puzzled. This was certainly a change from the time when he boasted about having his picture taken with her. Would she never be able to fathom the changeability of the man?

The statement was not to the liking of Walter

Gould. In spite of the involvement of Jim Fisk, and for reasons of his own, he had rather hoped that the story would reach the press.

"That was considerate of you, Fisk," he said without conviction, "but knowing the press they will get their teeth into it one way or the other."

"Perhaps," Fisk said slowly, "they should be allowed to print something of the matter, but more on the society pages than the front page, if you get my drift."

"No, I don't believe that I do."

"It would honor me, Mr. Gould, if you would allow me to give a small affair to welcome Lady Dorothy to our shores."

Walter Gould bit his lip impatiently, and scowled. He wished nothing to do with the man socially or otherwise, but how could he refuse after what the man had done? But for the moment he felt he had a safe scapegoat.

"It is we who should be honoring you," he said, smiling weakly, "but, as you can well understand, this wedding is crowding our social calendar considerably. Give me time, sir, to discuss the matter fully with Mrs. Gould and see what time might be available."

Jim Fisk was quite used to being brushed off by the likes of Walter Gould. Jim Fisk was also accustomed to getting his way, sooner or later, and would give Gould a small measure of time. Graciously he said goodnight to Dorothy and departed without shaking hands with Gould. His regard for the "insurance man" was nil—the man didn't even have the courtesy to see him to the door.

Letting himself out, he nearly collided with

Flora Gould. Plump, rosy and snow-capped, she blinked with limpid eyes at the man and pushed by him without speaking. The drag had given her a solid clue as to who would be visiting her home and she had stood for several minutes in the drizzling rain determining how to conduct herself. She had expected to confront Lucifer himself, and her brief sighting of Jim Fisk had been almost a disappointment. He appeared little different than a hundred other men who were associated with her husband in business. Fisk didn't look like a man who kept a mistress, but he was the first man Flora had ever seen who made no secret of keeping a mistress.

Being Walter Gould's senior by five years, Flora couldn't fathom him having a secret affair tucked away in some fashionable flat. He was too honest and loving a family man for such dalliances. No, she concluded, taking off her rain cape and hanging it on the hall-tree, there had to be an evil in Jim Fisk that was not apparent on the surface.

Then her heart began to flutter. She had been fearing this next meeting for days. She took a quick peek at herself in the hall mirror, smoothing her hands over the glimmering mauve satin with gigantic hoops and flounced up the froth of white lace bodice. Her prematurely white hair was caught in a net, and bedecked with little mauve bows. Under the hair her round face was still smooth and pretty. She looked more like everyone's favorite grandmother than the mother of the bride.

She sighed deeply and sailed on into the study, stretching out her big, warm hands with mock joyous pleasure, seizing Dorothy and pulling her up from the couch. She greeted the girl loudly, her voice never seeming to lower itself below a hoarse booming pitch, which seemed to be the only way she knew to be heard above the noise of her four children.

"Niece Dorothy!" she cried boisterously, blinking her round blue eyes at her, and hoping that she would not observe the inner nervousness and fear. "We are so glad that you've arrived safe and sound!" An incredible vitality expressed itself in her conversation. "But, Mr. Gould, the parlor is much more comfortable than your stuffy old study. Come along!" She dragged Dorothy irresistibly from the room, as an exuberant child would drag a puppy. Dorothy, momentarily stunned, clutched her hat, gloves and cape, and tried to keep her balance, trying also to protect herself from the whirling and bouncing hoops which buffeted her.

The room into which she had been dragged was large, awash with the glow of gas-jet lamps. The floors, of wide oaken boards, were dark and unbelievably polished, so that they were like brown mirrors. Over them were carefully scattered a few Persian rugs. The tiniest of fires burned in a black marble fireplace, and the white walls increased the sense of the chill and astringent cleanliness of the entire house. The furniture, too, was very austere and stiff; a mahogany rocker with an upright uncomfortable back, a horsehair sofa, a few tables covered by stiff linen or crimson velvet, an ancient rosewood spinet and a massive bookcase boasting formidable volumes that appeared never to have been touched. The ceilings were so tall that all the furniture was dwarfed to insignificance.

Dorothy could not help but think that the

crofter's cottage at the Castle Adare was better furnished. Everyhing here had a penny-pincher quality to it . . .

The penny-pincher in this case being Flora O'Flannigan Gould; whereas Walter Gould had a tendency to be somewhat of a penny-thrower. Twenty-three years before she had married Mr. Gould when he didn't have 'a pot to pee in, or a window to throw it out of.' The eldest daughter of twelve, she had just about given up all thoughts of marriage at age twenty-eight. Her main responsibility in life was to help her mother cook for her father, a lobster fisherman, and eleven brothers. She hardly knew another world existed outside of the back bays of Boston.

Walter Gould had tried his hand at a dozen different occupations during his first seven years in America, none of them very profitable. In 1847 the United States was at war with Mexico and inflation was running rampant. The insurance companies had come up with a new scheme to get small businessmen to insure themselves against the day when prices would fall again. As a fledgling salesman, Walter Gould was assigned the New England fishing industry and was having no luck. Timothy O'Flannigan took a liking to Walter and told him he thought he was trying to insure the wrong thing. People, not fish, were interested in protecting their families against the future.

Amazingly, no one had thought to bring the ancient tontine system to America. With fifty dollars borrowed from his future father-in-law, Walter set up his own company and began selling insurance to the fishermen for themselves, not their fish futures.

But Boston had its limits. It was rich, industrial and with too few poor. He needed mass humanity that had little hope for the future. The potato famines were pouring thousands of Irish immigrants onto the streets of New York and that's where he brought his wife of three months.

It took years for the immigrants' pennies to accumulate into profitable investment dollars—years in which Flora suffered in a cold-water flat and did her shopping in the open markets with the women whose husbands her husband insured. His largest contingent of customers was in Brooklyn and so that's where they lived. Walter would wear out a pair of shoes a week, walking thousands of blocks to collect the penny premium payments. Flora had to count her own pennies to see to the constant resoling of Walter's shoes. It was a habit pattern Flora was never able to overcome, even after they had purchased the brownstone and had servants. She was frugal about everything—except when it came to her daughter.

"I am so sorry Caroline is not here to greet you," Flora gushed. "She and her beau are taking in the theater this evening and then will have supper at Delmonico's. It will be the last night the dears have to themselves until the honeymoon. She is so excited about your visit, but we are so sorry about your dear mother's accident, aren't we, Mr. Gould?"

Walter Gould was seated in the rocker and was puffing contentedly on his pipe. He beamed with loving adoration at his wife. His emotion so softened and mellowed his face that it was hard for Dorothy to believe it was the same man she had first met.

"Now, mother," he chuckled, "you are going to give Dorothy the impression that you do nothing but prattle. Oh, I'm sorry. I hope you don't mind the informal address. I have been away from that rigid protocol for so long that it seems silly to me."

Dorothy had no choice but to allow him to address her in any manner he saw fit. She was a guest in a strange house, a strange land, and would have to bend to their manners and customs. Still, she could not help but resent his bourgeois attitude towards a heritage he had once been a part of.

"Walter," Flora scolded, "I may allow you to address niece Dorothy thusly, but please watch yourself in front of the children and our other guests. They will show her every respect due." She patted Dorothy's hand. "They are really quite proud to be related to a titled personage. However, they are a little mystified as to how you should be properly addressed."

Very thoughtfully she considered the point. She saw how it could be silly and awkward for people who were not accustomed to such formalities.

"I think Uncle Walter may have a very good point," she laughed. "I would hate to embarrass anyone. Mr. Fisk had a horrible time trying to figure out how to address me."

"Speaking of Fisk," said Gould, abstractedly. "He wishes you to consult your calendar and ascertain if there might be an opening for him to sponsor a little affair to welcome Dorothy to New York."

Flora said nothing. She merely stared at her husband as though she hadn't heard correctly.

"It was so nice of him to offer," Dorothy said. "He's such a nice gentleman."

"Gentleman?" Flora gasped. "My dear, there is nothing gentle about the man, from what I hear. He is recklessly indifferent to public opinion and surrounds himself by the worst possible type—actresses."

"Of that I am aware," Dorothy said. "There was one on board his ship who became quite jealous over the attention Mr. Fisk was showing me."

"Oh, dear," Flora stammered, fearing the worst. "What . . . what manner of attention?"

"What!" exclaimed Dorothy, sitting up straight. "I find that question both rude and uncalled for, madame. I resent it on the part of Mr. Fisk as well as for myself. I was shown nothing but the deepest courtesy and respect due a lady."

Flora blanched as though she had been slapped. Walter Gould's expression changed again and his expression was as bland and unreadable as ever. He said briskly, "Well, be that as it may, Dorothy. You have just met the man and must go on our good judgment as to his past. He has a passion for notoriety and a flair for using people to gain his own ends."

Dorothy sat back and studied the man intently. Could she go on his good judgment? She was rapidly coming to the conclusion that it was Walter Gould who wished to use her to gain his own ends, and did not want to share her with the likes of Jim Fisk. Taught never to avoid an issue, but to face it head on, she determined this was the time to make her position quite clear.

"Your words," she said cuttingly, "have a familiar ring to them, Uncle Walter. Lady Margaret informed me that you had a notoriety for trouble and a flair for using my father to gain you release after release. Is she as good a judge of your past as you seem to be of a man you have only met firsthand this evening?"

Walter moved restlessly in the rocker. He rued the day he had let Flora talk him into this foolish invitation. His wife wanted only the best for their daughter's wedding. Money they had, yes, but hardly any social position. A titled relative in attendance as an honored guest would not only help to elevate their position, but would assure a good attendance.

Although Walter had always used his brother badly, he had always feared the man's power and dominance. He had always considered his sister-in-law to be a rather weak and affectionless creature, automatically assuming his niece would be hardly different. But now he could see so much of his brother in Dorothy that he knew they had made a grave mistake.

He resented being compared with a man like Jim Fisk, but still knew it was a fair assessment. It was an age where you used people or were used by them. It was an age when America seemed to have abandoned completely all restraints on selfishness in a mad race for personal gain.

He was glad that the whirlwind entrance of his three sons gave him a respite from having to answer Dorothy directly. He was dominated enough by his own wife without having a ghost come across the waters to add to his misery.

Flora Gould had tried to raise gentlemen, although on the most part they acted like jungle natives let loose upon an unsuspecting society.

They could not talk except all at once, which produced an immediate round of punching, shoving and a rising boom in Flora's voice.

Dorothy was immediately aware that their antics were mainly show-off for her benefit, and it greatly amused her. She was not used to young men, except for the rather colorless coterie her mother and grandmother picked for her to associate with. The Gould boys were individuals unto themselves.

Twenty-one-year-old Brewster, a law student at Columbia University, was such a remarkable replica of the portrait of her father that Dorothy could not help but stare at him. "Black Irish" with massive bushes of eyebrows over languid bedroom eyes that suggested everything but promised nothing; handsome to the point of almost feminine beauty; quiet and unperturbed, unless in a verbal duel with his brothers.

Timothy O'Flannigan Gould, or "Timmy'O," was a nineteen-year-old reproduction of his maternal grandfather. Short, muscular, russet-haired and generously freckled, he exuded a Celtic masculine sexuality that was as yet untried. Not wishing to march in the shadow of his older brother, he was a student "of sorts" at the less prestigious New York City College.

In his senior year of high school, eighteen-year-old Adam Gould was a composite of the whole. The chunky baby fat of his youth was still being melted away, but would someday leave a lantern-jawed face of heart-throb quality. His razor-sharp brain was still carefully hidden behind a constant prattle of caustic wit. Being the baby of the family, he was more often than not the instigator of the devilment.

And again, Dorothy was struck by a subtle change in the personality of Walter Gould. The loving adoration he had shown toward his wife was now a jovial, bubbling comradery with his sons. He was as youthful as they, enjoying their antics to the fullest. His face was joyful, carefree, excited.

It made Dorothy feel guilty for her former words. Even she could see that in these rare moments he was trying to relive a youth that had long ago fled.

Flora Gould was unaware of this, and Dorothy could see that as well. The more the antics increased, the louder Flora's voice grew. Having helped to raise eleven rowdy brothers, she had prayed for nothing but girls. Granted one, she had devoted her life to her and left the boys to fend for themselves or to develop under the less stern counsel of her husband.

With Dorothy in the house she felt she had to take command of the situation, but she was beginning almost twenty years too late.

"But she is, mother!" Timmy'O insisted. "She's prettier than any we saw on the stage this afternoon."

"Walter," Flora said darkly, "I am scandalized. There is not much you can say to Brewster, as he is of legal age. But I will not have my babies seeing these bawdy shows! I must go and see to rooms for our guests. I expect you to have some stern words with these ruffians."

"Have you ever been to the theater?" Adam

whispered, as soon as his mother was out of the room.

"No," Dorothy whispered back.

"It's devilish fun," he chuckled. "Shall we sneak you away to one someday?"

"I think I'd like that, Adam."

"And you can get us in free, I bet," he said seriously.

Dorothy was puzzled. "How will I be doing that?"

"For you it will be easy. The man who rescued you, Mr. Fisk, owns the largest burlesque houses in town. All his dancers wear tights and then they . . ."

"Adam," Timmy'O hissed, "don't tell all you know."

Adam puckered up his moon face and stuck out his tongue. "You weren't even supposed to be listening."

"Well, I couldn't help but hear, fatty! And if you think you can get her into the theater without the help of the two of us, you're a pigeon-toed fool."

Brewster slipped down upon the couch with assurance and grace. With the polished grace of a collegian, he allowed his mouth to crack into a half-smile.

"Don't let the punks bother you, Dorothy. I'm sure that the festivities that Mother and Caroline have planned will be far more exciting than what they are suggesting. Of course, I have dibs on the first dance at tomorrow night's cotillion. I'm already promised, but I can break it for you."

In many respects Dorothy did feel like she was in quite a foreign land. Half of what they said she had to strain to understand. They talked at such a rapid rate of speed and had such a strange lilt to their words that she found herself nodding while not fully understanding.

But two things could be understood without words. Walter Gould sat smoking his pipe peacefully and never once admonished his sons as directed, and Brewster Gould's eyes suggested that he wished for more than just a dance on the next evening. She found his expression somewhat obscene.

She could not help but regard them with rising scorn. They were the hypocrites, and not Jim Fisk.

Dorothy came awake on a start. It took her a few moments to orient herself. The room was small, but the light from the single window didn't give much illumination.

"Oh, I just had to meet you!" cried Caroline, advancing toward the bed like a huge shadow. "I just knew you wouldn't mind me waking you. I'll light the lamp."

She had discarded her outer clothing except her stays and stood in her great white drawers, dripping wide bands of fine French lace. Her sturdy, over-weight legs were covered by thin black silk stockings. Her full bosom, splendid and so like her mother's, appeared about to burst the confines of her lacy chemise. Her large white arms were damp and glistening, her brown curls tied high on her head, her face moonlike and her blue eyes flashing with curiosity and mirth.

Caroline put the lamp on the night stand and wormed her way onto the foot of the narrow bed. Dorothy had to move her legs to make room for the girl's bulk. She was too plain to be considered pretty. She also had a tendency to squint her eyes when she talked, which was almost constantly.

"You were the talk of Delmonico's tonight, Cousin Dorothy," she giggled. "But I can see that you are far prettier than the reports."

"Reports?"

Caroline burst into raucous and ribald laughter.

"The waiters were keeping everyone informed of Jim Fisk's little set-to with his hussy. Mind you, she's a woman with an exquisite figure and perfect features, but Mr. Fisk went a little too far in comparing the two of you. You could soon hear the woman all over the dining area. Mr. Fisk wasn't much quieter. He finally stormed out, vowing he was cutting off Miss Mansfield's allowance then and there. Of course, everyone is just dying to get a glimpse of you now."

"This is horrible," said Dorothy, close to tears. "I won't be able to show my face in public!"

"Nonsense!" screamed Caroline, striking an attitude of exaggerated surprise, and glaring at Dorothy with a determined expression. "It is not horrible in the least. It is deliciously wonderful! There is not a person in New York who would dare turn down one of my invitations now. Oh, I'm so excited. At first I thought mother had planned too many affairs, but they will all be just perfect now because of you."

Dorothy, her lips compressed and her brow furrowed, silently struggled to understand her dilemna—she was to be showcased like some circus horse. But could she fault this less-than-attractive girl for wishing her wedding to be something wonderful and different? Caroline gazed at her with apologetic affection, and after a minute of deep thought, Dorothy smiled back.

"I'm afraid your mother has not informed me of the schedule."

"Isn't that just like her," Caroline sniffed. "She's going to fall to pieces before this is all over and ruin everything. Father is the real organizer and such a dear. Tomorrow night's cotillion is all his doing and he has a special surprise in store for you."

Dorothy felt there had been enough surprises and shuddered at what this one might entail. But Caroline was not party to what the surprise might be and launched into a full, detailed account of the next twelve days. Dorothy grew exhausted just listening to the list of teas, family dinners, formal dinners, intimate dinner dances, showers, bachelor parties, rehearsal dinner and wedding reception. Never one to have enjoyed such affairs in the first place, she began to abhor the coming days.

Then Caroline laughed lightly and musically and launched into a hearty discourse on one Clarence Dent, her intended. Love-sick down to her last ounce of fat, she began to confide little things that Dorothy felt were far too intimate for her to be hearing. It was totally embarrassing but there was no way she could shut the girl up without being totally rude.

When she was finally left alone, Dorothy found herself wishing that she could vanish totally and not be a part or parcel of this charade. She felt deathly ill. This wasn't her way of life. Unfathomable horror was in her heart, and a feeling of intense anger. Her estimation of Jim Fisk was somewhere now below that which she accorded the

Gould family. She abhored the thought of having been the topic of conversation in a public place. It was so common. She lay there a long time thinking of ways to disappear for about twelve days.

2

AS THOUGH MABEL were an unwanted encumbrance, she was relegated to sleeping in the basement with the cook and expected to accept certain "responsibilities" to lighten the work load of the rest of the staff. Mabel didn't mind the work, for it kept her mind occupied, but she did resent the obvious way she was being kept away from Dorothy. Being an outspoken woman, she made no bones about her feelings on America and her desire to return to "God's country." Flora Gould didn't want her attitude rubbing off on Dorothy.

A creature of a very strict routine in Ireland, Dorothy found the Gould household to be less than organized. The maid informed her that the "menfolk" had already breakfasted and departed, although Dorothy felt she was down quite early. As the maid wouldn't even venture a guess as to when the "womenfolk" might arise, Dorothy was left to eat alone in the drafty dining room.

She did not hear the kitchen door open, but at last she became aware that some one had tiptoed to the table. She heard an embarrassed cough. Sluggishly, she lifted her head and looked dazedly at Flora, who was standing beside her.

"You look tired, child."

"I didn't sleep well." She didn't know what hour

Caroline had left her, but she was sure she had slept no more than a couple of hours; and she was one who could never sleep past the rising of the sun.

"Look here," said Flora sullenly. "Mr. Gould says that I was out of line last evening. We have decided to cancel one of the family dinners and allow Mr. Fisk to honor you."

Dorothy pushed herself erect in the chair. She gazed steadfastly at the woman. "I don't want you changing any of your plans," she said quietly. "I want to cause the least amount of trouble possible."

Flora stared down at her incredulously. "Well, I'm afraid it's too late. A note has already been sent to Mr. Fisk giving him our only open date."

Dorothy stammered with real horror. "Then you must send another. If you'll ask your daughter, you will fully agree with me. The man made me the topic of public discussion last night."

"Caroline informed us of the same when she got home last night, my dear. Mr. Gould is a very pious man and saw nothing amiss in what was said. Perhaps you are making just a little bit too much of the incident."

Dorothy couldn't believe that she was hearing correctly. Had Jim Fisk suddenly grown a halo in the woman's eyes?

"That is your opinion," she said in a subdued tone. "I am not used to being placed in the limelight in that fashion. It is disgusting and repulsive to me. You may let the note stand, but I will make the decision as to whether I shall accept the invitation or not."

"But you will make us all look foolish if he goes

to the trouble of making arrangements for an affair and you do not show up."

Dorothy's heart hardened. "I don't think anyone can make you look more foolish than you really are."

Dorothy flounced from the room and Flora sank bonelessly into a chair. Disaster. She just knew she never should have given in to Mr. Gould on the matter of Jim Fisk. Even though the man was making Lady Dorothy's name a household word, it was not in her opinion appropriate to let him share in the festivities. She dreaded to think what his guest list would look like. No, she would just have to have another talk with Mr. Gould on the subject. She was nervous enough over his "surprise" guest for that evening as it was.

The cotillion, held in the beautiful formal ballroom of the Brevoort House, was a magnificent affair. There were only two hundred guests, but Walter Gould had spared no expense. For days the carpenters had been busy erecting arbors, creating an artificial pond with a little wooden bridge, stringing Japanese lanterns from the ceiling and placing potted bonzai trees and other exotic shrubs in artistic arrangements. The orchestra was seated within a redwood teahouse and the grand staircase leading down to the dance floor was garlanded with white and yellow mums. In an ante-room a repast had been laid out that inspired wonder and envy. Japanese waiters, clad in traditional kimonos, kept a river of champagne flowing to every table.

By and large it was a young group, but Walter

Gould had sprinkled the guest list with an ample selection of the rich and powerful.

It wasn't a party for Dorothy, it was tedious work. Hour after hour she stood on the receiving line while Walter fed names into her brain at such a rate that they all began to sound the same. Her hand became numb from being squeezed, patted and roughly shaken.

Even though the line was thinning rapidly, Walter stood scowling and wouldn't let the family go off to have a good time. It was Caroline who took pity on Dorothy and herself.

"But, father, you don't understand," she pleaded, exhausted. "There does come a time when ladies must adjourn to the powder room."

"Five minutes!" he snapped. "I'll give you no more than five minutes!"

"What's troubling him?" Dorothy whispered, as they scurried away.

"I think it has to do with his surprise, which doesn't seem to be arriving. I think he has his heart set on the President or First Lady attending tonight."

Dorothy wasn't too impressed. If the aunt and uncle were anything like the nephew, then she would be less impressed. She hated herself for thinking it, but she couldn't help but feel that Clarence Dent was dull to the point of being stupid. As thin and tall as Caroline was short and fat, he only seemed capable of standing pop-eyed on the receiving line while his enormous Adam's apple bobbed up and down like a yo-yo. She knew nothing about American politics but couldn't imagine how such a dullard could be the Second

Undersecretary of the Interior, whatever that was, in his uncle's administration.

As they walked along the balcony to the powder room Dorothy stopped short and tugged Caroline by the sleeve; down on the main ballroom floor a tall man lounged casually against a pillar as he openly stared at her.

"I don't remember him coming through the line," she said. "Who is he?"

Caroline shrugged. "Never've seem him before, but he's some looker."

"And horribly rude. Just look at that! He doesn't even seem to mind that I've caught him staring at us."

Caroline giggled. "At you, don't you mean? That's just like Clarence's 'evil' look. Makes me go all goose-pimply and just know that Clarence knows what I look like without a chemise."

"Disgusting!" Dorothy snapped and turned away.

Caroline wasn't sure whether Dorothy meant her comment about Clarence was disgusting or the man below was disgusting. She pushed it from her mind, because she was disgusted about something entirely different.

"You've just got to help me with mother, Dorothy," she cried, throwing herself down on a padded stool in front of the dressing-table mirror.

It took Dorothy a second to answer. Her mind was elsewhere. She couldn't get the man's piercing eyes out of her mind. They were the brightest blue she had ever seen and yet they were not cold. They had sparkled with something like a hidden mirth, as though he were well aware of who she was and the secret was amusing him.

"Didn't you hear me?" Caroline demanded.

"What? Oh, help with your mother."

"Oh, Dorothy, just look at the two of us. You look just like a sunset in your various shades of pink and mother has me looking like an odious cow!"

For the first time Dorothy looked at Caroline's gown. Violet and pale green! It was a ridiculous combination and the heavy hoops made the plump girl look like an overdressed washerwoman.

"She obstinately insists upon choosing my clothing," Caroline wept, "and gives me no credit for having any taste. Dorothy, please look over the rest of the wardrobe she has planned for me and try to talk some sense into her."

Dorothy nodded and couldn't help but think of the man with the light blue eyes. Mentally, she went over the other guests she had seen arrive and realized that Caroline's outfit was no more tasteless than hundreds of others. The women and girls were all overdressed and the men looked as stiff and formal as mannequins in a shop window. Only the man with the light blue eyes seemed to wear his clothing as though they were a part of him. He was the only one who looked like he *was* somebody of importance.

She had only seen him for a second, but she could still envision his striking ensemble. Beige from head to foot—the Eton jacket closely fitted to his broad shoulders and chest and allowed to flare open to expose the cascading ruffled shirt. The Edwardian trousers snuggled thighs and calves that must have known athletic endeavors.

But then her mind went blank. She had no face to go with all of this, save for his eyes.

Caroline giggled. "There you go again, Dorothy. Are you mooning over that looker? We can get you an introduction, if you like."

Dorothy flushed. "Nonsense! I think I've promised all my dances to Brewster."

"Ugh! How dull for you—and dangerous. You keep an eye on him, Dorothy. He may be my brother, but he's still a nasty-minded little twerp. He tried to get his hand up Mary Louise Peasley's dress at my engagement party and I could tell you about the time that I caught him—"

"I think it's time we got back!" Dorothy said shortly. She had no desire to listen to any more of Caroline's little revelations. She was beginning to think that sex was the only subject that the girl could converse on.

She tried not to, but still found herself peering down to the dance floor as they walked along the balcony. But there was no body to put a face to.

Walter Gould was near-apoplectic with rage. "You've kept him waiting," he hissed. "Get in line! Brewster, tell the door man he can make the announcement!"

Caroline began to shake violently with apprehension. But the announcement was not what she had been expecting.

Keeping in tune with the Japanese motif, the kimono-clad doorman clapped his hands three times and bowed.

"Ladies and gentlemen," he intoned loudly enough so that it carried down to the hushed ballroom, "the Honorable Windham Thomas Whyham-Quin, Fourth Earl of Dunraven, Viscount of Mount Earl and Adare."

The orchestra, forewarned of the arrival, struck up the Irish anthem.

Dorothy stood stunned and stupefied. She had not seen her second cousin in ten years. That the snobbish aristocrat would come across the ocean for this event left her mystified and suspicious. Was Walter Gould really out to win back a title?

The thin, balding thirty-three-year-old man walked down the line acknowledging the introductions with curt little bobs of his pale head. Being the Baron of the Scottish clan of Kenry, he was attired in knee-length kilts and a tartan sash that was held in place on his shoulder with his baronet crest of gold and diamonds. What greetings he may have mumbled were muffled by a mustache that was too large for his thin face and overshadowed a very thin lower lip and weak chin. No animation cross his face until he came to stand in front of Dorothy. Then a whimsical light flickered in his gray eyes and the mustache twisted oddly up at the right corner.

"So this is what developed from the freckle-faced little stringbean who used to frighten the sheep to death with her daredevil riding."

"Lord Dunraven," Dorothy intoned coolly, going into a deep curtsy.

"Splendid!" cried the Earl with genuine pleasure, striking his long bloodless hands together. "At long last I've gotten a Goold to acknowledge me!"

Dorothy rose slowly, her eyes pinpoint daggers. "Isn't it just the opposite, Windham Thomas?" she said acidly. "It is we who consider you have placed us 'a few grains below the salt.' "

Down the line she could hear Walter Gould's audible gasp. She waited while Lord Dunraven affected to give the matter close and serious thought. She was not surprised when he sighed resignedly, and said, with a humorous shrug, "And now, Lady Dorothy, we both seem to find ourselves quite far down the table, so to speak. I was amazed to learn that your mother reconciled her differences with Walter–"

"As she will be amazed to learn that you seem to have done the same. We have always been under the impression that you had little use for my father or his brother."

The Earl quickly took up her hand and pressed it to his lips.

"Well said, my dear cousin," he said with a chuckle, "but in you I find little that is Goold. You have the fire and dash and beauty of your grandmother. There is a true Quin, if there ever was one."

"You're quite right, sir," she admitted, reluctantly. She pretended to hesitate. "But, of course, my mother is of her stock, as well."

Walter Gould cleared his throat suggestively. He wanted them all to move down to the ballroom so that he could show off the Earl. Dunraven ignored him as though he were not even there. A connoisseur of beautiful women, he was more than pleased with Dorothy. Perhaps, he mused, his stay in New York would not have to be all business after all. He was so bored with women who would not stand up to him that he found her quite refreshing.

He offered his arm and whispered. "More about

our mothers later. Now, shall we show these colonists what they lack the most?"

Dorothy couldn't help but grin. They were both true Quins. They could fight tooth and nail within the family and still maintain a level of communication that did not require the spoken word. For fifteen hundred years the blood of Ollioll Olum had been filtering down to them. It was something that could not be bought, only cherished. Neither had to discuss with the other the feeling that this offshoot branch of the family was using them and their titles; it passed through their linked arms like a call to battle.

They poised at the top of the grand staircase, letting the applause soar and rise up to them; and still they waited until the orchestra cut the anthem short and broke into the Grand March.

Only then did they use the stairs as a coronation approach. It was the most majestic and regal thing the New Yorkers had ever seen. Deep in their souls was stirred an ancient feeling for the monarch splendor that their new land so greatly lacked. Most were generations removed from living under kings and queens, but the reverence for such tradition could never be completely washed from their blood.

The bride and groom-to-be were all but forgotten. This was pageantry that not even the New York theatrical producers could duplicate.

"Charming, dear cousin, charming," Dunraven murmured enthusiastically. "And now allow me to introduce my most valuable business associate in America, Paul Ely. Paul, Mr. Gould has promised me some introductions. Please escort Lady Dorothy on the Grand March in my stead."

Dorothy turned to look up into the amused blue eyes. Now she could really put a face with the beige ensemble. Curly brown hair trimmed loosely around a square face that was classical Roman. Powerful, commanding, handsome to the point of nearly being beautiful. His only disconcerting feature was a rapier-thin mustache that gave his mouth a faintly contemptuous twist.

Wordlessly, he bowed with a slow and artful grace and offered his arm and hand. Dorothy couldn't help a tremor as she gently placed her hand and arm on his.

His warmth penetrated her white gloves as though she were not even wearing them. For so tall a man he moved with a grace that seemed almost unnatural. With each turning and bow their eyes would lock. There was still the amusement there of having known who she was and it was beginning to unnerve her.

"I think they expect us to exchange with the bride and groom to be," he said and twirled her away into Clarence Dent's arms. Dorothy wanted to protest. It was the first time she had heard Paul Ely speak and it had taken her aback. His voice was low, soft and an artful mixture of his Alabama birth and the slow twang of years of Western living. Dorothy's ears had been so bombarded by New York nasalness that his few words had been a pleasant change.

"Ouch!" She knew it was a very unladylike expression, but that had been the fourth time Clarence Dent had stepped on her foot.

"Sorry," he gulped. "Ain't much of a one for the dance doings."

"Then I've arrived just in time," Brewster

smirked, tapping him on the shoulder. "I'll be more than happy to take over Lady Dorothy for you. Besides, father wants to see you over by the punch table."

As he swung her away, Dorothy was immediately reminded of Caroline's words. Brewster tried to draw her unconventionally close and let his hand move on her back in a most suggestive manner. She tried to ignore him and watched the artful dancing of Paul Ely. It was amazing, she thought, but the tall man was able to make Caroline look like she had grace and rhythm.

"Ah, my dear boy," Walter Gould beamed as he caught Clarence by the arm, "do come and meet our cousin. Lord Dunraven is absolutely amazed that a young man of twenty-five is already in such a high position of government."

Dunraven hid a smile behind his thin hand. He had actually just said that it was the worst case of nepotism he had ever encountered.

"Indeed! Indeed!" he said seriously. "Interior Department, I understand. That certainly gives us something in common, young man. I, too, have a great concern for the land and preserving it for the future. I believe that is your work, isn't it?"

"Some," Clarence said slowly. He felt as uncomfortable as he usually did standing in front of Secretary Columbus Delano. "I mainly work on the right-of-way claims for the railroads in the West."

"Ah, the glorious West," Dunraven said. "Do you know Colorado? A hunter and fisherman's paradise. Have you been there?"

"Once," Clarence stammered. "To help settle a claim between some miners and lumbermen."

Walter Gould was growing impatient. He had many more important men to introduce the Earl to than Dent.

"Very interesting," he simpered, "but we do have—"

"It *is* interesting," Dunraven corrected snidely, "to me. I was under the impression that the Homestead Act of 1862 curtailed everyone to just a mere one hundred sixty acres per man."

"It does, sir."

"Then I don't quite understand, Mr. Dent. Why would the miners and lumbermen be fighting over such a small parcel of land?"

"Oh," Dent said, as though he understood the whole conversation again. "That was different. The miners had duplicate claims right in the middle of the lumbermen's one hundred thousand acres."

Dunraven whistled. "Some parcel of land, to be sure. How was that brought about under this new Homestead Act?"

"That land is not open to the homesteaders, Lord Dunraven. It is held back for the lumber industry."

Dunraven was immensely pleased. He bit his lip to keep from smiling too broadly. Walter had promised him that Dent might be of service to him, but the man was a simpleton.

"And what constitutes a lumber industry?"

Dent shrugged. "I only approve the final application for land, sir."

"Well then, let's say a man knew of a place in the Rocky Mountains. Could he get as high, as, say three hundred thousand acres?"

Dent shook his head. "We've hardly begun to

survey that area due to the rugged terrain and we don't even have it open for homesteading. Now, if you had said the San Francisco Peaks, south of Denver, that would have been different."

"Would it now," Dunraven mused. "As a cousin, you wouldn't mind recommending a site I might find suitable for a lumber mill, would you?"

Walter Gould was quick to analyze the whole scene. "Oh, I'm sure Clarence would be more than willing to help you, Cousin Windham. After all, they will be just a young couple starting out with very little."

You conniving Irishman, thought Dunraven, fixing those wicked gray eyes of his on Gould, who returned the look with enthusiasm.

You wealthy money grubber, thought Walter, *you'll not be getting something for nothing.*

"There are forms and applications that must be submitted," Clarence said, on a rising doubt.

"Things that you can take care of, my boy," Gould said expansively. "Aren't you returning to Washington in the morning for two days? Time enough. Time enough."

"Yes," Dunraven said icily, "as long as he's aware of my needs. Shall we say one hundred thousand acres?"

He turned away without an answer. If there were difficulties, he would leave them up to Walter Gould. Dunraven was hardly a man who allowed himself to be ill-informed. He had had Walter Gould investigated from stem to stern after he had received the wedding invitation. He even knew the color of pajamas that Clarence Dent wore in his bachelor flat in Georgetown. He had developed a keen appreciation of Walter Gould's shrewdness. The wedding for him was window dressing, a sham. He detested New York, but it was the seat of power and money. He had the money, but needed a marriage of his own to wed it to power. For Lord Dunraven to use shirttail relatives to achieve his aims didn't in the least disturb his scruples. Actually, he had very few scruples to begin with. He was a believer in the up-and-coming theories of Darwin. The survival of the fittest had been a Quin concept for centuries. The fittest were men like Lord Dunraven who were out to grab the largest pieces of the pie.

"Sir," Walter Gould stammered nervously, "I would like to present you to the Earl of Dunraven, Viscount Windham Thomas of Mount Earl and Adare."

The stout man turned irritably in his chair and stared up at them with mean and piercing eyes.

"Got your note," he said curtly. "What do you want?"

Lord Dunraven fixed the man with the same nebulous stare he might use on a local banker in Adare.

"I was not expecting to discuss business on a evening such as this, sir. Tomorrow will suffice to present you with a letter of credit for deposit."

"Clerks can handle that," J. P. Morgan snapped indignantly.

"Not the Whyham-Quin funds," Dunraven said arrogantly. "I do not plunk a million pounds sterling down in front of a lackey. Good evening, sir!"

The sum staggered Walter Gould and brought the millionaire banker out of his seat.

"Perhaps you are free for lunch tomorrow, Lord Dunraven?"

"Perhaps I am," he answered indifferently. "You may check with my associate, Paul Ely, in the morning to ascertain my schedule."

And, as he had done with Clarence Dent, he walked away with things quite up in the air. He was quite pleased with himself. He had come into the room with no thoughts about timber land, but it was a stroke of sheer luck. He could leave his private valley project quite intact and pillage other forests for the lumber needed to build the dream that had been growing in his mind for months.

Tomorrow the great John Pierpont Morgan would fall all over himself to open his line of credit. Why not? His pounds sterling would translate into over four million American dollars, dollars he would spend in a very thrifty manner. After all, he was after what no man had ever sought before in the Western territories and he was unsure what three hundred thousand acres of that majestic land might cost him.

But he was no novice when it came to schemes of a villainous nature. He could acquire land in Ireland, England or Scotland at the snap of his coin-purse. But there he could intimidate with the power of his title. Here, he would have to rely upon others to intimidate for him.

Dorothy danced unceasingly with Ely, jostled by dancers who eyed her with speculative curiosity. Young ladies did not promenade all night long with the same gentleman.

Subconsciously aware, at last, of the stares and curiosity she excited, Dorothy declined the next dance.

"Tired?" Paul asked, as he found her a vacant seat along the wall.

"Hardly. I just don't want to monopolize all your time."

She made a quick appraisal of the flushed skin, the thin lips and firm, heavily cut nose, and for the first time she understood how handsome a man Paul Ely was. A moment later she forgot everything else as she recognized his look of admiration. "It's my time to do with as I please, Lady Dorothy."

"Oh, but the other young ladies should be given some consideration." She tried to sound casual.

"There's more than enough young men for them." He took both her hands and pulled her right back to her feet. "Shall we adjourn to the refreshment room?"

Ely's touch was warm; his blue eyes had a searching light, and she followed his suggestion as though he exuded a magnetic attraction that pulled her along.

"Have you been associated with Lord Dunraven long?"

"Only a few months," he said, as though it answered all.

Dorothy, never one to pry, had to assume that he was a man of importance, because the Earl would associate with no other.

To their surprise they were waved over to a table where the Earl was dining all alone.

"My first quiet moment away from the peasants," he chuckled. "Ely, fetch plates for Lady Dorothy and yourself. You will save me from Flora Gould's incessant prattle."

Dorothy laughed. "I thought she stood too much in awe of you to speak?"

"It proved to be only a temporary malady, my dear." He shot a caustic look at the next table of diners, who had stopped chatting to eavesdrop. Dunraven casually reverted to Gaelic. "I have never had much use for the Irish nobility because of their cheeky manner of snooping, but these people hardly know when they are being downright rude."

"Are you sure that some of them might not still speak the old tongue?" she warned, quietly.

"Hardly, my dear. Irish is a holy language which evil beings cannot speak. And speaking of evil beings, are you privy to what services this wedding will entail?"

"No. Does it really matter?"

He began to smile, but it was a shrewd and not overly pleasant smile. "I suppose it doesn't matter over here, of course, but I was curious. My father, you know, was received in the Church of Rome, but my dear mother is still a very earnest Protestant of a rather low-church type. Flora Gould strikes me as near the same type." Then he altered course very quickly. "Are you having a good time, my dear?"

"Thanks to your Mr. Ely. He's a remarkably smooth dancer."

"He is remarkable in many ways," he said drily. "Quite a hero in the Civil War. He recently guided my wife and me on a tour of the South and its sorry state."

"I was not aware your wife was with you."

Dunraven sighed. "Lady Florence Elizabeth is

not a very sociable creature, Lady Dorothy. She decided to stay with Judge Edmonds and his daughter Laura until the day before the wedding. They live in a delightful old-fashioned house on the shores of a lovely sheet of water, Lake George. Canoeing or wandering in the woods are more to my wife's liking than associating with people."

Ely returned with the dinner plates and his presence seemed to animate the Earl.

"I was just telling Lady Dorothy," he said in English, "of our recent trip to James River, Virginia. Remarkable! Remarkable! I cannot help but think that the most uncivil sword of civil war has cut deep into the Confederate soul. After five years the wounds have not healed, are scarcely skinned over. Pitiable! But our hosts were charming people. Reminded me of our own people after we were forced into the United Kingdom in 1801. They, like us, had lost their best and dearest. They were battered in mind, body and estate; but they are indomitable. The men-folk, laboring like—well, like their former colored slaves, only very much harder, tilled their land and kept the home going. But my real respect is for their women-folk. Cultivated ladies doing their best in manual work. I pray they do not become as we, my dear, rock-bound and conservative. Your mother would not agree, but we nobility are a dying race who pinch money from an ancient land and never think to put any of it back."

Dorothy looked up sharply. "And I cannot agree either, sir. The Adare farms are most profitable and are always being improved upon. We are respected because we are not absentee-owners."

"She is pointing her finger at me, Ely," Dunraven said, in a curt but polite tone. "Much the same way your uncle pointed it at you in the South. Why fight for a cause and then walk away from the land just because you are defeated? No, my dear, Ely has the right idea. As Ireland is dying, the South will long be dead. Out beyond the Mississippi is the future. Ely is a smart enough chap to be a part of that future."

As if she watched a new person, Dorothy noticed that one of Ely's dark eyebrows went higher than the other at the Earl's words; it gave an irregularity that made the symmetrical face more appealing—that, and also the way his hair, it seemed no matter how recently combed, hung in ringlets about his ears. Then she smiled—when Ely laughed at the Earl's appraisal of him, she saw that he did it in stages: the lips, the eyes, the low rumble.

Dunraven sat back highly amused. He had assigned his cousin to Ely so that he might be free from the arduous duty of escorting her and leaving him free for business purposes. He never once took into consideration that the girl might find the man appealing, but the soft rosy flush on her face was most revealing.

"Well," he said smoothly, "as I am not much of a dancer, I think I shall retire. Until we meet again, dear cousin. Ely, would you mind escorting me to the lift?"

Dorothy mumbled her goodnight, and tried to think of a subtle way of learning if Ely would return.

Ely could not refuse the Earl, for he had heard more command than request in the words, and read the man's meaning exactly.

"I think I should retire as well, Lady Dorothy. Thank you for a most charming evening."

Dorothy nodded. She began to tremble, and clenched her hands together on her knees. She tried to control herself, but in spite of her efforts she was pervaded by an intoxicating ecstasy and yet a fear that she would never see the man again.

She sat and watched them cross the ballroom, make their farewells to the host and hostess and begin the long ascent up the grand stairway.

Suddenly, the bloom was gone from the party and she wanted to depart as well. She could not look at her emotions with candor or honesty.

"Charming creature, what?" Dunraven asked, as they waited for the Brevoort House lift.

When Ely glanced at the man's profile, he saw that it was stern and harder than ever, with deep lines about the mouth.

"Quite," he answered simply.

"And she shall stay that way," Dunraven said candidly. "Being a former gentleman, I thought it more in keeping for you to attire yourself as just another guest, Ely. But don't lose sight of the fact that you are little more than my body-guard and mountain guide."

Ely was at first angered and indignant at his words. He didn't speak until they exited on the seventh floor.

"I was not doing all the chasing, Lord Dunraven. How do you suggest I handle the situation?"

"Discreetly," he said, in a changed tone. "Your association with me must remain a big question mark. In the event that it becomes difficult for me as a British subject to acquire American land, we shall have to fall back on your good name."

"That still doesn't answer my question."

"How shall I answer?" he asked, lightly, his eyes travelling over Ely's chest, his waist, his crotch. "Need I remind you that I have learned that you have tasted of life in its many forms during your past five years in the West? You yourself were most candid in revealing to me that of late your education consisted of the three W's—or, as you put it, wrangling, wrestling and womanizing. Around Lady Dorothy I will expect you to educate yourself to the single C—celibacy! The last thing I need is for Lady Jane Gould to come down around my neck over the lost virginity of her daughter."

Paul shrugged. He moved off toward his own room, but could feel the intensity of the Earl's eyes still upon him. He could play the gentleman, because he had been born to the role as much as the Earl. But the civil war had burned most of his genteel soul away; avarice, animals, carpetbaggers and "reconstruction" taxes had stolen away the Ely slaves, land and pride.

At twenty-one he had run—run from the hidden insurrection, the murder stalking the South; run from a down-trodden race dying in war-stricken houses, driven to crime in their misery. He never again wanted to see Alabama, had only consented to take the Earl to his uncle's in Virginia because the man was paying him an unbelievable salary.

His respect for the Earl lay only in what he could gain from the man. He knew that anyone who stood in the way of the Earl's ambitions would be struck down. He did not intend to be among the stricken, but still . . . it had been since before the war that he had met a woman to stir his desires as had this innocent little beauty this evening. His arousal had been even intensified on hearing the Earl reveal that she was a virgin. His interest in the Western demimondaines had long been on the wane.

"Discreetly," he echoed the Earl. Oh, yes, he could be most discreet, but could the lady in question?

The Goulds would not leave the cotillion until the last guest had collapsed. Brewster gallantly offered to take Dorothy back to the brownstone in a hansom cab. She knew it was an error from the moment they sat back into the seat.

Brewster moved close to her, and their thighs touched. He felt her faint recoil.

"Did you enjoy the dance?" he asked, lightly, his eyes traveling over her face, throat and bosom.

"It was nice." She averted her face, and looked out at the street, without truly seeing it.

Brewster smiled to himself and remained silent. He did not want to do anything overt until they were quite alone.

Dorothy thought she had averted a very bad scene until they were alone in the third floor hallway.

Brewster took her hand quickly. It was ice cold and rigid as steel. He felt the clenched curve of her fingers. He pressed firmly upon her hand until it relaxed out of sheer pain. He looked into her eyes penetratingly, and said with slow, cold intensity, "Who do you think you are fooling, dear cousin? You threw yourself at that man in a most wild and wanton fashion. Brazen, in fact. A bad piece, my mother is sure to call you."

Dorothy could only stare at him incredulously and wince at the pain.

"And don't give me that innocent look," he chuckled. "Right from the first I sensed that you had been with a man before."

"Unhand me," she warned darkly. "I will not stand here and listen to such trash!"

He was pleased at the indignant flash in her eyes. He liked a girl with spirit. He loathed the feckless debutantes who would lie weakly beneath him like a bag of meal.

"I think it's about time that you and I had a little frank conversation, dear cousin," he said quietly, but with a note of implacability in his tone. "As you can see, I possess as much, if not more, than the man you sought tonight."

He pressed her gripped hand right down upon his arousal and moved it about suggestively.

"Unhand me!" she repeated, with intense bitterness and scorn.

"Not until you promise that I may sleep with you tonight."

She stared at him, her face convulsed, and overcome with horror. She felt trapped and her mind wouldn't work. He took her other hand, held them both as if he were trying to prevent her from doing some mad and terrible thing.

He made his voice very quiet and steadfast. "I can give you a most enjoyable time. I'm told that I am very good and very gentle. Nor am I inexperienced. I can teach you things we can do with our naked bodies that you wouldn't dream possible. Depraved and wicked things, but delightful!"

He paused. His hold on her hands tightened. Such talk had always won the girls over before.

He could not understand her frigid silence, and his face went black with violence and anger.

"Am I not good enough for her majesty?" he cried. "Well, I'll show you!"

He tried to pull her forward for an embrace and kiss, but their arms were in the way and he had to release her. Before he could recapture her, Dorothy brought her knee sharply up to collide with his groin. It was an old trick the stablemaster had taught her to ward off the advances of the grooms. She had never before had to employ it and was ill-aware of its consequences.

Brewster doubled up in howling pain.

"Dirty goddamn slut of a bitch!" he gasped, falling to the carpeting and rolling about in agony. "I'll get you for this. I'll blacken your name good!"

Dorothy was silent for a long moment, then in a trembling voice, she murmured, "I think you'd best say nothing, Brewster. Caroline might be more apt to believe me than you."

Brewster sat abruptly up. His blue eyes were sharp and quizzical, glinting with sudden fear.

"What has she told you?" he demanded.

She was not about to admit that she had stopped the girl before all the dirty linen had been washed. His sudden fear gave her enough of a clue not to want to think on the subject any further. She just smiled knowingly, quickly entered her small bedroom and bolted the door.

Only then did she begin to violently shake. Her mind whirled with a strange, disoriented sensation, confused and aching. There was a beating pain in her head, which her throbbing heart chorused, and a nameless malaise in her body impelling hatred for Brewster and yet a feverish excitement.

The excitement mounted as she wondered what would have been her reaction if Paul Ely had been in the hallway instead of Brewster. Had she really gone after him in a brazen manner, or was it all jealousy on Brewster's part?

She dared not even undress until she heard the return of Caroline. Even then she feared there would come a knocking at the door in case Brewster had confronted his sister.

Sleep, when it came, was fitful. The nightmare played itself over and over again in her dreams.

Morning brought only more dread and fear. It was Sunday and they would breakfast *en famille.*

Her body was one long tremor in the quiet brown broadcloth frock and jacket in which she dressed herself. She felt guilty, and yet knew she had nothing to feel guilty about.

She could eat nothing for breakfast but some hot tea. Walter Gould and Clarence Dent sat at one end of the table quietly arguing. Flora sat at the opposite end, toying with her food as though reluctant to start a new day.

Caroline had been granted permission to sleep in and the boys seemed to be doing the same.

Then Brewster came bounding in, resplendent in a scarlet and black riding costume.

"Good morning to all," he chirped. "Isn't it a glorious fall day? How about a canter in Central Park after breakfast, Cousin Dorothy?"

Dorothy compressed her lips as she endeavoured to control her physical sensations. She couldn't believe he was acting as though nothing had happened.

Flora scowled. "Brewster, you know my feelings about riding on the Sabbath. And Father Flynn informed me at mass this morning that you have not been to confession in a month."

Brewster grinned broadly, heaping his plate high at the buffet.

"I have nothing to confess, mother dear!"

Dorothy nearly burst out laughing. She felt her tensions easing. If Brewster was going to handle the situation in this casual manner, then she dared not show her own fear.

"Thank you for the invitation, Brewster," she said calmly, "but I fear I didn't think to bring along a riding habit."

He sat down opposite her and winked. "And I can safely say that one of Caroline's would hardly fit your trimness."

"Brewster!" Flora scolded sharply, "That is a most unkind remark toward your sister. I swear, I don't know what has gotten into you of late."

"Perhaps it's what he hasn't gotten into," Timmy'O chortled, coming into the room.

Dorothy drew in a fearful breath. Her heart was an icicle in her chest. There was no doubt in her mind that Timmy'O knew everything.

"And what do you mean by that, young man?" Flora demanded.

Timmy'O laughed, going to the buffet. "It's a slang expression, mother. My dear, ego-handsome brother, didn't seem to fair too well with the belles of the ball. I could have done much better had you let me stay late. Oh, which reminds me. Could you have a little talk with Caroline? The walls in the third floor are so thin that she kept me awake half the night saying goodnight to Clarence. It was embarassing, to say the least."

Dorothy thought the couple had been most

quiet. Then, on a flash, she understood. Timmy'O had heard the scene between her and Brewster and was subtly being her champion. Her heart went out to the burly youth.

Brewster smiled with languid sweetness at his brother, but with a fair warning in his eyes. He was too shrewd a blackmailer himself not to have blackmail material ready in reverse.

"I fared well enough," he said acidly. "After all, one strike-out does not make the whole ball game."

"Depending upon where the strike is made," Timmy'O chortled.

"I do declare," Flora clucked, "I can hardly understand what you say anymore. I will not condone this slang in my house. Do you both understand?"

They understood. They understood each other much better. Brewster was not about to give up his quest for Dorothy, and Timmy'O was determined to thwart him at every turn.

Again, there was silence in the room. Then Flora smiled gently.

"Do forgive them, dear Dorothy," she said, in her sweet and contrite tone which she could use so effectively on occasion. "They are so thoughtless when they rattle on in that vulgar fashion. Would you really like to go riding in the park? I could well forget that it is Sunday."

"No, thank you," she said pleasantly. "I promised to go over Caroline's wardrobe with her this morning." Then she caught Brewster's eyes in a meaningful stare. "And you know how clothing can lead to girl-talk that can go on for hours and hours."

Brewster knew when he was boxed in. The

clever bitch, he thought, has gained allies too fast. For the moment, he would back off . . . but only for the moment.

Words did not have to be expressed to Timmy'O, his eyes said it all. He was as much enamored with Dorothy in a schoolboy way as Brewster was in a sensual way. But it was an endearment she could respect and not fear.

She decided not to say too much of the episode to Caroline. She feared they would create an outpouring of the girl's own confessions and those she did not want to hear or become a party to. Rather, they spent their time discussing Caroline's wardrobe, which Dorothy did find quite atrocious, and in girl-talk that had to do only with Caroline's forthcoming marriage.

But their closeted hours were enough to make Brewster begin to sweat and worry and fear their conversation.

"You don't suppose—" Brewster stammered.

Timmy'O rolled over casually on the bed he was sharing with his brother while Dorothy was making use of his room. "Suppose what?"

"That Caroline is telling her about the time that we—"

Timmy'O curtly cut him short. "What do you mean *we*, Brew? You said I was too young and would only let me watch."

"Damn! Don't get high and mighty with me, you freckle-faced twerp! How would your buddies at NYC like to know that you take the big—"

Again the younger brother stopped his flow of words. "Your ego is running overtime again, Brew. It was hardly big at the time and Adam and I seem to have survived your perverted education of our youth. I'm amazed that you could even think about sex after what she did to your balls last night."

"You sneaky little devil!"

Timmy'O laughed delightedly. "Sneaky and devilish, neither one, dear brother. As I told mother, the walls are quite thin. Adam and I are quite curious though. Where did you learn all these new techniques you tried to induce Cousin Dorothy with? Are you holding out on us?"

Brewster went into a pouting sulk. He was not about to admit that his sexual activities had been most pedestrian and unexciting. He had expected Dorothy, with her title and all, to be the far more experienced of the two. That she had treated him in a lower east-side way had at first angered him and then excited him, and now he was back to anger.

He would not let anyone get the better of him —he would just ignore them with snobbish indifference.

The entire Sunday night family dinner was an affair of snobbish indifference. The only outsiders at the table were Lord Dunraven and Dorothy. Dorothy was chagrined that Paul Ely had been forced to respectfully decline at the last minute. Flora was chagrined that it threw her ten-party seating arrangement out of kilter. Walter Gould was chagrined that his day-long battle with Clarence over the Earl's timberland request had been less than fruitful. Caroline was chagrined that Clarence was in such a nasty mood after fighting with her father all day and would be leaving shortly. Brewster was chagrined because he feared

Dorothy and Caroline had had a heart-to-heart talk. Timmy'O and Adam were chagrined just because the party was so boring and quiet.

Through soup, salad and fish, Lord Dunraven was a model of passive restraint, although he could have done murder quite easily. He could not but suspect Lady Dorothy of duplicity of the worst kind.

As the entree was served he turned and smiled at her boyishly. "Does the name Lord Barrymore mean anything to you, my dear?"

"It does," murmured Dorothy, satirically. "He's that rich American who granted himself the title and has been trying to buy up Limerick land to endow it with merit. He covets Adare land like no other."

"And your mother, I assume, has declined his offers right and left."

Dorothy laughed, "Up and down, as well. Quin and Goold land is never for sale. You should know that."

"I know nothing of the kind," he said shortly. "*I* am now the sovereign of that domain and will not be dictated to by petticoat foolishness!"

"I beg your pardon," Dorothy stammered, confused.

"Beg it all you wish!" he screamed, ignoring the startled expressions on the faces of the other diners. "You also will claim to know nothing of the cable I received this afternoon from Dublin."

"I claim so, yes," she said, mystified.

"Ha!" he chortled, pulling a yellow cable form from his breastpocket. "Claim all you want, but listen: Barrymore purchase under dispute. Stop. 1760 proviso enjoined by court order of Lady Jane

Goold. Stop. No purchase legal unless first offered to Quin blood. Stop. Advise. Stop."

"So," she said calmly, "what is out of order with that?"

"I will not have it!" he ranted. "It will cut my funds in America by half, without this sale. You had no right to inform your mother of my affairs!"

"Inform?" Dorothy gasped. "Sir, I am ill-aware of any of your affairs. But I applaud my mother's actions if she has refused to sell land to that avaricious landgrabber!"

"Idiot child!" he barked, rising forcibly from the table. "You have been sheltered from the facts. I passed through the troubled times in Ireland without much trouble to myself. How? If there was a trouble with the tenants about rent, I usually found a great solvent in unlimited talk and unavailability until they thought the grievances forgotten and then I would come and judge sternly. But the puppies think they have the Earl of Dunraven bested over this rent strike. Let's see how long the strike lasts if the land is in the hands of Barrymore."

"And you do not think the same would apply if the land were combined with my mother's?"

"I do not!" he said, wiping his hands vigorously on his napkin. "I have yet to see a woman who is capable of handling affairs best left to a man. You would do me a great service by contacting your mother and getting her to pull back from this odious suit."

"I cannot do that," said Dorothy, with that disconcerting bluntness of hers.

Dunraven bowed stiffly in Flora's direction and waved for his hat and cane.

Walter Gould ran after him like a lackey. Flora scowled as though the end of her world had come.

Studious Adam frowned thoughtfully and turned to Dorothy.

"What is a rent strike, Cousin Dorothy?"

"Many tenant farmers have been led to believe that their rents are exorbitant and cannot possibly be paid. It's true in some cases, but is not the case with our own land. A family man cannot make a living with the rents that are charged by most of the landowners. I fear that the rents will only go higher under a man like Barrymore. It will bring about bitter feelings and bad times."

Flora knitted her thick brows together and stared into space with gloomy anxiety. The tension between Lord Dunraven and Lady Dorothy was bound to have an effect on the wedding. She started to ask Dorothy to do as the Earl requested, then bit her lip. It was a job she must get her husband to do.

But to Flora's utter amazement, the Monday afternoon tea was a rousing success. People gave the simple rooms a certain elegance and Flora's heart warmed toward Mabel Allgood.

Accustomed to Lady Margaret's annual affair, the stout woman saw at once that the cook and maid were far out of their league. Without creating rancor she quietly instructed the cook on how to make the trays more pleasing to the eye. The clumsy maid was a hopeless case, so Mabel assigned her to the sole job of handling the front door and the taking of wraps. Donning her best black silk uniform, Mabel personally saw to the serving of the guests. Several dozen envious matrons would have hired her away on the spot if it had not been an inappropriate thing to do.

To the surprise of all, Lord Dunraven not only put in an appearance but was convivial and the epitome of charm. He was well aware that his manner with the ladies would be the talk of their own dinner tables that evening.

He was quite mistaken. A white-haired gentleman with drooping mustache, an unexpected house guest of the shipbuilder Arthur Payne, captivated the group with his dry wit and homespun humor. Lillybelle Payne was at first embarrassed in imposing an additional guest on Flora, but Flora was in such an elated mood that a hundred additional guests would not have upset her.

"I am not familiar with your works, Mr. Twain," Lord Dunraven told the man rather bluntly.

"Nor am I with yours," the man chuckled, "but we do seem to have one thing quite in common."

"Oh?"

"Our names, sir! You are better known as the Earl of Dunraven than by your real name and I'm stuck with Mark Twain. Only the folks back in Hannibal, Missouri—and my dear wife Olivia—seem to recall that I'm just Samuel Langhorne Clemens."

"You're too modest, sir," Caroline Gould gushed. "I just loved your *Innocents Abroad*. It shall be my guide for our honeymoon trip to Europe."

"See America first," he advised, "and especially the West. I'd rather see scenery than old buildings any day. European culture is like long forgotten bread—it's moldy."

"Then you're an advocate of the American West?" Dunraven inquired.

"It is America, sir. Still rough and rowdy and in knee britches. It hasn't quite reached puberty, as yet. The East has become a melting pot for what I call the 'Gilded Age'—gilded, sir, because it is dazzling on the surface and nothing but base metal below."

"But won't the Homestead Act turn the West the same?"

"Some smart thinkers down in Washington City thought it right wise to give every slave forty acres, a plow and a mule after our civil strife was over. Didn't take other smart thinkers long to buy them out and turn them back into plantations. Giving a man one hundred sixty acres is like giving him a patch of ocean and telling him that's the only spot he can fish in. That's mostly cattle and sheep country and not like the farmlands in the middle of the country. Won't take long for some other smart thinkers to start combining those one hundred sixty acres into something workable. Land is gold, except it's hard to carry it to the bank."

Dunraven smiled to himself. The man had just given him a great deal of food for thought.

If there was a disappointment that afternoon, it was only Dorothy's. It had been two days since she had seen Paul Ely and each time new guests arrived she expected to see him among them. Although the Earl was being very gracious toward her, she couldn't find the proper words to ask about Ely's whereabouts.

On Tuesday evening Lord Dunraven was dressing for a formal dinner in the gloomiest of moods, wrathful and full of resentment. His day had been spent primarily at the cable office. His solicitors in Dublin had failed him miserably. The proviso of 1760 would stand. He would have to sell the farms to Lady Jane at half the price Barrymore was willing to pay, or retain them and thus greatly reduce his capital for American investments.

He despised himself for having handled the situation so badly. To be beaten by a mere woman was appalling. He was left with no weapon to strike back with.

He turned at the entrance of Paul Ely.

"Paul, what have you found out about this Jim Fisk and his invitation for tomorrow evening?"

Ely pulled out a raft of papers from his breast-pocket.

"Quite some man," he said respectfully, as one successful crook discussing another. "He and his partner, Jay Gould, are called the Erie Ring and are tied in solid with the government of this city. They keep within the law with their skulduggery and fraud by having the law adapted to suit their needs."

Dunraven frowned. "What exactly is this Erie Ring?"

"It has to do with their control of the Erie Railroad. It took a fair amount in bribes, but I learned that Fisk and Gould were able to add more than fifty million to the capitalization of the Erie Railroad by printing their own money in the basement of the Grand Opera House, which Fisk owns. My sources say that most of the millions never reached the railroad treasury and what didn't find its way into the pockets of Fisk and Gould found its way into the pockets of those who could claim that they had done nothing that couldn't be legally justified, at least in the New York courts, which they seem to virtually own."

Dunraven whistled. "It's the most audacious, gigantic swindle I've ever heard of. I like the bounder already, but how did I come to appear on his guest list?"

Ely studied a newspaper clipping intently, priming himself for the blow-up he knew would be coming.

"He's the man who rescued Lady Dorothy off the *Shannon*," he said quietly, handing over the clipping.

But there was no reaction from the Earl as he read the account over twice. The article was less than kind to Jim Fisk and openly questioned if she would have been rescued had she been less than titled and extremely beautiful.

"I'll be damned!" he said aloud, incredulously, his heart beating faster. This was how he could win against Lady Jane. It would rock her to her starched petticoats if her daughter were to become involved with such a notorious individual. The reporter had been quite candid in reporting Fisk's little set to with his mistress in Delmonico's. That was all the clue Dunraven needed.

He turned on Ely with glacial calm.

"I've changed my mind, Paul. You will accompany me to this dinner this evening and all other affairs connected with this wedding. You are to make yourself attractive and appealing to Lady Dorothy."

Ely was surprised, and incredulous. He couldn't quite see the game the Earl was playing.

"What restrictions?"

Dunraven gazed at him in the inflexible silence

that so often intimidated weaker characters. His mouth lost its quizzical look. It became hard and fixed as stone, and the gray shining of his eyes was like moonlight on an ice pond.

"There shall be none, especially tomorrow night," he said, and his voice was low and brittle. "Your object, Ely, is to make Fisk jealous of Dorothy's attention to you. A jealous man is always willing to pay any price for what he desires the most. I want him very, very jealous."

Yes, it was a clever trick. Ely was being given a license for lust. He was going to enjoy the assignment to its fullest.

The thirty guests were lavishly served in a private dining room at Delmonico's. The names Flora had snagged were impressive: John Jacob Astor III and the August Belmonts; J. P. Morgan and Jay Gould; George Pullman and Leonard Jerome; the Marcus Stokes and their son Edward; Commodore Vanderbilt and Daniel Drew.

With the arrival of Paul Ely, Adam was sent to eat alone in the main dining room, which greatly annoyed him. He wished to see if there was going to be another fight between Lady Dorothy and Lord Dunraven. He held the man in contempt without really knowing why.

Paul Ely was glorious in a new Alexis overcoat of a dull cream color with pale green pants that were perfectly fitted to his muscular physique. He sported an elegant diamond ring (on loan from the Earl) and the Brevoort House barber had expertly groomed and shaved him. He looked so handsome that Dorothy found it difficult to take her eyes off his face.

"Did you miss me?" he asked with a devilish grin.

"Were you gone?" Dorothy answered nonchalantly, although her heart was hammering.

"Business has kept me fairly tied down, but I am going to make sure that my schedule leaves me free to partake of the rest of the wedding festivities."

"That will be good news to Mrs. Gould," she said a little bitingly. "It's always nice for a hostess to know if her guests are going to arrive or not."

"Ouch!" he said playfully. "I think I've just been soundly scolded."

Dorothy flushed. "I—I really didn't have any right to say that."

Ely quickly took her hand and pressed it to his lips. "I think you had every right. I've been a cad. I could have at least sent around a note thanking you for a most charming evening. I understand we are to be allowed to avail ourselves of Delmonico's excellent orchestra after dinner. I hope your dance card isn't filled."

Dorothy laughed. "I don't think Flora even thought of dance cards. This group looks more like eaters and talkers than dancers." Then her brow suddenly clouded.

"What is it?"

"Those people who just entered. I didn't know the young man was on tonight's list. He's Edward S. Stokes, an associate of Jim Fisk's. He was by the house this afternoon to get Flora's approval on Mr. Fisk's guest list for tomorrow evening. Seemed very late to be getting it, if you ask me."

"You don't sound too happy about tomorrow night."

"Frankly, Mr. Ely," she said honestly, "I am not. I haven't yet decided if I will attend or not, which has Flora in quite a dither."

Ely knew he would have to work on that situation before the night was over, but he thought there was another matter that should be discreetly handled first.

"May I get you more champagne, Lady Dorothy?"

"Only if you will do me a small favor," she said, smilingly. "Please drop the 'lady.' Mr. Belmont says it makes me sound like one of the horses at his racetrack."

"A favor requires a favor in return, you know," he grinned. "You must drop the Mr. Ely and just make it Paul."

"In that case, I am waiting for my champagne, Paul."

Ely paused for a few minutes at the service bar to extract some information from Walter Gould and had a brief whispered conference with Lord Dunraven before returning.

He took Dorothy to a corner of the room that was shrouded by potted palms so she would not be able to see what the Earl did with the information.

Dunraven was discreet. He talked at length with George Pullman about his new 'sleeping cars' while at the same time another portion of his brain was thinking about Edward S. Stokes, who recent information had confirmed as the spendthrift son of the prominent and wealthy Marcus Stokes. That the handsome young scion had a friendship with Fisk that had blossomed into a joint business venture intrigued him. As the varied group would require an 'odd-man-out' seating arrangement, he convinced Flora to place young Stokes on his left and Lady Dorothy on his right.

He then made sure that the waiters kept Stokes' wine glass constantly filled.

"I am certainly looking forward to meeting your Mr. Fisk tomorrow evening. From what I hear, a most remarkable man."

"Not remarkable," Stokes answered, his tongue growing a little thick, "just gutter-sharp." He looked around the table with an openly cynical expression. "No, I should have said *cesspool*-sharp. This society is mired in one dirty cesspool of vulgar corruption and there isn't a man at this table who doesn't express vacant and meaningless derision over its own failure."

"Aren't you being a little hard on your own peers?" Dunraven asked quietly, waving for more wine.

Stokes chuckled. "My so-called peers don't give a tinker's damn for decency. They merely want a system that will work, and men who can work it. They hate his guts, but every ambitious man in this room thinks Jim Fisk is one of those men who make it work. You won't find a one of them in attendance tomorrow evening. That would mean that their traditional moral standards had broken down. But that won't keep the likes of George Pullman from meeting secretly with Jim at Luigi's. That man is one of his troubles. We are still a society of short-line train service. Who wants fancy sleeping car accommodations to Chicago or San Francisco. Who goes there anyway? And look at that hungry trio at the other end of the table. Fisk made Gould a millionaire and now he is out to stab him in the back. He wants to avert personal disaster by reorganizing the Erie directorate—adding to the board such eminent capitalists as John Jacob Astor III and August Belmont. Hell, if my father ever were to reveal how those men actually made their millions, it would make Jim Fisk look like a saint."

Dunraven turned to Dorothy with a most perplexed look upon his face. He was well aware that she had to have gained most of the conversation.

"And you were worried about the greedy nature of Lord Barrymore, my dear? This man who rescued you sounds as though he could steal the whole of Ireland with the stroke of a pen."

"How absurd," murmured Dorothy. But she eyed the Earl reflectively. She didn't doubt for a moment that he might try to sell the land to Fisk at a greater profit than he might get from Barrymore. Because her mother did not know that she was involved, she had not been informed of the happenings of that day.

"Not absurd!" Stokes declared drunkenly, almost falling across Dunraven to address Dorothy. He fought to focus his eyes. "Hell, I know who you are! I should have realized it this afternoon. You're that Irish woman who got Jim to cut Josie off from her flow of funds. Damn, don't make no difference. Josie thinks more of me than she ever did of Fisk. Take him, lady, he's all yours." He had to choke back a sudden sickness that rose in his throat. The Earl quickly rose so he wouldn't be spattered.

"Hey!" Stokes called out, loud enough to make every head turn. "I got more things to discuss with you!"

Although responsible for his condition, the Earl looked down upon him with annoyance. "Then present me with your card, sir, and I shall call upon you when your condition is more lucid."

Stokes fumbled in his wallet and produced a card that the Earl took without comment as he moved away from the table. Dorothy sat for a moment staring straight ahead, even though the other guests were starting to rise from the table. She had heard and seen everything throughout the entire dinner. The Earl had coldly manipulated Stokes for every scrap of information he could gain about Jim Fisk. In spite of what Jim Fisk had done to her reputation in this very restaurant, she could not help but resent the Earl's tactics even more. If Jim Fisk was the cesspool of New York, then the Earl of Dunraven was every outhouse in Ireland.

"Are you ready for that dance?" a smooth voice said over her shoulder.

"Quite!" she said, quickly rising. "And put me down for every one tomorrow night as well!"

"Well," Ely chuckled, "that's a vast change from before dinner. What has enticed you to go?"

"There is an old Irish custom," she said, smiling sweetly. "One never walks away from their friends when the wolves are howling at the door."

"Wolves?" Ely chuckled. "I was not aware Ireland had any."

"We don't, as far as I know. Just as we don't have snakes, except for the two-legged variety, and they all seem to bear noble titles."

Ely determined it was best not to comment on her subtle change, although he could not help but quietly agree. That she was so quickly agreeing to attend the Jim Fisk affair took one burden off his shoulders, but he sensed added an even greater one. He was coming to realize that she was not as easily manipulated as the Earl thought. He was going to have to play fast and loose with her or lose his advantage.

Dunraven wasted no time in going to work on the information he had gained from Ed Stokes.

"I'm sorry, sir," he said expansively to Pullman, "that our pre-dinner conversation was cut so short. I am most interested in the equipment you have now as rolling stock for the railroads. Remarkable advancement in the luxury of rail travel. I shall soon embark on an excursion to Chicago, Cheyenne and Denver. What of your accommodations would you recommend for me?"

Pullman pulled on his full white goatee. He had spent the entire evening trying to convince Jay Gould and Commodore Vanderbilt that they had a need for his services. This was the first encouraging word he had heard all night.

"That depends," he replied slowly, "on your needs, sir."

"Needs?" Lord Dunraven chortled, as though he had millions to spend. "My needs are for pure luxury. I wish to show the majestic West to my peers. Sir, I am well aware that you are making your home in what is the hub of America—Chicago. But have you ever set your eyes more westward? I must confess that, notwithstanding the superior color of the sunset, to me there is something infinitely sad about the decline of the day; all things, vegetable as well as animal, sink so wearily to rest: whereas with the morn comes hopes renewed and energies restored.

"Needs," he went on, "are not just for me but for the Eastern reporters whom I wish to acquaint with the approaching dawn, flinging over all the eastern sky a veil of the most delicate primrose, that warms into the rich luster of azure, hiding the sad eyes of the fading stars. The yellow light creeping across the sky is followed by a breathtaking rosy hue, which, slowly creeping across the arch of heaven, dyes the earth and firmament with its soft coloring, and throws back the mountains and valleys into deepest gloom. Stronger and stronger grows the morn. Higher and warmer spreads the crimson flood. The mountains all flush, then blaze into sudden life. A great ball of fire clears the horizon, and strikes broad avenues of white light across the plains. The sun is up! A new day has come!"

Then Lord Dunraven grew gloomy. "It is a wearisome journey by stage with only a series of flea-ridden stops that are not suitable for overnight sleeping. I know, for I have made such a journey. But you, sir, offer no precipices, no torrents to run from, no avalanches to fear, no glaciers to cross, no sleepless nights, no greasy food, no danger in crossing the backbone of this vast continent."

Because of the publicity George Pullman felt he might gain from such a notable personage using his equipment he would supply gratis the "Pioneer," which had been used to transport the body of President Lincoln from Washington to Springfield, Illinois. The "Pioneer" could be converted from day to night use by folding down the upper berths, making the seats into lower berths, and separating the berths by curtains. For the further pleasure of the Earl's entourage Pullman would also supply his newly introduced dining car that had its own kitchen and something as yet not seen by the public—a parlor car that was like a private sitting room at one end, but housed four cubicle sleeping compartments at the other.

Dunraven had secured his rolling stock for a future promise of endorsement, but now needed the necessary rails to roll it across.

He determined that the Goulds, Astors, Belmonts and Vanderbilts would not be as easy a mark as the rather naive George Pullman. He would quietly wait to see how his campaign with Jim Fisk worked out the next night. He thought he had the bait in Dorothy to gain whatever he desired from Fisk. Dunraven did not know Fisk, however, and couldn't know that the man was governed by nothing but expediency and self-interest.

Dorothy sank back in the hansom cab and sighed. "It's been such a grand evening."

"It doesn't need to end," Ely said smoothly.

"All good things must come to an end."

Ely made a wry face. "We can at least have the cabbie take us back by way of the park."

Dorothy smiled indulgently. "If you wish."

It had been snowing for an hour. In the streets it seemed a cold, wet, miserable storm, but once the horse trotted them into the Central Park lanes, it was like a quiet fairyland. The falling flakes, caught in the glow of the streetlamps, seemed almost reluctant to join the ground mantle.

"Do you know, I was a full-grown man before I saw my first snow. It was about this time of year and I was a greenhorn trapper on the Cache de la Poudre. I stood in the camp for hours just letting the flakes hit my face. My excitement was as great as if I were a ten-year-old child." He laughed. "My enthusiasm was short-lived. The next morning we were buried in three feet of the white stuff. The trees looked like some giant had smeared frosting on their branches and the mountains had taken on a new face. I must have spent the entire day just marvelling at the change from one day to the next."

"I've never seen a real mountain, like the ones Lord Dunraven describes, and our snow in Ireland is mainly sleet, rain and fog. This is remarkably beautiful. I think someday I would like to stand and let it hit my face, too."

"No time like the present," he chuckled, pounding on the roof for the cabbie to stop.

Before she could object Ely was out of the hansom and giving the driver instructions to follow them along.

Dorothy was amazed to find it quite warm. She pulled the hood of her cape over her head and accepted it as quite natural when Ely took her hand. The ground was unbroken, so they forged their own path up one side of the gently rolling terrain and down the other.

They walked for a mile between the snow-shrouded trees. They made snowballs to throw at imaginary animals and laughed in the simple joy of being alive. They explored a glow of lights over a ridge and found four gas-lamps illuminating a pond that was not yet frozen over.

"I hear tell that they ice-skate here in the winter time."

"That's another thing that I've never done," she laughed.

"If you've done so little, what do you do?"

Dorothy pondered a moment before replying, then she said sullenly, "It suddenly seems quite routine. I ride each morning and visit with various tenant farmers. I have certain studies I must attend to in the afternoon and we always share our dinner with my grandmother. Sounds hopelessly dull, doesn't it?"

"No young men friends?"

Dorothy hesitated. "I come from a different world, Paul. Mother would be scandalized if she knew that I was out with you alone after dark. My young men friends, as you put it, are a very carefully selected lot who come to the castle for tea, an occasional evening of music or the joint reading of the classics."

"Sounds most romantic," he said sarcastically.

"Romance has nothing to do with it," she laughed. "In time they will be weeded out until Mother makes the proper selection of one to be my husband."

Ely scoffed. "And you will have no say in the matter?"

Dorothy hesitated again. A week before she could have been forthright in declaring that she didn't have a say in the matter. Now Paul Ely made her unsure of what her thoughts were on the matter. His very touch electrified her. His presence made her wish that they would never have to be separated. She had been miserable when he didn't show up for days and was equally miserable in trying to sort out her emotions toward him. She kept telling herself that it was just infatuation because he was so different and so handsome. No young men of her mother's selection could hold a candle to him. But she had to be reasonable. In six days' time she would be returning to Ireland. Paul Ely would have to be forgotten and tucked away as a fond memory.

"The man who marries me," she said, at last, "will be taking on quite a responsibility. We haven't had a man about to help run the property in ten years. That will play a large role in Mother's selection."

They didn't speak as they headed back toward the lane. Each were deep in their own thoughts. Ely didn't like the way things were going at all. He would feel that he had all but captured her emotions and then something like this conversation would make her slip back into her conservative little shell. He had to get her fully enamored of him before the next evening. It wouldn't do to have her go to Fisk's as Miss Prim and Proper.

Dorothy was day-dreaming. She was wondering what it would be like if Lady Jane could meet Paul Ely. Her mother would immediately recognize his fine qualities as a Southern gentleman, his resourcefulness as a Western pioneer, his position of importance as an associate of Lord Dunraven. Her mother would just have to see that he was the right man to be her husband.

As he started to help her into the hansom her foot slipped on the snowy step and threw her back. His arms encircled her as she started to fall and it brought their faces close together.

It was so easy for Ely to place his lips upon hers,

something he had not allowed himself to do with any of the Western whores. It was like tasting spring honey right out of the comb. Dorothy was warm and soft and fresh-smelling, nothing at all like the sweaty whores. Never had he desired a woman more.

Dorothy was melting as rapidly as the snow flakes falling on their faces. No man had ever held her before. No man's lips had ever touched hers. Her mind was a kaleidoscope of emotions. The strength in his arms seemed to overpower her and hold her trembling body from falling. His lips were firm and smooth, yet gently soft and enormously appealing. She never wanted this kiss to end.

"Let's go back to my hotel," he whispered.

Dorothy was brought out of her dream world with a resounding shock. For a moment it was like having Brewster Gould's arms about her and not Paul Ely's. A vein began to throb in her head, but she retained a composed tone.

"No, Paul," she whispered and gently pushed him back. "It's been a wondrous evening and I'm grateful. Please take me home now."

"All right, Dorothy, it's all right."

She had expected an instant argument, as she had gotten from Brewster. When Paul, kissing her hand, tenderly, helped her into the hansom and signaled for it to go on she felt the guilty party.

After a long silence she ventured, "I've made you angry."

"Real virgins don't make me angry," he said, langhing. "It's only the ones who pretend to be and aren't that upset me."

Dorothy blushed scarlet. She was not used to such frank sexual talk. Then she saw the humor in his statement.

"That's the first time," she said, "that I have ever been kissed." She grew somber and thoughtful. Then she said quietly, "This evening has meant more to me than just the kiss, Paul. I enjoy being with you more than any person I have ever known."

He nodded. "Well, that's one thing in my favor, I guess."

"I–I've been raised in a very strict and old-fashioned way, Paul. I–I just couldn't be like–like common women who–who–"

Ely pushed back his head and roared.

"Who give of themselves before marriage?"

Dorothy nodded and blushed deeper.

"Don't worry," he chuckled, "I'd never put you in the same class as a Caroline Gould."

Dorothy gasped.

It made Paul Ely laugh all the more. "You, my dear, are not only virginal but horribly naive. You can tell the way that girl walks that she has been experiencing the fruits of honeymoon for months. It's probably the only way she was able to snag that dullard of hers."

Dorothy felt an obligation to defend Caroline, but knew that her defense would sound shallow and false.

"Really," she said instead, "I don't think we should carry this discussion one step further."

"Afraid that you might want to start emulating her?"

"I won't even honor that statement with a comment, sir," she said coldly.

This increased Ely's mirth all the more. "Your biggest trouble, Dorothy, is that you need kisses and more kisses until you start beginning to feel like a real woman."

Dorothy turned sharply away and stared out at the snowstorm. She knew that Paul Ely was right, but she dared not admit it. She did want to be kissed and kissed and made to feel like a real woman. She wanted Paul Ely to be that man. But a force far more powerful than the present desire would keep her from bending to his will. She could not go against her upbringing that easily.

Paul Ely sat back with a curious sense of having been sated. Yes, he still wanted Dorothy physically, but the desire was now easy to wait upon. He had opened a door that she would find hard to close because his foot would be in it. He felt more confident than ever that he would have her within his hotel room before her departure.

3

LORD DUNRAVEN got off the elevator at the penthouse floor of the Summerville Arms and turned right. As a connoisseur of feminine beauty, he could not help but take note of the woman approaching the elevator. She had an exquisite figure and perfect features, large black-lashed eyes, magnificent glossy hair. Out of respect Dunraven tipped his derby and was rewarded with a gracious smile and a glance from her lustrous eyes that acknowledged his taste for beauty.

As there was only one door on the floor he was

sorely tempted to ask the butler for her name, as he handed over cloak, derby, cane and gloves, but determined that would be a little indiscreet. He would just have to figure a subtle way of gaining the information from Edward S. Stokes.

To his utter consternation the butler showed him directly into Stokes' lavish bedroom where he found the young man still quite abed.

"Dear chap," Dunraven stammered, "I mean not to intrude. Are you ill?"

"Oh, hardly that," Stokes said laconically. "I have just decided that I am not going to get up anymore."

Dunraven stared in total bewilderment. "I beg your pardon?"

"I have not gone off the deep end, if that is your worry. I have just had a most unpleasant little scene with a lady whose affections I thought were reserved just for me. I found her interests to be more monetary than romantic, so I have questioned the value of arising and decided that I shall just stay abed!"

"Really, Stokes," Dunraven said sternly. "There are other women about, you know!"

Stokes eyed him indifferently. "She is not the only reason I have come to this conclusion, Lord Dunraven. Life is a tedious bore. I get up in the morning and have all the trouble of dressing, loaf about my rooms a bit, dress some more and go out, and loaf about and have a cocktail and lunch somewhere; come home and shift into another kind of attire, and pay a visit or two, and have tea; home again, and undress, and dress all over again, go and dine at a club; come home and undress, and go to bed. Don't you see, man? Life is all getting up and going to bed, and dressing and undressing, and I am sick and tired of it. I have gone to bed. It is very comfortable, and here I mean to stay."

"But, Stokes, you do have business interests that you have to look out after."

"Did have," Stokes said drily. "My dear friend Jim Fisk feels I have appropriated too much of the partnership funds. His lawyers sent me a most amusing letter to that effect this morning. My, it has been quite a day."

"Well–I–uh–don't want to impose upon your rest, sir. Perhaps, when you are up and about again, you will call upon me at the Brevoort House."

Dunraven made a hasty retreat. Stokes was no longer any use to him and he saw no reason for wasting any more of his time.

He was so angry with the man that he walked along the bustling street in a fuming fog. He was also angry with himself for not securing the name of the woman who had thrown Stokes over. He still had two days before the arrival of Lady Florence and the woman's monetary request would not phase him in the least. For a woman like that he would open his tight pursestrings wide.

The sun had begun to melt the snow, leaving dirty slush in the gutters. A hansom cab came wheeling close to the curve and splattered Lord Dunraven's pant legs. The icy water brought him quickly out of his reverie and he was ready to storm at the driver when the carriage door opened and out stepped Walter Gould.

"Don't pay him a penny!" Dunraven barked. "The imbecile has soaked me through and through!"

"Lord Dunraven!" Gould beamed cheerfully. "What a remarkable surprise! I was just about to drop off Lady Dorothy and come in search of you."

"What about my pants?"

"I shall see to them," Gould muttered, not wishing a street scene with the glaring cabbie, who had probably already soaked a hundred people that day without once blinking his hard eyes.

Dorothy climbed gracefully out of the hansom and nodded a silent greeting at her cousin.

"Mr. Scribner will secure you a cab when you've finished with your purchases, Dorothy," Gould said, waving his arm toward the store.

Dunraven turned and looked at the shop's windows and frowned as though it were a seamy establishment.

"Books?" he scoffed. "What use do you have for books?"

"I read them," Dorothy laughed. "Our choice is so limited in Adare that Mother has given me quite a list to add to the castle library. I also have in mind several selections of my own. Thank you, Uncle Walter. I shall be some time, for this is going to be like a child going into a candy store."

"Utter foolishness," Dunraven grumbled, scrambling into the hansom. "My own mother doesn't read. What is this world coming to? Women are beginning to think they can do anything, Gould. Bah! It's that damn woman sitting on the British throne. She actually works at the job of being a queen and is giving women everywhere foolish notions. Well, why in the hell were you out looking for me?"

Gould smiled slyly. "Clarence will be back from Washington this afternoon, but he wired ahead some very interesting information. He's been able to secure some forest land for you. He'll bring all the necessary papers with him."

Dunraven suddenly forgot all about his soaked pants. "Excellent! Excellent! How much?"

"I'm unsure, except before he left he did mention the other grants were going for $1.25 an acre."

"Absurd!" Dunraven exploded. "That would be one hundred twenty-five thousand dollars! Can't he do better than that?"

Gould shrugged. "He can't, but perhaps *the man* coming up for the wedding could be of service to you."

Dunraven eyed him shrewdly. "Is that fact or more wishful thinking on your part?"

Walter Gould grinned broadly. "It was also in the telegram. Clarence's aunt and uncle are most anxious to meet you."

Dunraven sat back, reflectively. "And I won't mind meeting the President. Not at all. You've done well, Walter, but then you have profited handsomely by my name."

"I have profited?" repeated Gould, with incredulous amazement and outrage. "Whatever do you mean, sir?"

Dunraven chuckled wickedly. "I mean that I am not blind to the venal society you pant after, Walter. Society, bah! It is a close-knit little fraternity that controls the land, the minerals, the mills, the factories, the railroads, the banks and even the government. My good name has given you a gilt-edged card of membership, shall we say. Can you deny that it has not opened whole new areas for your insurance salesmen to exploit?"

"Well, I—uh . . ."

"Exactly!" Dunraven chortled. "You are probably already counting your new millions." He spread his hands expansively. "Well, as the old proverb goes, Walter: one hand washes the other and both wash the face. I now need you to wash my face."

Gould suddenly colored violently, and stared at his cousin. But he said nothing. He had used the man grossly and prayed that paying the piper would not be too expensive.

"I have great need," continued Dunraven, with obvious inner amusement, "for a most capable male secretary with accounting ability—ability that I am sure you must possess in your various offices. So that we understand each other quite clearly, dear cousin, you have blessings in this land that we do not enjoy at home. We are taxed quite heavily to keep good Queen Vicky upon her expensive throne. I shall require one set of books for my eyes only and another for the eyes of the Lord Exchequers agents, who by now have already probably smelled out my large transfer of funds to Mr. Morgan's bank. Oh, their grubby Union fingers stretch even across the oceans."

Gould sighed. It was not as disastrous as he had anticipated. "I think I have just the man for your needs. He is young, although he has been with me for five years, and unattached."

"Splendid! Of course, you will keep the lad on your payroll and give him to me only on loan."

Gould was so choked with rage that his face turned crimson. Dunraven smiled, and shrugged sadly.

"It is not as if that will make you a pauper, my dear cousin. But there is an element of justice in all of this. You are the one who made me open my eyes to the American way of doing business. Can I help being such a fast learner? Now, when can I meet this young man?"

"Right away," Gould said in a tone of gloomy regret. "I'll drop you at your hotel and send him right along when I get to the office."

The Earl was taken with the young man at once. As well as being a connoisseur of feminine beauty, he was also a devotee of muscular handsomeness in the male species, although he had never been one to go in for buggery in school. It was a personal fetish with him, fully believing that thin, waspish men—such as himself—were more prone to be cunning, sly and disloyal. But a burly man, with the air of the outdoors about him, could be most trustworthy.

Rufus Brogan, who was exuberant and heartily simple of temperament, for all his cunning and agreeable duplicity, was awed by his assignment.

"We shall be leaving for the West in four days' time, Mr. Brogan. As you will be gone a minimum of six months, Mr. Gould will see to whatever salary advance you might need for winter clothing and lodging expenses in Denver. Once we are travelling, I shall acquaint you with what secretarial and accounting needs I shall require. That is all!"

Rufus Brogan rose and bowed stiffly. He was

going to like working for this man very much. He was straightforward and precise and from first impression not constantly shifting in mood like Walter Gould. And the man was fulfilling his life-long dream. In twenty-five years he had never been more than twenty miles away from Manhattan Island. He didn't care what this titled gentleman would ask of him, he would do it without question.

Yes, Windham Thomas was learning very rapidly. He had very few positive eggs in his basket, but was already acquiring a loyal staff to make sure that none of them became cracked. He was becoming just like the rest of the—his mind paused and searched for the exact description of these men he found himself emulating more and more—and then it came to him.

"*Landgrabbers*," he chuckled. "For without the basic land what else would they have? They would not have the fur pelts to sell; they would not have the gold and silver to strip from the earth; they would not have a place to build their railroads, or mills, or factories, or shipyards, or banks, or insurance companies, or anything else. Without the land you have nothing. And I shall have the land!"

Flora Gould had paid little attention to the address on the invitation until the two rented Victorian carriages brought her entire family entourage to stop before the brightly illuminated fine brownstone residence on Twenty-Third street between Eighth and Ninth Avenues.

"Oh, husband!" she gasped, nearly going into

the vapors. "We'll be scandalized entering this establishment."

Walter Gould, only slightly more at ease than his wife, had understood the address from the very beginning.

"Flora," he soothed, "when Mr. Fisk entertains, he always invites his guests to Miss Mansfield's home."

"And what guests!" she wailed. "Walter, did you see that horrible list?"

"I did," he said, with cunning calm, "and we shall just have to make the most of it."

Walter Gould fully intended to make the most of the whole evening. Every judge, councilman, commissioner of fire, police and sanitation, every ward boss and political hack, including Boss Tweed himself, would be in attendance. If New York society would not come to Jim Fisk, he would create his own by calling in every political I.O.U. that was outstanding.

Walter Gould had to literally pry his wife from the carriage. In that house were men who controlled ten thousand policemen, eight thousand firemen and six thousand garbage collectors—and not a one of them with a tontine insurance policy. He could make more contacts in this single night than all the Morgans, Belmonts, Astors, Pullmans and Goulds could give him in a lifetime.

For Brewster, Timmy'O and Adam the house was intensely titillating. They had never before been within the house of a kept mistress and prayed for the worst to happen to them.

Caroline and Clarence Dent had engaged in a prolonged "matinee" upon his arrival from Washington and couldn't have cared less where they were to spend the evening. They were both exhausted.

Dorothy was apprehensive, but not because of any knowledge of the address. She just feared that Paul Ely would not attend after her treatment of the night before. He had been such a gentleman in saying goodnight to her that it had made her feel even guiltier. She just knew that he now hated her for being so completely prudish.

The house was a surprise to some, a disappointment to others. Jim Fisk's fondness for barbaric splendor was lacking here—the house was a true reflection of Josie Mansfield's uncommon good taste.

The rooms on the main floor were already thronging with a wide variety of guests—most of them politicians, who always seemed to arrive early and stay late where free drinks and food were available. None of them had really come to see Lady Dorothy or the Earl of Dunraven.

But when Dorothy was announced the noise and laughter quickly subsided. Fisk rushed forward to greet here, abashed that he had forgotten what a stunning creature she was. He was joyously happy that she was dressed so stylishly for his party. Dorothy had dressed only to please Paul Ely, but she looked so lovely that her appearance was creating quite a flutter.

In her burnished hair were perched jaunty little green feathers. Her gown was of the heaviest green silk, cut *à l'Impératrice,* and having deep flounces of white lace over Milanaise bands of light green satin. A superb green velvet mantle covered her shoulders.

"What an honor and privilege it is to see you again, Lady Dorothy," he beamed. "And may I present your hostess, Miss Josie Mansfield."

The two women knew that they should be mortal enemies straight off, but Fisk had taken the precaution of warning Josie that she was not, by the slightest smile or word or flicker of eye, to allow her jealousy to spoil the evening. Josie, who preferred herself first over any one else, found herself respecting Dorothy's beauty and costume, rather than envying it. To show her feelings she executed a most graceful and theatrical curtsey.

As Dorothy was acknowledging the salute the Earl and Paul Ely made their entrance. The introductions got a little confused and Josie curtsied to Ely and shook Lord Dunraven's hand.

It hardly phased the Earl. He stood mentally stunned and stupefied to learn that the woman he had seen leaving Stokes was the hostess for the evening. Josie took Dorothy and Paul into the main parlor with the Goulds. Dunraven hung back with Fisk.

Dunraven turned courteously to Jim Fisk. "That is certainly some woman."

"Woman?" Fisk said, thinking he referred to Dorothy. "That is no woman, sir, that is a real lady."

"Oh, no," Dunraven chuckled, "I was not speaking of my cousin, but of that other divine creature. I'd like to hear all there is to know about her."

Fisk said with venomous quiet, "It is hardly any secret in New York, Lord Dunraven, that Miss Mansfield is my mistress!"

Dunraven stared at the man, his narrow and

colorless face darkening. Suddenly Stokes's comments of the evening before now made sense. This was not in keeping with his plan for the evening at all. How could Fisk grow jealous of Dorothy being with Paul Ely if he had a mistress on his arm? The same black devil that Lady Jane had always maintained was lurking somewhere in the soul of the Earl came springing to the surface. He cared not whose lives might be affected to gain his own ends.

"My congratulations, sir," he said coyly. "She certainly has improved upon her position since this morning."

Fisk scowled, but said nothing.

"I had a business appointment this morning," continued Dunraven, with just a touch of malice, "and saw the lady leaving the same penthouse I was due to enter. I was most taken with her, as you can well understand would be the case of any gentleman seeing her for the first time."

"Stokes?" Fisk queried darkly.

"Why, yes," Dunraven said, with mock surprise, "that is indeed the gentleman I called upon. To be most honest, I met him at a dinner party last evening and was led to believe that he could be of great service to me in bringing about our introduction this evening. But, alas, I arrived to learn that you two are no longer associated."

Fisk looked up now and regarded the Earl with that bland and evil look of his, derisive and mocking.

"You wished business with me, Lord Dunraven?"

Dunraven looked at the big man standing before him in the foyer, at his pale and murderous eyes, at his square, lined face and greased down hair. Then he said, "It would be inappropriate for me to raise such a question now, sir. I feel most guilty in having blurted out such damaging information."

Fisk snapped his fingers and a young man seemed to appear from nowhere.

"Jamey," Fisk demanded, "what do you know of any connection between Josie and Eddie Stokes?"

The young man blanched. "Well, Jim, I—"

"Out with it!" Fisk barked savagely.

James McFarland knew better than to lie to Jim Fisk.

"I hate to be the one to tell you, boss, but it's no new thing. Stokes was here most of the time while you were in Europe. After you cut off her allowance, and she pleaded to come back, it became a secret thing, or so they thought. This hurts, boss, but you'd best know it all. The town is snickering and ridiculing you as a cuckold for lavishing your wealth on a flagrantly unfaithful mistress and her lover."

"Thank you, Jamey," Fisk said, pondering and knitting his shaggy brows. "You will keep what you've just said to yourself. I will not have this evening ruined for our honored guests."

McFarland could not believe his ears. He had expected a stormy scene of the worst kind. He had seen Fisk's short-fused temper blow too often and got quickly out of the man's sight.

Fisk turned to Dunraven, who had been listening in grim silence, his eyes sparkling.

"This may sound strange, Lord Dunraven, but you have done me a great service. My staff seems to feel that I should be the last man to learn of anything said about me. Would you join me in my study for a private drink?"

All thought of bringing about a connection between Dorothy and Fisk vanished. Dunraven had Fisk right where he wanted him and could handle matters quite on his own.

"You are most beautiful tonight—" Ely said, bowing. His clear blue eyes expressed a courteous interest, but in his deep voice she detected a note of patronage.

She stood stiffly, waiting for the Goulds to go on into the buffet table, noting the ruby-eyed owl stickpin in his glossy satin cravat, the newness of his gray broadcloth suit, the massive gold watch chain which glinted across his striped waistcoat. Everything about him reeked of wealth.

A waiter passed with a tray and she reached for a champagne glass. She was becoming quite addicted to the "bubbly."

"Permit me—" said Ely, taking the glass and handing it to her. For only a second their hands touched in the passing, but a current coursed through her that nearly made her drop the glass.

They stood drinking in a long and peculiar silence. Dorothy's eyes glinted angrily as she waited for Paul to make a comment. Ely, who was playing the scene as though following a script, smiled faintly and sipped at the champagne.

It was Dorothy who was forced to speak first.

"Well?" she goaded him, a nerve in her cheek twitching with impatience.

Ely, pleased with his cunning, laughed mirthlessly. "Well?" he echoed. "Is that a continuation of last night's discussion?"

She frowned, tapping the rim of the glass with her fingernails, and pretended to give the matter great thought. "I wish I knew more about you."

His smile became broader. "What is there that you don't know about me already?"

"Don't be cruel, Paul. I don't know your line of work, your thoughts for the future, whether you are spoken for already—"

This caused him to roar with laughter. "After what you said last night, I don't see why those things would matter to you."

"Please, Paul," she begged. "I wish some of last night had never happened, or happened differently. I'm so confused and all you can do is laugh at me."

Ely sobered quickly. The door was opening wider.

"It's too damn noisy in here! Let's go over into the library."

Dorothy followed without hesitation. Ely had been on her mind all night and all day. Her feelings were becoming so entangled that she could not sort them out. Even in the reading matter she had selected for herself, she had gone far afield on one selection and became highly embarrassed when Mr. Scribner's eyebrows arched at the title. But *The Loves of Amy Blakely* proved to be less educational on the information she sought than she had anticipated. She was not a poor little Cockney wench using a sultry body to climb out of the gutter and into a Duke's bed. Amy's tactics, Dorothy felt would not work on a Paul Ely. She couldn't snag him into a marriage by claiming to be carrying his bastard son. But one aspect from the novel she felt she could employ.

Almost as soon as Paul had closed the library door, she wrapped her arms about his neck and pulled his head down so she could hungrily kiss his eyes, his cheeks, his mouth. Cunning little Amy had made her see that this man was to be hers. Now he was more than just her first kiss, she wanted him to be her very first man and forever.

Ely felt the door opening wide. He kissed her, brushing his lips against her forehead. She relaxed in his arms with an audible sigh.

"Oh, Paul, I've been so miserable. Every moment I'm away from you is so terrible."

"It doesn't have to be," he said soothingly, smoothing back her hair and gently kissing each cheek.

Dorothy pulled back and stared at him wide-eyed. "Do you mean that, Paul? Are you growing to love me as much as I am growing to love you?"

She hated the way it sounded coming from her lips. Amy had been much more convincing.

Ely pulled her close, so she couldn't read his eyes. "I've loved you since the moment I first laid eyes on you," he lied smoothly.

"Oh, my darling, why haven't you said anything?"

"What would have been the use? Your Mama is going to select the man for you."

She hugged him tight. "We can change that, Paul. I just know that my mother will love you just as much as I when she gets to know you."

Ely smiled to himself. "I'm sure that she will,

but when will she get the chance? We leave for Colorado right after the wedding."

Dorothy could feel him slipping away just as Amy's first love had slipped away. She couldn't let it happen that way.

"Then I'll just run away and go with you!" she declared positively.

It was the last thing in the world that Paul Ely wished, but he thought he had her almost in a position to fulfill his own desires. He kissed her again with loving tenderness.

"Would you do that? Would you really do that for me?"

"Yes! Yes!" she cried. "I hate this horrible feeling of being in love and not being able to do anything about it."

"Then why should we wait?" he enthused. "Let's run away tonight. All they are doing tomorrow is rehearsing for the wedding. They won't miss you."

Dorothy had a moment of sane thought. "But they will miss me tonight."

Ely had to think fast. "No, they won't. I'll send a cab to the Gould's after midnight. It can bring you to my hotel and we can slip across to New Jersey in the morning and be married."

Because he had actually said that they would be married, Dorothy was too rattled to question what would take up their time between midnight and the morn.

"Oh, my darling, yes, yes!"

Now it was Paul Ely who kissed her hungrily. He had never before felt so victorious. He had no doubt that once he had her within his hotel room he could convince her gullible mind that there would be no harm done in their starting to be husband and wife as long as they were getting married in the morning. He still had not figured out how he would be able to get out of the actual ceremony, but he had all night long to work that out in his brain.

Dorothy was numb with happiness. She was being even more daring than Amy Blakely and she didn't care. She had never felt so passionate, so alive, so free. She wanted to sing, and dance, and shout out the news that she was in love, really in love.

She floated from the library. She was so gay and happy and bubbling that it made Flora Gould raise a quizzical eyebrow.

Jim Fisk, who had come to a most agreeable business arrangement for both himself and Lord Dunraven, took her in tow and made sure that she met every person present.

Dorothy didn't mind being separated from Paul —she had her whole life to be with him now.

Never had she been more charming, gracious and affable. Bill Tweed thought it highly amusing that she would compare him with the likes of Santa Claus. She was referring to his countenance and he thought she meant his good works among his constituents.

Satisfied that he had gained all he could gain, Dunraven left early and took Ely with him.

Jim Fisk was reluctant to face what he knew was coming that evening because he was still infatuated with Josie Mansfield; but he would be a cuckold for no one.

He kept the party going until even the political hacks could eat or drink no more and Flora Gould was almost asleep in a chair before the fireplace. Finally, he had no choice but to release his last guests and cohorts.

"Lady Dorothy," he said warmly, touching her hand to his lips, "you have done me proud this evening. This city is yours for the asking."

The only thing she wished to ask was for some time back. The grandfather clock in the foyer was striking a quarter of twelve as they went out to get into the carriages. Not only would they never reach the brownstone by midnight, but it would take forever for the family to settle down for the night. Her nerves were getting edgy and she had to elbow Brewster when he tried snuggling too close. Declaring total exhaustion she scurried to her room and huddled in the narrow windowseat, praying the hansom cab had not already arrived and departed.

In actual fact Paul Ely had not even ordered one as yet. He sat in the gloating Lord Dunraven's suite and had all but forgotten Dorothy for the moment.

"It's almost too good to be true," Dunraven chortled. "For a percentage of the lumber operation Fisk will advance half a million and hold the paper on the farm lands until Lady Jane makes good the purchase price. He has plans to build a railroad down from Colorado to the New Mexico Territory and shall require great quantities of lumber. But the most important aspect of our agreement, Paul, is that he is sending West with us a man by the name of Trevor Cleveland. Cleveland is a master at land acquisition. He was able to acquire for the Erie a ten mile right-of-way on each side of their tracks. He was also on General Grant's staff during the war."

Ely pursed his lips. "That will make it easier to obtain the President's ear."

"To be sure. Now, my boy, tomorrow is going to be quite a full day. First thing in the morning I want you to take this letter from Fisk around to the various rail offices he has listed. They will schedule and stamp the letter so that we will have free access to their lines for our Pullman cars. Damn, I wish we didn't have this confounded wedding hanging about our necks. I would leave the moment Lady Florence arrived tomorrow, if I had my druthers."

The mention of one lady reminded Ely of another. He took out the gold pocket watch and was amazed to see that it was already a quarter of one. He mentally shrugged at his oversight, then determined that it might even be better to make Dorothy wait an additional night. He had learned at an early age that when a woman started desiring him she wasn't going to stop for any reason. Besides, he was experiencing a mental climax of a far different kind. Any doubts he may have harbored about the Irishman were now washed away. The man was going to make his goal and Paul Ely would be standing right there to help reap the profits. His duties, at the present, were rather mundane, but he knew the Earl had other plans for him in the future. He was determined to show his family that their antebellum wealth and position was nothing compared to the heights he could gain.

"It is amazing and sad," Lord Dunraven said after long thought. "Every nation of this civilized world has an inbred pride in their land and their heritage and their people. Here, they are uncaring of past or future. Like starving animals they gobble and devour at the trough called America. Nor do they seem to care what other animals come to gobble her up with them. Even though they are benefitting me greatly, I cannot help but be a little amazed at such ingratitude, such ugliness, such greed and stupidity. Perhaps your uncle was quite right, Paul. The North may someday learn that they really lost the war, because they killed off the only noble breed that America really possessed."

Ely fully disagreed. Cotton may have been king, but cotton was still hard, dirty work for the plantation owner as well as slave, and it didn't make anyone noble. To him the nobility was a myth born from defeat and was as stupid as those who still hoarded away their Confederate money. Neither nobleness nor the money was ever going to buy them anything. He was out to emulate every person Dunraven had put him in contact with—he would grab what he could while the grabbing was good.

4

BY TWO A.M. Dorothy gave up her anxious vigil, although each time the clomp of horses' hooves would echo on the cobblestone, she would spring from her sleepless bed and peer down at the gas-lit street.

Her mind was a quagmire of horrible thoughts and fears. Was Paul sick? Had he been in an accident? Had the Earl somehow found out their plans and was thwarting it? Had he determined that he did not love her after all and was not man enough to come and tell her?

No! No! No! She cancelled out the thoughts as soon as they arose and then worried about the new ones that took their place.

By dawn she was exhausted and haggard. But a new thought renewed her hope. Paul had not been able to contact her because of the late hour and now he would be able to do so without anyone questioning.

The house stirred early, because this was the beginning of the two most hectic days of all. Because of that hope, Dorothy also arose so that she could intercept the message when it did arrive.

Paul Ely had been quite correct on one point. She would not have been missed that morning. The house was in total turmoil and confusion. Everyone was taking breakfast on the run and paid little or no attention to Dorothy sitting sipping her tea.

She felt as though she had consumed a gallon and still no messenger came to the Gould's door.

Although the morning seemed to evaporate for everyone else, for Dorothy the hands on the clock seemed to jump back twice for every tick forward.

She barely touched her lunch, but no one noticed. Last minute problems were arising so fast that everyone seemed to gobble and run without comment.

Carriages rolled constantly on the cobbles of the street, but their stopping at the brownstone was to deliver wedding gifts, not messages for Dorothy.

To keep her mind occupied, she helped unwrap the gifts and register on an ever-growing list who they were from and what they were. She privately thought most of them vulgar, but things that would please Caroline inordinately. She became conscious of Mabel Allgood hustling around more than any of the rest of the household staff, and as caustic as she knew the woman might become, she just had to share her doubts with someone.

"Mabel," she whispered, catching the woman's arm as she sailed past the unwrapping table in the foyer, "I need to talk with you."

"Holy caterpillar!" Mabel gasped, reaching immediately for Dorothy's forehead. Then she sighed, noting that the girl's forehead was cool. "Thought you were sickly for the moment. Can't say as you shouldn't be, with all this nightly partying. Shameful, I say, but my voice is not heard any farther up than the basement."

"Mabel, I need to talk to you," she repeated urgently.

"What you need is sleep, young lady. Go take a nap and I'll come to you later."

"Mabel, now!"

"Child, everything about this mad-house is now, now, now! That cow of a bride cannot fit into her wedding dress, the suit pants for the boys haven't yet been delivered and no one in this household seems to know how to put a length of thread through a needle's eye. I need me a hundred leprechauns at the moment, so let me get back to you later."

Dorothy didn't argue. She knew that Mable would not have been much help anyway. The welling tears were making a bright dazzle before her eyes. She was beginning to fear the worst, and still did not want to admit it.

Another carriage clomped down the street, another clang came from the bellpull. She didn't even look up as the maid answered. Her anticipation had long since vanished.

"How do you do," a quiet voice addressed her. "The girl tells me that you are Lady Dorothy Goold. You might recall me as Florence Elizabeth O'Hearn."

Flushing deeply, and hastily brushing away one or two ribbon strings which had stuck to her bodice, she turned to the speaker. She saw a slight woman of simple dress at her side, smiling down affectionately at her. She did not recognize the woman, and recovering herself, hastily rose.

"How ungracious of me," the woman continued, "I should have said that I am now Lady Dunraven. Naturally, since we have not met in years, you wouldn't recall me."

"How do you do?" Dorothy murmured, almost inaudibly.

"And how glad I am to see you," Lady Florence said, beaming. "I am in a dither. We came in the carriage from Lake George, rather than take the train, I am trying to find my husband and this is the only address I have."

Dorothy heard Lady Florence's voice and nothing else. It was so musically Irish that it seemed to fill the air about her, and little darting thrills of home ran over her legs and arms and young breasts. She had the oddest impulse to hug and kiss the woman.

"He's staying at the Brevoort House," she stammered, her voice too loud in her embarrassed ears.

"Glory! I hope it's not far. If I must sit in that carriage much longer I am going to have bunions in all the wrong places."

Dorothy heard herself laughing, the first time all day. "Well, we can't have that. Come, we'll find ourselves a cup of tea or something."

"That would hit the spot," she sighed. "Girl, tell the driver to deposit my luggage here. I'm not moving another inch until I'm good and ready."

The woman took Dorothy stoutly by the arm and was ready to be led away. She, too, was exhausted. New York was a frightening experience for her, and she was grasping onto home ties as desperately as was Dorothy.

The dining room table was laden with gifts, so Dorothy ventured on through the pantry to an area of the house unknown to her. The cook took immediate offense that such as they would even consider taking their tea at the servant's eating area, but both women immediately agreed that the windowed alcove, looking out on the back garden, was more than charming. In all the years that Clara Cummings had cooked for the Goulds she had considered it no more than an oil-clothed table to hurriedly eat her meals upon.

Lady Florence leaned her elbows on the table in unladylike fashion and studied Dorothy with frank affection. "It was certainly silly of me to be asking if you recalled me. How could you? You could not have been more than seven or eight the last time my family visited Adare Castle. We were then in India for many years. We only returned last year for my marriage to Lord Dunraven."

Dorothy could not help but be amazed that this was the Earl's choice for a bride. The woman, for all her surface sweetness, was simple and colorless. Her clothing was dowdy and plain. Her light brown hair was plastered back into a tight bun under the poke bonnet; her features so conventional as to be easily lost in a crowd, except for the pleasant sparkle of her hazel eyes.

"I am aware," she went on without faltering, "that it was the desire of the Earl and Lady Agatha that no members of the Goold side of the family be invited to the services. I was motherless by then, Lady Dorothy, and my father long overdue to be retired from the Colonial Service. I'm afraid that even though his advancement from Baronet to Baron to Viscount to Earl was justified, he had become most senile and would not have recognized either Lady Margaret or Lady Jane had they come to visit."

"Excuses aren't necessary, Lady Florence."

"I was making it sound that way, wasn't I? In actual fact I was trying to learn what animosities you might hold for me."

Dorothy raised an eyebrow. "I have no reason to hold any."

Lady Florence sighed. "You will never know how dear those words sound to my ears. I've not been home to Ireland since our marriage eight months ago and find that I am not a great lover of America or Americans. I was overjoyed to learn Lady Jane was coming to New York and then crushed by the news of her accident. But my joy is renewed in finding you here. Now I can suffer through this experience with less fright."

The cook brought them a plate of cold beef,

bread, salad and a pot of steeping tea. Dorothy was not aware of eating, though she watched Florence intently as she filled her plate. The woman projected an aura of warmth and happiness.

"Now, tell me all about the wedding plans," said Florence, eating as though she were starved. "The Earl is most remiss in informing me about such matters."

"I can certainly understand why. He and his business associate have been quite busy with their own affairs."

Lady Florence laughed lightly. "The story of my entire honeymoon and marriage, my dear. I don't believe Windham draws a breath without thinking of some new scheme or another. But I didn't expect my life to be any different. Living in India for so long I was held back from marriage until age thirty so that it could be proper for me and political for father. Only to you would I admit that I am still searching to know my husband. Living out of our luggage hasn't made it any easier."

"And now you will be right off again to Colorado," Dorothy said sadly.

"Will I?" The woman didn't even pretend to mask her surprise. "You see, I am told nothing." She sighed. "Well, that is the system we were born to, my dear. When the husband says 'jump,' you are on your feet before he is finished speaking!"

There was a sudden quenching of the light on Dorothy's face. She began to murmur, and Lady Florence leaned across the table the better to hear her. Dorothy had dropped her eyes, and was twisting her napkin in her hands.

"I'm beginning to see what is lacking in the system. It almost denies that there is such a thing as love."

"That, my dear, comes to each of us as we grow to know our mate and bring forth our children."

Dorothy lifted her eyes now, and they were full of anguished tears.

"But why can't love come first, if you've found the proper man?"

Lady Florence felt a strong tenderness for Dorothy that could easily translate into protectiveness and love. She was hearing her own words of ten years before echoed back to her. She too, in her youth, had not beeen able to understand why love could not come first. He had been a dashing young officer in her father's regiment, and she had been overwhelmed that he looked beneath her simple exterior to perceive the interior beauty of her mind and soul. It had been the most glorious six months of her life—until the romance was discovered. He had been dispatched at once to the farthest border patrol and she had been sternly warned never to try and see him again. Lord and Lady Starnes were not about to let her waste her life on a "young pup" who would take years to rise in the grades. And now, she thought, as she looked at Dorothy's anguished face, she couldn't even recall the young man's name. But the love she had carried in her heart for ten years was a painful and lasting memory.

"Would you care to discuss him?" she asked quietly.

"I didn't say there was—" Dorothy started to protest.

Lady Florence reached across the table and took

up one of her little hands, so white and thin and trembling.

"You didn't have to say it with words, my dear. Is it a recent development?"

Now she stammered as she struggled to retain coherence over her wild emotions. She had to get it out of her system or go mad. "Since coming to America. He's like no man I've ever met before. He loves me as much as I love him, Lady Florence. Last night he was to send a hansom for me and we were to elope this morning."

Lady Florence released her hand. The situation was farther along than she had anticipated. There were certain aspects that she did not like, but she said nothing.

"The cab never came," murmured Dorothy. "I've had no news since and have worried myself into a real stew. I was even contemplating going to him when you arrived."

"How old are you, Dorothy?"

"I will be twenty-one March the next."

"A marriageable age, to be sure. Would you like me to meet the young man?"

"Oh, but you already know him! He's Lord Dunraven's business associate, Paul Ely!"

Lady Florence Elizabeth was not born to mince words. Her first love had at least been an officer and a gentleman—but Paul Ely! She knew him as nothing but a scoundrel.

"I do know him," she said sternly, "but hardly as a business associate of my husband. He is a hired bodyguard and hunting guide. A cowboy of sorts, if I remember the term correctly."

Dorothy looked her full in the eyes. "I don't believe you. He is a Southern gentleman and an elegant dresser."

"And a peacock is the filthiest bird you can have roaming your garden. He may have been born in the South, my dear, but his actions while we were there hardly classify him as a gentleman by my standards. I cannot understand Lord Dunraven allowing the man to pawn himself off on you in such a deceitful way. I am most distressed by this, Dorothy. In lieu of your mother not being here, I intend to investigate this matter to the fullest. Now, if you will inform me of Lord Dunraven's whereabouts and the schedule I am expected to fulfill, I can get started at once."

Dorothy answered dully. "We'll have to get you transportation to the Brevoort House. This evening is the wedding rehearsal, followed by a supper. Lord Dunraven will have the address for each." And then all at once her expression became blank and sad. Slowly the truth was beginning to filter through her strong desire that the woman had to be wrong.

Numbly, she saw Lady Florence away and, disregarding the stack of gifts that had arrived during the tea, she pulled herself up the three flights of stairs to her room.

She looked at the windowseat with hatred, as though it were a part of the onerous plot. Dorothy saw all of Ely's lies with a gray numbness of despair in her heart. He was no better than Brewster Gould, only much more cunning. Only then did she begin to fathom what would have happened to her between midnight and dawn. She would have become just as trashy as Amy Blakely. To vent her anger and hurt pride upon something tangible, she took the novel from its hiding place and tore it into shreds. She had almost been duped by common love.

She felt so humiliated. She saw that she had cut her own throat. Had she retained her self-dignity, she never would have allowed herself to fall into such disgrace. Oddly enough, for the moment, she blamed only herself for being such a fool.

Lady Florence Elizabeth feared no man or situation, least of all Lord Dunraven. Despite her rather colorless exterior, she was a very shrewd lady indeed, and it took her only an instant to be advised by her own intelligence to proceed slowly, and watch her every step.

"It was all for her own protection," said Lord Dunraven quietly. "The man who rescued Lady Dorothy off the *Shannon* is an infamous womanizer and was beginning to show her undue attention. As the scandal would have touched the whole family, I made Ely into something that he was not to escort the girl about and keep her away from this Jim Fisk."

Lady Florence did not believe a single word of this, but pretended that she did, and shook her head somberly.

She knows I'm lying, thought Dunraven. Damn it, why all this mystery, this skirmishing? What had Ely done that he was not aware of?

"So," she said flatly, "a purse was made out of a sow's ear? I fail to see why you could not have escorted your cousin, instead of stooping to such duplicity."

What the hell is she up to? thought Dunraven, knitting his thin brows. He did not believe in discussing business affairs with his wife. It was none of her damn business. She was a social asset, the future mother of his heirs and nothing more. If his scheme was as successful as he knew it would be, he would not even have to rely upon her fifty thousand pounds a year dowry. But he had to answer logically, because she did not let loose of a topic easily.

"It would have been out of the question. I had business to discuss at almost every one of the affairs—business that I did not think appropriate for the ears of Lady Dorothy."

She drew a deep breath, and looked at her husband with stern resolution.

"At the inn where we took breakfast this morning, Windham, they had the city newspapers. Laura read the Judge and me the society page account of this Mr. Fisk's party of last evening. I've always said that you should read more and then I wouldn't have to question why the reporter infers that you are planning to do business with a man you paint so blackly."

"Woman," he scolded, "kindly stay out of business matters that do not concern you."

"Oh, I intend to," she said sweetly, "but not out of this sordid affair you have burdened us with. I would know straight out, sir, if you properly instructed Mr. Ely as to his conduct or gave him *carte blanche* authority to play the cad!"

Dunraven was trapped. He could answer truthfully on both counts, but one or the other would come out sounding like a lie.

"My dear," he said, in a deep and worried tone, "it all has to do with the business proposals I am putting together at the present time. You might as well know that Lady Jane has been giving us some little trouble over the sale of some farm lands. Until that could be finalized, I wished for Ely to keep Lady Dorothy occupied. If she has reacted like a typical emotional female, I cannot be held responsible."

Eight months of marriage had not allowed him to see how shrewd a wife he possessed.

"I am ashamed, sir," she said in a thin and shrilling whisper. "You were going to allow that girl to be compromised just so you could vent more of your petty revenge against Lady Jane."

"I did nothing of the–"

She stopped him short. "Quiet, sir, until you have all the facts. Whether you sanctioned it or not, the man was glib enough to worm his way into the girls affections and proclaim his love. As a sheltered child, she saw no reason to disbelieve and waited throughout the night for a cab that was due to pick her up at midnight. This morning they were to leave this hotel and elope for marriage. As an honorable man, sir, I ask you what a dishonorable man would intend to do with a young lady throughout the night until he could make good on his morning promise?"

There was a sudden, pregnant silence in the warm and pleasant suite of rooms. Lady Florence sat as still as a statue. But there were streaks of rough red on Dunraven's sallow cheekbones and his eyes were so narrowed that they could not be seen.

"As the man was with me until the wee hours of the morning," he said darkly, "I cannot help but believe this is all a figment of a very wild imagination."

"You may believe what you wish," she said softly, "but you will shackle your little minion from having anything to do with Lady Dorothy henceforth. Now, I wish to rest for awhile and then dress for the evening." At the bedroom door she turned. "And I strongly question why you would want to keep the man in your employ." She shut the door softly.

Dunraven was white with rage and hatred—rage at Ely for handling the whole thing like a stupid ass, hatred toward his wife for thinking she had the right to meddle into this affair and tell him what to do. He would reprimand Ely severely and tell him to stay clear of both Lady Florence and Lady Dorothy. But he was damned if he was going to fire the man just because his wife told him he should. No woman, not even his mother, had ever dared try to rule him and no woman, especially not his wife, was going to be given the opportunity to start now.

Paul Ely sat very quiet listening to the Earl relate Lady Florence's accusations. Then all at once he burst into a shout of wild laughter. He bent almost double, shaking his brown head until his thick, curly waves of hair were greatly agitated. He thought the whole thing quite priceless and only nodded a half-hearted agreement to stay away from the two ladies.

As Dorothy was not a part of the immediate wedding party, she thought her excuses to Flora would be quickly accepted by the overly agitated woman.

"But you can't," remarked Flora crossly. "You won't know where to sit in the cathedral tomorrow and it will make me a place short at the restaurant."

"Two short," Dorothy said dully. "I don't think Mr. Ely would dare—will be attending tonight."

Flora was just about ready to pounce on that statement when she saw Dorothy's feverish face and dull sunken eyes. She came closer, the better to scrutinize the girl.

"What's the matter with you?" she demanded. "You look ill." She pressed the back of her cold hand against Dorothy's burning cheek.

"I'm not feeling too well today, Aunt Flora," she admitted.

Flora scowled. "Good God. I hope you aren't coming down with something. Not with the wedding tomorrow, and everything. I think I'd best send for a doctor, to reassure me."

"That won't be necessary," answered Dorothy, curtly. "I just need rest and want to be alone."

"Well, alone is exactly what you will be. I've got to take everyone with me tonight so that they know their duties tomorrow. Thank God for your Mabel Allgood. She is such a gem. Oh, I'd better tell cook to lay you out some supper. Changes, changes, always changes. I'm just grateful that I have only boys left."

Dorothy closed the door after her, went up to her room and waited for the house to vacate.

But even when it did, she was given no peace. The doorbell jangled so often with arriving wedding gifts that she was exhausting herself running up and down the stairs. Finally, she determined it would be far wiser to find the prepared supper plate, take it into the front parlor and be near the door.

She surprised herself by having a fairly good appetite. She had thought earlier that she would never want to ever eat again.

"Drat!" she said, as the door bell jangled again. "One would think that she was a real princess with all these gifts. I'm coming! I'm coming!"

"Oh, no!" she mourned, breaking into tears, "how dare you come here? Go away!"

As he had anticipated he might someday have to do, Paul Ely got his foot into the door before she could shut it.

Then he said explosively, "I'm not leaving until you hear me out!"

"There is nothing you can say that I care to hear."

"Not even that I love you?"

"That, most of all I don't want to hear," she cried. "Go, or I shall start calling for the police."

"Call!" he shouted. "Call out the whole force! Arouse the whole neighborhood! Perhaps with them as the judge and jury I'll get a better hearing than I've been given by your blue-nosed cousins!"

"Hush!" she snapped, pulling him inside and slamming the door. "Haven't you embarrassed me enough without announcing it to this entire neighborhood?"

"Embarrassed?" he growled. "What do you know about embarrassment? What kind of trumped up story did you tell Lady Florence?"

Freckles began to pop out on Dorothy's nose and the green flecks in her brown eyes were like flashings of St. Elmo's fire. But when she spoke her voice was rapier thin.

"Only the simple fact that your hansom cab never arrived last night and I have not heard from you since, until this very moment."

"Let's be frank," he said. "Do you mistrust me? If you do, blame your cousin. He kept me occupied until three this morning."

Dorothy's eyes met Paul's, and she saw the fiery blue in the young man's eyes, the boldness of his look, the resolute determination.

"Have I said I distrust you?" she asked coyly. "If I distrusted you, you'd never have gotten in."

Ely's expression spoke of smelling victory again at hand. He had anticipated that Dorothy would have foregone the rehearsal and dinner just to avoid him. He had also anticipated that if he was just manly enough, just positive enough, that he would catch her in such a mental frame of mind that he could twist her easily and have her in bed within minutes. He gave his thigh a sharp blow with the palm of his hand.

"Now we can cut out all the damn nonsense you're hearing from everyone else. That old harridan has never wanted me around. She was always nasty to me in Colorado and treated my kinfolk down South worse than we ever treated the slaves."

She smiled sweetly, knowingly. "What's the matter, Paul? Wouldn't she let you guard the Earl's body or take him on hunting trips as a guide?"

There was a sharp silence in the room. Ely's face became congested and his eyes flashed fire. His mouth settled into sullen and resistive lines. Dunraven had not informed him that he had been fully unmasked. He felt naked and momentarily unsure of himself.

But it was not in the character of Paul Ely to remain unsure for very long. He allowed his face to take on a hurt, pouting expression. He cleared his throat.

"You make that sound almost criminal," he said slowly and somberly. "It's been good, clean, honest and well-paying work. It's all the Earl had for me at the time, but that is going to change. Now that he's going to start on his project, I'm to be his right-hand man. Why else do you think he dressed me so good and built me up in the eyes of the men he was associating with? I'm going to have to work with them, just as much as he, and he couldn't have me looking like a nobody. Did you see Jim Fisk's lackeys? They jump at the snap of his fingers. Have you ever seen me jump for the Earl? No! He respects me for what I'm going to become. Do you think he would have let me near you if he didn't respect me as a man and a gentleman?"

He was smooth. He was very smooth. He could take a dotted i and turn it into a full sentence in his defense.

"It was still deceitful," she said quietly.

"Hell yes!" he roared. "Deceitful as hell, because I was under direct orders. I was to escort you about just to keep you out of the Earl's hair. I'll confess to that. I'll also confess that I thought it was going to be boring as hell because you were such an arrogant, snobbish little prig. But, damn it, I didn't know I was going to fall in love with you. Yes! That's honest! Love! I've never said it to a woman before. I've had my share, but they've never gotten under my skin as you did. Dammit, I'm only human! You stir my blood until I can hardly stand it! I schemed to get you, but it didn't work. Then when I do have a moment of honesty and make plans to marry you, that lousy bastard has to get in the way and keep me like an errand boy after school. And he's had me doing one thing or the other all day, until I got back to the hotel and was hit square in the face with these charges."

Dorothy sat listening, but was still not sure. Brewster had tried force, Paul Ely words. She was not about to get burned again.

"What more can I say?" he pleaded. "I fell in love with you as a woman I came to know, not for any title or wealth that you might possess. I'm the man. I'll provide the wealth for my woman." He hesitated. "The only problem is that I was living in a dream world created by the Earl. I was trying to be something in your eyes that I was not. But I will be, Dorothy. Six months on this project and I can be wealthier than my father was before the war. But I can't do it unless I have you and your love to strengthen me. I can see that now."

Still Dorothy remained silent. She was more confused in her mind now than she had been before. He had confessed to what he had not been, and thus made himself more than he ever was. Love doesn't die in a moment, but like a spring flower shocked by a late frost it takes it a bit longer to blossom back into full bloom.

"What are your plans now, Lady Dorothy?" he asked.

She frowned.

"The first thing," she said, "is for you to stop calling me Lady Dorothy, again. And then I need time, Paul. Which means, I suppose, that I have to change certain people's opinions of you."

"Then you do still love me?" he asked impulsively.

"I don't know," she said honestly. "Was I just in love with love, or was it really you?" She could not help but think of Amy Blakely again. "If love is nothing more than sex, then every woman in the world would be nothing more than a harlot."

Ely stiffened as if he had been slapped. Sex was all he desired from her, and all she really had to give him in return.

She saw his reaction and bowed her head for an instant and mastered her tears. She had been taught how to do that to be a proper lady. She had practiced a great deal of it in the last twenty-some hours. But there was still a lot of woman under the Whyham-Quin-Goold veneer.

"Paul," she said gently, "do you still want me to go West?" The hunger in her soft brown eyes was as visible as their color.

"What I want you might not understand, so let's be frank. I've known whores and Southern belles. I've never known a woman like you. I don't give a damn what that milksop and his prudish hag say. They probably don't fornicate anyway. Tonight I want to have you, to be with you, like I have never done before." He gave her a slow, sensuous smile and started toward her before her rattled brain could dredge up an appropriate denial for his request.

He looked deep into her eyes. Then he wrapped his arms forcefully around her back and waist and pressed his open mouth to hers. The kiss was long and meaningful. Dorothy felt a stirring in her stomach that she had never felt before. A field of butterflies ascended to the bright blue sky. Her fingertips tingled. The blood in her veins rained torridly hot, then as chilly as an Irish fog. She was shaking when he pulled away with a curse. The bell was jangling.

"Don't even answer it," he snapped. "Let's just sneak on up to your room."

"I'm the only one here," she insisted, "I must answer it." She started away and then called back over her shoulder. "It will probably be just another wedding present."

He sulked along behind her. He could not stand much more of this frustration. Every time he had her primed to go, something came up.

"Timmy'O," she gasped, "what has happened?"

"I forgot my key," he said sullenly, pushing past her.

"That is obvious," she said, "but what about your face?"

His battered and bloodied face was forgotten when he saw Paul Ely standing in the foyer. "What in the hell is he doing here?" he demanded.

"He came by to talk with me," Dorothy answered honestly.

"Well, I don't want the son-of-a-bitch in my house!" Timmy'O screamed.

"Stop it!" Dorothy gasped. "What kind of talk is that?"

"Better than he deserves," the boy sneered. "He's the cause of the whole fight I've just been through with Brewster. And his being here makes me believe I got bloodied up for nothing!"

Dorothy blanched. She didn't need to be told what manner of obscene things might have come out of Brewster Gould's mouth. But she did not want a repeat of the argument in the foyer.

"That's quite enough," she insisted. "Timmy'O, go to the kitchen and I will be right there to see to you. Paul, I'm sorry, but I'm afraid I'm going to have to say goodnight. Will I see you tomorrow at the wedding and reception?"

"I suppose so," he said laconically.

"Good. The reception should be over by about two. Let's go back for a drive and walk in Central Park. We seem to be able to get our thoughts expressed more clearly there." She reached up and kissed him tenderly on the cheek. "Don't worry about Cousin Florence. I can handle her. Everything is going to be all right."

"I'm sure that it will be," he smiled weakly and went out the door.

Dorothy stood for a moment mentally hugging herself. It was going to be all right. Paul had been honest with her and reaffirmed his love. She had been such a silly goose for worrying all day long and bringing Lady Florence into it. As she had suspected, Lord Dunraven had been the one who kept Paul from sending the hansom for her last night. She hugged herself again, because she felt so joyous.

Beyond the door, if she could have seen Paul Ely's face, she might have felt quite differently. He stood for a long moment scowling and then it turned into a devilish grin. Mentally, once again, a thought had sated his frustrations. He need not now lie to the Earl about the girl. He had been most chaste with her. His sexual desires for her had been burned out by insurmountable objects and events. He could go home and play with himself and get more enjoyment than with this continuous struggle to get Dorothy into his bed. As beautiful as she was, she was not worth the effort and patience. He checked his wallet and hailed a passing hansom cab. There was a bar in the tenderloin section where he could get everything he had wanted from Dorothy for a few bucks and end up without a marriage noose about his neck.

He planned on getting very drunk, satisfying his sexual appetite, and not showing up until the train was ready to depart on Monday morning.

"All right," Dorothy demanded, getting a basin and wash clothes to clean up Timmy'O's face. "What is this all about?"

"That damn Brewster," the freckle-faced youth scowled. "He said you'd be back here at the house screwing that bow-legged mick."

"Timmy'O," she gasped. "I'm leaving the room at once if you continue with such language!"

He eyed her narrowly. "Don't give me that shocked talk. I heard what Brewster said to you in the hall. Now, that *was* shocking."

"I don't wish to discuss it!" she said piously, reddening.

"Why not? It happened. You can't change that. So be honest. I know how you beat off my stud of a brother, but you really made me feel like one of Boss Tweed's ward hacks coming in here tonight. Dumb and stupid."

"Then you are dumb and stupid," she said soundly. "For if you believe that anything was going on between Paul and me when you arrived, you have a very dirty and nasty mind!"

"Really?" he said cautiously.

Her mind was gripped by an unbreakable ribbon of desires and truths. He had been her champion, before and, how, tonight, as far as she could gather—and she could not allow herself to tell him lies or half-truths.

"No," she said sadly, "because of the love that I feel for him I was just about ready to give him whatever he desired."

Timmy'O was quiet for a long time. "Do you really love him?"

"My heart tells me so."

"But what about your gut?"

"*My what?*"

"Here!" he yelled, pounding his stomach. "My stomach has been tied in knots since you came into this house. Unless your stomach is tied in knots over him, then it's really not love."

"Thank you, Timmy'O," she giggled. "You have just reduced my indigestion to its real symptom. My stomach, too, has been tied in knots since meeting Paul Ely."

Timmy'O shrugged. "Well, I guess you just knocked me out of the ball park."

"Hardly," she chuckled. "You will always be special to me and I already envy the girl lucky enough to get you."

She leaned across and gave him a long and thankful kiss full upon the lips.

"Wow!" he gushed. "I feel like I've just been rewarded for slaying the dragon."

If that was the case, Dorothy hated to see what the dragon looked like.

5

AFTER MANY REFITTINGS, Caroline managed to get into her bridal finery. The wedding dress was a marvel of French lace and ivory silk, bustled and draped lavishly. The ancient lace veil billowed about her like a diaphanous cloud. Fortunately it took away from the girl's natural largeness.

Guests were arriving, filling the cathedral pews with brightly colored gowns, whispered greetings, gleaming tall hats and canes. The tempo of the church increased deliriously with the arrival of President and Mrs. Grant. They were given the place of honor on the groom's side of the aisle.

Opposite sat Dorothy in soft green lace, Lady Florence in her usual earthen tones and Flora, harried and teary-eyed, in blue silk. Lord Dunraven, in cutaway and pin stripes, sat restive and bored. The massive pipe organ entertained the guests until the appointed hour. Dorothy was flamboyantly beautiful in comparison with the day before and kept peering about expectantly. It finally dawned on Lady Florence who she was searching out.

"He'll probably not be here," she whispered sharply. "Windham says his room was not slept in."

Dorothy looked down. She slowly pressed the palms of her gloved hands together. She spoke in a low voice, "Then it is my fault, Lady Florence. He came to me last night and confessed all. He still wants me for his bride and will work hard to prove himself worthy. I should have kept him with me last night. He is probably off sulking and embarrassed to face you."

Lady Florence drew a deep breath, and looked at the young woman with stern resolution. But the strains of the wedding march were swelling from the organ and kept her from speaking her thoughts at the moment. The music rose triumphantly.

Lady Florence saw none of the entrance and heard little of the solemn mass. She hardly glanced at the bride and her distinguished bridegroom. Her mind was fixed solidly on the problem of Dorothy and Paul Ely. It could not be handled in the same manner as her parents had handled her first love. No woman, she determined, should have to suffer with a faceless ghost and a constant question mark as to how her life might have been under different circumstances. But even as the veil was lifted for the groom to kiss the bride, she still had not fully solved the problem in her mind.

The reception passed like an evil dream for Dorothy. She enlisted the aide of Timmy'O to take a cab from the Waldorf-Astoria to the Brevoort House and search out Paul Ely. The young man's report was dismal. Neither the house detective nor Timmy'O could rouse the man out of his drunken stupor.

Guilt assailed Dorothy. She wanted to rush to Paul, but Timmy'O persuaded her that it would do little good. Time was now becoming the enemy. With their scheduled departure in the morning, she saw everything slipping away again.

The reception was too brilliant, too crowded, too noisy. Brewster, with his twisted broken nose, became obnoxiously drunk; more guests came to be seen than to see; the Waldorf had to hurriedly borrow champagne from other hotels because of the unexpected high consumption for so staid a gathering; Flora continued to worry until the pain in her head increased to frightful proportions. By the time Caroline and Clarence departed on their honeymoon, Lord Dunraven was about the only person who was smiling broadly.

He had found that he and the President were men cut from the same cloth. They each had gained stature not only because of their egotism and ambition, but because of a quality few men took advantage of. Each had gained by hatred and a cold blooded ability to step on others and never look down.

On the surface Ulysses S. Grant was a quiet, unassuming man, with almost a shy manner. In spite of the spoils system around him, Grant was an honest man, but had enemies in the Senate that he hated.

"Your dream is greatly similar to my own, Lord Dunraven. Vast portions of this beautiful land should be put under federal control and taken out of the hands of the homesteaders. *My* Congress calls it folly. Perhaps, if your experiment worked, they would have to change their tune. Of course, the three hundred thousand acres you desire poses problems. The Utes claim all of the Northern Colorado Territory as theirs under prior treaties. If you will supply them with transportation I can supply you with a man each from Interior and the Bureau of Indian Affairs to put these claims quickly to rest."

"It will mean a delay in my departure, Mr. President, but I shall be more than glad to take them along."

"Won't be more than a day, Lord Dunraven. When I bark, most men don't hang around to see if I also bite. Ah, Trevor, let me say again how good it is to see you. The White House seems to intimidate my old friends from coming around to see me. You will have a fine man here in Trevor Cleveland, Lord Dunraven, a fine man, indeed."

"He has already shown me his worth, Mr. President. He has proposed that the forestry land that I have been granted be established as a 'development area for new lumbering techniques and reforesting.'"

"Why is that?" Grant asked.

Trevor Cleveland eyed him shrewdly. "Such development is by Executive Order, Mr. President."

Grant grinned broadly. "Which will add an additional man to your growing entourage, Lord Dunraven. Such an order requires that the land be surveyed by the government. Trevor, you find the right man for the Earl and I'll sign the order when I get back to Washington. Senator Sumner may have kept me from buying the Dominican Republic, but he can't keep me from giving away land to preserve it from being hacked to pieces as they've done to our Eastern states. If I thought I could get away with it I would close all of our ports to further immigration. Two million new people since the war. Too many! Far too many!"

Dunraven was so happy that he was hardly listening to his wife as they returned to the hotel in a landau.

"Windham, you have not heard a single word I

have been saying about this situation between Lady Dorothy and Paul Ely."

Dunraven opened his cruel slash of a mouth, and smiled as though he thought the matter had been all settled.

"Well?" he was goaded to say, with impatience.

"It would seem, Windham, the cunning Mr. Ely did not take your advice and went to the Gould's last night and confessed all to Lady Dorothy. He has her all a-twitter again with thoughts of marriage."

"Preposterous! The marriage would be a scandal and put me in a very unfavorable light!"

"I could not agree more. We must do something to stop it."

Dunraven laughed gently. His little eyes, so cunning and bright, sparkled mirthfully. "Which is quite simple, my dear. We pack Lady Dorothy off to her home and I threaten to discharge Ely if he attempts to contact her."

Lady Florence shook her head. "That is not the solution, as I see it, Windham. Ely is a fox. And like a fox he will double back on his tracks. Dorothy has got to be made to see the scoundrel that he is."

"I wish you luck, my dear. She and her servant woman are due to sail tomorrow for home."

"It cannot be done with just words, Windham," she said sternly. "That is why I seek your permission to cable Lady Jane this afternoon."

"Are you daft, woman?" he gasped. "We are trying to forestall a scandal, not bring it fully out into the open."

He listened to his own words and thought how

strange it was that a few days before he had been formulating what he was now trying to eliminate.

"She will be told nothing of this," she said coldly. "Please give me some credit, sir. She will only be informed of our journey to the West and my desire and need for a female companion. Because of the conflict between you two, I feel the cable should come from me as the personal request of an old friend."

Dunraven smiled slyly at his wife's plan. "I'm sure that Lady Jane will not give you any objection, put that way, but how do you propose to handle Lady Dorothy and Paul Ely?"

"Like a female fox," she said, in an odd and very slow and purposeful voice. "I do not think the man is sincere and am sure he will unmask himself. As Dorothy is an intelligent creature, I see little difficulty in convincing her that the conventional thing is to allow this romance to have a proper period of courting. How can she refuse? After all, we will be allowing her to be near the man she claims to love, and with a degree of parental approval. What she won't know is that we shall keep a close eye on the courting process."

"You shall keep a close eye," he amended. "I shall be too busy with my own affairs to partake in your little game."

He sat back and could hardly restrain his laughter. This was even better than his original scheme to entangle Dorothy with Jim Fisk. If Dorothy still fell from grace, it would now be on the shoulders of his wife. It would be too bad if the women's old friendship suffered a setback. It would just show them all that women should never intrude upon his affairs.

* * *

The Pullman cars were lavish to the point of being overdone in plush, gilt, silver and mahogany. The sitting car easily accommodated the secretary-accountant, Rufus Brogan, Trevor Cleveland, Morris Phipps from Interior, Palmer Hoyt of the Bureau of Indian Affairs and Captain Jacob Hartman, a surveyor from The Army Corps of Engineers. There were ample sitting and sleeping berths to also accommodate Paul Ely, but because of his recent escapade Lord Dunraven, in a fit of pique, exiled him to the coach section of the regular train.

Next came the dining car with galley and cook, snow-white linen and napkins for each table, fresh flowers, silver, cut glass and china service, three black waiters and a small bar and lounge area.

The third and last car was too extreme to simply call a parlor car. Its front half was a formal sitting room whose furnishings put John Jacob Astor III's Louis XIV collection to shame. The rear half was comprised of two spacious drawing rooms with permanent bedroom-berth alcoves and two compartments, left and right, that were less specious. Their berths had to be made down at night by the parlor car porter, but they did possess, like the drawing rooms, closet-sized toilet and washroom facilities.

The drawing rooms, naturally, went respectively to Lord Dunraven and Lady Florence. The roomettes, as the porter called them, were to have been for Dorothy and Mabel Allgood. But when Lady Jane cabled back her permission for Dorothy to accompany Lady Florence, the strong-minded Irish woman put her foot down. Mabel Allgood had no desire to set foot one inch farther ino America and returned as planned on the ship that left on Monday.

The Tuesday morning departure from Commodore Vanderbilt's new Grand Central Station was like the exodus of an Eastern potentate. The entire social register of New York, and then some, were on hand.

You would have thought that Flora Gould was seeing off her own daughter the way she wept and carried on over Dorothy. Walter Gould thought he was solely responsible for putting everything together for Lord Dunraven and loudly boasted of their relationship.

Lady Florence, who loathed travel of any form, quickly entered the train and took refuge in her private drawing room.

Dorothy shook Brewster's hand coolly and then gave warm kisses and hugs to Timmy'O and Adam. Too late, she was beginning to see how she would miss those two bubbling spirits.

She turned to have two dozen long-stem roses thrust into her arms by Jim Fisk.

"Ah, lovely, lovely lady," he cooed, kissing her hand, "that I were much younger, or you a trifle older, what an outstanding team we would have made!"

"I'm so sorry to hear of all your troubles."

"It is certainly selling newspapers," he chuckled. "Too bad I don't own a couple. Dear Josie is now resorting to blackmail and threatening to publish compromising letters which I am supposed to have written her. Knowing my gift for gab, I probably did, and they will make most amusing reading for the public."

On a heartfelt impulse, and a strange premonition in her heart, Dorothy went up on tip-toe and kissed Jim Fisk on each cheek.

"You're the sweetest, kindest, most genteel gentleman I have ever met. I may never meet you again, but I shall never forget you."

Jim Fisk turned away with honest tears in his eyes. He could buy off judges, juries and governments, but no amount of money could buy the respect he had just been given for nothing.

And Dorothy's premonition was quite correct, she would never again see Jim Fisk. The Prince of Erie would so embroil himself in legal suits, libel suits and countersuits with Josie Mansfield and Edward S. Stokes over the next four months that not even the Tweed judiciary could bring him mollifying revenge. The immorality of his private life, so vulgarly and needlessly flaunted before the public, would cause him to surprisingly resign his vice-presidency and directorship of the Erie Railroad.

And when it finally appeared that Josie and Eddie would win their libel suit, the fickle public changed its outcry and a Grand Jury indicted the two for the attempted blackmail of Fisk.

But the public was too late. Fisk, ascending the long flight of stairs to the second floor of the Grand Central Hotel looked up to see Eddie Stokes coming at him with pistol in hand. Stokes fired, point-blank. Fisk cried out in fear and pain, stumbled, fell down, and struggled to rise to his feet. Stokes fired again, saw Fisk fall down the staircase, turned to flee and was captured.

Fisk, who was at the hotel to meet Jay Gould, Bill Tweed and his lawyers was soon surrounded by them and carried to a room where physicians worked to save his life. Gould, a highly religious man, seeing the end was near, wanted to send for a priest to administer the last rites.

Fisk waved the thought away. "Once in my life I was called a genteel gentleman. That's good enough for me to face St. Peter with."

The next morning, January 7, 1872, Jim Fisk, Jr. died—still harboring that thought.

The vastness of America overwhelmed Dorothy. The grip of winter was closing in on the land and making the leafless trees of the farmlands appear as eerie skeletons. The byways and communities seemed deserted and forlorn, Pittsburgh already a gray-sky-sooted city that reeked of burning coke and smelted steel. Day and night they were hauled across the expanse of Ohio, Indiana and Illinois. Dorothy's excitement waned, mainly from loneliness. Lady Florence never left her drawing room and made it well known that she desired no company. Lord Dunraven and his entourage spent countless hours in the first car discussing his plans in such exacting detail that it became boring for all but the Earl. Dorothy never saw Paul Ely and thought he was avoiding her because of their last meeting. She tried not to let it upset her, because she knew she now had plenty of time to make amends.

The switching yards of Chicago's Union Station were enormous. The three Pullman cars were backed onto a siding and uncoupled with such a jolt that it knocked the book right out of Dorothy's hands. She leaned over to pick it up and then straightened to stare out the window. The main part of the train pulled back onto the line and then backed into the station. The tracks were so close that she found herself looking directly into the faces of the coach car occupants. They in turn gawked back at her luxurious surroundings, the likes of which they had never imagined possible.

Then, to her total surprise, she was staring at a face that was not that of a stranger. And Paul Ely stared back at her in shocked disbelief. He had not been informed that she was on the trip and it boggled his mind. Daily he had attended the meetings in the sitting car, but had never been invited to the dining car or parlor car. He knew he was not in the good graces of the Earl at the moment and had purposely kept a very low profile. But the sight of Dorothy opened all manner of speculation and his ego-centered mind could narrow in on only one conclusion: she was chasing him.

The coach car was gone in a mere second and Dorothy raced out to the rear observation platform to see where the train was taking Paul and to find out why their cars were standing still.

The aroma in the air almost gagged her. The stench of cattle dung was so strong that it nearly burned the eyes. She saw the red and green lights of the train vanish into the long car-barn tunnels and her puzzlement grew.

"Good Lord!" Dunraven gasped, stepping out to the platform. "They have left us right in the middle of a cattle pen. No fresh air, this. Come back inside, my dear."

"What is going on?"

"We are being switched to a train that will take us to Omaha and then onto the new Union Pacific lines to Cheyenne. We shouldn't be here more than an hour or two."

"But, but," she stammered. "I just saw Paul in one of the cars of that train."

He had all but forgotten about Lady Florence's little game and his decision to punish Ely.

"Quite true," he said casually. "He will switch to the other train that will come to pick us up."

It was not a satisfying answer, but all she thought she would get at the moment. She was about ready to enter her roomette when the Earl stopped her.

"Our other guests have also gone on to the station to see a bit of Chicago, although I can't understand why. It's a horrible little city with cows boarded right in town. It needs to be razed and started all over."

His wish would come true the next year when the city would burn, killing three hundred and leaving ninety thousand homeless.

"But," he continued smoothly, "I am getting off my point. Lady Florence is still bedridden and I think it is time you stopped taking your meals in your cabin. Won't you do me the honor of coming along to the dining car and having supper with me?"

Dorothy nodded and nearly laughed. As she had never before been invited to the dining car, she had just automatically accepted the trays delivered to her by the porters. She was so starved for human contact that even the Earl would be a welcome relief from her dull routine. She had already devoured almost every book that she had purchased.

Although the food was quite the same as she had been eating, the atmosphere and service gave it a totally different flavor. She sat back and relaxed.

"Look here, dear cousin, I shall have to call upon

you when we reach Denver to help with Lady Florence. A charming woman, but too long in the provinces of India."

"What manner of help?" she murmured. She leaned back against the plush chair and regarded him with the brown luminosity of her eyes. Her burnished hair framed her lovely face.

"Of a serious nature," he said, and regarded her again as he had been doing throughout the meal. He had never fully appreciated her beauty and grace until comparing her with his wife. As long as she was on the trip he thought it only right that he put her training to use for his own advantage. "Denver has more of a social life than one might expect. You would be of great help to me by counseling Lady Florence a bit on her dress and deportment as the wife of a lord."

The pretty face became meditative, with a curious sharpness about the faultless features, a curious tightness around the soft rosy mouth.

"That should not be too difficult," she said musically. "This project means a great deal to you, doesn't it?"

"At the moment it means everything. It is said that some are to greatness born, others seek after it, while it is thrust upon some. I have always felt myself quite neutral, due in large part to my father. He, being an ardent Roman Catholic, naturally desired my conversion, earnestly and sincerely. The controversy it plunged me into was quite something. Told on the one hand that Roman Catholicism was the sure road to indescribable agony, and on the other that it offered the only certain means of escape, the inevitable consequence was indifference. I hardened into disbelief in anything and everything. I was an only son, and thus granted every little whim, while my sisters were granted none. Everything that is in Ireland is not a part of me, but of my father and grandfather. This project shall be entirely mine and take me out of my neutrality."

Dorothy hardly saw him as neutral, but she was seeing him in quite a different light. She really didn't know this side of the man at all.

"That hardening into disbelief, is that what prompted the silence between you and my mother?"

"Hardly," he said laughing. "Our family were vehement opponents of your mother's marriage. As your mother and father were first cousins there was no land to be gained in the marriage whatsoever. The only profit out of the whole production was you."

Dorothy couldn't help but laugh. "How utterly silly a reason for such a long-standing family feud. It's archaic."

Dunraven frowned. "You may wonder how archaic if you persist in your romantic little venture with Paul Ely. Lady Jane's reaction will be pure Whyham-Quin, I assure you. As he will be bringing no land into the family, he will be strongly opposed."

"But he will be gaining land, working for you, will he not?"

Dunraven blinked foolishly. If Ely had given her such an impression, then the man was more of a fool than he suspected. No one was to gain land but Lord Dunraven. He determined to find out exactly what Ely had told her and then his mind froze on a new thought. Could the man have actually grown serious about the girl? For Dorothy to fall from grace was one thing, but to even consider having her bring Ely into the family was preposterous.

"Only time will tell," he said, so as to not commit himself. "Now, I really must get back to my paperwork."

Long after midnight, when the Pullman cars had been recoupled to the Omaha-bound train, Paul Ely sat in the near-empty coach car whistling abstractedly to himself. The whistling was low and impatient, yet thoughtful, and his light blue eyes were almost obscured by his thick, frowning eyebrows.

"Damn the bastard!" thought Ely, savagely pounding his knees with his fists. Dunraven had come to him the moment the trains were coupled and had been strange and abstract with his questions. He had been quite honest in asserting that he had known nothing of Lady Dorothy's presence on the train until that evening and equally honest in declaring his lack of desire for marriage at that time, to any female. But he was just as dishonest in avowing that he had made no rash promises to the lady and had never once discussed his future as far as Lord Dunraven was concerned.

Dunraven had taken it all at face value and once again advised Ely to stay away from the woman. That was like telling a pack of dogs not to go after a bitch in heat.

By the time Ely got to the first Pullman car, where the other guests were already asleep in their berths, he was in a very bad temper which even the thought of Dorothy could not dispel.

The porter roused in his seat and eyed Ely suspiciously.

"Ah'm sorry sir, but ain't nobody 'llowed in dem back cars."

"I'm Lord Dunraven's bodyguard," he snarled, "and have business with him."

The porter shrugged. He didn't know what a bodyguard was, but he had seen Ely in on the business meetings. He also recognized a Southern drawl when he heard one and wanted no part of such a man in such a fit of apparent rage.

The silent galley and luxurious dining car greatly increased his rage. He had been eating catch-as-catch-can in the various depots across the country. He was being made to look like a fool and now began putting all the blame at Dorothy's feet.

He entered the third car and stopped short. Curled up asleep on a petite-point divan was the parlor car porter. Here his story wouldn't work and the man would march him right to the door of Dunraven's drawing room.

Ely crept by the man, trying to orient himself as to the location of the car in which he had spied Dorothy. This automatically excluded the two left hand doors of solid mahogany. This left him the questionable choice of the two right hand doors. He assumed that Lady Florence was aboard, but was now in doubt about Mabel Allgood. He could just picture the scene he would create by walking in on either of those sleeping ladies. They would scream first and ask questions later.

Again, he measured in his mind the train window in which Dorothy had been sitting and went to the far right door.

A cold perspiration broke out on his forehead

and his hand began to shake as he reached for the solid silver latch. In spite of his frustration and determination, he began to have doubts about being thwarted again. He just knew that the door would be locked before he started to depress the handle. But it went all the way to the bottom, made a faint click, and the door was swinging inward.

He didn't hesitate, but stepped quickly through and closed it softly behind him. He looked about him with his usual distaste, only since boarding the train had he come to realize how much he had detested this trip and its fancy surroundings.

He had been conscious of the fine figure he had made in such elegantly rich clothing, but felt far more masculine in his twill trousers, cotton flannel shirt, rough-hide boots and mackinaw jacket.

Now, the luxury of the roomette seemed to set him apart again. This was not his world, with the dark maroon plush seat and extendable mahogany table, the flickering gaslight sconces, the alcove berth made down to accommodate . . .

The alcove was in semi-darkness, but not so dark that he couldn't make out the supine figure lying, with covers thrown back, in the overheated compartment.

He had nearly frozen, night after night, in the chilly coach car, while Dorothy slept with not even a sheet covering her. To see her thus washed away his anger and renewed every desire he had ever felt toward her.

This was not one of his recent whores. This was a scene he had never before experienced. She lay flat on her back, an arm thrown casually over her head, the burnished hair cascading over the pillow like rolling seawaves. The brilliant red nightgown was sheer to the point of being non-existant. It had been an impulse buy while Dorothy had been shopping wtih Caroline for honeymoon lingerie. She had never dreamed that another human being would ever see her in the daring costume.

Ely was privileged to see what a gorgeous creature she actually was and it momentarily stunned him. Divorced from petticoats, stays and breast binders she gave the image of a leggy figure: long thighs, rather narrow hips, hourglass waist and with shoulders of a proportion to counterbalance the rest. Her breasts, always diminished by the cut of her wardrobe, were now seen as full and firm and pointed. Beneath the ıed sheer fabric her femininity seemed like a dark-forested island.

Ely's south went dry. He began to perspire profusely. A terrible excitement filled him. He looked at her with blazing eyes, as if dazzled by what he beheld. What had so long been denied would not be denied again.

He was not even fully aware that the mackinaw was already off his back and that one foot was pushing away the boot from the other. He was just filled with vehement passion.

Dorothy stirred and rolled toward the wall. Paul Ely had no desire to merely view the curve of her back and buttocks and his clothes now came flying off.

Slowly, cautiously he sat the edge of the berth and swung his long leg up onto the inches left to him. The movement was starting to arouse Dorothy so he quickly rolled onto his side and nestled into the curve of her body.

Coming out of a deep sleep Dorothy was unsure

if it were a dream or reality. Something bulky kept her from moving. She turned her head as far as it would go and caught a small portion of Paul Ely's profile. It was reality and she opened her mouth to protest. Immediately she found it clamped shut by his big hand.

"Don't scream! It's just me!" he whispered, urgently. "At last we are alone!"

She tilted her head more and gazed at him with the strange and frightened face of a woman, aware of the passion he would now be demanding; frightened by it; drawn mysteriously by it.

"Don't look so damn scared! You wouldn't be chasing me if you hadn't expected this to happen sooner or later."

His words forced her swift recovery from momentary confusion. She dragged his hand away from her mouth, and rolled as far as she could onto her back.

"But only if it happens after we are married!"

He rose to his knees, hovering over her, and caught her by her shoulders. His fingers went deeply into her soft flesh. He was no longer going to be denied, not again talked out of it by her. His passion could not stand another refusal.

But his sudden movement, the added weight of his body and the still-unperfected locking device to secure the berth in a lowered position kept him from uttering his demands.

With a fierce snap the spring lock broke, throwing the berth up and backward. Ely's head crashed into the overhang of the unmade upper berth and, momentarily stunned, he felt himself falling.

Dorothy didn't have time to scream or gasp. The

mattress was slipping down beneath her, back into the storage well, and the weight of Ely's body was forcing her own body to follow its slide.

The berth box slammed against the bulkhead and locked in its upright position. They were entombed within the well. Fortunately, being the last compartment in the car, the well had been designed for luggage storage behind the berth, luggage space unused for Dorothy was the only occupant.

Dorothy struggled to get out from underneath Paul Ely, who was still stunned from the knock on the head. In pushing him away her hands became aware of his total nudity. She tried to pull as far away as possible.

Ely's senses were returning. Slits of shafted light entered where the berth was imperfectly fitted to the bulkhead. He reached up and tried to push the berth back down. It would not budge and he cursed.

"Damn stupid thing," he muttered.

"There has got to be a way," Dorothy said, a note of alarm creeping into her voice. "Pound on it!"

"A lot of good that would do," he growled. "They probably make these damn contraptions so the jostling of the train won't knock them down. I can't see, but there is probably no way that it releases from this side."

Dorothy lay quiet in the semi-darkness for a long moment and then she began to giggle as she saw the comical aspect of the situation.

"What in the hell is that all about?" he asked, in his incisive and softly ruthless voice.

"I was just thinking of the shock we are going to give the porter in the morning," she chuckled.

Ely shook his head numbly. This would really cook his goose with Lord Dunraven.

Then, as though reading his mind, the comical aspect faded and the full import dawned on her. The porter would not only be finding a man within her berth, but one sans clothing. She would be compromised, though guiltless.

Now she was truly frightened. In the shafted light she looked at Paul's vivid and desperate face, crowned by its disordered, thick profusion of curls.

"Do—do you think," she stammered, "that we can keep the porter from saying anything?"

Ely's frenzy of rage, misery and despair suddenly vanished. "Of course," he chuckled, "after all the man is just a nigger and I've been dealing with darkies most of my life. The proper words from me and the bastard won't dare open his mouth." He swung his head. "So, it is just you and I for the rest of the time."

Ely reached out forcefully and dragged her back against him. She struggled with him as best she could in the confined space. His mouth found her lips and tried to part them with his tongue. She clenched her teeth and tried to push him back, but he persisted. Sensing her displeasure he closed his lips and returned to kissing her as he had done before. Now, for her, the contact was heady, provocative.

She admitted to herself that Paul's nearness stirred her desire. The impropriety of it tickled her fancy perhaps because Lord Dunraven slept in the next drawing room.

He made the kiss more intense as his hand sought and found the curve of a breast. Anticipating her reaction he held her head firmly to his with one hand and let the palm of the other come squarely down under her nipple. Around and around, over the gossamer fabric, he rolled his palm until the nipple erected sensuously.

The feel of his hand was so new to Dorothy that she relaxed rather than tensed.

Paul felt the reaction and sighed. He was fully aroused, quaking with need. Gently he began to unbutton the top of the nightgown. His mouth closed around a swollen nipple. His hand snaked under the nightgown and onto her stomach. He inched his hand down, his breathing heavy.

Finally he could feel the downy hair touch his fingertips.

Now she did tense, lacing her fingers through his hair, she tried to pull his mouth from her breast. His neck muscles hardened into knots and he let his hand fondle her with more ardor. Strange nuances of delight began to spread through her body.

"Damn!" he breathed. "Stretch out as much as you can—hurry!"

"No!"

As only a true cynic can enjoy life utterly, he didn't even hear her utter the word.

He swung above her, and when his rigidity met her femininity, he felt intense pleasure at hearing her gasp and plead against the sharp, excruciating pain. Only once before in life had he been faced with the problem of a virginal wall. He had been fourteen and the chocolate-hued plantation girl but twelve. A few thrusts had solved that problem, but not now. He reared back and pushed himself forward with a mighty thrust.

The scream in the small chamber nearly burst his

ear drum. Then Dorothy instantly went limp. The fainting blackness came over her so swiftly that she wasn't even aware of drifting away.

It utterly delighted Paul Ely. An urge for total dominance had been growing within him over the past five years. Prostitutes had a tendency to intimidate him and become the master of the situation. They had only one thing to offer him and he didn't think that was too damn much.

Dorothy didn't intimidate him and he would be the master of the situation. He would have his way with her as she lay senseless, and make her pay for every gutter whore who had made him less than the man that he knew himself to be.

Vaguely, as she came around, she had a faint memory of her last word, "No!"

Now her head hummed and screamed the word, until she knew she could never utter it again.

She did not know how much time had passed, but she came to herself with a shivering start. Paul Ely still lay within her, but he was limp and sated.

There was a burning in her pelvic region, but it was not from pain. The euphoric passions within her had been aroused during her faint and then left to hang in unreleased limbo.

Sensuous tingles curled through her loins; her nipples ached where his mouth had been upon them. She was frustrated, and that, too, was a new experience for her. Her flesh burned like fire one moment and was clammy cold the next. She heard herself breathing heavily. She hungered for something with an almost savage desire, but knew not what it was.

Paul Ely rolled away, and seeing her eyes were

open, accosted her with a superior expression. "Ah, milady is awake."

Then Dorothy, to her intense astonishment, said, "Is that all there is to it?"

Paul's expression became so ludicrously blank and shocked at this remark that Dorothy became even more confused. She hated it when she did not have full knowledge of a subject and was made to feel foolish.

Ely, accustomed to putting on his clothing and leaving a sexual encounter without further ado, was caught wordless. Her comment seared into his brain like foaming acid. He read into it another personal affront, as though he had been inadequate.

His rage rose to the point of murderous intent. His heart seemed to pause in its beating. Now his body was incandescent with heat from his rage, his mind preternaturally sharp and clear, so that Dorothy became the epitome of all women who had no other role than to give him pleasure.

He was just priming himself to lash back at her, as he had never found the courage to do before, when there was a resounding click within the chamber and the berth began to fall forward.

"Lawdy me!" shrilled the porter, with a high-pitched laugh. "Thought something were amiss when you didn't come back through the sleeping car."

"What right do you have to come snooping after me?" Ely asked, and now his burning eyes gleamed with a different kind of anger.

"Mis'tah Pullman's rules, suh," he said without fear of retribution, but carefully averted his eyes so he couldn't be accused of looking upon a white man's nudity. "Besides, dis 'ere door were the only one standin' open."

Ely cursed himself for not having locked it upon his entrance. Again, everything was extraordinarily sharp and clear, as if magnified. He had not only been accused of being inadequate by a woman, but had been caught in the act by a goddamn black nigger! He rolled from the berth and began pulling on his clothing in a frantic rush. The words that he had fashioned earlier in his mind to keep the rescuing porter in his place wouldn't come. He was being put through a duble insult of the worst kind.

In an effort to retrieve the situation, he said coldly, "Does an open door still give you the right to enter, darky?" Then he spun from the room and was gone.

But the mischief had been done. The porter's face had become as still and pale as granite. Wordlessly, he remade the berth, his heart as bitter as wormwood. He had been a free man since 1855, and two of his sons had served in the Union Army, but he knew that some men would consider him a slave forever because of the color of his skin.

Not having served anyone but the men in the sleeping car, he knew nothing of the woman more than the gossip he had picked up from the parlor car porter. The gossip had impressed him about the quality of the ladies his porter friend served. His impression was doing violent flip-flops. That a woman such as this could have anything to do with such a hateful man saddened him.

He finished his work and bowed his way out of the room.

Dorothy stood silently, unaware that her nightgown was unbuttoned half way down, allowing a very full view of her breasts; a view that the porter had chosen to ignore.

She had always evaded questions of conscience, of self-examination, as her father had done before her. It was the only aspect of his character that she really possessed. Now she knew that she was like him, soft and weak. She had none of her mother's steel, not even her mother's violence. She wished, vehemently, that this scene had never taken place. She had not really fought against it. She had not tried to defend her reputation in front of the porter. She had only been able to question why the sexual encounter had been so bland and uninteresting, while the unsated part of her screamed for something that she did not understand.

This is absurd, thought Dorothy. I must be going mad. She controlled herself, and spoke in a hoarse, weak voice to the walls, "But who is there to discuss it with?"

DOROTHY WALKED up and down the narrow roomette frenzied and confused.

She had always had a logical and analytical mind, but now she saw that it had been incapable of dealing with certain human emotions. Against human passions, logic was useless: a feeble voice crying against a hurricane wind. The door that Paul Ely had opened for himself was also giving her quite a different vista of the world. He had destroyed her neat little philosophy about marriage, sex and love.

She experienced no resentment, no anger, against Paul Ely for the seduction. She was trying to understand it as a measure of his love, and that she must learn to love him that way in return.

And then, in the chaos of her mind, she tried to fathom the unfulfilled feeling within her.

It wasn't a feeling that was going to be quickly answered. Paul Ely had experienced physical release and the conquest of Dorothy. Mentally, he didn't have to think beyond that point. The door in his mind had been closed on the subject as surely as the door of the roomette. The encounter had been no more erotic than if Dorothy had been a whore, and he never thought about them a second time. He didn't need the advice of anyone to stay away from Dorothy. As far as he was concerned she had ceased to exist.

With the switching of the Pullman cars to the Denver Pacific Railroad at Cheyenne, Lord Dunraven's excitement became that of a little boy on Christmas morn. When Lady Florence refused to share these moments with him, he turned to Dorothy.

A cold resolution and intense clarity had come to Dorothy. She was profoundly sure that the Earl had gained information about the berth accident and was again keeping Paul from her. She would just have to make Dunraven see how wrong he was about them. A curious elation rushed over her at the very thought. Her step was with resolution as she entered the dining car.

"Ah, dear cousin," Dunraven called out merrily,

"come sit for lunch and partake of God's great beauty."

After thousands of miles of flat winter farmland, plains and never-ending prairies, Dorothy at first saw very little difference in the terrain. Then, as she settled into a plush chair opposite the Earl, she looked beyond the rolling plains. At first she couldn't speak, but just stare.

The horizon was broken, as far as she could see, by a towering, ragged granite line, etched by winter-white tracery upon its purple-gray hues.

"This is called the Front Range," Dunraven enthused. "That saber-toothed jutting is called Long's Peak. Over fourteen thousand feet she soars into the blue. This is her backside. Just wait until you see her magnificent face. I'm told it is breathtaking!"

The other men began filtering into the dining room for lunch. Dorothy searched each face expectantly. There was no familiar face.

"Lord Dunraven," she said on a rush, "why doesn't Paul Ely dine here?"

Dunraven either didn't hear her or pretended not to. "Would you believe that before our eyes are over a thousand peaks that are over ten thousand feet in elevation? This sight thrills me, but wait until you see them from my valley."

"Are you purposely trying to keep us apart?"

Dunraven turned from the window and blinked. "What?"

"I was asking about Paul Ely?"

"What about him?"

"Don't play coy with me!" she snapped in exasperation.

Dunraven composed his features and cleared his

throat. "Lower your voice," he said, delicately, in a thin sad tone. "The matter is of no concern to these other gentlemen and I will not have you making a scene. For your information, Paul Ely remained in Cheyenne on business. I hardly find that coy on my part. Now, as we shall be in Denver in a couple of hours, I suggest you order your lunch."

Dorothy sat back. She was convinced that there was something extremely peculiar about the whole situation. She, too, could play coy.

Dorothy sat very still and let the Earl rave on about the land. She was polite, ladylike and did not intrude, except for necessary comments to his questions. It was a pleasant, lengthy lunch and gave Lord Dunraven another view of his cousin. He thought what a great asset she would be to the man she would some day marry back in Ireland.

Then, mainly for the benefit of the other gentlemen, he began to extoll the virtues of Denver, the Queen City of the Plains.

Dorothy found the braggart city spread out brown and treeless, surrounded by an equally uninteresting plain.

The railroad had just been completed five months before and the depot was still under construction. The railroad was bringing the city back to life. Although mainly constructed of brick, its streets were unpaved and without sidewalks, but they were far more littered than those of New York.

It was all so primitive that it left Dorothy aghast.

Dunraven deposited the men of his entourage at the Imperial House, still an unfinished two-story structure that had not been destroyed in the fire or flooding of Cherry Creek five year earlier. It was no Brevoort House, to be sure.

But Brown's Bluff was a different world. Here the few houses were pretentious. Built of large sandstone blocks, replete with turrets, bays and leaded windows, they were surrounded by heaving copings with either white marble lions at the entrance or cast-iron deer on the lawn. The Blackhawk, Central City and Leadville "gold" millionaires were building according to their own "American gothic" tastes.

Unbeknown to Lady Florence, her husband had leased the mansion in which they had been guests the summer before. She had found it a drafty cavern then and was not about to change her mind now. And to make matters worse, in spite of his otherwise efficient planning, he had overlooked having a household staff included in the lease.

The house was cold, dusty, foodless and without indoor plumbing.

Wordlessly, Lady Florence selected a bedroom for herself and retired, leaving the problem entirely in the hands of her husband and Dorothy. Lord Dunraven, admitting for once that such a matter was "woman's work" quickly deserted the ship and returned to the Imperial House and his cohorts.

Freezing in the November-chilled house, Dorothy set about doing chores she had not been trained for. The fire would not start, the room filled with smoke and she became a sooty mess putting it out again. Standing in the center of the large living room, ready to weep, Dorothy heard a heavy knock.

Throwing open the heavy oak front door, her

smoke filled eyes saw what her mind wanted her to see.

"Oh, Paul!" she cried, rushing out to hug him, "I'm so glad that you are here!"

The tall, handsome youth pulled back in total embarrassment.

"Hey lady," he stammered, "I ain't who you think I am."

Dorothy stepped back and blinked. There was about his height and configuration everything to suggest a duplication of Paul Ely. His curly hair was of the same brown tones, his eyes as sparkling blue, his face as romantically handsome, but now she could see that he was quite junior in age to Paul Ely.

"I'm so sorry," she whispered, her own embarrassment growing.

"That's all right, lady. I'm here seeking a Lord Dunraven."

Fifteen-year-old Lloyd Folsom sized up the situation and took over at once. He dispatched Dorothy to clean her face and hands while he went to the shed to find drier firewood, plunged his hands into the mess she had made and got the fire to work, cleaned the soot from the room, and went on horseback to purchase basic supplies from Solomon's Mercantile. And later the youthful kindness did not diminish, and it was to Lloyd that Dorothy owed much of the comparatively easy settlement in Denver. Lloyd had a widowed sister, Mary Folsom Eddy, who was glad to take the job of cook and maid, although it irritated Lord Dunraven that her two children were also included in the package. Lloyd availed himself as woodchopper, chore-boy and general handyman. His friendship with Dorothy strengthened through the harsh winter months. Stricken with puppy love far worse than what the Gould boys had felt for her, he was her undying slave.

And it was all to the benefit of his initial reason for visiting. One of the major cornerstones that Denver had been founded upon was gossip. David Folsom and his half-brother Frederick Folsom Austin had a carting company that was idle and nearly broke. They wanted the Earl's lumber mill business.

To Dunraven's chagrin, he was finding that a great deal of Denver "business" was conducted in Charley Harrison's Criterion Saloon. Outwardly a charming Southerner with fingers in several legal pies, Harrison also maintained a large staff of henchmen who kept his fingers in all manner of illegal pies. It had been through Charley Harrison that the Earl had found Paul Ely the summer before. Harrison also introduced Dunraven to Folsom and Austin.

The Earl looked at the two men keenly. Harrison was seldom so effusive in his introductions.

"Well," Dunraven drawled, "it amazes me that you all seem to know my business before my luggage is even unpacked."

David Folsom pushed his wide brimmed hat back at a jaunty angle and leaned on the bar. He looked ten years older than his forty-five years, his weathered face tanned almost to shoe-sole hardness. For twenty years he had been carting supplies to and from the mining towns and was no lover of the new railroad.

"Well," he drawled even more slowly than Dunraven, "ain't no big mystery, sir. My widowed daughter, who I hear your missus is hiring as a cook, keeps company with the telegraph operator. For a week the messages have been piling up for the gentlemen you brought with you from America."

"From America," Dunraven laughed, "but this is also America."

Folsom leaned to the side confidentially.

"Ain't nothing more than a territory they don't take interest in except for the wealth they can take out of it. They'd have given it all back to the Indians by now if Nate Hill hadn't figured a way to dig out the deep gold and smelt it locally. That's going to make the strikes of '58 look damn small. The deeper they go, the more shoring timber they'll need."

"That's great," Dunraven said, his voice heavy with sarcasm. "But I have other uses for the timber I plan to fell and mill."

Folsom shrugged. "Look, Lord Dunraven, ain't no business of mine what you want the lumber for, I just want the contract to haul it to wherever you say. My rates are right and I keep my equipment and mules in prime condition."

"I see," Dunraven mused, again thinking farther into the future than they. "I shall need an outfit to cart equipment to the mill site once it has been selected and surveyed. But would you have difficulty getting the lumber up to the South Park region?"

Folsom frowned thoughtfully.

"Why," he asked quietly, "would you want lumber up at that old Indian summer camp ground?"

Dunraven smiled. He could see that Folsom was no fool and could be a man of great worth to him.

But to his way of thinking the Criterion Saloon was a hangout for a mob of cutthroats who might try to chisel in on any overheard deal.

"Mr. Folsom, as you have informed me of a new cook at my residence, I hardly anticipate that she will be able to supply supper for this evening. So that we might carry on this conversation, would you and your brother be my guests for a bite nearby?"

It was an invitation that David Folsom could not afford to turn down, but the fashionable Corkscrew Club on Eighteenth Street was far out of his league. He was a work-hardened teamster and the fancy trappings made him nervous and uncomfortable. Fred Austin, fifteen years his half-brother's junior, was the business agent for the carting firm and found the surroundings much to his liking and to his secret tastes. Normally shy and inarticulate around his rough-hewn brother, he felt very comfortable around the polished gentlemen.

"The land you mentioned," he informed Dunraven, "is under dispute with the Indians because of settlers moving in before it has even been surveyed for homesteading."

This was very unsettling news for the Earl. "How many?" he croaked.

"Must be five to seven families have moved in and built cabins and corrals. Don't know how they are faring this winter, but they all plan to plow and plant come spring."

Dunraven's appetite vanished. "That will utterly ruin it for me, Mr. Austin. How can I have gentlemen hunt and fish if they have to ride across plowed fields and jump fences?"

"Is that what you are looking for?"

Dunraven realized that he had voiced his dream aloud. To win over this duo he knew he could not backtrack, but would have to go on truthfully.

"Yes, gentlemen, I wish that valley and mountain area for a lodge and unrestricted hunting. It has been an age-old tradition in England, Ireland and Scotland to have such private game preserves, but alas they have dwindled in size and the game has become almost nonexistent."

"Then I think you're looking in the wrong place," David Folsom said, speaking for the first time since entering the club.

"Have you a better suggestion?"

"Might," Folsom said quietly. "There's a place to the northwest I haven't hunted for about five years. Game is plentiful and trout play leap-frog over each other in the streams."

Dunraven studied the man in silence.

"How far?" he asked finally.

"About seventy miles. Well, I'll take that back, now that we have this damn railroad. Only about thirty-some miles west of the depot in Longmont."

Dunraven's stomach began to twitch with nervous excitement. "I had the opportunity to meet Kit Carson last summer. He told me of his early trapping days in that region. Would this be near the peak that they call Long's?"

"Long's stands guard over the whole valley I'm talking about."

Dunraven gulped. "And no settlers?"

Folsom shook his head. "Was a family in the park when I hunted there. Estes by name. But in '66 they tired of pioneer life and sold out to ole Mike Hollenback for fifty dollars, a yearling steer and a yoke of oxen to take 'em back east somewhere."

Dunraven could hardly keep his voice steady. "And this Hollenback, does he still have the land?"

"I think he's dead," he answered indifferently.

Dunraven sat back, calm and collected. "Perhaps, when we get the mill fully operational, we might take a little hunting trip. Eh?"

Folsom nodded, because he still did not see the full significance of the conversation. But Fred Austin remained very quiet. He wanted out of the carting business in the worst way and saw that opportunity in the dapper form of the Earl.

Dunraven went back home at last, his head spinning. The situation was so perfect as to be almost unbelievable. It was obvious that the land hadn't as yet come under government survey. Why in God's name hadn't he thought about it after talking with Kit Carson? Then he recalled Carson's explanation of it being nearly inaccessible . . . yet, apparently, one family had gotten in and homesteaded. And didn't he want a place that was nearly inaccessible to keep other homesteaders out? He would take up the whole matter with his entourage in the morning.

He was saved from the tangle of his thoughts by his arrival home. The door was dutifully opened by Mary Eddy. She, more than the gaslamps, had brought a warmth to the dull house.

David Folsom's eldest child at twenty-eight, she was a slim dark creature who was decidedly pretty. She welcomed Dunraven as though she had been in his employ for months and not just hours. But it was not the woman who caught Dunraven's attention, but the children who were dusting and cleaning although it was well after dark. Then Lloyd Folsom made an entrance with an armload of fresh firewood, just as Dorothy came sailing down the curved staircase to make the proper introductions and explanations.

Dunraven was greatly impressed by the industry of the fifteen-year-old youth and approved of his magnetic dark beauty. Young as he was, his bearing was manly. Dunraven saw more of his uncle in him than his father, and hoped that Fred Austin would prove to be as industrious.

Nobody but Lloyd had a chance to be industrious for nearly the next two months. The snowstorms started coming at two-to-three-day intervals, until the town was nearly paralyzed. Christmas eve and day the temperature dropped to thirty below zero and seemed to freeze there. Social function after social function, planned to honor the return of Lord and Lady Dunraven and Lady Dorothy, were cancelled, rescheduled and cancelled again. The trains stopped running, food supplies started to dwindle, and Dunraven's entourage in the Imperial House nearly went crazy with boredom and what Lloyd called "cabin fever."

It was little better on Brown's Bluff. Dunraven's dark mood began to affect the entire household. Mary's ten-year-old son and eight-year-old daughter feared the man more with each sighting and his hatred of them grew to the point of volcanic explosion. Only Mary Eddy seemed to be able to approach the man and gain a decent word from him, because she alone realized they were both suffering from the same malady. The drafty house had given Lady Florence a violent cold and for two months she stayed abed under tons of quilts and comforters. And because the snow, Indians and buffalos scratching themselves on the telegraph poles had disrupted all service to Kansas City and Cheyenne, Mary's telegraph operator boyfriend drank away his frustrations at the Criterion Saloon.

Dorothy staved off her frustrations, because she still didn't fully understand them, with the artful help of Lloyd Folsom. Snowshoeing to the bluff each day with their supplies, he always brought along a sunny smile and news about the rest of the snowbound town. In the morning he would help her care for Lady Florence, who came to look upon him as something closely akin to St. Patrick. In the afternoon, and again at his suggestion, Dorothy would take Lonnie and Lureen Eddy to her room and read them asleep for their afternoon nap, although both protested that they were too old for a nap.

Lloyd, to quiet their argument, would come and sit for the reading as well. Lonnie and Lureen never talked back to their Uncle Lloyd, although he was only five years their senior, and thus did the house escape from Dunraven's black mood for a few hours, at least.

Lloyd would sit spellbound, captivated by Dorothy and enthralled that she could read the printed words that he and his niece and nephew could not. It was magic to him and Dorothy was the beautiful magician who could bring it all about.

And when Dorothy began to grasp their illiterate state, she did not embarrass them with her knowledge, but secretly began to prepare a text that would help them learn how to read.

The daily activity kept her mind and body occupied. She blamed the weather for keeping Paul Ely in Cheyenne and away from her. She was not aware, as Lord Dunraven was, that Paul had come back into Denver on the last train south before the storm.

But the weather kept the Earl from learning that Ely spent the majority of the two snowbound months in the establishment of Ada Lamont. The notorious madam found nature's atmosphere a boon to "indoor sports" and promptly began calling herself "Mme. La Monte." Almost daily she doubled and tripled the prices on her girls until men like Paul Ely were as destitute as the worst bums on Larimer Street. Credit? Not even Prince Albert, carrying Queen Vicky's crown in hand, could buy any pleasure there without cash in hand.

The bell rang and rang until Dorothy feared it would wake the napping children. Even Lloyd had dozed off and she couldn't imagine where Mary might be not to hear it. She raced down to the foyer and threw open the door. When Paul Ely saw her his eyes lighted with sardonic joy.

"I'm honored," he said. "And delighted. And—"

"You are drunk," Dorothy finished for him. "You look as though you haven't bathed or shaved in weeks."

"But you are still lovely," he slurred, "and mystifying. But then you always were."

"What is it you wish?" she asked, ignoring his comment with the cool indifference of her upbringing, her heart breaking anew.

This was not how she had dreamed of their reunion. His arms were not around her, his lips were not upon her, but this was not the man she remembered either.

Paul Ely stood gaunt, red eyed and filthy. Although he would not admit it, the two-month binge that he had been on was the true measure of his real life. In a drunken stupor he could forget what real life was all about and imagine that the prostitutes of Mme. La Monte were something that they were not.

"What do I wish," he sneered, sarcastically, making it neither question or statement. "Money! Money, from his great lordship! He's left me sitting down at the Imperial House for nearly two months with little more in my pocket than I left New York with!"

The words hit Dorothy with more force than the January winds howling without the house. For a moment she stood frozen, as though standing in the blizzard itself.

"I see," she said quietly, swallowing the words she really wanted to utter. "Please be seated and I'll have a word with Lord Dunraven."

Woodenly she put one foot in front of the other as she ascended the curving steps, and each one seemed to echo an indictment of Paul Ely from the past. She had never met a man who could play his part so well. One face to her and another to the rest of the world. She felt sick, but controlled. Her mind was so distracted that she did something she had never before thought of doing. She entered Lord Dunraven's chamber without knocking.

It was cold, dank and held in drape-drawn darkness.

Dorothy started to call out and a noise stopped her short. There was something familiar about the noise, as though she had heard it before. Then suddenly, she realized she had—it was the same as the sounds she had made in the train roomette. But these were not cries of pain, of virginity lost or of terrible physical agony. These were different notes of weeping. They were joyous.

She wanted to call out to them, but couldn't find the words to express a disgust that was bottomless. She turned slowly and went to her own room to take money from her purse.

"Lord Dunraven is busy," she told Ely, handing him the money. "This should hold you for a few days."

Ely grabbed at the money, snarled at the small amount, and departed without a single word.

Dorothy was almost weeping now and then she caught herself. Oh, damn all men's black souls to bitter hell and may they burn forever! I'm not going to waste my tears on the likes of them. I'm going to get busy and keep busy and burn these memories right out of my brain.

7

SPRING CAME EARLY to the plains that year. More mansions began to mushroom up on Brown's Bluff. The lateral ditches on each side of the street were filled with the melting ice water from Smith's Lake. The height of the lake enabled the water to run by gravity down to Brown's Bluff. Water, to Dorothy, meant an end to the drab, brown winter. It also meant mind-occupying activity. Although she had enjoyed schooling the children, the house had been confining and she had tried to avoid Mary and her cousins as much as possible. She feared that Lady Florence would read her mind through her eyes.

With the help of Lloyd she purchased a horse

and sidesaddle. When the days were warm enough, and the buds not yet burst forth, they would ride out to the Platte River and dig up cottonwood saplings from its shallow banks. On other days they would go to Cherry Creek to secure shrubs and its native cherry bushes.

Fred Z. Salomon, who was building a new home several doors away, saw Lloyd plowing up the front yard and digging an irrigation ditch back from the lateral canal. Although his business interests were now far more widespread than just his mercantile store, he never forgot a single unsold item on his shelves.

"Son," he called out, "If you're thinking of seeding a lawn why don't you stop at the store. I've got bags of it left from last year."

Dorothy had considered she would have to dig up clumps of wild grass along the river banks and wait and wait for them to spread, but the Prussian immigrant's words sent her scurrying toward his downtown store.

Salomon was amazed that Lady Dorothy had come herself and personally waited on her, although he kept the members of the Board of Trade waiting an hour for him. He wanted to see Denver grow and bloom and had heard from his friend David Moffat of the vast sums of money the Earl of Dunraven had transferred to the First National Bank. During the harsh winter days many men such as he had begun to speculate that the Earl's deposit far exceeded what he would require for a mill operation, and Denver's needs were great.

Dorothy was ecstatic. Not only did Salomon have burlap bags of rye grass seed, but hundreds of brown packets of flower and vegetable seeds.

It was a project to which Dorothy devoted almost all her time. Lady Florence was up and about and taking charge of her own home. Lord Dunraven and his entourage, ever since the first spring thaw, were off and away to survey the forestry land, begin the construction of the mill and hire timbermen and millers.

There had been no need for haste in seeing the northwest park region that spring, for, as Paul Ely told the Earl after he had made a quick inspection trip, "Man by the name of Griffith Evans bought out the Joel Estes holdings from Hollenback. He and his family are the only ones in the whole region."

For want of a better way of thinking of it in his mind, Dunraven mentally called it Estes Park and dreamed of the day that he could add Earl of Estes to his other titles. But one dream had to be accomplished before a second could be begun and he was already running five months behind schedule.

Dorothy was, at first, amazed and dumbfounded. Because of the fertile unused soil, and the city being a mile high, the grass seed germinated to a sea of lush green in only seven days. Other women homesick for flowers and greenery began to follow her example.

By the time the hot humid days of summer settled on the plains the trees were growing, the gardens flourishing and the Brown's Bluff lawns were being praised for their greenness.

Because it was the first thing she had ever accomplished on her own, although she gave Lloyd credit for the backbreaking tasks, Dorothy was as playful as a kitten, and full of a youthful passion for the project that was practically inexhaustible. She became brown as a chestnut and didn't worry about the freckles the sun had painted on her nose. Never one who cared for sunbonnets or hats, the sun lightened her hair to the soft shades of early morning sunrise.

She composed long letters about her projects to Ireland and received back answers of glowing praise, and longing for her return. She surprised even herself in not wishing to return until she saw her gardens totally finished and fruitful.

Lord Dunraven, on the few weekends he did venture back into Denver, was surprised at the change in the house and its people. Surprised? The truth of the matter was that the Earl was shocked.

On a Sunday afternoon carriages and strollers by the hundreds would saunter by to behold the beauty and were making his name a household word. But nature and happiness, of a sort, had also turned Dorothy into a different manner of beauty that made him begin to have thoughts that he knew he should not entertain. But he was surrounded by ardor, so it was hard not to have such thoughts about the third adult female in the house.

All his life the Earl had taken his pleasures where he found them, lightly and without thought. Mary Eddy was not a woman of decent morals and strict upbringing and had decided that she no longer wished to keep company with her telegraph dispatcher man friend and coveted only the Earl. This was very pleasing to the Earl's ego, but presented him with great problems of secret bed-hopping.

He had always considered that he would marry a paragon of purity for child-bearing. He had expected the same shyness, timidity and propriety that Lady Florence had shown throughout their first year of marriage, but instead he found during his brief returns . . . ardor.

"Children!" Lady Florence laughed, when he mentioned her change. "I was most careful when we were doing nothing but traveling. But, as it seems we are to be rooted here for awhile, I've determined it is time to start a family."

Rooted was not the word Dunraven would have used. He felt stuck in a quagmire of stupidity and fawning servility.

Captain Jacob Hartman surveyed the one hundred thousand acres of forestry land and flat refused to even go and look at the Estes Park region. Trevor Cleveland hustled him back to Washington and went to have a look for himself. He was quite enthusiastic that the area would contain well over the three hundred thousand acres that the Earl desired, but he was used to acquiring straight stretches of land for railroad rights of way and this problem rather baffled him because the area was unsurveyed.

It also posed a problem for Palmer Hoyt. He had spent the winter and spring negotiating with the Ute tribes for the more accessible South Park region. Now he had to go back and start all over again. Then he began to question if the Earl knew what he was about. The Utes had not used the area in over sixty years and were unsure what use it would be to the white men. It did not possess buffalo, the early French and English trappers had nearly depleted the beaver ponds, and the elk and deer herds were not large enough to supply the Utes in a summer encampment.

It puzzled them and puzzled Palmer Hoyt even more. He had not seen the land and only had Trevor Cleveland's report to go on. He had no point to start negotiating from and had to jump in cold.

He frowned as they nodded agreement to his first proposal: one hundred horses and one hundred blankets. The Utes had anticipated only a quarter of that amount and didn't want him changing his mind. As they were army horses and blankets up for auction the total cost to the Earl was less than a thousand dollars.

Hoyt shrugged and went back to Washington. He had opened up South Park for ranchers and settlers and would let Lord Dunraven worry about his new region. He had done all he was supposed to do.

Rufus Brogan seemed to be the only one of the entourage that was quite contented with his assignment. He didn't care if he ever saw the east again. He found the Earl a remarkable man to work under and devoted himself to the man wholeheartedly.

September was an unusual month for Windham Thomas. The first lumber was sawed from the mill and carted to Denver and sold to Fred Salomon green for curing. Rufus Brogan's dual books could now start a credit column.

In September Lady Florence announced that she was with child, with a March arrival. Mary Eddy made the same pronouncement, but only to the Earl.

As he had done in Ireland when trouble was brewing, the Earl found great solvent in unlimited talk and unavailability. He took his long-awaited hunting trip to Estes Park and left the matter entirely in Dorothy's hands. Nor did he seem embarrassed in informing her of all the facts and to what limit he would pay to keep the news from Lady Florence.

But it was embarrassing for Dorothy, especially worrisome when it came to Lloyd Folsom. She had fully anticipated returning home to Ireland that fall and didn't want to saddle Lady Florence with a whole new staff.

Mary Eddy grinned at Dorothy and her brother. "Thanks, hon," she said sassily. "First time I've ever had a hundred dollars in my hand all at once." Then she turned to Lloyd.

"If you had your choice," she said acidly, "would you rather go back to work for Paw or moon around here?"

Lloyd Folsom's face was a battleground for his emotions. What his sister had done didn't shock him—that was how she had snared her first husband. But he didn't think he had any choice in the matter. He just automatically assumed that he would be fired right along with her and he was miserable.

"I would like you to stay," Dorothy said softly, to ease his doubt.

"But not me?" Mary inquired with bittersweetness.

"I don't think it would work, Mary, but I do wonder what you will do."

"Don't worry about me," Mary chuckled. "I've already got Dan Rafferty convinced it's his kid and we're going to get hitched. About time I had a father around for my other two. You got them spoiled with all this book-readin' crap. Time they went to work. Lloyd and me been workin' since we were ten and so can they." Then she looked at Dorothy sourly before sailing out the door. "Just remember that you're a lady and my kid brother is only fifteen. I don't want him learning any hanky-panky yet."

Dorothy turned as scarlet as the boy.

"I'm sixteen now," Lloyd declared, as though that eased the embarrassing moment for each.

And I am twenty-one, Dorothy thought foolishly, and you are still a little boy in my eyes.

Lloyd smiled and pointed toward the large kitchen range. "Lunch we could probably handle," he said, "but not dinner. There's a Mrs. Ferguson who used to cook for Mr. Evans when he was governor of the territory. I could talk to her, but she doesn't do cleaning."

"Fine," Dorothy said, thankful that their friendship was smoothly jumping the hurdles Mary had placed before them. "Perhaps she might know of a cleaning girl and . . . Lloyd . . ."

"You don't need to say it," he cut in quickly. "All we have to say to Lady Florence is the truth as Mary expressed it. She's getting married."

"That does simplify the whole matter," Dorothy said, and gently kissed Lloyd's youthful cheek.

"I'll go see Mrs. Ferguson right now," he smiled, his heart bursting with pride and love. He would have walked on red-hot coals if Dorothy had commanded it.

As it was, Dorothy did have to cook dinner that evening, and it was a disaster. But Sarah Ferguson arrived before daylight the next morning, and proceeded at once to take over the whole residence.

By noon she had her unmarried niece uniformed and dusting. Dorothy was utterly pleased with the duo. They were affable, stout, jolly and both as ugly as mud fences. She would not have to fear Lord Dunraven getting either of them with child. But she knew he would also be quite pleased because Sarah made the simplest foods taste as though prepared for Olympian gods and dowdy Primrose Ferguson, who reminded Dorothy more of a spruce tree than a primrose, polished brass and silver to a mirror finish.

Dunraven's pleasure, at the moment, lay in three other areas. Paul Ely, who had been "on the wagon" for three months, could again be trusted as an associate. Griff Evans, the homesteader, was more interested in hunting and guiding than plowing up the land and the two men developed an instant mutual admiration society.

But his third pleasure was the most enthralling. He stood on the castellated fringe of the Estes Park basin and gazed down at the open rolling land, the winding rivers with the majestic purple hills in the background and the great snow-crested range beyond. And, as he had been told, the sheer-faced Long's Peak did stand like a sentinel over it all.

It was a perfect location for his concept of an English-style game preserve—isolated from the world by a ring of mountain ranges, air as crisp and invigorating as the icy stream water to the parched tongue. The rainbow trout did seem to play leap-frog in the streams, and, if not enough for the Utes, at least Dunraven was pleased with the number of deer, elk, bobcat, Big Horn sheep and bear that Griff Evans tracked for him.

Time lost all meaning for him as he explored far

and wide and dreamed his dream. Still, dreams have a way of being pricked by stark reality.

The Utes' agreement with Palmer Hoyt had reached the ears of the clerk of the Arapahoe County Court in Denver. Instead of studying for his forthcoming bar examinations, the young lawyer was also in the region on a camping and hunting expedition. Alexander Q. MacGregor was much impressed by what he saw and rushed back to Denver to learn how the land could be obtained.

The region was large enough that Dunraven and Evans were not even aware MacGregor had been about. But the Earl did become aware of something that for the moment left him beyond speech.

"Cattle!" he gasped. "Where in God's name did they come from?"

"Been here on the stock range all summer," Evans answered innocently.

"But whose are they?" Dunraven demanded.

Evans, not one known for quickness of mind, didn't see why the normally affable man was suddenly so angry.

"I look after some of 'em," he drawled slowly, "and some belong to Jimmy McLaughlin."

"I was led to believe that you were the only man in the region."

"Near about. Jimmy and I each know our share of the land by mutual agreement and ain't got no fight. Cattle don't fight either. The ones I see after belong to George Brown and W. C. Lothroup in Denver."

Black rage mounted in Dunraven's face. His dominion was being trampled upon by cattle and strangers. He squinted and counted three riders driving the huge herd down to the rolling meadowland. Slowly, he turned back to Evans.

"That's all the hunting for this season," he said. "But come spring I'd like to bring along some friends from Ireland and England. We will camp, of course, but you and your good woman may have to see after some of our needs—for a price, of course."

"We're used to that," Evans beamed, "and the Denver men who come up hunting in the spring never seem to argue about Griff Evans' prices."

Dunraven looked about and it was as though someone had strewn litter on land he had thought virginal. It was nearly the middle of December and he began to blame himself for letting grass grow under his feet. He allowed his black rage to cool, rubbing his greedy fingers together. After all, the land was still unsurveyed and thus not open for legal entry of others. He considered Griff Evans a man he could easily control and would just have to learn about this James McLaughlin in due course. But he now knew that merely standing upon the land was not the same as owning it.

If Dunraven's black rage had been cooling Dorothy's had been steadily boiling and she felt as if she were about to explode in her anger. For three months they had heard nothing from Lord Dunraven and had no way of finding out if he was alive or dead. Lady Florence's middle period of pregnancy had been most difficult, made worse by her fear and worry over her husband.

Dorothy, who had anticipated being home for

Christmas, could have boiled the man in oil. She felt trapped, stifled and greatly concerned over Lady Florence. She didn't know the first thing about a pregnancy, but was an astute student in the hands of Sarah Ferguson. Even so, it was obvious that nothing was going to make the woman completely well short of some positive news of the Earl.

The trap closed tighter about Dorothy and she could say nothing to the Earl upon his return. Coming down the canyon to the plains, the Earl's horse had slipped and dumped them both into the icy winter waters of the St. Vrain River. The horse had to be destroyed and the torrents had carried away all the Earl's gear and extra clothing. He caught a chill, cowering in Paul Ely's sleeping blanket, while his clothing refused to dry before a feeble campfire. Reduced to a single mount, they were twice as long reaching the train depot in Longment. By then the Earl was running a fever and suffering with ague, but stubbornly refused to stay in the small village. By the time Paul Ely had him to Brown's Bluff the man was near delirious with pneumonia.

All the fury that Dorothy had been storing up to use against the Earl was poured over Paul Ely instead. He listened to her bombast silently and then shrugged.

"Go to hell, lady!"

That night Paul Ely fell off the wagon.

Even though the doctors gave him little chance for survival, the Earl spent his Christmas in bed, and most of the month of January, 1872, proving them wrong. As he seemed to grow stronger, Lady Florence grew weaker. Dorothy was constantly back and forth from sickroom to sickroom, until Sarah began to fear for her health as well.

But illness or no, the Earl was not inactive.

"Rufus," Dorothy scolded, "how many times do I have to tell you that he is not supposed to be disturbed?"

The handsome young secretary-accountant sighed as he had sighed a hundred times before. "Lady Dorothy, what am I supposed to do? He sneaks out messages by Lloyd for Paul Ely and myself. Paul is drunk half the time and that makes double work for me."

"All right," she said reluctantly, "but try not to upset him like yesterday. He was a bear to handle after you left."

Rufus grinned. "Today is a good-news day."

Rufus was becoming somewhat of a politician and a grabber of secondary power. He didn't mind doing Paul Ely's work, for it gave him a better overall picture of what the Earl really desired—plus, it was making him indispensable.

"Paul is still drunk," he explained. "He nearly fouled up the deal with George W. Brown yesterday. But that's not what I came to tell you."

"Still," Dunraven said sullenly, "let's discuss him first. You tell him for me that I want him dead sober by the time I am out of this bed or I'm washing my hands of him!"

Rufus Brogan nodded, but had no intention of saying anything. He, more than anything else, was responsible for Paul's latest drunken spree. Paul was jealous of Rufus—and the importance of his assignment—and Rufus was not above rubbing salt in the wound at every opportunity.

"Now," Dunraven went on, "how badly did he mess up the Brown deal?"

"Not so badly that I wasn't able to salvage it," Rufus boasted, although he had given Paul the wrong information for the man in the first place. "Mr. Brown has suddenly taken a strong interest in real estate and building in the Longmont area. A hotel, I think, is his secret dream." Rufus smiled wickedly. "Shall we say a hotel that would serve any of your friends who might wish to rest overnight before starting up to your region."

Dunraven looked at him wonderingly.

"He was quite pleased," Rufus explained further, "at the "cheap" lumber prices I was able to quote him. However, I made it quite clear that the quoted price would remain as such only if it was paid for in cattle and everything connected with those cattle."

"And Lothroup?" Dunraven enthused.

Rufus grinned. "It would seem, Lord Dunraven, that William Calhoun Lothroup is the County Clerk of Denver and a man always looking for monetary reward. Of course, he is most willing to sell his share of the cattle and everything connected with it, for he considers it a coin purse investment. His wallet concerns him more."

"I told you I didn't want anyone else involved—" Dunraven began.

"I don't think you can do without him, sir," Rufus cut him short quietly, but firmly. "The man is a personal friend of the Surveyor General for the territory and that gentleman's brother-in-law. The brother-in-law, a Theodore Whyte, is an independent land agent. I took the liberty of meeting the man on your behalf and feel you will find him much to your liking."

"Reasons?" Dunraven snapped, but not out of anger. He was getting totally bored by his confinement and Rufus Brogan was the only visitor to the sickroom who gave his mind a challenge. He was becoming quite fond of the young man and the manner in which he tried to emulate and sometimes out-guess him.

"The reasons are many, sir. First, it seems to me that Theodore Whyte could gain a copy of the survey long before the recording of same. Next, the man knows every surveyor employed by the Surveyor General and could advise on who would be the most "trustworthy" for your benefit. Also of some importance is Mr. Whyte's information that although the Surveyor General has no money with which to have the survey made, under an Act of Congress, you, as a private party, would be allowed to pay for the survey and receive a receipt from the Surveyor General which receipt could be used as the equivalent of cash payment of land to the government."

Dunraven sat back among his mounded pillows and did a bit of surveying of his own. Theodore Whyte sounded most interesting, but the Earl's interest, for the moment, was centered on the young secretary-accountant. He was proving to be a very valuable employee, and was not trying to make of himself an associate like Paul Ely. It was a situation between the two men, he determined, he would have to watch most carefully.

"Very good," he mused, "but I sense that there is something else on your mind . . ."

Rufus was impressed by the Earl's intuition—

but sorry that he was forced to reveal an unpleasant aspect of the deal.

"Well, sir," he said unwillingly, "once the survey is recorded the area shall become subject to entry and homesteading in 160 acre grants."

"I'll be damned and in hell first!" Dunraven roared.

"Whyte has a thought on the subject," Rufus answered quietly. "Although it is most illegal."

"Damn the legality! What is it?"

"The filing of the grants by others and your immediate purchase back."

"That's too damn dangerous!" Dunraven said fiercely. "The law says that they have to start improving the land with a cabin and corral. Once they see my land they will renege on selling it back to me." He cursed. "And the thought is not original. Jim Fisk and others proposed the same to me back in New York. Unworkable! Utterly unworkable!"

"I have to disagree," Rufus muttered, his voice suggesting that he was unsure of the ground he was about to step upon. It could suck him under to oblivion or greatly improve his standing in the Earl's eyes. "Couldn't men be found, like Paul Ely, who would sell their souls for a drink of demon rum?"

And then, suddenly, Dunraven had the missing portion of other men's suggestion. It illuminated his face, and he stared at Rufus as though he were a mental wizard.

"Think upon this," he said softly, "and don't dare give me an answer for several days, or until you are quite sure of your answer. Except for the men we trust, who by their good name and position can garner larger blocks of acreage, we shall need men who have no desire to even see the land and less desire to sell it back acre by acre. Nor must I be connected. It shall be a matter for you and this Theodore Whyte. Think on it!"

Rufus Brogan didn't need to think on it. His mind already had the plan mapped out to the last acre, but now he could breathe easy and sit back and wait. He was suddenly the lord and Dunraven the follower. He prayed for a long recovery period so that he would be able to fully eliminate Paul Ely, personally select the trusted men, and turn down the less trustworthy men.

But before he could start turning the Earl into the biggest land-grabbing blackguard in territorial history, he needed certain license to set in motion events that would leave grand juries shaking their heads in bewilderment for the next hundred years.

"And the survey?" he asked softly.

"Pay for it! Pay for it!" the Earl roared. "You know I have the money! Let's get this thing started, so we know how to finish it!"

Rufus smiled boyishly. He rose and bowed. In his mind Paul Ely had just died. He was the official voice and *alter ego* of the Earl of Dunraven from that moment on. A wish had become a reality for him.

Since his return Windham Thomas had concerned himself more with his own health than that of his wife. After all, he had concluded, she was only having a baby and he had come near to death with pneumonia. Women had babies every second of the day and night. That was their only reason for being, so he was a little mystified at her lie-a-bed state when he had been *really* sick.

But this night he could forgive her "feminine ailments", because Rufus Brogan had made 1872 come alive as the year of his fullfillment. He could discount the bitter newspaper accounts of Ulysses Simpson Grant's "nepotism." Hadn't he been the first to silently and publicly dredge up the ancient word to describe the offices that the President filled with near and distant relatives? Neither Clarence Dent nor the President were any longer of service to him, so he shrugged off the reports.

Nor did it faze him greatly to read of the demise of Jim Fisk at the hands of Eddie Stokes. Fisk's half million was safely tucked away in the vault of the First National Bank of Denver and who knew how long it would take for the courts to unravel that man's financial affairs. And even then, he was a British subject, not accountable for death claims from a "colonial" court when the collateral was "empire" property. For the first time ever, he blew a kiss to pudgy, pompous Queen Vicky.

But the physical condition of Lady Florence greatly shocked him.

"What the devil—" he began.

"Get Dorothy," she whispered, "I think my time is come!"

"Nonsense!" he growled. It's been seven months!"

Lady Florence stared back at him, her face white and frightened, glistening with fevered traceries of sweat. He saw her twist painfully, and his jaw dropped open.

"Something is wrong," she whispered, a note of fear creeping into her voice. "Go for the doctor, Windham."

He was instantly back across the hall and diving into his clothes, pulling the bell cord and cursing.

"Hell of a time not to have live-in servants. Damn, why don't I even know Dorothy's room? Bloody mess!" ....

In the hall he was met by a sleepy Dorothy. She had taken to sleeping in Mary Eddy's old room so she could hear the bellpull during the night.

"Go to her!'" he roared. "I'm off for the doctor!"

"The baby?" Dorothy gasped.

"Yes! Just don't stand there! Go do what women are supposed to do!"

Sarah Ferguson's education had not proceeded to this point. Dully, she prayed that he wouldn't be long in getting the doctor.

After what seemed an eternity to Dunraven, but what was actually only a space of minutes, he had a horse saddled and was leading it out to the street.

Before he could mount, his way was blocked by an arriving horseman who stumbled drunkenly from the saddle.

"Dunraven," Paul Ely sneered, "just the man I seek."

"Out of my way!" the Earl bellowed. "I've no time for you now!"

"Then take time! I need money!"

"Idiot! My wife is having trouble with the child and I must get a doctor!"

For a split second he considered sending Ely on

the mission, but his trust in the man had nearly evaporated, and he didn't want to waste another second in foolish argument.

"Get into the house!" he snapped. "Wait for me in the kitchen!"

He didn't wait for any rebuttal. The horse raced down the deserted street, its hoofs striking fire on the frozen gravel. Paul Ely stumbled to the back of his house, his thoughts black and bitter.

"I feel so inadequate," Dorothy stammered, cleansing the fevered brow with a cool cloth.

Lady Florence smiled weakly. "Don't fret, child. You've been an angel to me. It may be an old wives' tale, but the doctor shall probably call for lots of hot water and sheeting. Busy yourself with those tasks."

Dorothy was reluctant to leave her, but thankful for any little chore to keep her busy. She cursed herself for not accepting Lloyd Folsom's offer to stay within the mansion as long as it was a sick-house. She was sure that he would know what to do. Her faith in the boy's ability had grown daily.

She stopped short at the kitchen door and a portion of her troubled brain relaxed. Someone was poking about in the banked kitchen range and she automatically assumed that the Earl had stopped at the Folsom house before going on for the doctor.

"You?" she gasped, swinging through the door and stopping anew.

Ely didn't even bother to turn around. "Damn cold in here!"

Dorothy's instant anger didn't let her feel it. Wordlessly, she marched around the cavernous kitchen selecting pots and kettles and taking them to the sink. Furiously, she began to work the handle of the well pump, but it only grumbled and spit.

"Needs a prime," Ely said snidely, pushing her aside almost harshly. He took a ladle of water from an oaken bucket, removed the pump cap and poured it down while slowly working the handle up and down. The water began to gush forth into a kettle. When it was three-quarters full, Dorothy pulled it away and placed a large pot under the spout.

"What's all this for?" he asked, as she took the kettle to the range, which was starting to roar in the same manner that Sarah could get it to work.

"Hot water," she answered simply.

Ely chuckled, but continued to pump. "Hell, that's supposed to be a job for the expectant father, just to keep him out of the way. All it will really be good for is to make a lot of coffee."

Dorothy was tempted to say that was exactly what *he* needed, but bit her tongue. "If you know so much, what should we be doing?"

He brought the pot to the range, a slow grin cracking his thin lips. It was the first time he had ever heard her admit she didn't know something and he suddenly felt superior.

"Linen and towels will be needed, but that's plenty of water, except for some in the coffee pot. I've seen lots of nigger brats born on the plantation and it will be hours yet."

"But this one's ahead of time!"

"Ain't no real set time for a baby to come. Some is early and some is late," he mimicked plantation argot.

This reassured Dorothy somewhat, but she still

wished it had been coming from a more stable authority. The bellcord jangled at the same instant that they heard Lady Florence's scream echo through the house.

They raced up the stairs, but at the door of the bedroom Dorothy put out a hand.

"You'd best let me see if she is decent first."

"Damn decency!" he said sternly and pushed on in.

Lady Florence was just coming out of her faint, her face a mask of pain and fear. When she saw Paul Ely a look of surprise flashed into her eyes. Feebly, she tried to pull the sheet back over her blood-drenched nightgown.

"It's all right," Dorothy soothed. "He is here to help."

She looked anxiously at Paul for instructions. His lie was rapidly catching up with him, his brow contracted in tight furrows of worry.

"Examine her!" he breathed.

Lady Florence went tense as Dorothy nervously peeled back the soiled nightgown. Ely did know that the muscle-tensing was the worst thing in the world for her to do.

"Give me that basin so I can clean her up and go get some brandy!"

"Don't you think that you've had—"

"It's not for me," he growled. "The baby's coming! We've got to get her to relax!"

But he did not know exactly what to do next. It was characteristic of him that he was going to see the lie through and never once considered that Lady Florence or the child might die at his bungling. Gently, he began to clean her up and move her to a drier portion of the bed. He felt of the rotund belly and found it infuriatingly still. Her body was wracked by another mighty eruption of pain.

"Calm yourself, please!"

Ely's hands began to shake and he knew the situation was far more serious than he could handle. He silently left the room and waited for Dorothy in the hall.

"I can't do it," he said simply.

"Can't?" she exploded. "Why, because you're too damn drunk?"

"These last few minutes have made me cold sober! There's something wrong with the baby."

"Then we've got to help until the doctor gets here," she demanded. "If you can't do it, then tell me what to do!"

He looked into Dorothy's frightened eyes.

"I–I don't know what to tell you," he stammered.

"What are you saying?" she gasped.

"That I lied," he confided quietly, because he didn't want Lady Florence to her. "I only saw it a couple of times and then I wasn't supposed to be watching. It wasn't like this, they just seemed to pop out. This I've only heard of."

Dorothy stood momentarily transfixed, her mind wanting to hate, but there was no time for such a private emotion.

"Thank you, at least, for the truth," she heard herself saying. "But at least you have more knowledge than she or I. Here is the brandy. Now, what else can you remember that we shall require?"

She was so calm and composed that he could hardly believe it. "Scissors, thread, towels and some of that hot water."

She spun away before he could advise her of the dangers that they faced. Almost numbly he re-entered the room and nervously poured some of the brandy into a glass. Lady Florence had no use for it, she was again in a deep faint. He almost swallowed the entire contents himself, but with shaking hand put the glass down on the bedside table. His stomach turned at the mere thought of it.

Dorothy burst open the door and hurled herself into the room. She took in everything at a glance and felt her own stomach begin to churn.

"Don't look," Ely growled, "and don't you dare faint on me! Wring out a towel in the hot water and put it on her belly. Then, gently massage the belly downward, but don't watch what I have to do!"

Dorothy obeyed and disobeyed. She could not help but watch. Ely marvelled at her courage and stamina. As she calmed, so did he. He tried to pray, but had forgotten the words to use.

It went on forever, the soft, shallow sounds of their breathing, and Lady Florence's intermittent moaning. Slowly Ely was able to inch forth the wrinkled little object and even more slowly turn it to unsnarl the tangled umbilical cord. It was small and mottled blue and badly deformed. It was a sight Dorothy prayed never to have to see again and one that she vowed never to put into words for the ears of Lord and Lady Dunraven.

Paul Ely had just finished tying a thread knot about the cord when they heard horses in the drive. A moment later Doctor Horace Lentz came bounding into the room.

His examination of the situation was brief.

"Cut it, man!" he snapped. "We have only one patient to save now!"

He bent down to Lady Florence's pain-ravaged face, marvelling that she was not a corpse as well. "You stay," he said sternly to Dorothy, "and keep putting those hot towels on her body. You, man, go down and get some coffee into that raving madman who came after me. But not one word to him, mind you!"

"My son!" Lord Dunraven shrieked. "A drunk and an idiot have killed my son!"

Fearfully Doctor Lentz tried to explain again that the situation would have been the same even if he had been there. The baby had been dead for hours and even two more months would not have been sufficient for it to fully develop. Horace Lentz saw it as a merciful act of God. Lord Dunraven saw it only as bungling on the part of Paul Ely and Dorothy.

"You might ask after your wife!" Lentz snapped.

Dunraven's face went ashen with new fear.

"Have they killed her too?"

"They have saved her life," he said sternly, "and don't get any other foolish notions in your head. She will need a couple months' complete bedrest, but the young lady seems a capable nurse."

"The young lady is returning to Ireland post haste!" Dunraven exploded.

"Then I suggest you retain a different doctor," he said, his voice heavy with disgust. "Like some pompous god you took me away from a dying woman's bedside last night, just because you think that money and power can buy you anything. Well, it can't buy your wife's return to health. She needs someone around her that she knows and can trust. Do as you wish, which you probably shall. But should your wife die, I shall hold you personally accountable in my prayers!"

Doesn't he know that they have killed my heir? Dunraven raged inwardly. Doesn't he care? Well, he cared. For the moment he would be a patient man. But patient men have very long and spiteful memories.

8

THE CHANGE in Paul Ely was remarkable. That he had helped to save a life put him in great awe of Lady Florence. It was strange the hold she now had over him, Dunraven thought. Thank God for that. Now he really had a weapon he could use against him. And, a sober, clear-thinking Ely he had plans for—until he was ready to dump him.

The cattle had to be rounded up and counted before he could purchase them. There was no better man for the task than Paul Ely. Besides, he wanted the man away from his wife and Dorothy.

Windham Thomas kept quiet in his patience, but again avoidance was his ally. As soon as he was able, he divorced himself of the Denver scene and went to wait for spring at his sawmill.

Lady Jane gave her daughter little choice but to be patient as well. The woman, upon reading the letter of the tragic event, wired Dorothy right back that she was to stay with Lady Florence as long as the woman had need of her.

So, Dorothy began to work her second spring in the mansion's gardens. But the joy was short-lived. Lloyd Folsom had turned seventeen and his father thought it time for him to become a teamster on one of the lumber carts. A light went out in Dorothy's life.

A light was nearly going out in another young man's life. Over a dinner of mutton and ale, A.Q. MacGregor nearly lost his appetite.

"As quick as that, Bill?" he asked despondently.

D.C. (Billy) Oakes grinned. "Quick? Me and Kellogg been up there since February. It should be approved and ready for entry by the end of summer. But don't tell no one. One party wants to get their hands on the whole thing."

"That's my worry. I wanted a slice of it first."

"Alex, you're crazy! Ain't land good for anything!"

"Am I? Then you'd best stick with surveying, Bill. I don't know what you called it, but there is a valley I saw what I called Lumpy Ridge, and to the west was a canyon that was black as midnight."

"Hey, I know the spot. There's a rock outcropping that looks just like twin owls perched on a limb."

"That's it," MacGregor said enthusiastically. "But how do I get it?"

Oakes shrugged. "Get up there and homestead it before the survey goes through. The act of preemption will cover you on 160 acres."

"That's not enough." And he sighed. "And I'm due to leave for Wisconsin for my marriage."

"Marriage?" Oakes hooted. "When did this come about?"

"Last summer. A young lady I met who was here with a sketching party from the University of Wisconsin. We've corresponded and the date is set."

Oakes pursed his lips. "Tell you what I'll do, Alex, as a wedding gift of sorts. Come by the office when no one is around and I'll let you look at the plat maps. File on what you want and I'll back-date it. But remember, it's only 160 acres for a husband and wife."

MacGregor grinned. "We're not married yet."

"And you each must have relatives."

That evening claims were filed for A.Q. MacGregor, Maria Clara Heeney, Georgianna Heeney (her mother) and W.C. MacGregor (Alex's father)—a six-hundred-and-forty acre beginning.

War had been declared without either side knowing a shot had been fired. That each man was of Scottish ancestry would only tend to prolong the stubborn battle and eventually accord it a place in history books.

"No," Dorothy wailed. "I want to go home!"

"No?" Dunraven's face was filled with astonishment. He had come to regard her as almost one of the servants and he wasn't used to being rebuffed.

"No, thank you, Cousin Windham. I do want to go home, and after all Lady Florence is quite her old self."

"Oh!" Dunraven said. "Very well, consider it from a different angle. The hunting guests who arrive in Longmont tomorrow are all males. I do desire for my wife to see my valley, but don't wish to see her left alone while we are off hunting."

Dorothy started to shake her head, but the

humor of the situation struck her with irresistible force. He had to play the role of being a husband, but wanted others to accept all of the tasks involved. And she knew that although Lady Florence was quite strong again physically, Dr. Lentz's announcement that she might never bear another child cast her in moods of deep depression. Who was she not to give another month of her life to the woman? Besides, she too had a desire to see the distant mountains up close.

"All right," she smiled, "for the month I will stay."

Dunraven smiled wickedly. He had not anticipated any other answer but this.

It was like the gathering of an uncoordinated circus parade. Austin and Folsom Carting Company had supplied, through a large advance of money from the Earl, horses, pack mules, tents, cots, folding chairs and even a Chinese cook. Some mules were laden with straw packed crates of wine and Scotch whiskey. No safari into the jungles of Africa went better equipped. The six visiting baronets and lords seemed a thoroughly likeable group, their ridiculous British hunting costumes excepted.

Dorothy was delighted that they had brought her favorite mount up from Denver.

"May I help you up?"

She lowered her parasol and turned. A sunbronzed Paul Ely stood grinning down at her boyishly.

"Paul," she gasped, "I didn't expect to find you on this little excursion."

"Without me it just might go in circles."

"It seems to need some leadership," she laughed.

"We thought you were still off on cattle business for the Earl. Lady Florence often wonders why we don't see you in Denver."

"That," Ely said, lifting her easily up to the side-saddle, "is very easy to explain: I didn't know if I would be welcome. I didn't mean to be such a cad, truly I didn't. You must believe me!"

Dorothy thought her wounds were healed—and she didn't want to reopen them. But he seemed so changed. Quiet, gentle and far more handsome than she could recall.

"I do believe you," she said gently.

Ely stood very still, looking up at her.

"I hope so," he said sadly, "because on the range I've had time to see that I am hopelessly in love with you."

Dorothy stared at him incredulously.

"Now, really, Paul," she began, "we've been over that ground before."

"But not honestly!" he said, almost angrily.

"Please," Dorothy said, "please don't! You can't know what you're saying—it's impossible!"

"Impossible? Hardly that. Let us say . . . difficult. First I have to convince you that I have changed, that I mean neither harm or embarrassment to you or your family. Now I think I can win Lady Florence over to my side. All I'm asking, Dorothy, is for another chance."

"Please no more," Dorothy pleaded. "You're getting me all confused again."

"Good! At least that is some response. Oh, here is Griff Evans with Lady Florence and her mount. Good day, Lady Florence. Griff, I'll ride the lead with the ladies. Lord Dunraven can stay with his group, and you can lead the pack train. We should get into the St. Vrain before nightfall, if Folsom's mounts are sturdy."

Dorothy went into a shell of silence. She sat her horse and listened to the gay platitudes pass between Lady Florence and Paul Ely. She had never seen the woman more animated or happy. He was indeed the prodigal son in her eyes.

Once off the plains they climbed up around the base of a reddish-brown gigantic cliff outcropping that resembled the prow of a ship and then dipped down to the gently rolling St. Vrain River. For an hour more they followed its cottonwood-lined banks, halting on a wide curve beneath towering redrock cliffs that were constantly changing hues with the setting sun.

Paul Ely realized at once Lord Dunraven's first mistake. The guests conducted themselves as such, accepting the Earl's offered afternoon drinks and leaving the erection of all the tents to Ely and Griff Evans. Even the Chinese cook stood expectantly until fires were started for his pots and kettles. Nor did Ely see why so many individual tents were required. The dinner was cooked and the lamps were burning before he and Evans had the last tent erected. He was glad they would have to put up only one more time on the trail before they would go up permanently for the summer.

After dinner Dunraven started serving his guests drinks again and Lady Florence and Dorothy started to make their excuses.

"Goodnight, Paul," Dorothy said. But Paul caught her hand.

"Wait," he said. "You haven't told me if you would give me another chance."

Dorothy thought quickly, wildly. He's so

changed. Oh, why wasn't he like this long ago—before the train—oh, yes, before he destroyed me in the train . . .

"Please," Paul Ely whispered.

Why not? Dorothy reflected. If Lady Florence could change her opinion of the man, couldn't she?

"Please," Paul said again. "Come take a walk with me. I promise I won't even touch you."

"All right, Paul," she sighed. "But please just talk."

And talk he did, all through the spring sunset that lasted until after nine o'clock. Herding the cattle had brought him back to what he should be doing with his life. Dunraven's valley was an ideal range, as long as the herd was not too large. Once the herd was purchased and the land acquired he would see to them for Dunraven, until he could acquire his own.

"Then he doesn't have the cattle, as yet?"

"Almost, but this other guy, McLaughlin, is holding out."

Dorothy frowned, puzzled. "And the land? I don't know why, but I was under the impression that he had secured it already."

"I'm not told everything," he said grimly, "but I guess Windham is working on it this summer. He's got to get it in 160-acre grants."

"Couldn't you do the same?"

"What do you mean?"

"If the valley is as large as Lord Dunraven claims, then it seems to me there is plenty of room for you to also fill and at least have the land for your ranch."

Paul's big jaw dropped.

"He would skin me alive and call it a double-cross."

"Fiddlesticks! This is supposed to be a free country, isn't it? It's no more his land to file upon than it is yours or mine. As a matter of fact, what would keep me from filing a claim?"

He sat there looking at her, his eyes widening and darkening in his handsome face.

"You'd be making a mistake," he said hurriedly. "He'd buy up all the land around you and squeeze you out."

Dorothy's brows rose sharply.

"I get so sick and tired of people talking about him as though he were some kind of god who should be feared. His title doesn't make him any more of a man than you, nor does it give him any more rights than you. Are you any better off than when you first started working for him? No. He'll dangle a carrot in front of your nose until it's withered and rotten."

Paul Ely was beginning to feel uneasy, almost traitorous. He knew that Rufus Brogan had been pushing for his dismissal, but the Earl had given him an opportunity to prove himself.

"I'll just have to take my chances," he said softly.

"Why? If you want to quit him and get started on your own, I'll loan you the money."

Women had offered Paul Ely money before, but not quite in this way. He chuckled. "It would take a heap of money."

"Nonsense! My ears have not exactly been glued shut while the Earl was home sick. It's only $1.25 an acres. I have over a thousand dollars in the bank at Denver. Surely $200 for the land and $800 for building and cattle should get you started."

"Look, Dorothy," he said humbly, "I don't know what to say. I appreciate the offer, but I better wait to see how the ground lies."

"The offer may not be made again!" she said coldly.

"I—I know," he whispered. "I think we had better get back."

Dorothy stood in her tent for a long time after he had said goodnight. He had been truthful and had not tried to touch her or kiss her. He is changed, she thought. But is he changed for the better? Before, there had been more of an independent quality about him and no fear of the Earl of Dunraven whatsoever. Had he lost some of his manliness?

"Well?" Dunraven growled.

Ely accepted the mug of bourbon offered him, his first drink in months, and stretched his long legs out before the open fire. Everyone else was in the tents and night sounds filled the air. He hesitated. He was really unsure of how to answer.

"Different!" he said at last. "Quite different than you anticipated."

"Well," Dunraven repeated, impatiently.

"To tell you the truth," Ely said slowly, sipping at the bourbon, "I don't think her interest in me goes beyond friendship."

"Friendship?" Dunraven chuckled. "In what manner?"

"She offered me the loan of a thousand to get land and cattle and quit working for you."

Dunraven looked at him with some astonishment.

"I should have known," he snarled. "Of all the low, contemptible tricks . . ."

"I think she was being honest."

"I'm sure that she was," he sneered.

"Why do you hate her so?"

The question caught Dunraven off-guard and his cheeks flushed with wrath. Then, because he held Ely in the same disdain as Dorothy, he calmed himself. "It is not a question of hate," he said quietly, "but of family honor. She's a slut!"

Ely started to protest, but Dunraven waved him to silence and filled his mug anew with bourbon.

"Do you think me blind and deaf and unable to bribe certain information from black porters? Oh, I don't blame you for going after her in the pullman berth, for that is your basic nature. But for her to consent disgusts me."

Paul Ely smiled to himself. For the first time he could read the lie on the man's face and determine the truth. Dunraven was jealous and coveted Dorothy for himself and was using him as a stalking horse.

Ely almost laughed aloud. In no sense of the word could Dorothy be called a slut, and he knew it. He also knew how his manliness measured up against the Earl's and knew that the man would get nowhere with the woman—that is, not without *his* help.

He could afford to keep silent with each of them. Dorothy's offer had been nothing in comparison to what he anticipated gaining from the Earl. But he would keep all of his options open, for he saw them each as sly and clever people who thought only of themselves.

Well, he could be just as sly and clever. He poured out the rest of the bourbon upon the ground. He was not going to fall off the wagon. This was one trick of the Earl's he was onto immediately.

"Do you like Paul?" Lady Florence inquired of Dorothy, as they rode higher into the jack-pine forests.

"I think that he's changed," Dorothy said soberly.

"Or are we looking at him through different eyes? I must admit that I am most confused. America must be changing me. Really, have you met such insufferable boors as the Earl has invited along? No wonder the Empire is so detested abroad. They are not very good diplomatic representatives, to say the least."

Odd, Dorothy thought, that the woman did not see that her own husband was part and parcel of his six guests. They were all the Earl's contemporaries and made her feel uncomfortable—all mid-thirty lecherous men, thousands of miles from the watchful eyes of their spouses and each casting secret looks in her direction as though she were the most sensual being they had ever encountered.

It wasn't so much what they said to her, but the tone in which they said it. One by one, they had come riding up to share a few words with the ladies. Most of their comments went over the head of Lady Florence, but Dorothy noted that Paul Ely blanched a few times. If it was a game being played by the Earl, Dorothy was ready to meet it head on.

"You're quite right," she said, but making sure

that her words reached Paul Ely, "but, then, they are men away from home who feel they do not have to abide by the social rules any longer."

"Dorothy," Lady Florence gasped, "you're making me blush."

"Then be honest with yourself. They would all be much happier if we were not along. They wish to partake of the manly world to which we do not belong: the hunting, the fishing, the drinking, the coarse talk. We are intruders and as such remind them of the other world and bring out their worst thoughts about women."

"Well," she answered sternly, "I am happy to say that Lord Dunraven is not like that!"

Paul Ely, without turning, smiled to himself and Dorothy wondered what the good Earl would do if Mary Eddy came riding around the bend in the trail in one of her more daring dresses.

Then Dorothy thought ill of her own thoughts. America was changing her, as well. What had happened to her naïve simplicity? Was she becoming so cynical that she could not look or listen to a man and not see a Brewster Gould, Paul Ely or Lord Dunraven behind their mask? Or was she maturing and seeing the world as it actually was—divided into unequal parts for male and female?

Lady Florence still accepted such a world without questioning. Could Dorothy? She wished that she could, but she couldn't. She wished that she could say that she still loved Paul Ely, but she couldn't say for sure. He was changed, but she was also changed. Caution was now her byword.

The camp was pitched on a rolling hill with the river a hundred yards below. Now it roared down over boulder bedrock and filled the forest with its musical lilt. Except at dinnertime the camp was deserted by all but the women and the Chinese cook. Griff Evans called it "buck fever." Not more than an hour after the tents had been pitched one of the Englishmen came excitedly back from a walk to report the spotting of a large herd of elk. It was no surprise to Evans for they were camped in Big Elk Meadows, an ample game area, but his caution went unheeded. They were there to hunt and could care less that the mules could not carry another ounce of cargo.

The women were long in bed by the time of the hunters' return. Griff Evans should not have feared, for all they brought back were enormous tales of what they shot and did not fall. Their excitement had carried them beyond the desire for food, but not drink. As long as Lord Dunraven played the willing host they drank and laughed and told succeedingly taller tales.

Paul Ely, who had forgotten the effects of bourbon upon an empty stomach, and his staunch resolve, was one of the first to weave his way to his tent, undress and collapse.

Windham Thomas had cautiously controlled his drinking, watching guest after guest make their drunken departure, until he alone sat in front of the dying fire.

The evening could not have gone better had he planned every second. He rose, stretched and walked toward a tent. He was a man who prided himself on having a thorough grasp of everything about everyone who surrounded him. He squatted down and peered into the tent. A wide grin cracked his normally dour face.

Ever since the train ride and Paul Ely's drunken

bouts, he had learned that the man had developed a fetish for sleeping with his clothing off. Carefully, so as not to disturb the snoring man in his long-johns, he extracted Ely's clothing and took them to his own tent.

With a fiendish giggle he made himself appear as much like the guide as possible.

Dorothy had been through the dream in a hundred different variations. The shadow that came to her was always Paul Ely, although she sometimes mentally fought for it not to be him. With Paul as the object of her dreams it always ended as it had in real life—a misty nothingness without conclusion.

And, as now, the dreams were always so real and lifelike. They were always shadowplays in which his clothing and odor were the major clues to his presence. And his hands. His large, sensitive hands gently caressing and searching out every curve of her body until it was tingling with a million little needlepoint pricks of anticipation and excitement.

Fighting to wake herself and stop it, and yet desiring it to continue, she would become almost like an observer as the nightgown would be unbuttoned and her breasts laid bare. Knowing what was coming next her nipples would begin to harden in anticipation even before they were touched. Her back would stiffen and arch, pushing her breasts upward invitingly—swollen, jutty, her nipples now expanded like field-ripened strawberries. Soft lips seemed to open warmly around them as her body writhed sensuously in the building ecstasy.

Dunraven, amazed that he had been able to proceed this far without arousing her, opened the whole front of the cotton nightdress. His light touches on her belly were provocative, purposely avoiding the seat of her need, enjoying the view of her nearly naked figure, her spreading, milky thighs, so wondrously contoured and rounded. He tickled his fingers along the inner planes of her legs, feeling her tremors of desire. Waves of woman-fragrance invaded his senses. In the frenzy of his own lust he ripped off Ely's clothing and then he calmed himself.

Her little shivers of pleasure made him feel intensely masculine, pleasing his ego, and making him see the importance of prolonging the foreplay. As long as she remained asleep, which he did not expect to be much longer, he could continue to play the Paul Ely role.

He continued his provocative game until she trembled all over. Only then did he stroke her arching mound and fondle the warm, tempting zones of her need. She writhed.

It was time.

He angled down between her thighs, and she gave a low moan of semi-awareness.

The pain was going to come and with it the ending of the normal dream. Her mind rallied against that. This time she wanted to know the full ending. Subconsciously she lifted, seeking him. And suddenly she found him, without ever using her hands . . .

The moist, heated contact made her shudder. She raised, her breath catching in her throat. She was dilated and there was no pain. There was also no pain because of the difference in girth between the two men. The expanding of her velvety-hot cove was accompanied by a series of sweet shiverings around him.

He drove in deep, and suddenly he felt the first wave of her intoxicating tremors, the delicious claspings and tightenings . . .

By damn, if only Florence was like this, he thought.

A sharp cry came from her throat. The dream had ended and reality begun. Still, it took her several seconds to ascertain that this was not a Pullman berth and that Paul Ely was again atop her. She lay quiet, torn between anger and an emotion she could not name. Reality was proving little different than the dreams. Inconclusive for a finale of some manner or other.

Sensing the change in her mood and body, Dunraven gently began to kiss her nipples and slowly withdrew, planning a quick reentry.

It was all that was needed. Her whole pelvis seemed to explode, pushing hungrily against him, and then the swift, unbridled spasms of her climax tore at her reserve. With each throb she whimpered, shuddered, her thighs gripping him, her breasts heaving . . .

This is what had been lacking. Now she could name it—passion. Her love for Paul Ely came soaring back as though it had never been dead.

Dunraven cursed to himself. She had left him high and dry and frustrated. He would just have to peak her again.

When the fury of her release quieted her, at last, she opened her eyes and reached out her hands to stroke the head nestled on her breast. Instead of rich, luxurious curls she came in contact with thin baldingness.

A sick terror seized her. She saw Lord Dunraven as clearly as if her fingers had been given sight. Her heart began to beat heavily, like an ominous drum. Her ears filled with its mounting and menacing sound. From some inner reserve of strength she gathered power and determination. Without warning she rolled him away and quickly rose.

"What the hell?" he roared, reaching out to grasp her, but connecting only with a tent pole. "Come back down here, bitch!"

Then his other hand encircled her ankle and began to tug. Dorothy jerked back, but Dunraven's grip was too tight. Frantically, she tried to use her other foot to kick him away. He caught it in midflight and twisted her off-balance. As she fell, a scream involuntarily escaped her lips.

Dunraven, in his own frantic attempt to reach her mouth and stifle the noise, crashed into the tent pole and cracked it in two. Cursing savagely, he tried to hold up the cascading canvas with one hand and rejoin the broken staff with the other.

"Help me, you silly little ass!" he shouted, but Dorothy had no desire to come anywhere near him.

Her scream had aroused the camp and kerosene lamps began to be lit. Paul Ely, who immediately suspected no more than a small animal getting into the tent of one of the women, reached out for his clothing without lighting a lamp.

Confused, he sat up and his head nearly sailed off his shoulder. He groaned and felt about for the lamp and some sulfur matches. Disoriented, he could find neither.

"Tent collapsing," Griff Evans growled, sticking his head through the tent flap.

"To hell with my damned clothes," Ely mumbled

and crawled out of doors. He nearly blacked out when he stood upright. He had nearly forgotten what a miserable feeling it was not to be able to sleep off a drunk. His head felt like every tribe in Africa was sending drum messages through his brain. The second scream nearly tore his head off anew.

Because the English gentlemen guests thought it only proper to don robe or outer garment before venturing into the midnight blue, Evans and Ely were the first to arrive at the collapsing tent.

The second scream had been caused by the weight of the canvas buckling the second tent pole and causing the whole structure to collapse inward. Pawing for release, neither Dorothy nor Dunraven could find an escape route.

Ely pulled rope taut stakes from the ground on one side and crawled beneath the canvas.

"Crawl over here," he commanded roughly, thinking he was dealing only with Dorothy.

A form moved toward him in the darkness and he reached out to help it along and raise the canvas for its escape. His hand came in contact with something that suggested that the form could be nothing more than male. Bewildered, he raised the canvas quickly to see what was amiss.

The guests had now fully gathered with their lamps, making the area as bright as full moonlight. Among them stood Lady Florence, wrapped in a full-length fur coat.

Lord Dunraven, on all fours, blinked against the brightness as though it were nothing more than the rising sun. With casual aplomb, as though he were not totally naked, he rose and dusted off his knees. With a haughty and disdainful nod to his guests, and not a single glance toward Lady Florence, he marched toward his tent as though everything were quite ordinary and understandable.

Ely, still holding the canvas aloft looked back. The lamplight illuminated the collapsed tent in oddly segmented sections. As dull as his mind was at the moment he could make out that Dorothy was almost nude and that his own clothing lay piled near her in a heap. His eyes travelled from one to the other as his mind burned away the cobwebs of truth one at a time.

"Why you dirty little whore," he snarled. "You've denied me, but you've been giving it to that bastard all along."

"How dare you—" Dorothy started, but instant darkness closed off her words. Even as he had been speaking Ely had been reaching for his clothing and crawling back outside.

And like the Earl before him, clutching his clothing to his chest, he haughtily marched off in his longjohns.

Wide-eyed and bemused, the guests looked at each other knowingly and made a prompt withdrawal. The hunting party was proving to be more enticing than thy had dreamed possible. Their own chances with the entrancing Lady Dorothy had just sky-rocketed. Imagine, they chortled, she was quite capable of handling two men at once! With such activity the collapse of the tent did not amaze them at all.

Only Griff Evans stood mystified. When he moved forward to extract Dorothy from the tent a stern voice stopped him.

"Leave her!" Lady Florence commanded. "And leave us alone!"

Her voice seemed to echo throughout all the aching bones of Doorthy's skull within the canvas. It was such a horribly impossible situation to explain. Somehow she was able to get her nightgown rebuttoned about her and find the area in which the other two had made their escape. She prayed that everyone had departed, but such was not her luck. Lady Florence still stood outside the tent, a secret and cunning look on her face, and in her condition it had something malefic about it.

Dorothy started to speak, then, coloring heavily, was silent. But Lady Florence, the imperturbable and logical, looked steadily at her and said in a calm tone: "Mary Eddy always claimed that you pushed for her dismissal for all the wrong reasons."

Dorothy answered with loud and hasty impatience. "Certainly, she would say that! She was paid well not to disclose that it was Lord Dunraven's child she bore!"

Lady Florence bestowed a look of real hatred and contempt upon Dorothy for this indiscretion, for, according to ancient code, such matters were not openly discussed. Gentlemen, after all, were granted a certain license of freedom with the servants.

In an effort to bring the situation back to the moment, she said coldly: "That is an entirely different matter. How dare you embarrass us all by bringing about this disgraceful scene?"

Dorothy's face became as still and pale as granite. Fever was running like a fiery liquid through her veins. She spoke, and her voice was hard and clear.

"Since when has a man entering a woman's tent and forcing himself upon her become a disgraceful scene for only the woman? Is your husband to go scotfree of any blame?"

The two women exchanged swift looks. Dorothy was momentarily embarrassed, and, in consequence, was infuriated with herself. She should not have felt ashamed or guilty, but did so. But Lady Florence, poised and restrained as always, mistress of herself as always when it came to feminine protocol, was not too disconcerted. The eyes fixed on Dorothy were wicked and smooth and blue as opal.

"I may ask this of you, Dorothy: Why all of your passionate denials of Paul Ely of late? . . . and yet, I come to find you entertaining both Paul and my husband at the same moment."

Never before, in all her sweet and gracious life had Florence used such calm and deadly words to any one. A product of a class structure, which had been rigidized even more by the caste system of India, it was highly embarrassing for her to make such an accusation. But in her Victorian heart she knew that such a scene would never have come about unless the woman in question had weak morals.

Dorothy's eyes did not drop at the woman's steadfast regard. Their brownness took on a molten gold quality, as if incandescent. The words had struck her like repeated blows, and she felt a great aching anguish in her heart. But she did not look away from Lady Florence.

"Now," she said, "we see your true heart, don't we, Florence? I don't know all of your husband's plot, but I've seen enough tonight to realize that it is dirty and disgusting. Perhaps you aren't woman enough to keep him from other women, but I am woman enough to keep him away from me."

Their eyes locked together. Then, very slowly, Lady Florence smiled. Her lips curved in a lovely meditation, without looking away from Dorothy.

"What plot could you possibly mean?" she asked, with honey sweetness, even tenderness. "Is that a clever way to cover up your own lustful ways? Don't place yourself so high and mighty, my dear. Unless you wish a full reporting of this to your mother, you will steer clear of *all* of the men in this camp until I can make arrangements to have you sent away!"

Dorothy, ashen with terror, gaped at the departing woman. She wished her mother to learn none of this because she would be too heartsick to explain the real truth. Her thoughts were clamoring. She was sick with their import. Everyone seemed prone to paint her scarlet and care little about Lord Dunraven's part in the affair. Could she get Paul Ely to convince Lady Florence that he had only been a party to the rescue? And would that even really matter?

One by one the camp lights flickered out. Not a single *gentleman* came back to help her re-erect the tent. She struggled to lift back the canvas and pull forth the blankets from the cot. She wrapped them about her shoulders and sat down on the canvas to sort out her thoughts.

The whole thing was contemptible! It had all happened so fast that it was almost like a part of a horrid and frightening dream. Then she smiled internally.

"At least it answered one important question,"

she mumbled to herself. "Even if it was the wrong man bringing about the answer."

She wished, vehemently, that this scene had never taken place. It had compelled her to show fear in the face of Lady Florence. A half-truth would sound like a whole-lie in her mother's ears. She felt that her mother, like Lady Florence, had probably never fully experienced passion and therefore could never fully understand what she had just been through.

She straightened and gazed steadfastly up at the stars.

"But, I must make Paul see the truth first."

9

LADY FLORENCE's light voice, with its lack of resonance and depth, was very seldom taken seriously by her husband.

Now her voice, as she confronted Dunraven and Paul Ely, was so strong, so passionate, so ringing with threat, that they stared at her in complete stupefaction.

"No!" she cried. "No! I have held my silence through this entire long, miserable day! Her tent is not to be pitched in this camp!" She made a desperate motion with her hands. "Or anywhere in this entire valley. She has deceived me in the worst way. I want her taken back to Denver, at once!"

Dunraven shook his head slowly and sombrely. During the night he had had a change of thought and of plans. He had not gained any real revenge by seducing his cousin, only awakened a lust that had gone unsated. He was not about to let her leave until his vanity had been satisfied.

"Now, my dear," he said soothingly, "you are making too much of this whole matter. Nothing really—"

"Enough!" she snapped, cutting him short. "I am no fool, Windham Thomas! Just be thankful that I am lady enough to know that all men are weaklings when it comes to hearing the call of a temptress. That does not mean that I forgive you, but recognize my family obligation to take away the temptation. I feel duty-bound to protect Paul in the same manner. But if either of you insist upon keeping her here, then make arrangements for my departure—all the way back to Ireland and its consequences."

Dunraven began to shout, all at once, as if his self-control was totally gone. His face was contorted. He struggled into his saddle.

"Damn you, woman! I'll give you what you want! I'm sick of it all. And of all of you! You all get in my way with your constant pettiness!"

He flung his horse about so violently that it kicked gravel up into their faces. With a shout, he galloped off, waving for the hunters to mount and follow him.

Paul Ely shook off the entrancement that had seized him at Lady Florence's look and words, and his hands doubled murderously into fists. Dunraven had left him holding the bag. The order had not been stated in so many words, but he knew he would be the one expected to escort Dorothy back to Denver. He was the one who felt deceived.

"She has been shameless," she said, with pious coldness. "She as much as admitted it to me last night. Paul, please help me in this matter. I can't stand to look upon her face."

The tragic appeal in her voice, her face and her eyes, would have moved a more reasonable man. But Paul Ely was not being any more reasonable than Lady Florence. He grumbled a half-hearted agreement to the request and strode away.

Pleased with herself, Lady Florence smiled and entered her tent. She was not new to handling such sordid affairs. After the death of her mother she had had to keep a most watchful eye upon her father to keep him away from loose women. It was in the nature of the weak beasts, she had always concluded. She considered women most depraved who gained any enjoyment from the act whatsoever. It had one God-given purpose and should be feared and respected in that light.

Paul Ely was not intimidated by either Lord or Lady Dunraven. He would let them do the dirty work of telling Dorothy she must leave and then he would follow their orders, if he could be found at the time.

When all but Dorothy's tent was erected he told Griff Evans to go and see to his family and then saddled his own horse.

It was the moment Dorothy had been waiting and praying and hoping for. Throughout the day she had avoided everyone on the trail. Lady Florence had stuck to Paul Ely like glue and Dorothy didn't think it would do her much good talking with Lord Dunraven.

As soon as Griff Evans had selected the campsite, at the fork where the Fall River and Thompson foamed together to create the Big Thompson, she had hurriedly dismounted and climbed the nearest bluff. Sitting in a field of purple, yellow and white spring crocuses, she had watched the confrontation, well knowing she was the reason for such a council.

That Lady Florence had won was apparent in the manner of Dunraven's angry departure. And that had stirred Dorothy to new anger. Even without hearing their words she knew that Dunraven had admitted to nothing.

"Oh," she had stormed, "if only I were a man!"

But had she been a man she would not have been in such a situation.

For the next hour she fixed her eyes upon Paul Ely, and she saw no one else. He had to hear what she had to say. He had to believe that she was blameless and take her away from all of this. Her concentration on his working form had something inhuman and ghastly in it. She was almost trying to enter his mind from such a great distance.

When she saw him start to send Griff Evans away, she rose and started to run down the bluff. She didn't want to arrive before Evans departed, but at the exact moment that Paul would be alone.

She didn't have to worry about Griff Evans tarrying. The whole day had seemed to crackle with monstrous passion and tension. He wanted away from these "weird" people, if only for the night.

Paul Ely had just put the last cinch in the saddle when he saw Dorothy running across the meadow. Everything darkened before his eyes, and he saw nothing but the entrapment of being caught by Lady Florence and having to take Dorothy away.

Having been the victim all his life of sensual emotion, and rarely reason, he did not understand what he was experiencing, nor the cause of the fixed pang which stood in his chest like a sword. All he could see was that Dorothy was ruining his chances with Lord Dunraven and had not given him a better offer in return. Jealousy was not even a word in his vocabulary. He felt only madness and rage and frenzy.

Without even a turn of his head to acknowledge her strident call, he jumped to the saddle and rode furiously downstream.

Dorothy misread his departure. She thought he meant to get out of eye and earshot of Lady Florence and she raced to where her mare was tethered. Her frustrations mounted when she saw that the beast had been unsaddled and she turned to see where the sidesaddle might have been placed.

Then she froze in stark disbelief and terror.

Lady Florence, who had heard her call, stood a few feet away. Her slight body appeared to expand with the vehemence of her thoughts and her hatred. She flung up her arms and aimed the rifle at Dorothy.

"Florence!" she gasped. "Think! Think for just a moment, in the name of God! I can ride after Paul and get him to prove how wrong you are!"

"You baggage," she said, with slow virulence. "You could get any man to say what you wanted him to say with your hussy promises. Get away from that horse!"

Her words brought a profound quietness to Dorothy's senses. Every ounce of Goold and Whyham-Quin blood came surging to the surface. This woman was only what she was by a giant step up the marriage ladder, while she, Dorothy, possessed the natural birthright. She was mentally and physically exhausted by this silly folly.

"Madame," she said icily, "you are an imbecile! I own that horse and aim to mount it, saddle or no! And when that mount gets me back to so-called civilization I now intend to scream out what I was too foolish to scream out last night. No matter the consequences to myself, I'll broadcast far and wide that the Fourth Earl of Dunraven, Viscount of Mount Earl and Adare, is most capable of incest and rape!"

"You liar!" Lady Florence screamed and pulled the rifle trigger.

The roar of the blast momentarily stunned Dorothy. Warm, sticky blood gushed across her breast, but she knew it was not her own. The death cry of the mare announced who had taken the fatal shot, even before it crumpled to the ground.

Dorothy turned swiftly to Lady Florence, who smiled at her gently and maliciously, and with triumph.

"Ride out now with your lies!"

A cold resolution and intense clarity came to Dorothy. The woman was never going to believe her and was never going to let her tell her story. Only on the *Shannon* had she come near death before and that terror seemed minute in comparison to this.

Slowly, she turned and started to walk away, each second expecting to hear the bark of the rifle. She was actually a little amazed at the woman's fierceness.

But the mischief had been done. She was now without a horse and would have to find Paul on foot. The fever of the moment was still running hotly through her veins. Her breathing did not return to normal until she found a stepping stone path across the Thompson and rounded the first rocky bluff.

Silence. No sound of anyone following her. Only the drone of a bee moving from spring flower to spring flower. No sign of man's hand anywhere in the world.

Ahead of her, eastward, the land dipped sharply, the vast meadowland a verdant blanket for the river to meander through like a snake unsure of which direction it wished to travel.

Dorothy was of a similar frame of mind. At the far base of the meadow the rocky hills soared silver-olive, silver-tawny, silver-violet, gashed by ravines. Out of one such she knew they had ridden that afternoon, but looking at it backwards made it all seem quite different. She tried to pinpoint the spot.

Although it had not been mentioned at the time, she had seen a distant cabin and grazing cattle as they had come down off the mountain. Cattle, at that moment, indicated the logical direction in which Paul Ely would have ridden.

She looked the other way, south, where the meadow rose again to rolling pine dotted foothills, only to explode almost immediately into heavily forested, towering walls that seemed savage and deserted. But she was certain that at their base would be the little ranch.

With no path to follow, she created one of her own that began to rise, gently at first, and then fairly steeply, with the meadowland now completely closed from her view. Trees closed in overhead; the pine-needle bed became thick; her steps were muffled except for a soft crunch.

Feeling she was rising too high, she angled back to a downhill direction. Now she could travel at a fair speed, although it was a good hour before she came to the bottom of a narrow valley.

For a moment the mountain silence and solitude and strangeness disoriented her sense of direction. Shadows of high cirrus seemed to constantly change the faces of the ghostly ridges in every direction. Shielding her eyes she peered upward and began to turn about.

Looming over a jagged piling of gigantic boulders, as though watching her every move, was a landmark she could recognize.

She gave a sigh of relief and smiled back at the granite-sheer east face of Long's Peak. She would keep it on her right, go over the next ridge and have the meadowland below her again.

In a few moments her plan fell apart. The ridge was twice as wooded as the one she had ascended and closed her in from all sighting of the towering mountain. She kept to what she thought was a steady path forward.

It was darkness, in the end, that stopped her. It had come suddenly and swiftly, the clouds blanketing down over the mountains as though by a magic hand and bringing along a cool breeze. The rain fell like a downy mist, although it suggested it was fluffy spring snow in the higher regions.

Dorothy knew that she was lost, but had no sense of panic. Little of the mist was invading the bower-sheltered woodland floor and on a bed of pine needles she sat back against a treetrunk to wait out the storm and gain her bearings again.

Suddenly, the whole thing became so laughable. She had never been in such a ridiculous situation in her whole life. They were all adults acting like spoiled children, each wanting their own way.

Dorothy might not have thought it so laughable if she could have heard the accusations being hurled against her back at the camp. Because the Chinese cook spoke no English, Lady Florence could relate the happening as she desired. If she could not win one way, she would win another.

"My love, don't shake so," mumbled Lord Dunraven pleadingly.

"Oh Paul, I thought you would hear the shot and come back," Lady Florence sobbed. She turned blindly to Paul Ely, who took her hand and held it tightly. His face was quite red and peculiar. Dunraven listened calmly, with a faint half-smile.

"She must have taken the gun from your tent, Windham," she said timidly and hoarsely. "When I told her that Paul was going to take her back to Denver, she just went crazy and shot her horse. I feared for my own life, but she went running off."

"With the rifle?"

"I don't know," she lied. "Now I insist that you find her and take her away. I am most frightened."

"Now, now," Dunraven said, striving for lightness. "It isn't as bad as that, my pet."

He paused. She was, after all, he thought, a hot-tempered Goold and he had taken very ungentlemanly advantage of her as though she were little more than a servant girl who could not strike back at him. He thought of Dorothy with the rifle and was terrified. He spun away to do a weapons count, but would not have thought to look behind the luggage in Lady Florence's tent.

"Perhaps it is bad," he quietly told Paul Ely. "Before the storm really breaks we'd best split up into two search parties—I would suggest armed, as she apparently is. I don't want any of our guests hurt unnecessarily."

Ely leaned forward, spoke softly and forthrightly: "Why would she want to shoot any of us?"

"You should know that well enough," he said brutally, wishing to put a face on the matter that would arouse Ely as well. "You've sniffed after her enough. She has faddle-daddled each of us with her wily ways. Last night it was supposed to be just a little chat about you, or so I thought. She started her faddle-daddle game and I am only human and male. But as soon as I was naked she starts to scream and make threats against the two of us. I am to allow her to marry you or she will ruin both of us in the eyes of my wife. Now, after this latest business with the horse, I am certain that the girl is more than a little balmy in the brain."

Ely looked at him, and his mouth tightened. "It doesn't make sense. Why shoot the horse?"

Dunraven spread out his hands resignedly. "That's true. Logically, you might say it was so she couldn't be sent away from you. Do you wish to keep her here and marry her?"

"Hell no! I've played the game just as you've wanted, but the rewards have been damn slim."

Dunraven was silent. He gnawed his lip. Now, he could see, Dorothy was becoming enormously troublesome to his affairs. If his first guests returned to England with far-fetched tales it could make his whole scheme a laughing matter. Never once did he consider that his own lust had brought about all the turmoil. Dorothy was a thorn that had to be plucked from his side.

Then he flung out his hands. He said dully, "I can't let you go after her without all the facts, Paul. Do you have her with child?"

The look that passed between the two was a thin rapier of darting mistrust. But Ely remained sober, and very serious.

"You are well aware the only time I've had her was on the train," he said with stern gravity. "The time element makes her claim false."

Dunraven did not speak. His look was more black and lowering, as he worked to bring Ely farther into the scheme he was developing moment by moment.

Then he said explosively, "And you are without an ounce of defense! That is the threat she will take to Lady Florence against you! After last night, seeing you come from the tent in longjohns, she cannot help but believe that there have been other times. Well, now do you see the importance of getting her away?"

The damned Irish bitch! thought Ely, with evil fury. Now he saw the reason behind her offering him money for land and cattle. She had cast, and she had lost. He was not about to be marched to the altar at the point of a shot gun. He suspected Dunraven as the father of her child but he had to side with him, even though the thought of it was sickening.

"I think I know the direction she might have gone," he said darkly. "Give me two men."

Dunraven tried to bluster, sheepishly. "Don't go losing your head, Paul. I—I wouldn't want her harmed."

Ely shook his head slowly and somberly. He knew exactly what the Earl wished protected. "No. But the safety of your guests comes first."

Dunraven nodded. He ran the tip of his tongue over his lips, and his narrow face narrowed still more. If an "accident" happened, there would be no blood on his hands. He had eight witnesses as to the dangerous nature of the woman.

When the parties were formed, Dunraven went from guest to guest, as though taking each into his personal confidence over the matter. None were aware of what had been said to the other, but Ely suspected.

Dorothy had slept—some—though she was stiff when she finally woke. She couldn't tell if it were late or early. The light which shafted through the forest was pearled, but without sun. Was it sunset or sunrise?

The thought brought her fully awake. Paul! Surely Paul should have been back to the camp by now and learned of her absence?

She raised her head cautiously, and tried to awaken the wrist and arm she had been sleeping upon. Then, in spite of the numb arm, she sat up abruptly.

There came a crashing through the underbrush that increased to a frightening roar. Before Dorothy could react a buck elk and eight of his cows came charging through the trees. Almost too late they smelled her and their panic was doubled. With eyes flaring they leaped fallen logs and frantically sought alternate escape routes. The enormous bull bugled furiously to keep his harem together, and Dorothy marvelled that he could dash between the trees without even entangling his widespread antlers. But one large cow, nearly ready to drop her calf, either didn't heed his call or was too heavy to be as agile as the rest of the herd and charged directly towards Dorothy.

Neither beast or girl had time to completely avoid each other, but the cow had sense to jump at the last moment. But the jump was not high enough and the cloven hoofs struck her stomach and leg with a violence that knocked the breath out of her body.

For a time she lay still, breathing in the scent of the pine needles in which her face was buried, and waiting for the pain in her leg to subside. Then she thought she heard the pound of horses' hooves, and she tried to sit up; but when she rested her weight on her left hand it gave way, and she collapsed with a gasp of pain.

The hoofbeats came nearer, and stopped; a man's voice cried out:

"It's too thick in there! Let's ride around and cut them off! Magnificent beasts, eh wot?"

Dorothy was ready to call out for rescue when the answering voice stopped her.

"No!" Ely shouted. "You've the whole summer to hunt! Dunraven wants the girl tonight!"

There was a ribald laugh from one of the hunters. "Always was a cheeky one, but not in this case, lads. That little Irish piece is not what the bloke led us to believe. I'm on holiday and have no desire to go home in a pine box."

"Don't be listening to Dunraven's nancy-do talk,

lads. The Earl just wants to keep the cutting of that meat for his own bed, and with a wife like that who could blame him? But if I come across that lass alone, don't expect me back until morning."

"You there, man, settle the matter. Is the lass dangerous or just playful?"

"Both!" Ely announced, not wanting them off the chase any more than Dunraven had wanted him off the chase. "She would probably kill the Earl on sight, but might show real gratitude to any man who found her on an evening like this. And from experience, I can tell you that she really knows how to show gratitude."

The back of Dorothy's hand was pressed so hard to her mouth that her teeth hurt it. She dared not call out for help. It was unthinkable, but Paul Ely was almost giving them license to search her out and rape her. She didn't understand his comment about the Earl; although her opinion of him and his wife was pretty low at that point, she certainly wasn't interested in murdering either one of them.

It was one word that convinced her she didn't know all of what was going on. Who was calling her dangerous and why? A mindless panic swept through her. She was alone. The words suggested that even Paul Ely had been persuaded against her.

She became motionless and silent. Kill, she might, if one of the hunters had come upon her. They, after all, had reverted to type and were little more than predators of other species. She could be the same, if the occasion arose.

It was a stupid thing to think, she finally determined; like telling the wind not to blow. She was weaponless and a woman. Her only course of action was to avoid the hunters and find her way to the ranch for the help and shelter it would afford.

Exhilaration on the thought seized her, and she was on her feet and running. Speed, speed, that was what she wanted! To reach the ranch first and tell her story without lies.

That was her only thought for several hours. She kept at a steady walk. The trees slid past in a blur, mile upon mile without change. She might have rested except for the cold mixture of rain and snow that was now falling heavily. The landscape was rocky, the descent now steep. The ground beneath her feet no longer needle gray, but smooth white. The snow was only a thin layer yet, but it was dangerous. Twice her leather soled boots slipped on the ice. Then the weather changed.

She strained her eyes always to find the mountain landmark. It was under thousands of feet of clouds and wind driven snow—one moment hail-like, then icy pellets driving into her face and body. And always, always the air grew darker. Night was almost complete when she saw that she was down in the valley and could hear the gentle rush of water in the distance.

She realized then the utter futility of her struggle. The odds were all against her; there was nothing in her favor. The weather, her female constitution, her poor sense of direction, even the time of day, all made failure a forgone conclusion. And to make matters worse, behind her she heard the rapid advance of horses' hooves.

"No," she screamed against the storm, "none of these shall dismay me, none shall rouse a doubt in my mind. Only one thing matters! To reach safety before it is too late!"

When she turned to see if the rider was gaining, the wind whipped the hair across her face, blinding her. She was dizzied with the mad rush of wind.

As soon as she reached Fish Creek she knew it meant further trouble. The stream cut through two cliffs. She would have to wade the icy waters or climb again.

Although the selected route was difficult for her, she reasoned it would be impossible for the man and horse. It was getting close enough so that she could hear the horse slithering and slipping. She could not make out the voice of the rider who urged the horse on, but she suspected it to be Paul Ely. Sick with despair, she clawed her way to the rocky summit and looked back.

A second horseman was coming fast along the creek bank. Distance and swirling snow kept his face hidden, but his horsemanship and impetuosity told her she had been wrong before. This had to be Paul Ely.

The disaster seemed to come all at once, like a lightning flash. There was a mingled shriek from the first rider and horse, a crashing fall down the cliff side, and then the most dreadful of all sounds, the screams of an injured animal.

Dorothy stumbled to the precipice and caught the rough trunk of a tree for support. Below she could see the fallen beast, but not the man, and could hear the second rider crashing into the water toward the scene. For the first time, her anxiety to reach the ranch was dulled by another feeling—remorse. Her folly had injured the horse; it might have killed the rider. Then she could see the second rider as he jumped from his mount.

It was not Paul Ely. It was Lord Dunraven.

The first rider came trudging back from downstream.

Dunraven was so angry that he spoke to the English hunter as he might have spoken to a servant. "You fool of an idiot," he shouted, right into the man's face. "This is one of my finest beasts."

"I was following the lass's tracks," he said placatingly.

Dunraven didn't answer or ask if the man was hurt. His hands were busy under his coat. The last of the light from above shone dully on the object in his hand. He leaned forward. The cries of the injured horse rose to a pitch, and stopped.

Dorothy bowed her head and clutched the tree with hands that had lost their power to feel.

Dunraven scowled. Then he shook his head.

"Let's get back! The storm is getting worse!"

"What of the lass?"

"What of her?"

"She couldn't be too far—" The words died in the man's throat and he peered incredulously at his host. "You can't just leave her out in this!"

"Can't I?" He glared at the man. "She's cost this excursion two horses and nearly your life. You aren't hurt, are you?"

He shook his head, with the slow motion of a man too exhausted to speak on the one hand and too dumbfounded on the other. Then he looked about helplessly.

"But—" he stammered.

"There are no buts about it," Dunraven glowered. "This is not jolly old England, man. This is the American West. The survival of the fittest! She created the folly, not I. It will save us all a great deal of embarrassment if she does die of exposure, which seems to be her only fate on such a night. I will not have another beast or a single guest suffer the same fate in a futile attempt of searching her out. Come! Let's get out of here before we both catch our death!"

Dorothy could see that the man had been lying. His stumbling walk was due to more than fatigue. But hurt or no, he was of little use to her as long as Dunraven was his companion.

The whole situation seemed so ludicrous and strange and confusing. What folly? What embarrassment? Why so little regard for her rescue and safety? She had been the one forced to flee Lady Florence for fear of her life! She had been the one chased by the hunters because of her fear of the overheard words!

Die from exposure? She was not about to die and let Lord Dunraven get away with his bully-boy tactics.

Soon she was out of the shelter of the rocks, and the wind and snow flung themselves at her in a wild fury. She felt none of it. The heat of anger and determination to survive were like barriers against them. She didn't know where she was going, but she kept the sound of the creek constantly on her right. It had to drain eventually into the meadowland, she soundly reasoned. She plodded on, leaning more and more heavily on the support of a stick she had extracted from the snow, and at long last she saw, through the pine branches which now surrounded her, the yellow square of a lighted window.

The cabin was a low, small place, huddled in the shelter of a steep rock slope. That was all she could see of it through the storm. She had to pound against the door for a long time before it came open a crack.

"I'm Lady—I'm Dorothy Goold," she called against the wind. "I've been lost!"

The door inched farther open. The woman appeared small, her lifeless gray hair plaited into double braids that hung over the blanket wrapped about her shoulders. The first reaction on her pinched face was concern, of that Dorothy was sure. Then, though she did not move her head, Dorothy got the impression that she had cast a quick glance into the cabin's interior. Then rough, hospitable hands pulled her inside and put her down before a roaring fire.

Dorothy was drenched through, but the woman seemed nervous about offering her more than a stool in front of the fire.

"I'm sorry to disturb you."

"No bother." But now Dorothy could see that she did look uneasy.

"Your husband is gone?"

This time the quick glance went to the back door of the cabin.

"Out in the storm," she said without emotion. "Saving calves from the freeze that will come 'fore morn."

Only then did Dorothy notice that three young calves lay in a strawed corner staring curiously at her and their strange surroundings. At least they had someone who cared for them and went looking for them in the storm, she thought bitterly.

"I am from the camp—" Dorothy began.

"I'm aware," the woman quickly interrupted. "I'm Mrs. Evans."

"Aware?" Dorothy hesitated, feeling defeat sag her down. That she was the wife of Griff Evans and *aware* meant that someone from the camp had been by to report. Suddenly she didn't feel that she would get help or truth as she had so hoped.

"I see," Dorothy said. "Then someone from the camp has been by looking for me?"

Martha Evans saw no harm in answering that question. "That cowboy, Paul Ely. Came by near suppertime to warn . . . to tell us you were gone." She had almost made a slip and quickly turned away.

"Warn?" Dorothy quickly asked. "Warn you about what?"

The woman seemed to shrivel inside the blanket. "My husband don't cotton for me to mess in matters that ain't mine, Miss Goold."

Dorothy wondered, as she spoke, how often tact and truth go hand-in-hand.

"In this case, Mrs. Evans, I seem to be involved in that warning without knowing why. I am very confused."

Martha Evans was a God-fearing woman who had never seen a prostitute in her life. Her husband had all but called this woman such and she had never before had reason to doubt the word of her husband. But in that moment she doubted, and doubted the words from Paul Ely's mouth even more. She was also confused. The woman wasn't armed as far as she could see.

"Mr. Ely says you ran off to the woods with a rifle after shooting a horse."

Dorothy gasped. "That's absurd! A twisted lie! What infamy!" She gasped again. "If you want the real truth, Mrs. Evans—" Then she caught herself and blushed. "I'm sorry, Mrs. Evans. That was rude of me to impose upon your hospitality. I shouldn't involve you in this matter. It seems to become more and more complicated."

Mrs. Evans hesitated a moment and then quickly took the blanket from her own shoulders and wrapped it about Dorothy. "Good Book says not to judge unless you want to be judged. Keepin' broth hot for my man on the fire. I'll ladle you a bowl."

"I don't want to cause any problems, Mrs. Evans."

Her face split into a smile, and the dark eyes lighted. For the first time Dorothy realized she was not an old woman, but just aged beyond her years.

"Already got me a problem in letting you in. Bowl of venison broth ain't goin' to make it worse."

Dorothy hesitated, feeling ashamed. She did not want to get the woman in trouble, but now she could smell the savory aroma and realized her own hunger. She had eaten nothing all day.

Her embarrassment grew as she eagerly accepted a second bowl of the spicy soup, laced with thin slivers of deer heart and liver. It warmed her from head to toe and made her feel as though she had devoured a full-course meal.

Martha Evans was of simple stock. For five years her association with the outside world had been limited to three shopping trips to Denver. She had not expected to associate with the "ladies" in the Dunraven party, especially after what her husband had informed her had transpired on the trail, but if her Lord Jesus Christ could take unto his bosom

Mary Magdalene, then she would be a hypocrite for doing less.

Fifteen years of marriage to Griffith Evans had made her a good and silent listener. But she also had the common sense to ask the proper questions, at the proper time, until she and Her Lord were certain they were dealing with the wrongly accused and not the damned.

"Marty?"

It was a man's voice calling from outside the back door. Dorothy knew that the repercussions of her being there would fall squarely on the woman's shoulders.

Martha, near the door, turned quickly, to ward off an entrance. But the door was already opening.

"All is well," he said shortly. "And as for the woman—what is the matter?"

Martha made some little hushing gesture, indicating that she was not alone. "Someone is with you?" he asked sharply.

"It is the English lady from the camp, and—"

"*The English lady?*" The swift intake of breath was almost explosive. "Have you no more sense than to invite her in when Griff told you—"

"Things are not as they would have us believe. Come in. I need your help."

Dorothy heard his breath go in, as if he had shut his mouth hard on whatever he had been going to say.

He was a powerful-looking man in his late forties, broadly built and swarthy, with the glow of good outdoor living on his skin. His face was square, going to fat a little, with high cheekbones and the inevitable moustache; a typically Western cowboy face. He seemed shy and embarrassed.

"This is our neighbor, James McLaughlin," Martha said.

Dorothy was already giving him her nicest smile; it was in her interest to win a second convert to her cause.

"How do you do? I'm Dorothy Goold. I'm sorry, I know I shouldn't have imposed myself upon Mrs. Evans, but it was the only lighted window in the storm."

McLaughlin's embarrassment grew. Cattle, mountains and horses were his friends, because women left him stammering like an idiot. He stood stiffly just inside the door, watching Dorothy as though she were the first woman he had ever seen.

"Griff is late," Mrs. Evans said. The statement sounded tentative, like a question, as if McLaughlin might have known the reason why.

He shrugged, and grinned sheepishly. "Perhaps he's gone back to tuck in the Englishmen."

"He did not . . . help you with more calves?"

"No. Just those."

Martha sighed. "Then he needn't know. Jim, you will have to take Miss Goold on home with you for the night."

Jim McLaughlin gasped as though she had just suggested he commit adultery. "But I'm a bachelor!"

"And she is a *lady*," Martha said sternly. "And she is also horseless," she added, as though the two went hand in hand.

He dug his hands deep into his pockets as though to protest, but Dorothy could see that Martha Evans had a quiet power over the big man that would stifle his words to silence.

Dorothy turned, her eyes brimming with tears.

"Thanking you seems so inadequate, Mrs. Evans."

Martha Evans always considered herself an emotionless woman, but she suddenly found herself grasping Dorothy and hugging her.

"Go with God, child! Go with God!"

The McLaughlin cabin was only three miles back up Fish Creek. Dorothy had been within a thousand yards of it early on in the evening, but it had been lampless and dark.

After the Evans' cabin, she did wonder what a bachelor cabin would look like. Without being asked, she slid down from his horse, and followed him indoors.

The cabin had two rooms, with no door between them, merely an oblong gap in the wall. The living-room, opening straight off the yard, was scrupulously neat, and very poor. The floor was of earth, beaten as hard as a stone, with a decrepit, balding bearskin rug covering half of it. There was a small stone fireplace in one corner, in which McLaughlin immediately built a wood fire, and across the back of the room ran a wide ledge, three feet from the floor, which served apparently as a bed-place, and was covered with a single quilted blanket patterned in rose and green. The walls had not been recently whitewashed, and were grimed with several winters' smoke. Here and there, high up in the plastered walls, were niches which held ornaments, cheap and bright, and faded tintype-photographs. There was one in a place of honor, a girl of perhaps twenty. She wasn't pretty, or common, just rather nondescript.

Dorothy turned. The fire was blazing and she was quite alone. McLaughlin came out of the inner room with an armful of clothes. He dumped them across the plank table and looked at the picture, with what Dorothy took as scorn.

"Correspondence bride," he said emotionlessly. "Clothes arrived, but not her." Then he grinned shyly. "Ain't her finest, I reckon, but they are warm and dry. I'll be sleeping in the barn, in case you need me."

Dorothy watched him go, a strange mixture of emotions written on her fatigued face. She had never know a man like him before—a gentle sort of man who was all giving. She could not help but think that the girl in the tintype had made a grave error in not becoming his bride.

She was asleep almost the instant she crawled into the bed.

10

THE SMELL OF COFFEE and bacon awoke her. It was a clear, blue sunny day. Robins chirped on the windowsill where Jim McLaughlin had scattered some bread crumbs.

"Come eat," he said as a greeting. "Griff Evans was here hours ago. Told him I wouldn't wake you to go with him. Told him it was the responsibility of someone from the camp to fetch you. Got chores, now."

He was almost breathless after stringing together so many words. After he had gone, she sat down at the rough-hewn table and ate slowly.

He was right, of course. He had handled the situation the way only a man could. She didn't want to go back like some found criminal. But she was going to have to go back and face them squarely, embarrassment or no. This was a hard new world she found herself in. One had to learn to fight, physically as well as morally, and the former a woman had to learn to do in her own way. Lord Dunraven was playing by ancient rules which excluded women of all rights, even the right of self-protection from men like him. It wasn't right, but how could she fight him when he was judge, jury and the accused all rolled into one? She sighed and stood up. As she went out the door, Paul Ely came riding hard into the yard. His handsome, well-tanned face was wrinkled in an anxious frown.

He scrambled out of the saddle and came toward Dorothy. "Dorothy, Dorothy, I'm so terribly glad to see you safe! I just got the word from Evans that you were here."

"I know, Paul."

"Are you all right? I mean, you're not hurt?"

Dorothy forced a smile she was far from feeling. His concern was too oily and glib. "I'm all right, Paul."

"Good. Then let's get you back. Everyone is very concerned."

"Are they?" she asked narrowly. "Well I am concerned, too, Paul, and would have some truth before I budge an inch. About my horse? About the animal way the hunters were chasing me in the woods?"

Paul shook his head. This was not going at all as he had expected. He said, "Well, after all, Dorothy, you really can't blame them in a way. They all saw you carrying on with the Earl."

Dorothy eyed him coldly. "And who was it told them I would show them gratitude for finding me on such a night?"

Ely's jaw dropped in astonishment. "You heard that?"

"I heard everything!"

"Damn, can't you see that I was only saying it to spur them on to find you?"

"I think," a voice said softly, rounding the corner of the house, "you could have found different words to use, Mr. Ely."

Paul Ely spun and glowered at Jim McLaughlin. "Stay out of matters that don't concern you!"

Dorothy lifted her head. "It does concern him, Paul. Without his shelter I might have died of exposure, as Lord Dunraven prayed would happen."

"Leave it to you to find a man's bed to warm yourself in," Ely snapped.

"I don't like your implication," McLaughlin said angrily. "Apologize!"

"Watch your step, McLaughlin!" Ely warned. "I can have you cut out of the cattle deal with the snap of my fingers!"

"Do it!" growled McLaughlin, with a snorting laugh. "But I would like to see you cut me out of something I haven't agreed to as yet!"

"*What?*" said Ely, hoarsely. For the moment Dorothy was all but forgotten. He paused. "Griff Evans has all but given his word."

McLaughlin shrugged. "Evans' word belongs to him, but my cattle belong to me."

Ely gaped at him, scowling. "Then you better start moving them out of this valley, because you are trespassing on Dunraven land!"

"At this very moment, Ely," he said, with sudden sharpness, like an acid under the honey of his voice, "you are trespassing on my homestead. I've seen no proof that Earl owns anything. Now, would you like some help off of *my* land?"

"Come on, Dorothy," said Ely, with bitterness, as though she had caused this problem, as well. He flung up into his saddle and looked at her with eyes full of contempt and hatred.

"She's not going," McLaughlin said quietly. "Not with you, at least."

The bitterness and hatred swelled in Ely's heart. Dorothy was going to foul him up with the Earl again and he would not stand for that.

"You are biting off more than you can chew," he said in a quick and breathless voice. "She is related to the Earl and under his charge. He's not going to think kindly on your not turning her over when he has ordered it."

McLaughlin started to answer, but Dorothy held him back.

"Then take him my message," she said, in her sweet and contrite tone which she could use so effectively on occasion. "I am not his chattel, slave, not even his hired servant. I am quite of age, although I suddenly realize I have not been acting it of late. Paul, you're an ass! And you can tell the Earl, for me, that he is an ass and a fool as well!"

Ely was seriously flustered. "He'll be back for you himself!"

McLaughlin waited until he had ridden completely out of view. "I–I didn't know you were related," he stammered.

"Second cousins."

McLaughlin frowned on a puzzled note. Dorothy

could read his expression like an open book. She put her head in her hands and laughed helplessly.

"Miss, what's the matter? Are you all right?"

Dorothy sobered. "Yes, I'm all right. It was just the look on your face. Friends you can pick, relatives you are stuck with."

He stared out at the sky for a few moments. Then he said, "I don't think you should be here when the Earl comes."

Dorothy sighed, "You're right. I didn't mean to drag you into my problems."

McLaughlin flushed. "I wasn't sending you away, if that's what you thought. Seems, the more I hear, I might have problems with the man myself. Does he have the whole valley?"

"I'm really not sure, Mr. McLaughlin. I was under the impression that it all had something to do with the purchase of the cattle."

McLaughlin pondered gravely. "Can you travel in Mary McChesley's clothing?"

"Yes. But where?"

"Denver," he said tonelessly. "I'd best be seeing if what is mine is really mine."

Dorothy nodded agreement. Her heart turned over inside her. There was something terribly touching about this gentle giant, but along with it there was also something commanding. He was not impressed or daunted by the Earl's title or power. He was the type of man who would give Dunraven a run for his money.

Lady Florence gloated over her easily won victory. Dunraven, though shrewdly doubting that his wife had told him the complete truth, nevertheless recognized the real truth of the problem. He was consumed by the deepest and most enraged anxiety. Dorothy could ruin him. Oh, not as a man, because his peers would just consider that he had taken what was his due. But should Lady Jane get wind that he had used consigned land for the Fisk loan, then she would use every power available to her to make him look the blackest sheep of the lot.

He frowned dramatically at Paul Ely. "Well, now, run off with another man, has she? She's still so upset with the two of us that I don't think she's given a thought to her position. Makes the two of us look mighty base, I'd say. I'll not be having her depart for Ireland in such a mood, Paul. Get to Denver and stall her until my return."

"She won't listen to me," he said suddenly.

The mood changes of Paul Ely were beginning to exasperate the Earl as much as the fear that his wife had started to lose her mind, but he smiled sweetly.

"She can't resist you, dear chap. You have only to fondle her breasts gently, and kiss her nipple passionately, and beg her to listen to reason. You know how you sexually arouse her. When she sees that her obstinacy is causing you such distress, she will not want to leave Colorado."

Ely regarded him in brooding and violent silence. On the long ride to Longmont his brain was a study in turmoil. He did not desire Dorothy as a wife or mistress, but wanted no other man to possess her either. Dunraven's words suggested the worst to his mind—he *had* possessed her in the tent before its collapse. He now vividly pictured her with Jim McLaughlin. But his hatred did not go against the men, but the woman. He kept reducing her in his mind to something that he understood—a whore.

In Longmont he entered the first saloon available. A week later he was still there.

It was just as well that he had not gone to try out his wiles on Dorothy. She was angry, frustrated and mystified.

In that early summer of 1873 there was a growing feeling of uneasiness in the world of business. Even as far west as Denver there were rumors that the great businesses were dangerously overextended. The steamship lines would not give her a definite sailing date. They would only wire back the advice that she should come to New York and take her chances.

She wired Walter Gould for assistance. He mistook her message to mean financial assistance and dropped the telegram in the wastebasket. He was losing thousands of insurance customers a day and was stopping his program of expansion. He foresaw a very bleak winter around the corner.

But it was the cable from Lady Jane that mystified her:

> WINDHAM DEFAULTED ON LAND PAYMENT. MONEY TIED UP IN AMERICAN LITIGATION. WHO IS JIM FISK JR.? WILL NOT ADVANCE MY PURCHASE MONEY TO THROW GOOD AFTER BAD. MAN WON'T ANSWER ME. YOU MUST.

Dorothy was wondering what answer she could give when the bell chimes pealed.

The man filled the doorway like an overstuffed walrus, and just as oily and slick.

"Lord Dunraven," he said commandingly. A hint of recognition flickered across his eyes and he quickly added, "I'm David Moffatt of the First National Bank of Denver."

The name, more than the face, made Dorothy remember him. "I'm terribly sorry, sir, but Lord Dunraven is still in the mountains."

"Oh!" He seemed greatly surprised. "Upon hearing of your return, I automatically assumed the Earl would be with you. There is some rather urgent business that must be taken care of, Lady Dorothy."

"I'm afraid I would not be of much help to you."

"I see," Moffatt said thoughtfully. "But on the other hand, you might. Might I indulge upon your time and privacy for a few minutes?"

"Please step in, Mr. Moffatt."

Now she recalled why the name was familiar. David Moffatt had been the bank clerk who had been so solicitous in the opening of her account. But not to recognize the man was understandable. The clerk had been dowdy and sackcloth-suited. Moffatt's present suit and manners were impeccable in style and cut. A hint of bay rum wafted after him as he took the lead to the salon. From behind Dorothy was reminded of Jim Fisk and again she found herself marvelling on how such bulky men could move with such easy grace.

"I am sure," Moffatt said, upon turning, "that you are aware that Lord Dunraven is desirous of obtaining certain Northern Colorado properties, Lady Dorothy."

She nodded, and motioned for him to be seated.

"Thank you. A certain parcel has come to my attention, in an undisclosed manner, and needs transferring to The Estes Park Company, Ltd."

"Would that not be," Dorothy said slowly, "a matter to be handled by Mr. Whyte? He is the Earl's land agent."

Moffatt smoothed down his walrus moustache appreciatively. He had heard that the Earl's cousin possessed brains, as well as beauty. He appreciated a woman who didn't hide behind mock femininity.

"Look, Lady Dorothy," Moffatt said—nothing on earth would induce him to use other than her formal title—"because you are the Earl's relative, I feel I can speak most candidly. The manner in which Mr. Whyte and Mr. Rufus Brogan are beginning to obtain land for the Earl is not for me to question, but a matter in which the bank does not wish to involve itself. Recently, I have been made the bank president and have my personal reputation to consider, as well."

"My congratulations," Dorothy said sweetly. She was being genuine, but was also stalling to see if this information could help her in answering her mother's wire.

Moffatt preened. "I would be less than honest if I didn't admit my handling of the Earl's accounts helped to elevate me to such a position. Oh . . . ah . . . of course, your account, as well."

"You're being modest, sir. If you give personal attention to all your customers, as you seem to do for us, then you certainly deserve your reward."

Yes, Moffatt mused, he could speak freely with such an intelligent creature.

"So, you see, dear lady, this land parcel puts me in a very embarrassing situation. It really should not go through the bank or through me personally. I thought to quickly transfer it over, gain a valid signature and the claim price. As the Earl's corporation is organized under the laws of Great Britain, it would have to go to the corporation through his signature."

"Then I fail to see how I can be of service to you, Mr. Moffatt."

He smiled sagely. "I am credited, Lady Dorothy, with a brain that seems to retain an overabundance of trivia. Correct me if I am wrong, but your account was opened with a letter of credit on the Castle Adare account of the Bank of Dublin."

"Quite correct."

"I am just now in the process of transferring funds back to the Bank of Dublin for payment on the Whyham-Quin Farms mortgage and a down payment on the interest charges on the Fisk loan. Because bankers must know everything, this will lift the cloud over the Whyham-Quin farm lands being transferred to Castle Adare lands. A family matter, but still governed by rather stern British banking regulations."

Dorothy sat back and smiled. "I am most impressed, Mr. Moffatt. You seem to know our family matters almost as well as I."

They studied each other with growing interest—Dorothy, because she had gained a world of knowledge without having to confront Lord Dunraven; Moffatt, because he now thought she had known all this information and was just a very shrewd fox.

"That is the key phrase, dear lady. Family matter. As Castle Adare and Whyham-Quin matters are so closely involved at this time, I see no legal stumbling block in your signing for this parcel of land and paying for it. As a British subject it would be legal under their corporate laws as a relative, and you can sign it over to Lord Dunraven upon his return."

Dorothy sat very quiet for several seconds. Her mind was abuzz with questions, but Moffatt was not the man to present them to. "How much land?"

"A total of 2,650 acres."

Dorothy couldn't help but laugh. "Mr. Moffatt, you must surely know that my bank account would never cover such a purchase."

David Moffatt knew that this was one time he did not have to abide by his primary rule of "playing sharp and saying nothing."

"Lady Dorothy, all that is required is your signature and the $5 filing fee. Frankly, it is a rather unethical acquisition of so large a parcel, but it is a valley higher up in the region that would be overlooked by the homesteaders for years."

"Then, I too must be candid," she said, still a little numb and flustered. "How do you hope to gain by being so generous with the Earl and me?"

Moffatt laughed, a rich booming sound. "Am I not already gaining from the Earl's deposits that I may invest in other quarters? The East is dying financially, but the West is still rich and will grow richer off of such men as the Earl." Then he grew serious. "Personally, though, I think Whyte and Brogan squander some of the money foolishly. A reasonable person could gain the land for less."

"Such as myself," she said coyly, but only for information.

"Why not? It's all in the family and family money."

"Not quite," she said very truthfully. "My account is quite separate from that of the Earl and is being safeguarded for my return home funds."

"Fiddlesticks, my girl! You strike while the striking is good! It's the ones who have the brains and the ability to grab first who will reap the profit. Buy now! Sell back to your cousin, if you like, and at a profit. I lose nothing. It reduces one account and swells another!"

"There's sense in that," Dorothy said thoughtfully. "Still—"

"You do what I tell you!" Moffatt ordered. "When you come to the bank to sign the land papers, I'll have the loan ready for you. I'm not sure of your balance at present, but would an additional five thousand dollars be adequate?"

Dorothy stared at him. "Quite adequate," she whispered.

"Good! Now I must be off. But my mind's at ease now, knowing your signature will be on that land. As you seem to be back in town for the summer, may I allow Mrs. Moffatt to arrange a dinner party in your honor?"

"Yes," said Dorothy, her mind off on an oblique, "that would be nice."

After Moffatt had gone Dorothy stood in the foyer thinking. What am I doing? she wondered. I should be packing to return home, not letting people arrange dinner parties and "borrowing money." She didn't know the first thing about borrowing money and paying it back. A Goold never borrowed or lent.

She suddenly remembered something Lady Jane had once said—an odd, fleeting remark: "A banker is your friend as long as he is playing with your money. Start playing with his and he becomes the devil's advocate."

Well, she mused, she was already surrounded by devils and their advocates. Why not give them a little bit of their own in return?

Before she could change her mind she sailed back to the library and began composing a return wire:

> ON DEFAULT HAVE BANK CONTACT DAVID MOFFATI, FIRST NATIONAL BANK OF DENVER, IF THEY HAVE NOT ALREADY HEARD. YOUR PURCHASE SAFE. INVESTING LAND HERE. HOME BY FALL.

And I hope I am! Pray God I know what I am doing!

David Moffatt was reluctant, but finally agreed to give Dorothy the address of Theo Whyte's office on the proviso that she go by carriage.

It was a world like she had never before entered. The street clung grimly to the selling of three commodities—whiskey, women and used household wares. It was unpaved, and every other shop showed a broad expanse of dusty street in front of it where the frugal businessmen had refused to pay the fee for the watering cart. Dorothy did not even glance at the houses of prostitution or the saloons. Instead she was fascinated by the unbelievable number of second-hand stores, bulging with the broken dreams of would-be gold miners who had sold everything of value for a few pennies in the name of survival, their old world treasures glutting the fly-stained windows like the chests of Ali Baba. Hawk-eyed salesmen lurked just inside the shadowy interiors waiting for fashionable carriages, such as her own, to find their way down from Brown's Bluff. Each anticipated the stoppage of her carriage at their door, each were disappointed.

Dorothy was also disappointed as the carriage turned onto Wyncoop Street. The second-hand shops vanished.

Now, she thought in exasperation, why would he have offices in an area where there are nothing but saloons?

The saloons were as noisy as though it were midnight and not midday. The narrow street had not been watered at all and a dust pall seemed to hang constantly in the air. It, too, was a street of broken dreams. Despair was so apparent in the shuffling walk of the vagrants and drunks filtering from saloon to saloon that even the carriage horse seemed to slow its gait and slump along. The carriage driver began to doubt that the woman had given him the right address.

As the carriage began to approach the given address a customer sallied forth from a saloon whose appearance was so comical and strange that Dorothy was drawn out of her thoughts to regard him. He was a tall, lean old man who moved with an amazing sprightliness. He was clearly no recent immigrant but a longtime native of the west. He was wearing buckskins which hung in overlapping folds on his bones. The trousers ended a good four inches from the top of his boots, and the sleeves of the leathery jacket revealed only finger tips. On his head he wore a brown felt Stetson which was so large that its shadow obscured all but his mouth and chin whiskers. His mouth was fixed in the lines of a sly smile. To Dorothy there was something familiar about the mouth, but she couldn't quite place it.

The old man turned into the saloon at which the carriage stopped. Now the carriage driver was skeptical.

"Sure you got the address right, miss?"

Dorothy hesitated. "Yes, but . . ." She would have to go into the saloon. Nothing could have been a greater ordeal for her. Slowly, reluctantly, she climbed down from the carriage. Then she said hurriedly, "You will wait for me?"

"Ain't about to leave you here alone, miss!"

That gave her some courage and heart. Still, she felt so out of place. It wasn't just a question of being a woman entering such an establishment, but the manner of her dress. She had so wanted to make a good impression on David Moffatt with style and flair and richness that she would certainly be quite out of place in this seedy establishment. She stood out like a single flower in an otherwise dead garden.

The watered lavender silk seemed to cling suggestively to her bosoms and legs; the wide-brimmed straw hat with trailing lavender ribbons was decorative, but almost too wide for her to keep in place as she went through the swinging doors.

And once inside she almost turned and fled. The small saloon was packed with filthy, bedraggled men of all ages. The smoke pall was as thick as an Irish fog and the odor of stale beer, whiskey and unwashed bodies was nauseating.

But about it all there was a feeling of business-like organization. The men were bunched in three queue-like formations, straggling across the room to two wooden tables or along the bar. At the tables sat Theodore Whyte and Rufus Brogan, in costumes not much dissimilar to the men approaching them.

Dorothy was disconcerted. She didn't know if she would be expected to join a line or march on forward. Then she noticed that the comical old man was pushing his way right up to Rufus Brogan and she determined to do the same. The old man's audacity was being met with grumbling and caustic comments. Dorothy's advance created stunned awe and a parting of the ranks as though Moses were standing there waving his arms for her. It was done so silently that the men at the tables were not aware of her approach.

Brogan regarded the old man with a disgusted sneer. The old man loitered, feeling in each pocket for something. Then he proffered a badly soiled piece of paper and extended a trembling hand for payment. Rufus dropped five gold pieces into it, and turned away with a suspiciously casual manner.

"Where's the other half?" demanded the old man in a high-pitched creaking voice.

"What's the matter with you?" demanded Rufus with a wholly disproportionate display of passion. "That's all you get!"

The old man pointed an indignant forefinger to the paper on the table. "It says fifty dollars!" he shrilled.

"That's right, but only when the deed is recorded," was the rejoinder.

"No you don't! That could take weeks or months!"

"Well, if y'ain't satisfied, gimme back the money and I'll tear up the paper."

The old man would have none of it. "Give me my other half!"

"That's all you get now!"

"Give me my other half or I'll call the police!"

All activity had stopped at Theo Whyte's table. The crowd was pressing forward so hard to hear the argument that Dorothy was being jostled and her hat pushed forward over her face. Whyte was growing furious with the bumbling Brogan. He didn't want that part of the scam becoming widespread. When the winos, drunks and derelicts approached his desk for instructions they were so eager to get their hands on some money they only half-listened to his terms. Still anxious for drinking money, few questioned the half payment. The scum of the earth or not, Brogan did not handle them with the diplomacy that Whyte thought necessary.

He looked up, to take command of the situation himself, and gasped.

"Lady Dorothy! What in God's name are you doing here?" Then he barked. "Get back, you idiot! Let her come behind the table!"

For the moment it brought the argument to a standoff. Dorothy shoved back her hat and accepted Whyte's hand to help her between the two tables and a better breathing space.

"Thank you, Mr. Whyte," she sighed. "I was unaware that these would be your office accommodations or I might have sent word first."

"I wish that you had," he said, with a sigh of displeasure. Now more than ever he wanted to make short work of the old man. Dunraven was purposely out of town so that he could claim no knowledge of the fraud Whyte was bringing about. He wanted Lady Dorothy to learn no more than was necessary.

"Pay him!" he hissed at Brogan and tried to steer Dorothy away to a door behind the tables. Dorothy hesitated. She wanted to see the old man get his due.

A flicker of pleasure crossed the thin mouth as five more gold pieces were offered. Then, becoming aware of Dorothy, his whole lean frame seemed to freeze in place. He turned and fled with a gait that belied his age.

My God! Dorothy gasped to herself. "That's Jim McLaughlin!"

Now her priorities were suddenly changed. She wanted to catch up wtih the man and find out what he was about.

Daintily she put a hand to her forehead. "You will have to excuse me, Mr. Whyte, but this place is making me most faint."

That was the last thing Whyte wanted to happen. "Then, quick, come into my office."

"No! No! I have a carriage waiting."

The weasel-headed little man seemed unsure of what to do and looked at her and then at Rufus Brogan uncomfortably. "Rufus, see Lady Dorothy to her carriage." His beady eyes glared at the young man as much as if to say, "And find out why the hell she came here!"

Rufus resented the look. He had already determined in his mind to ask such a question, although he already had a theory in mind. To him Theo Whyte was lower than the scum they had to deal with each day. He knew that Lord Dunraven would not condone some of the unethical practices being employed, but all he was allowed to do was act as paymaster. Whyte had the only key to the "inner-sanctum" office and Rufus was not allowed to see how the work was progressing. He was sorry that Dorothy had not gotten a peek.

"Is Lord Dunraven well?" he asked, as he steered Dorothy out of the saloon.

"Quite," she said. "Enjoying his hunt and all."

"I'm surprised to see you back so soon."

Dorothy laughed. "I don't think that I am suited for so much outdoor activity."

Rufus laughed politely. Their relationship had always been a little standoffish. He had always considered her an ally of Paul Ely and so automatically his enemy. He wanted none of that feeling to show now through his veneer.

"Then I would assume that Lady Florence returned with you?"

"No. I would assume that she is hiking and hunting."

As he helped her into the carriage, his eyes grew wide with disbelief. "Hunting?"

The delay in getting to the street had been exasperating. Dorothy tingled to know what game Jim McLaughlin was playing. But he was nowhere in sight. It was obvious that Rufus Brogan was dying of unabashed curiosity, so she decided to play his game first, but get in a few licks of her own.

"Do you know how to contact Lloyd Folsom?" she asked, settling back regally onto the carriage seat.

"I see him almost daily. Why?"

Dorothy laughed lightly. She wanted the incident to sound almost unimportant. "I shall require him to find me another horse. Lady Florence is such an expert marksman that my horse seems to have become her biggest trophy to date."

"You don't mean it?" Rufus chuckled.

"Oh, but I do!"

Rufus grinned broadly. Dorothy had struck the right chord. The secretary-accountant had never had much regard for the Earl's wife or her ability, less after she elevated Paul Ely to near sainthood. This little bit of gossip about her tickled his fancy.

"I will send Lloyd to see you today. Now, is there anything else I might do of service to you?"

Dorothy looked at him keenly. Rufus was seldom so effusive. He wants something, she thought, wants something bad . . . Well, Rufus might be an easier man to deal with than Theo Whyte.

"Well," she drawled, "I really came to see Mr. Whyte." She hesitated. In this, as in all other forms of gambling, she was learning, you started the bluff and let the other person finish it for you. "The Earl thought . . ." She hesitated again.

"Lady Dorothy," he said hurriedly, "If it is something the Earl wishes you to do, I am much better qualified to handle it for you than Mr. Whyte. He is, after all, handling only one little phase of the *whole* operation."

"I never thought of it that way," Dorothy said sweetly. "And, after all, I have known you much longer, haven't I?"

"You certainly have," he said enthusiastically. "Now, how can I help you?"

Dorothy smiled and looked about at the men milling in and out of the saloon. "Perhaps, Rufus, this is not the time or the place to discuss business. Some of these men might not be as stumble-brained as others think. I am staying at the house on Brown's Bluff. Would you care to join me for dinner? At seven o'clock perhaps?"

Rufus preened importantly. By calling him by his first name she had elevated him to the position he felt he deserved. And he admired the tact and diplomacy she used in not saying, but fully implying, that Theo Whyte was not to learn of the dinner invitation.

"It shall be my pleasure, Lady Dorothy," he said, smartly closing the carriage door and importantly giving the driver the Brown's Bluff address as though it were commonplace for him to do so.

The driver clicked his horse forward, more confused than ever. Not only to normally eavesdrop on his passengers' conversation, this one had been such to let his wife untangle that night. He wasn't sure why the ill-clad youth kept putting the word "lady" before the girl's name, but he had his own dark suspicions—especially after she invited him for dinner to "discuss business."

Rounding the corner onto Seventeenth Street, he nearly jumped from his skin at Dorothy's command to stop. He looked back to see an old geezer running to catch them and jump into the carriage as nimble as a youth.

"Jim McLaughlin," Dorothy cried. "What in the world?"

"I thought you might have recognized me," he chuckled. "I hope you didn't say anything to Brogan."

"Not a word."

Then McLaughlin saw that the driver was staring at them in open-mouthed wonderment.

"Drive on," he said harshly and shook his head to warn Dorothy to say no more for the moment.

Now the driver's mind was really rattled. He didn't cotton to any form of hanky-panky in his carriage and had the full fare not already been paid for by the gentleman at the bank he would have been half tempted to put them both out at once. But he still kept his ears peeled for any little tidbit he could take home to his wife.

He was greatly disappointed. The only other piece of information he gained was when he turned off Broadway to climb the Colfax hill.

"That's where I am staying," McLaughlin said softly, pointing to a little white-framed house with a wrap-around porch and bountiful gardens. "It was my mother's. When my paw died I brought her out here from Ohio. She hated it, so I sent her back home to her friends. Guess women just don't take to this type of living."

Dorothy knew that he was also speaking of his urequited love and so held her silence.

But Dorothy could not control her silence or mirth as they entered the foyer and Jim McLaughlin tried to remove the false chin whiskers.

"Wherever did you get them?" she giggled.

"It would seem that some men will sell anything for a drink. For a dollar an old prospector whipped out his knife, sliced away half his scraggly beard and handed me this mess. I wish the horse who gave up his hoof for the glue had it back. Ouch! That hurts."

"Come into the kitchen and we'll heat some water to soak it off. I'm really curious to learn what you were doing there."

He grinned at her. She was the first woman, outside of Martha Evans, who he could feel comfortable around.

"I'm curious as to your presence, as well."

"Oh no you don't. I asked first!"

McLaughlin slumped down in a kitchen chair as Dorothy put the kettle on the range.

"I could hardly believe it when I went to the land office, Dorothy. Men filing claims like gold had been found on that land. But you saw the manner of men that they are—bums of the first order who would never abide by the homestead laws."

"Excuse my ignorance," she interrupted, taking the seat opposite him, "but what are the laws?"

"Once the land is claimed you are given a year to start putting a home or improvements upon the land and then five years in which to pay off the $1.25 an acre."

"I see. Go on."

He blew air through his lips as though it had been some sort of nightmare. "When I got up to the counter and saw the plat map I thought I was safe because what I thought was my land had big red X's through it. But some snot-nosed kid tells me they are now claimed by three other men. I was about ready to tear the place apart, when this old geezer pulls me aside and tells me that others have been given the wrong plat numbers also. That really confused me, so I followed the old man back to that saloon. I ain't too bright, Dorothy, but it didn't take long to figure out what they are doing."

"You must be bright, because I still don't get it."

"It looks complicated, but they have to keep it simple because of the rum-dumb brains they are dealing with. You come into the first line and listen to Whyte mumble about what payment you will make for taking a piece of paper to the land office, giving them a five dollar gold piece, having the paper signed and bringing it back for payment."

"Ah," Dorothy enthused, "the five dollars being the recording fee."

McLaughlin looked at her wonderingly.

"See, you are getting the idea. Of course, a lot of those five dollar gold pieces are getting no farther than the next saloon, and the paper getting torn up. That's what is really fouling up Whyte. I surmise that he has a duplicate plat map in his office and can't really know where he stands until the end of each day. And that's not helping because once a man sees that his buddy actually did get a handsome sum, and he didn't tear up the paper, he borrows a fiver and goes to the land office the next day. So, some of the land has two claims against it."

"But what of your land, Jim?" she asked anxiously.

He grinned wickedly. "That double claim business is what gave me the idea. I went in to Whyte first as myself and got one of his slips. Glad my Maw made me learn letters and figures. I just added to his slip that a transfer was to be made putting my old acreage back into my own name. I did it twice more, making myself look different each time. Of course, I never returned those three slips. They're my proof that what is mine is mine."

"But I thought you could only get one hundred and sixty acres."

"The whole thing is illegal, Dorothy. Who is to say that I didn't buy them from those three guys who were originally recorded? This whole thing is going to get so snarled up that it will take a parcel of Philadelphia lawyers to figure it out."

"But why go back again in this disguise?"

He chuckled. "Two reasons, I guess. They're taking those poor men. Hell, fifty bucks is a fortune to them. That's why they don't quibble over the twenty-five, and, in case you didn't notice, that's a free bar he's running to keep them from screaming too loud about the other half. A drink in hand quiets them down right quick. First I wanted to see if I could embarrass them into the full payment because I doubt if the second payment will be made to the majority. But my fifty in gold will never be spent. That's insurance money. If Dunraven tries any funny business to get my land, then that's my evidence in court to blow his whole scheme right out of the water."

Dorothy slowly shook her head. She still didn't fully understand the whole thing. "How?"

He smiled quietly. He thought he was boring her with all his talk. "Water's boiling."

"Damn the water!" she exploded. "I want to know how the whole scheme works!"

James McLaughin, at that moment, was beyond speech. This was a different type creature sitting opposite him. Her skin was aglow, her eyes snapping. In spite of what he knew she had been through, he never suspected this kind of fire and drive to come from her. She was almost a little frightening. Commanding women always sent him back into his shell.

Dorothy saw at once she had gone too far with him. She put out a small hand and let it rest on his arm.

"I'm sorry, Jim," she whispered. "I didn't mean to be rude."

"I understand," he said grimly. Then he thought he saw the reason for her outburst and concern. "Do you have money tied up in that land?"

"Yes," she answered simply, although at the moment saw no reason to reveal that it was a mere five dollars.

"Then you had better know," he muttered, his voice far off and deep. "It's going to end up being a gigantic land fraud. When those old men sign for their money it's really a bill of sale for the land. The government plat map will have hundreds of names on it all legal-like, but the land will really belong to The Estes Park Co., Ltd."

"I understand," she answered just as grimly as he had before, "but doesn't he still have to pay the government the $1.25 an acre?"

"Sure, but what is money to him?"

Dorothy couldn't help but wonder about that. It didn't sound to her as though his financial affairs in Ireland were too stable. But that, again, was a family matter and not for the ears of Jim McLaughlin.

He was out of his facial disguise by the time Lloyd Folsom arrived with a double surprise—a new horse and Sarah Ferguson.

When Lloyd was halfway through the door, he stopped abruptly at seeing McLaughlin, and the joy drained visibly from his face. He and McLaughlin regarded each other with instant awareness. They were both secretly in love with the same woman. For Jim McLaughlin it was a double shock. It was only in seeing Lloyd's eyes that he realized his true feelings toward Dorothy, and he was unsure whether he should put his heart in jeopardy again. But Lloyd was too young to read that look. He came forward once more, walking slowly, awkwardly; and when he was close put out his hand.

"Hello, Lady Dorothy," he said.

Dorothy didn't see the change in Lloyd or the looks between the two men. He was still her friend and boon companion. But the "little boy" now stretched over six feet, with a broad chest and timber-toting shoulders and arms that made Jim McLaughlin look small in comparison. His jaw had lanterned with the melting away of the last baby fat, setting his clear blue eyes around a straight aristocratic nose. Others, who had daily contact with him, did not see the handsomeness he was acquiring, but Jim McLaughlin saw it as competition that his gangling looks would have trouble against.

Dorothy held his hand lightly for a moment, before she pulled the youth forward into her arms.

"Hello, Lady Dorothy!" she mimicked him. "That's a fine thing! I thought we had done away with the lady business. Oh, Lloyd, the horse is superb! And Sarah is a godsend. I opened my mouth with a dinner invitation and you all know I can't boil water without burning it."

"That's a bunch of horse-radish!" Sarah chortled, pushing her huge frame into the foyer and giving McLaughlin's attire a stare as though she didn't consider him the proper dinner guest for her to come and cook for.

"Forgive my manners," Dorothy said quickly. "This is James McLaughlin, who brought me down from Estes Park. Jim, this is Sarah Ferguson and Lloyd Folsom."

Sarah squinted up into his face and nodded politely. Proper clothes, she thought, and he wouldn't be half-bad. "I'll see to the kitchen and what I may have to send Lloyd to fetch."

Lloyd made no move to follow her. He had suddenly recognized McLaughlin from the saloon and curiosity cemented his feet to the floor.

McLaughlin cleared his throat, knowing it was time for him to make his exit, but reluctant to do so.

"I'm going back to the ranch tomorrow morning," he said, "and I was wondering what you were going to do about . . . well . . . when the Earl returns, and all."

"I expected to be gone," she said, quite honestly.

Both men stared at her as though she had dealt them a death blow.

"But now," she continued slowly, "my plans seem to have changed, and I've given it not the slightest thought."

"Well," Jim said sternly, "you can't consider staying here. I won't hear of it, after the way that he treated you. My mother's house is vacant and I'll not take no for an answer. It is yours to use as you see fit!"

Tears sprang to Dorothy's eyes. "Thank you, Jim," she gulped. "You have become a dear and sweet friend, in a very short time." On an impulse, she rushed forward and kissed him on each cheek.

Lloyd Folsom wanted to scream out in fury at such a show of emotion. Jim McLaughlin turned a sunset scarlet and made a hasty exit.

"The horse is yours also," Lloyd blurted, to equal McLaughlin's offer as best he could.

"And I'm waiting to hear the price," Dorothy said, not used to the subtleties of men vying for her affections.

"It's a gift," he declared hotly, "just like his damn house."

The point still did not register on Dorothy's naïve mind. "Now, Lloyd," she soothed, "the loan of Mr. McLaughlin's house will cost him nothing. That horse did cost you."

"I can afford it!" he insisted. "I've been making nearly fifty dollars a day working for Mr. Brogan."

Dorothy frowned. "Running claims to the land office?"

Lloyd glanced up at her. Was there a note of reproach in her voice? He couldn't tell, but he couldn't lie to her, either.

"I have."

"How many times and under what names?"

She saw the expression of surprise on his face. "How do you know so much?"

"That doesn't matter, Lloyd," she said gently. "Just tell me the truth."

"About five times and from names they have me take from tombstones in the graveyard."

"Tombstones?" Dorothy echoed blankly. "But none of your own family names?"

"Seems they must be holding them for the last."

"Are they?" Dorothy said callously. "Seems with honest names they are afraid to use them legally. Honestly, Lloyd, has it been twenty-five each time or fifty?"

He gulped. She did know more than he realized. "Twenty-five," he whispered.

"Then they have used you just as badly as the others. Damn their black hearts! This thing stinks more and more. You will never see the rest of your money due."

"But-but they owe it to me," he stammered.

Dorothy felt a swift surge of pity at the sight of his crestfallen face. Then she looked at him more closely. This wasn't a gullible youth that had been twisted to do their chores. He was now a man.

"How well do you know their operation?" she asked quietly.

"Quite well. Sometimes, when he is behind, Mr. Whyte even pays me extra to mark up his wall map from the returned papers."

"Does he, now? And you must be getting to know the men at the land office quite well."

"Oh," he boasted, "I've known them right along. One was my sister's boyfriend before the telegraph operator."

Dorothy hid a smile behind her hand. Not only did Mary Eddy seem to get around but her new husband remained a profession and not a name.

"Tomorrow," Dorothy said. "Tomorrow I want you to do things differently. Without Whyte knowing it, I want you to place claims in the name of your family members. You, your father, uncle and sister. I'll pay the charges. But don't let them sell it to anyone."

"I don't understand."

"Lord Dunraven wants all of that land, Lloyd. You have been getting it illegally for him at $25 a claim. Get it for yourself legally and he will have to pay your price to get it back!"

"That's blackmail!" he said firmly.

"No, Lloyd," she said fondly, "it's business, the way the Earl does business."

"But," he pointed out, "I'm underage. What good would it do me to get property in my name?"

"Then, as soon as you get the four claims, put them all in your father's name. That will be just as legal as what the Earl is doing. More so, for you're American citizens."

"All right," Lloyd said with a shrug. He trusted Dorothy enough to do whatever she told him, and he wanted to show Jim McLaughlin that he could do something for her that Jim could not do. Impatient to shine in her eyes, he conned his friend in the land office to record six claims for him that afternoon. The bribe cost him half of what he had made from Whyte and Brogan, but to win favor with Dorothy it was worth it. Then he went against her advice. Instead of signing the land over to his father, he consulted his uncle, Fred Austin, instead.

"My God!" Austin gasped, his handsome face lit with respect. "You wish to put it all in my name?"

"Uncle Fred, don't tell Paw, but he ain't too sharp when it comes to business. You know and I know that Rufus Brogan cheats him on every wagonload of lumber he hauls for Lord Dunraven. You and me will handle this deal and make it all back, okay?"

Lloyd was the type of son that Fred Austin dreamed of having some day, if he ever got out from under his older brother's shadow enough to marry. The man possessed no vanity, so he was unable to see that the extremely handsome youth could have more readily passed for his son than that of his brother.

* * *

Dorothy now saw little reason for the dinner party, but still selected her ensemble with utmost care. Knowing that Rufus was a social climber she selected a dusty rose gown with a princess style bodice, tightly fitted to the waist and the pedlums cut in tabs trimmed in deep rose velvet, and with a low, square neck. She tried three different bustles under the skirt until she found the one to accentuate the proper silhouette of regality she wished to convey.

Nor was the importance of the dinner lost on Rufus Brogan. He arrived in an expertly tailored frock coat of robin's-egg blue, white linen vest and midnight blue trousers of an extremely narrow cut. He had been barbered to a fault.

"How pretty you are this evening," said Rufus, beaming at her affectionately as she glided down the curving stairway to greet him. "And how happy I am to get away from that degrading place for an evening."

Dorothy stopped and openly stared. The figure possessed Rufus Brogan's voice, and nothing else. She had never thought of him as a tall man—nor even as a man—though he stood over six feet, and his face, beneath the slightly wavy black Irish hair, was as though she had never seen it before—features of elemental strength, rather than pretty handsomeness, she thought. A man who looked like he was someone and was secretly amused that he looked that way.

She smiled sweetly. "Then I am happy for your sake, Rufus. I don't think I could stand that place for an hour, let alone day after day. Come. As I am aware that you are a non-drinking man, I've asked Mrs. Ferguson to lay dinner on at your arrival."

He raised an eyebrow. "How in the world were you aware of that fact?"

"Observation, I assume," she laughed. "I don't recall you ever having wine with your meals on the train."

"That is some memory," murmured Rufus. "That's nearly three years ago."

"Surely not that long," Dorothy said, indicating the end of the table at which he would be seated, but allowing him to follow her and seat her first.

"It will be this coming November, and to think that I came here for only six months."

"As did I," she answered a little sadly.

"Oh, but I don't regret a day of it," he said with enthusiasm. "Although your Uncle Walter regrets each and every day of it."

"I beg your pardon?"

"My salary," he chuckled. "By some arrangement made between Lord Dunraven and Mr. Gould, the insurance company is still responsible for my yearly salary."

Dorothy's face split into an enormous smile.

"I think that is jolly good," she chuckled. "Family wolves devouring each other."

Rufus frowned. "Do you really see the Earl as a wolf?"

"Look at the manner in which he is devouring those poor drunks and derelicts, Rufus. Isn't that eating off the misery of others?"

"I'm afraid I must correct you, Lady Dorothy," he said slowly. "That plan, to a great degree, was originally mine, with only Lord Dunraven's wave of the hand approval."

He started to say more on the subject but stopped so that Sarah Ferguson could serve the soup. It was a hearty vegetable from fresh produce she had had Lloyd pluck from her own garden plot.

"I must say," Rufus went on, as though there had been no break, "that I am not so proud of my plan at the present, nor do I think that the Earl would be."

Dorothy thought differently. Her knowledge of her cousin's operations was exceedingly vague, but she was beginning to know the man. He would go to any measures to get his own way.

"Has something gone wrong with your plan?" she asked innocently.

"In a word, Theodore Whyte." He flushed. "Excuse me, Lady Dorothy, for such ungracious manners. The soup is excellent and I should not be imposing a business topic at your dinner table."

My, Dorothy thought, someone has been polishing this rough stone into a gem.

"Nonsense," she protested. "As there are but the two of us, we can pursue whatever dinner conversation we desire and, please, be less formal and drop my title."

He shook his head doggedly. "That I could never do, Lady Dorothy, any more than I could rightfully call Lord Dunraven Windham. It just wouldn't be proper."

Suddenly, her thought of the morning returned: he *wants* something. His dress, his polished manners, his desire to be quite proper were all a facade for her benefit. The evening became interesting again.

Sarah replaced the soup bowls with a garden crisp salad and cold fillets of rainbow trout garnished with lemon wedges.

Playing the proper guest, Rufus waited for

Dorothy to open the conversation anew. She went right back to the same old brick-bat.

"I'm afraid today is the first opportunity that I have had to meet Mr. Whyte, although he was here at the house to see Lord Dunraven."

Rufus grinned. "I shall never forget the first day Lord Dunraven met the man. He told me later that it was his firm belief that thin, waspish men such as Whyte were more prone to be cunning, sly and disloyal."

Dorothy hid her grin. Lord Dunraven had perfectly described his own self.

"And the man has daily proved the validity of the Earl's point," Rufus went on. "He is cunning enough never to give the men adjoining block or plat numbers, sly enough never to let me see the map in the office to know where we stand and it is my personal belief, is disloyal to the Earl when it comes to the payment money."

"You mean like today, in not wanting to pay that man his second half?"

"Exactly. I was only refusing on Whyte's strict orders. Lady Dorothy, I am responsible for the books and where every dollar goes. Whyte insists upon making the second payment to the men himself. I don't believe he is making those payments but is pocketing the money."

"Can it be so much?"

"We have already deeded over eight thousand acres. That would be close to fifteen hundred dollars that should have been made as second payments."

He was looking at it from an accountant's point of view. Dorothy was looking squarely at the fact that Lloyd Folsom had been cheated, and fifty or sixty other men besides.

"I know that does not sound like a great deal of money to you, Lady Dorothy, but think of it in terms of Lord Dunraven's reputation. Should these men ever sober up and begin screaming, it would be heard all the way to Washington."

"You're speaking, of course," Dorothy said coyly, "of the names on some of the claims who do not have bodies any longer?"

"What?" he gasped. "Where did you get such a notion?"

"Really, Rufus, I *did* have to stand in that horrible place for some little time and I am hardly deaf. I heard two of the men discussing the names that they had taken off tombstones in the graveyard."

Brogan's chiseled face went ashen with fear. He spread his hands wide.

"Lady Dorothy, Lady Dorothy," he implored, "I am aware of none of this!" Although it had been his suggestion at one time to Whyte. "*I* have nothing to gain by tricking Lord Dunraven. Why, I am banking on my future with him."

Dorothy saw her advantage to gain her own desires from the man and pressed it.

"Look, Rufus, that doesn't make sense. I saw you there, remember? Don't tell me that you haven't seen the same people come back time after time."

"No," he said miserably, "I'm not there all the time. Other duties take me away and then Whyte runs both desks. And when I am there, I hardly ever look up, unless something unusual happens, like today. I can't stand the sight of those drifters and bums. This is America! There is plenty of honest work for all men who have the guts to put in a full day. I—I don't drink for a very good reason, Lady Dorothy. I spent too many nights listening to my mother cry herself to sleep because my father was drinking up his salary check down at the tavern. One day he was so drunk he walked right in front of a delivery drag and team. Ironic, but it was delivering kegs to the very tavern where he would have gone to swill it down. I want to make something of myself, and I resent them for not wanting to do the same."

They were silent for a long time over the roast leg of lamb, mint jelly, new potatoes and peas in cream sauce, candied carrots and fresh rolls. They each needed the silent time—Rufus, because he had opened pages of his past to an outsider, something he had vowed never to do in his life; Dorothy, because she was taking an entirely new measure of the man. He had a heart and soul after all, and it was the very weakness she had been looking to exploit.

"What you say," she said quietly, "makes it most difficult for me to obtain the land that I was seeking."

"I don't see why," he said hotly. "Just march right in there and tell that dirty, bloodsucking little leech what it is you desire!" He blushed at his daring words.

Dorothy sighed. She had him in the exact mood she wanted.

"That helps only me, Rufus. It doesn't help my cousin and it doesn't help uncover Mr. Whyte's dishonesty—which is an unproven fact."

Dorothy hoped she had been convincing.

"He will deny all, of course. Oh, the Earl will skin me alive for letting things get into this disgraceful state!"

Dorothy doubted that, but clearly saw what it was Rufus desired of her. Lord Dunraven was absent, she was present. She could gain access to Whyte's office; Rufus could not. But Dorothy did not want to become that personally involved. No, she wanted it handled in an entirely different manner.

"Rufus," she said, on a long thought. "Why does Lloyd Folsom come to that saloon daily?"

It was an innocent enough question. "He runs errands and keeps Whyte's map up to date for him."

"Errands?" she said, on a raised eyebrow. "Does that include running slips to the land office?"

"Not at all, Lady Dorothy, not at all."

Dorothy smiled. It was obvious to her Lloyd only ran the slips for Theo Whyte. "Then that is our answer, Rufus. Lloyd can somehow talk Mr. Whyte into letting him earn some extra money by running my slips."

Rufus's face cleared, but a nagging doubt clung like a burr in his mind.

"Suppose," he said, "it's not a parcel of land you would want?"

Dorothy thought her words out carefully so that she could cover up for Jim McLaughlin's own scam and also protect Lloyd.

"I will want three parcels, Rufus. One in my name, one each in my mother and grandmother's names. It stands to reason that I would want them all together." She smiled anew. "It would stand to reason that Lloyd must know that map quite well. Could he not put a different number on that slip before he gets to the land office? It does come back to you and then again to Lloyd to mark the map. We wait. If he does not pay Lloyd the additional seventy-five dollars when the deeds become mine, then we have evidence to place before my cousin."

The nagging doubt was gone now in Rufus's mind. He had wanted to be sure. Even if Whyte got smart and paid Lloyd they would still have proof that he was not above using the same person more than one time. He would again shine in the eyes of his idol, Lord Dunraven.

"I'm convinced," he said. "What do I do now?"

"*You* don't have to do anything," Dorothy warned. "The less you appear to know about this the better, until we are ready to pounce. We don't want the wolf scared away from the chicken coop."

Rufus grinned broadly. She was more than fulfilling his aspirations of that evening. Of course, he was ill-aware that the wolf Dorothy intended to pounce upon was his idol and not his foe.

"Excellent, excellent meal," he said, rising.

"We'll take coffee in the library."

Over coffee, other aspects of Rufus Brogan came to the surface that utterly amazed Dorothy.

As a boy he would walk all the way down from the Bronx and spend countless hours in the libraries and museums; would sneak in behind the wide hoops of some fat lady to stand in the upper aisles to listen to the opera; hide among the potted palms in the Brevoort House lobby and study the manners and customs of the ladies and gentlemen. At twelve he became a runner on Wall Street so that he could learn figures and how money was made. He became so adept at working figures in his head that he could almost instantaneously tell a broker on the floor what it would cost him to buy 869 shares at 6 and 7/8ths. Then he turned fifteen and was given an accounts position. It was love at first sight. Now he could see the figures that had only been in his head. They were his symphonies, his poems, his novels, his works of art.

Salary had drawn him away to Walter Gould and utter frustration. The insurance books were static, plotting uninteresting pennies, nickels and dimes. Even Walter Gould's personal second set of books were grade school primers when he was used to Moliére.

"So, you see, I am born again. I am working with a true gentleman who has a most admirable and challenging project. Oh my, look at the time! I have certainly overstayed my welcome."

"Not at all," Dorothy said rising. "I've enjoyed every minute of it. I've never been to the theatre, you know, and your storytelling of the plays and opera certainly brings them to life. In another age you would have been a court bard, I am sure."

In another age, Rufus was totally convinced, he would have been as titled as she, or more so. Then he would have been worthy of her.

Then swiftly, deftly, and hardly without thinking, he stepped forward and took her in his arms.

Dorothy started to struggle, but thought better of it. She needed him momentarily as an ally and not a foe. So she resorted to what she thought he would expect from a lady. She allowed him to kiss her, but made no response at all. She was like a statue of wood, her lips cold, unmoving, until at last he drew his face away.

She was shocked at his expression. It was exalted.

"That was sublime," he gushed, "although I

would not have blamed you had you slapped my face. But standing there you were Moliére's *Les Precieuses Ridicules,* needing only the touch of male lips. I feared that barbarian Ely might have changed you. I am heartened!"

Quickly, he formally raised her hand and touched it lightly against his lips and then turned and fled.

Dorothy stood silent and stunned. Except for the kiss she might have been saying goodbye to one of her coterie in Ireland. Educated, suave, mannered and frightfully unromantic under all of the polished veneer.

Then Dorothy laughed at her own thought. Wasn't Rufus Brogan the exact mold into which she had wanted to fit Paul Ely?

From the story that he had told earlier on in the evening about Moliére's play she thought Rufus had been most inaccurate in his statement. Moliére had her pegged. She had been a sophisticated, snobbish, spoiled and arrogant feminist. Paul Ely had taught her to be a woman.

But reasoning came in that moment for which she would have to give Rufus Brogan credit. She would never be able to make Rufus a romantic figure like Paul, nor Paul a sensitive, understanding human like Rufus.

Neither one of them, really, were meant for her.

"Damn," she muttered, at the peal of the door chimes. "If that is you back, Rufus Brogan, to ruin the determination I just set in my mind, I'll kill you!"

She flung open the door and stared straight into the glowering face of a stranger.

"If y'er not the 'ousekeeper," he snapped, " 'oo might ye be?"

Dorothy blinked at his affrontery woodenly. He was no taller than she and thin as a rail. He glowered at her from slate-gray eyes, intent and more than a little hard. He was bareheaded. The wind lifted his thick, sandy-red hair and stirred the pleats of his kilt. The slender, sharp nose seemed to sniff at her and the inflexible mouth grew harder.

"I am not the housekeeper," she said coolly, "and demand to know who you might be."

"Ye fule of a woman," he shouted, right into her face. "What ails ye, to demand of Sandie, Lord Dunraven's gillie? Six weeks I am from Dunkeld 'n lothin' this moor a'ready. Where's imself?"

Scots boiled Dorothy's blood, especially when they were insufferable male body servants. "He's seventy miles northwest," she said icily. "If you hurry with your kit you might catch up to him."

His stare back was just as icy. "I dinna get yer name, mistress, but I dinna need it. You must be the baggage being sent awa' yerself, and yer troublesome ways."

"Sir," Dorothy said calmly, controlling her temper, "I am unaware if you are a raving lunatic or just an ordinary madman. I am Lady Dorothy Goold, Lord Dunraven's cousin, and insist that you leave at once."

He grinned wickedly. "I told ye I dinna need yer name. I got it in 'is lorship's cable. Now, get the auld'ousekeeper out fer me luggage."

"There is no housekeeper."

"Aye, Sandie'll patch that over tomorrow." He pushed right by her as though she were as fragile as paper. Then he turned back, his wooden face did not change expression. "Tell the cabbie to fetch and tote, ah'm g'inna find a room fer meself."

He was nowhere to be found when she returned. Dorothy was unsure of what to do. He certainly acted like every gillie she had ever known and there was no mistaking that he had been around Lord Dunraven long enough to acquire *all* of his bad habits—a knack that male servants seemed to pride themselves on.

One thing she was sure of, she would ask Sarah Ferguson to start staying in the house at night.

As she was extinguishing the gaslights in the salon the mantle clock struck midnight. Dorothy frowned on a sudden thought. The last train from Cheyenne arrived at eight. Where had the man been for four hours?

The downstairs locked and dark she started up to her room, extinguishing the stairway candle sconces as she went. At the top of the stairs she turned toward her hallway and nearly screamed. He stood there grinning at her, displaying a row of brown, broken teeth.

"Aye, I thocht as much," he muttered in a croaking voice. "Peekin' an' pryin' aboot the 'ouse, as if to see what ye can snitch before I oust ye."

"Now look here, Sandie," she exploded, "I've had just about all of you I am going to take. I have no reason to steal and I don't intend to be ousted, as you put it!"

"Och, I ken weel see what yer after, ye fule of a lassie! Ah'm being with thirty years an' been with 'is lordship since fifteen. Isn't me first time to get an unsavory lass oot of 'is bed and 'air. Sandie's got 'is ways, he 'as. Now, lass, he's wed wi' a fine lassie. Leave 'im be or run me wrath."

Dorothy stomped away, with her mind seething words she wanted to scream at her cousin rather than his hired servant. *Six weeks.* She could hardly recall what had happened six weeks before to cause Lord Dunraven to send for this man and give him such foul instructions. And all the way down the hall the sound of Sandie's sarcastic laughter followed her.

This was the woman who had killed his Lord's heir, and that was reason enough for Sanford McDuff to hate her from the start.

11

BEFORE LONG Sandie's caustic manner infected everyone who came in contact with the house. Sarah's niece was so intimidated by the man that she started and shrieked if anyone came upon her unawares, and the formidable Sarah was reduced to tears over his comments on her cooking. Like a lord and master he took over possession of the front door and therefore control of who did and who didn't see Dorothy.

Lloyd was disallowed front door entry and sent to the back like a delivery boy. David Moffatt refused to be interrogated by the man and left in a huff. Dorothy came upon him browbeating Rufus Brogan and thus learned about the man's missing four hours.

"Can you imagine such gall," she told Sarah and Lloyd in the kitchen. "That man actually went from window to window spying on me while I had dinner with Rufus."

Sarah, busy at the range, looked over her shoulder.

"Don't surprise me none," she said. "That man seems to know everything that is said or done in this house."

That was now becoming Dorothy's major worry. How much had the Scots gillie heard that he could relate to Lord Dunraven? It was apparent that she could no longer conduct any business in the house without the man snooping and spying about.

"Dorothy," Lloyd whispered, "you've always got the McLaughlin house."

She straightened up and looked at him with her heart in her eyes.

"Lloyd," she whispered back, "oh, Lloyd, I had all but forgotten!"

Lloyd hadn't forgotten—it was still a thorn in his side. But he would much rather remind her of Jim McLaughlin than have her stay another moment around the scowling Scotsman. He had much to tell her, but now didn't dare.

Primrose Ferguson came into the kitchen and held a whispered conversation with her aunt. Her eyes widened in utter dismay as Sarah whispered back firm instructions and then she bustled away.

Wordlessly, Sarah crossed the room and wrapped a shawl about her shoulders.

"What are you about?" Dorothy whispered.

Sarah Ferguson's eyes twinkled. "No need to whisper. Himself just took off like a shot. Primmy just told me that word came that the Earl had a run-in with a mountain lion and is in some doctor's private home in Longmont."

Dorothy felt nothing. It was her second cousin and she felt no urge to even ask how badly hurt he might be. It was almost like hearing about a stranger.

"Still," she stammered, "what are you about?"

"I'm about to get you out of this place. Primmy is already packing you, lock, stock and barrel. Lloyd, get your arse in gear and go borrow a wagon and team from your father. I'm going on over to Molly McLaughlin's house to see what it might need. Miss Dorothy, send Primmy along to start cleaning as soon as you are finished with her. Always did hate working in this damn kitchen! Stove don't draw right!"

Dorothy sat very still and watched them depart. There must be something a person can say at a time like this; but what is it? What are the words? Say: "What dear, wonderful friends you all are!" That really didn't express all the emotions in her heart. Words hadn't been coined to express those emotions. Oh, Paul, Paul why couldn't you have shown me the same consideration and love? But you only showed me deception, and I've got to live out my life knowing I love a man who doesn't love me . . .

The loser again was Rufus Brogan. Paul Ely was dried out once again and sent back to the range and the cattle. Dunraven thought that Theo Whyte was doing an excellent job and would hear no word against him. Sandie made sure the Earl received a very distorted picture of Dorothy and her dinner party for Rufus. For the Earl it was very disturbing news. He soundly reprimanded Rufus for associating with his enemy and nearly fired him in his rage.

Dorothy learned of it through Lloyd and her rage boiled.

"I don't know who has the filthiest mind, Lord Dunraven or his gillie."

The humid August days and airless nights were beginning to affect everyone's nerves. David Moffatt soon learned that he had erred in having Dorothy sign for the two thousand six hundred forty acres and quietly took his family for a vacation in the cooler atmosphere of Pike's Peak. But for everyone else it was like a thunderstorm were brewing. Dunraven was nearly ill each time he looked at Whyte's map and saw the little pockets of land that didn't belong to him. He wrongfully blamed Rufus for allowing it to happen—which Dorothy also learned about. There was something electric in the air, some pressure building up to an unknown climax.

Fredrick Austin felt uncomfortable. Dorothy sat in the quaint little sitting room of the McLaughlin house and studied him like a fish in a bowl. Lloyd sat silent and concerned. He was putting his whole faith in these two people that he trusted the most.

"So, Theo Whyte is offering five dollars an acre," Dorothy said.

Fred ran a hand through his unkempt hair. It made him look even more like an older version of the young man who sat next to him.

"It would be a sizeable chunk of money for the lad," Fred said flatly.

"You don't sound too sure, Mr. Austin. Are you suggesting that he hold out for a higher price?"

A week before she might have thought it a quite handsome offer. But, she too was being pressured into selling, but not directly by Theo Whyte. With David Moffatt out of town the Earl was riding roughshod over the minor bank officials and threatening to withdraw all of his assets unless Dorothy's loan wasn't called in at once. She had slightly less than twenty-five hundred dollars left, and she had no intention of touching this last reserve, no matter how caustic the officious little men became who now pounded on her door daily. Of the land she felt she could legally sell, five dollars an acre would only be half enough to cover the loan. Her desire was to hold out until she could discuss the matter with David Moffatt. Plus, she was angry with herself for having so hurriedly signed for the loan without learning all its conditions.

Austin gulped. What was in his mind he hadn't even discussed with his nephew. He didn't know the workings of Dorothy's mind, except from what he had gained from Lloyd. He knew she had a very strong influence over the boy, and feared that she wouldn't like what he had to say at all.

"Well, miss," he said slowly, "I went and took me a look-see of this land a couple of weeks ago. Seems others are getting the same idea as me. Must be three to four families starting cabins and barns up there.

Dorothy sat up suddenly.

"You mean from those drifters and bums?"

Fred quickly looked to Lloyd to answer the question.

"They haven't been using them much since the Earl came back to town, Dorothy. The grasshoppers have been eating up the farmers' crops and many of them are near destitute. Whyte has been hiring them to come down from Longmont and Greeley and Boulder. For more crop money, they're swearing that they are homesteading.

"But some of them aren't turning in their paper to Whyte and are actually going up to homestead," Austin emphasized anew, hoping to soften his own announcement.

"Despicable!" Dorothy said, ignoring him. "It is just like them to feed off of a different kind of misery to gain the land. Lloyd, do you have any contact with these men?"

"Every day. They don't know their way around, so I have to take them to the land office."

Dorothy grinned. "Good. I think it would be a very wise move on your part to let them know what you have been offered for your land. Fifty dollars, bah! That won't get them new seed crop money or carry them through the winter. But if they demanded more money for land that is really quite legally theirs, I'm sure the good Earl would be forced to pay the piper, if he wants it all so desperately."

Gloomily, Fred shook his head.

"Then you are advising us to sell Lloyd's land?"

His tone made Dorothy study him more intently. She saw a shy, sensitive man who had been too long under the domineering hand of his older step-brother. She was sorry that she didn't know him better, because Lloyd spoke so highly of his abilities. But she didn't feel right advising one way or the other.

"No, Mr. Austin," she said slowly, "it is not my place to give such advice."

"Thank you," he said quietly. "Lloyd, it may take me a lifetime to pay you the same as Lord Dunraven is offering, but I think we should hold onto that land and get even more. I've got enough money put away to get the lumber and supplies we'd need to have a cabin built by fall. I've got a hunch that if Lord Dunraven wants it so damn bad, then there has to be some kind of money to be made up there."

Lloyd frowned, and then shrugged almost dejectedly. "That's fine with me."

Dorothy was getting to know his moods quite well and read this one exactly.

"It seems to me that you both need to start a life of your own apart from David Folsom. A cabin would go up much faster with two men working on it."

"Excellent!" Fred laughed. "As partners they can't beat us! Thank you, miss, for having Lloyd get that land in the first place."

Thank you, Dorothy thought to herself. Just like Jim McLaughlin, she knew that they would never sell the land. It was the best monkey wrench in the world to foul up the Earl's scheme.

But she also knew she was giving up something dear and precious in the bargain. For Lloyd's own advancement she was sending him away. It was a hard thing to do. She had come to rely upon him for so much.

"Wait!" Lloyd breathed. "What about you, Dorothy?"

The tenderness on his face was beautiful to see. It was deep and honest and loving.

"I shall be fine," she whispered. "After all, I do return home in the fall."

Suddenly, with terrifying certainty, she knew that this was her only course of action. Lord Dunraven was too strong, with too much capital for her to buck. She had boasted too strongly in her letters home and was too proud to ask for help from that quarter and admit defeat. She had blundered badly on the loan and would just have to handle it as best she could.

She lifted her fine head proudly. Fred Austin started to comment and stopped himself. No words needed to be spoken. And, even as his heart sang with joy, he was sure that never again would he see anyone as radiantly beautiful as this woman.

12

NOW THE LANDGRABBING became a desperate battle of wits and financing. Lloyd Folsom's rumor spread like wildfire at midnight. The 'imported' claimers were mostly transplanted New Englanders who had an inbred distrust of anything British and coined a caustic little term of their own. They had to deal with Theo Whyte and the Estes Park Co., Ltd., but knew that it was for the benefit of Lord Dunraven and his English Company.

More and more men began to hold back their slips until it was becoming a minor revolution. Ironically, Lord Dunraven called it sheer greed, but the root of the matter went much deeper than just trying to thwart him. Daily, *The Rocky Mountain News* painted a gloomier and gloomier picture of the Eastern financial market. If disaster was coming, the men wanted gold in hand.

Dunraven became so fanatical in his determination to get the land without highway robbery that he ordered Whyte to return to the original scheme, but under new rules. The drifters and bums were to be given a free drink *before* they left for the land office and only men who could sign an X for their signature were to be used. Dunraven would just let the thirty-odd farmers who were holding out retain their plots until they were starved into submission.

"Damn you," he snarled at a cowering vice-president from the bank. "What do you mean you can't move against her loan at this time?"

"We never noticed before, sir, but Mr. Moffatt secured it against the payments due from your account to the Bank of Dublin as against what funds will be due to you from the Castle Adare."

"That's not banking," Dunraven exploded, "that's shyster double-dealing in a matter that doesn't even involve the woman. You tell Moffatt to get his fat ass right back here and straighten this out! I want my land back and that loan called in!"

His black rage at everyone became so fierce that Lady Florence quickly departed with Mrs. Augusta Downing and party for an Eastern shopping spree. Her departure did not help his mood. Lady Florence had come to fear another pregnancy and had refused him her bed throughout the summer. His ego being what it was, he thought he was still being punished for being caught with Dorothy, and that increased his resentment towards both of them. He wanted an heir that year, and, Church of Rome or not, he would have an heir or a new wife.

At the end of the summer Rufus Brogan came

back from a quick trip to Estes Park in a highly disturbed frame of mind.

"Four to six families have cabins started and will be ready to winter in by October."

He dared not say that one of the cabins was being built by Fred Austin and Lloyd Folsom.

"Blasted bastards!" Dunraven shrieked. "Show me their locations on the map!"

Rufus smirked at Theodore Whyte. "I can't do that, sir. Mr. Whyte does not allow me access to the map."

"What?" the Earl bellowed, glaring at the rolled sheets beneath Whyte's arm. "Roll those damn things out on the dining room table and don't you ever again keep information from my private secretary."

The long-standing feud between the two men was now a clear-cut battle line. The Welsh engineer calmly rolled out his maps, but his heart was plotting destruction for Rufus Brogan.

Rufus took methodically recorded notes from his breast pocket and started to acquaint himself with the map. He looked back and forth several times and then began to scowl.

"Something is horribly wrong here," he said.

"Nothing is wrong with my map," Whyte insisted pompously.

Rufus saw where he could draw the first blood and quickly.

"The land office map records these four parcels under A.Q. MacGregor, but you show one listed for W.E. James. There is also duplication on these three parcels, this one here, and these over here."

Without even looking, Whyte tried to sound knowledgable. "What difference does it make? We still have the land no matter what name it is under."

But Lord Dunraven had been looking and his face was growing scarlet. "Do we?" he snapped. "How in hell's name did the Goolds get hold of three parcels and who are these other three names in those squares?"

Rufus naturally held his silence as though a golden angel who could do no wrong.

Whyte's weasel eyes narrowed to nervous slits and he carefully answered only the last part of the question.

"Wilson H. James," he read on a squeak, "George Robinson and Samuel Payton. Well, sir, they are three of the farmers who are holding out on us."

"Well, now," Dunraven wheezed, "isn't that just lovely? My cousin, somehow—and I'm still waiting for an answer on that one—gets in three claims that are also held by the revolutionaries. She may be a woman, Whyte, but at this moment I would venture to say she has more brains in her fingernail than you have in your head. Her claims outdate these three and would win in any court. I want those three bought out at any price and I want the bill of sale dated prior to her claim."

"But that will open a floodgate for the others," Whyte insisted.

Dunraven glowered as though his intent was murder as well. "If need be, yes," he stormed. "But what else does this map tell you?"

Whyte leaned down close, searching for an answer that wasn't readily coming to his mind. He was silent.

"Are you blind?" Dunraven hissed. "Rufus, do you see anything?"

Rufus smiled to himself. He had been on the

land and, seeing the full map for the first time, he knew exactly what the Earl was driving at. He relished being able to draw the second blood as well.

"If you speak of the holdout farmers, sir, I think I see your point. They still possess the papers on about five thousand acres. But those acres surround or box in the other claims that we are not deeded on or are trying to control."

"Now, isn't that simple, Mr. Whyte?" Dunraven asked ruthlessly. "So, for a moment, if your pea-sized brain is capable, let's think backwards. For a year I have had lumber curing to be transported there this spring. I've invested ten thousand dollars for an architect to design the buildings I want constructed. A contract is ready to be signed with John Cleave to supply the necessary workers. The only thing I seem to lack is a man capable of getting me the land to put it all upon."

The silence in the room was almost deafening.

"So," he went on slowly and thoughtfully, "we think forward again. Rugus, you will take over the negotiations with Brown and Lothroup. I want that settled this week. Everything. Cattle, houses, fences, everything. Although we can't own it outright, as yet, that will give us control over the seven thousand acres of cattle land set aside by the survey. No one can then lay a claim on it or squat. Give Paul Ely full control over the cattle. He'll know what to do from there. Then send word that I want to deal *personally* with Griff Evans on his land. He'll come running when he knows what I have in mind. Now, hop to it!"

Rufus left reluctantly. He wanted to be in on the kill.

Dunraven was too sly for that. Theo Whyte knew too much to be fired at that dangerous moment, but he was not about to be let off scot-free. The Earl continued to study the map soberly and let the room become agonizing in the complete silence.

"What," Whyte stammered, "should I be doing?"

Dunraven pursed his lips. "I would first like to know how my cousin and Frederick Austin got their hands on so much land. That is almost one thousand five hundred acres."

"Well, sir," Whyte breathed laboriously, "Rufus was also handling—"

Dunraven crashed his fist into the table. "What I hate worse than a liar or a cheat is someone ready to scapegoat! You handed out the slips! You marked the map! You had the men sign the land over! Rufus? *Rufus?* He just pulled your chestnuts out of the fire for you! Now own up!"

Theo Whyte could only surmise, but was quite correct in his surmising. He had to admit using Lloyd as a runner and a map-marker. He failed to mention that he allowed Lloyd to mark the map so that he could sit and get mellowly drunk at the end of each day. He really knew next to nothing about the map.

Lord Dunraven had to turn away and smile. It quite obvious to him that Dorothy would have been the master mind to have pulled such clever wool over the eyes of Whyte and Brogan, to say nothing of Moffatt and the money to finance her purchases. He couldn't help but feel genuine family pride. She was a true Whyham-Quin. Resourceful, daring, unafraid. Had he allowed her and Lloyd full control over his land acquisition, he felt he might now possess the full three hundred thousand acres—and without question.

But family pride or no, she had to be squashed. Three of her five parcels were not only in question but prime to his needs. For the moment he wouldn't worry about the acres under Fredrick Austin's name. He could handle that through David Folsom, or the loss of the carting contract.

"I fail to see," he said rudely, "why you continue to stand around with your finger up your bugger!"

"I'm waiting to hear what you would have me do, sir," Whyte gulped.

"Need I repeat myself? Buy out those damn farmers!"

"And Lady Dorothy?"

"Did I mention her to you?"

"No, sir."

Dunraven's silent glower was message enough. Whyte was to leave well enough alone.

Because the land butted into a mountain, Wilson H. James had been granted 170.23 acres. Twice Whyte made offers that were gruffly refused. Twice Whyte presented the refusals to Lord Dunraven, which was a gross error on his part.

Five minutes after walking into the mansion on Brown's Bluff, Wilson H. James walked out $1800 richer.

Theo Whyte's office was stampeded the next morning. Stupidly, Whyte let it be known that he wished only to talk with George Robinson and Samuel Payton first. Both wanted as much, or more, than James had received. Whyte didn't want to pay as much.

They left in a furious mood and spread the word.

Rufus smiled to himself and made sure that Dunraven got the news.

But some of the men were growing desperate. Two settled for $900, two for $800 and one for $700.

When Dunraven came storming into the saloon, Whyte felt quite proud of his day's work. Back in the office, which Rufus was seeing for the first time, Dunraven burst his balloon.

"Those are not the parcels I wanted first. You are causing this thing to become common gossip all over Denver. As you seem to be able to think only in terms of twenty-five dollar and fifty dollar payments get back to your drunks. Rufus, do as we discussed on the way over here."

Oddly enough, Rufus didn't feel triumphant. Whyte was, after all, trying to save the Earl's money, even though he was making a mess of the whole situation.

Whyte, however, felt totally defeated and placed all the blame on Rufus Brogan. He recalled the gossip about Rufus and Lady Dorothy and made a mental note to have a little chat with gillie Sandie.

Rufus wasn't thinking about the past, only the present and future. He rounded up Robinson and Payton and got them away from all concerned ears. Because they were in tandem, they settled for two thousand dollars each. But unlike Wilson James, Rufus didn't let them run back to the pack with their good news. He carted them off immediately to the train depot, bought them one-way tickets out of town and waited to wave them a goodbye.

More of a diplomat than Whyte, he was able to

save the Earl money. He had the advantage of telling the men that he had seen the land, which they had not, and could fluctuate the price accordingly, never having to pay out more than one thousand five hundred dollars and in most cases just one thousand dollars.

Still, it took over thirty-nine thousand dollars of the Earl's money to acquire the majority of the five thousand acres.

Then, on September 8, 1873 the telegraph wires began to hum ominously. The New York Warehouse Securities Company had closed its doors.

The last holdout farmers came to Rufus in a panic. He was in the driver's seat and picked up their claims at thirty-two cents an acre.

Theo Whyte arrogantly boasted he had seen this coming all along and that was why he had been stalling on paying such huge prices for the land. His boast went against him.

"I see," Dunraven said heavily. "I fail, however, to understand why you didn't share your crystal ball with us at the time. Men work *for* me, not against me."

Rufus was becoming saturated in the man's blood.

On the thirteenth, the first of Lord Dunraven's erstwhile landgrabbing backers pulled in his sails. Daniel Drew, as the senior partner of his firm, announced the firm's bankruptcy. The next morning the *Rocky Mountain News* listed those other companies who were rumored to be in danger.

This news brought David Moffatt back to town in a highly agitated mood. The bank was highly overinvested with its customers' capital. He prayed that one company would remain as the rock of Gibraltar in the financial world.

Windham Thomas Whyham-Quin was praying for the opposite. Jay Cooke and Company had obtained control of the Jim Fisk estate, and Lord Dunraven's mortgage to the man.

During the next four days Rufus Brogan was given quite a new assignment. Two and three times a day, each time going to a different clerk, he quietly began withdrawing the Earl's money in dribs and drabs until every empty dresser drawer in the mansion was bulging with nearly half a million in gold coin.

Landgrabbing was forgotten for the sake of moneygrabbing.

Not even the President of the United States could save the giant. On the eighteenth Jay Cooke & Company sank into the sea of insolvency. With it Lord Dunraven sank into debt, unless he was able to pay a few cents on the dollar. His bank account balance proved that he could not, although someone forgot to check his land value assets. And who cared to check? "The Club" considered him a member.

Dunraven was not competition to them out West. The Goulds and the Vanderbilts just wished to rid themselves of competitors so that they could devour the fallen carcasses without cutting into their private treasuries. But one Gould, who should have been a Goold, was not a giant that would remain towering. The unwise investment of insurance money was bringing the tontine system to a screeching halt.

Walter Gould went to a closet in the spacious brownstone and looked at a pile of shoes that had been soled and resoled. They had walked him hundreds of thousands of miles for pennies that had grown into invested millions. He sat down among them with tears in his eyes. They would never walk him another mile because he was too old and too tired and had invested with all of the "right" people at all of the "wrong" times. Unbelievably, one rainy morning in September had washed away twenty-five million dollars in insurance investments.

The tears were not for himself, but for all the little people who had put their trust in him and his tontine. As though he willed it, his heart just stopped.

David Moffatt wished he could still his palpitating heart. By begging, borrowing and nearly stealing he kept the bank doors open, almost. For days on end he refused to cash even the banks own checks. His anger over the Dunraven withdrawals had him nearly in fits, but he had no control over a customer wishing to withdraw his funds, even if it had been done in a very sly and devious manner. Then an interesting item on the telegraph caught his eyes. The British-controlled house of Drexel, Morgan & Company had taken over Jay Cooke's.

Bustling over to the mansion he found only the hostile and uncommunicative Sandie at home. Dreading his next stop, he quietly instructed the carriage driver to take him to Whyte's office-saloon. Within blocks of the place his heart began to sink. Hundreds of men, in all manner of dress, stood silent and expectant. Theo Whyte was king of the heap again. He needed but to open his saloon office for a few hours each day and gain all the men he desired for five dollars to ten dollars a claim, plus a *single* free drink, coming or going.

Although he recognized a face here and there, he tried to avoid their eyes. His very girth made him feel guilty of the lavish lunch he had consumed earlier at Charplot's.

Although the sign boldly announced "out to lunch" he vigorously pounded on the saloon door to the snickers and jeers of those in the line. He was wheezing by the time Rufus Brogan admitted him, and he demanded to see the Earl.

He was a caller Windham Thomas had been expecting, but hardly at this location. Because Whyte and Rufus were already in attendance, the Earl did not go out of his way to exclude them from the meeting.

Desperate men make desperate concessions. David Moffatt was *very* desperate. To gain back the Earl's full account he had no choice but to stand and be berated, chastised and cursed in less than gentlemanly tones. His opinion of the man dropped to nothing, but he was there for something. No matter who was hurt in the long run, he was out to save his bank, first and foremost.

"I made a grave mistake," he admitted reluctantly. "I'll go at once and have her sign the land back over to me."

"No, you blithering idiot," Dunraven fumed. "Only do as I command! Am I destined to be surrounded by morons? You will only bring the legal pressure of the bank to bear on the payment of that loan, the confiscation of any assets she may have to cover it, or any other means available to you."

Theo Whyte found the whole conversation exceedingly irksome. He had already gained enough information from Sandie to brand the woman as a harlot and traitor to the Earl's cause. He had only refrained from speaking his piece until he was back strong enough in the Earl's favor and until he could pin Rufus to the same cross. Throughout this conversation he had watched only Brogan's face and felt very smug about what he read from it. He knew the banker would cave in to the Earl's demands. Then the Earl's final instructions jarred him.

"But, Moffatt," Dunraven warned, "You will not go against her until tomorrow. I want Rufus to get certain confessions out of her first."

Whyte's anger seethed at the departure of the banker. Again he was excluded from the whispered conversation between the Earl and his secretary-accountant. He would have been amazed at the mild message that was conveyed.

"Do nothing," Dunraven chuckled. "I just want to see if he is capable of doing more than sit on his fat ass."

Rufus intended to do nothing for Moffatt or Lord Dunraven. He waited until the Earl had departed and then made his own hasty exit. He was not aware that Whyte followed close behind. It was time, so Whyte thought, for the blood to start flowing in the opposite direction.

Rufus was not aware he was being followed until he came out from making a withdrawal at the First National Bank for "a dear friend." It was a withdrawal he had to demand or close the Earl's account forever.

The dear friend was, of course, Dorothy Goold.

But in spotting Theo Whyte, Rufus quickly resorted to the lessons learned during his upbringing in the Bronx; he led the man back to nothing more sinister than his own quarters on Broadway.

Whyte, a man of strong convictions once his mind was centered on what he considered a truism, marched right on up to Colfax to Brown's Bluff.

Dunraven listened to Whyte's half-baked charges and scoffed.

"Whyte, you are a total ass! Sandie has been with me since the age of fifteen and has no other master but me. Where I am concerned, male or female, he is a highly emotional and jealous being. He would tell tales on Queen Vicky if he thought she was casting a lusting eye in my direction. I gave not a bat's eyelash to his lurid story about Rufus and Lady Dorothy. The laugh, old chap, is on you."

Whyte went away in a horrible mood. He had made the worst type of fool of himself.

Dunraven chuckled to himself and began to dress for a social visit. Whyte had done him a great service, but not great enough to acknowledge and reward. Although he gave Dorothy credit for being quite capable, a certain segment of his ego would not admit that she had done it alone. There had to be a man standing behind her and advising her. He had come to the conclusion in his own mind that it had to be James McLaughlin. Never Rufus Brogan—that was laughable, unthinkable. Rufus was as true blue to him as was Sandie. Theo Whyte was just trying too hard to get back into his good favor.

An hour later he was almost to the marble facade of the Horace DeWinter mansion when he checked his pocket watch. He was adequately early for dinner and had time for one short social call before making his appearance.

Five minutes later he walked into the McLaughlin house as though he owned it. It didn't surprise Dorothy; she had almost been expecting it.

"I have already had a visit from David Moffatt," she said grimly. "What do you want, Cousin Windham?"

"Couple of things. First, I want to make my apology. I have not treated you as a true kinswoman, nor have you, exactly, treated me as a true kinsman."

Dorothy looked at him, a puzzled expression creeping into her eyes. "I'll overlook that last, but go on."

"It has come to me that your mother and father were not so wrong after all. Second cousins can be quite suited to each other, even first cousins. As you know I am a great one for believing in astrology and the occult. I even believe I heard my father speaking to me as I dressed this evening, although I ignored it at the time. I am no longer ignoring his voice, Dorothy. Our stars are crossed. I shall start paperwork at once to divorce myself of Lady Florence. Will you marry me, then?"

"No!" Dorothy exploded.

"I thought that would be your first reaction. Well, I know it will take time . . . you know the ways of the church. But you need not be denied the enjoyment I gave you on the way to Estes. Who will question you as being my mistress until the time that we can marry?"

"I question it," she answered hotly.

Dunraven studied her with unconcealed amazement. "Nonsense," he chortled. "You must admit that I have given you more manly pleasure than you have ever received in your life. You thought that I was that muscle-bound Paul Ely, and I was not. I was more man than he could ever hope to be." He chuckled anew. "And you were more woman than I have ever had beneath me. Can you deny any of these facts?"

Dorothy could deny and be a hypocrite and liar. He had given her more manly pleasure than she had ever received in her life. She had thought that it was Paul Ely. But she could not bear the thought of being beneath Lord Dunraven ever again. And marry him? Never!

"You took my breath away," she said coyly, stalling for time to think.

"As David Moffatt must have," he answered, without being coy.

"That was a shock," she said truthfully, but not as truthful as she felt. Until his arrival she had been shaking with mortal dread. Then she decided to take her truth one step further. "Perhaps, Cousin Windham, I am not accustomed to these American banking laws." She sighed and became fully feminine and vulnerable. "I've done something you will not approve of, because I didn't understand interest and principal and due dates."

Well, Dunraven thought, perhaps his foe was not as formidable as he thought. His face was as bland as though he did not know what she was talking about.

"Is there something that I might help you with?"

Dorothy wanted to scream out at his arrogant attitude, but she remained as calm as a breezeless pond. "Perhaps. I made a five thousand dollar loan and find myself overextended. I do have land to back up the loan, however."

Dunraven's Adam's apple jerked in his throat. His ego could not condone one more second of doing business with a woman.

"Land," he snapped, "that you got in your name under false pretenses, I might add!"

Dorothy relaxed. The enemy had signaled his poker hand.

"That is only your opinion, Windham," she said sweetly. "After all, I did pay the going price for it."

"*Five dollars?*" he bellowed.

"The going price," she countered. "After all, I was keeping it in the family."

"Admirable of you," he choked. "Right admirable of you. Now I want it back forthwith!"

"Of course," she said gaily. "Only, Windham, the price is now five thousand."

Why did I come? Dunraven thought miserably. Why didn't I leave this to Rufus? I don't desire her as a wife. Why did I think she would be gullible and jump at such an offer? Well, she would just have to learn that he was the Earl of Dunraven.

"What sheer nonsense, my girl," he laughed. "Why do you think I would fall for such a stupid scheme?"

"It's simple," she said softly. "You have no choice. Had I not been here when your default payments came due, you might be a penniless pauper right now. Check, Windham, and you will see that not a single pound of my mother's money would have come into your account if I had not been here to wire her my approval. You owe me one, Windham, without a confining marriage."

"I'll see you in court," he sneered.

"Fine," Dorothy simpered. "I have the deed and the pay slip. What have you?"

It was a reality Dunraven couldn't ignore. He had tried everything and had failed on all counts. Then he smiled and shrugged.

"You really are a true Whyham-Quin. You have won. Get the papers and sign them. I shall pay your five thousand mortgage."

Dorothy hesitated. No matter how cruel he had been to her in the past, it still seemed like an excessive amount of profit. Then her heart hardened. What price should she put on her life, that he wanted to let die of exposure? She got the deed from her desk, signed it and handed it over with a sigh. She was really quite glad to be rid of it. She was free and clear of its burden; free and clear of the mortgage; free and clear of her cousin and still had eight hundred acres of land.

"Thank you, my dear," Dunraven intoned with courtly courtesy. "And now, what are your plans?"

"Not to marry you," she laughed, feeling suddenly light-hearted.

"No," he said soberly, "I never expected you to accept that offer, although we would have made a remarkable team both in bed and in the business office. Is it back to Ireland?"

"Those have been my plans for some little time."

"Then this is probably our goodbye."

With a quizzical little grin he bowed and marched to the door.

Dorothy watched him depart with mixed emotions. There had been no messages for her to carry home with her, which was most customary. There had been no parting goodbye on behalf of his wife, no matter the trouble between the two women. Not to try and patch up a family quarrel before parting was an omen of the worst type of luck yet to come. Dorothy felt a cold shiver creep up her spine and she tried to shake it off as an old superstition.

But an hour later, when there was a furtive little knock at the front door, her pure Irish heart nearly stopped beating. The devil or death would be the only two callers coming after such a visit.

It was neither, but perhaps worse.

Rufus Brogan slid through the door as though the devil were on his tail and death were but minutes away. He was ashen and greatly agitated.

"Stay away from the windows," he warned. "I've waited over an hour to make sure that he, or someone else, didn't return."

"Rufus," she gasped, "what is this all about?"

"Hush," he whispered. "Not here, not now. How soon can you get fully packed?"

Dorothy stared. "I've never really fully unpacked since leaving the mansion."

"Good," he said sternly. "Let's get you fully packed. David Folsom will be here within the hour with a wagon to fetch you."

Dorothy looked at him in dismay.

"I am not taking one step, Rufus Brogan," she said with gentle dignity, "until I learn what all this prattle is about."

"Please," he begged, "while you pack."

"So!" Dorothy said an hour later, almost in a state of deep shock. "I knew that he left here too quietly!"

"I was the one who was supposed to come here,"

Rufus whispered. "His only concern was to get the two thousand six hundred forty acres back from you. He has no intention of paying off that mortgage." He gulped. "He fully wants you to default and run up against the law and Mr. Moffatt."

"But that doesn't have to be, Rufus. I can still sell the acreage to make up the difference."

Rufus's head came up slowly, and his eyes, looking at Dorothy, were miserable. As quickly as possible he told her about the double filing and how Dunraven had paid five thousand eight hundred dollars to gain the three parcels and have them back-dated. Her other two parcels would not bring more than $500 each.

"Ruined!" Dorothy was shocked.

"No, not quite. I was able to pull some strings and get this out of your bank account. It's not all. Only one thousand five hundred dollars. It should see you home. Now, I've got to get back before questions are asked."

"Back?" Dorothy protested. "You would go back to that wicked hypocrite? Rufus, he's the most—" She stopped, seeing the torment on his face.

"Don't make my position worse," he moaned. "I know all of his sins, because I've been a part of them. I've become as greedy and selfish as he is, except for . . ." He turned his black Irish eyes, glossy with tears, upon her. "I couldn't let him allow Mr. Moffatt to do to you what he wanted. But you could still fight him, in a way."

Dorothy nodded grimly. "I'm waiting," she said.

"Possession is the majority of the law. If you got someone to start a cabin on that land for you and could fight for your rights . . . It's no good. He's got you all boxed in. The only reason I was able to talk David Folsom into picking you up was because of his threat over his step-brother's land. David doesn't threaten easily. His comments about the Earl are not fit for your ears, and you know the things they say about Lord Dunraven."

"I'm beginning to understand," Dorothy said. "But I don't understand you, Rufus. Why all of this, for me?"

"I know what you are thinking. But I haven't turned traitor, Dorothy. I find myself with divided emotions. You are each right and you are each wrong. But that doesn't change the love I've come to feel for each of you. You each have invested some of yourself into my life and I am eternally grateful."

As he left her he was the perfect gentleman and only lifted her hand to his lips. But his eyes spoke the whole truth. He would never love another woman until he could find one to match her.

It was not as auspicious an exit from Denver as her entrance. She could look back up at Brown's Bluff and see the glowing lights of many more mansions than had been there a few years before. Now everyone had lawns and trees and flower gardens. It was a growing island set apart from the financial woes of the rest of the country. The rich were rich enough to survive the storm and the poor would do what they had always done, just get poorer without anyone really caring.

She felt bad in leaving nothing more than a hastily written note for Sarah Ferguson. That was not the way she wanted to say goodbye to an old friend, but David Folsom packed her into the high-sided lumber cart as though he feared the instant arrival of the militia.

Dorothy reacted to the fears of others because she was a little numb. Her experience was strictly European. She had read too narrowly between the lines of what Rufus had said about David Moffatt and the bank and could almost hear the gates of pauper's prison closing on her. How then would she communicate with her mother to unravel the web she had woven? Like one of the melodramatic heroines that Rufus had told her about she felt saved from the villain at the last moment.

With a start she came out of her reverie.

"Mr. Folsom! We are blocks beyond the train depot!"

"Yep!" he intoned emotionlessly. "Last train left more'n two hours ago."

"But-but—" she stammered.

David Folsom turned and caught her in the steel gaze of his gray eyes. "I ain't ever liked you much," he said with candid honesty, "but Mr. Brogan paid me a fair price to get you out of town before dawn. Trains will be checked by then, so I'll cart you to Longmont. Ain't much more to be said."

And he said nothing. Dorothy thought it just as well, her opinion of the man had never been too high either. Besides, she had thoughts and plans of her own to consider.

She was going home! She would be able to kiss her mother and hug her grandmother! She could ride again daily through the farms and down into the peat bogs! *Home!*

A delicious thrill crept through her. She began to picture in her mind scenes that had become a vague memory. The castle, her room, the rose garden, even the foggy mornings when she and her horse seemed to be the only creatures alive in the whole world.

She fought to keep awake, but she was so mentally tired and her thoughts were making her even more drowsy. Her eyes grew heavy and her chin fell forward onto her chest. Although the September night was warm, she never felt David put his own mackinaw jacket about her shoulders. The gentle roll of the wagon northward kept her in a comfortable slumber for hours.

The lack of movement awoke her. The eastern plains were being divorced from the night sky by slivers of gray and faint fingers of orange. Everything about her was still cast in weird shadows. There was a single sound. Then she realized the form of one of the shadows and the sound. David Folsom was standing down beside the front wheel relieving himself.

Dorothy sat still for a moment, amazed at her own quiet, unembarrassed reaction. Wordlessly, she slipped down off the opposite side of the wagon and went off into a tangle of overgrown cottonwood saplings. Never once did she even question whether David Folsom might be watching her.

"Thank you," she said, scampering back up onto the high seat and folding the mackinaw on the seat between them. "But it is really quite balmy."

"Indian summer," he said, clucking the horses forward again. "It might stay this way, or it might snow tomorrow. Funny country."

"But you love it, don't you?"

"I respect it," he said laconically. "It can take

care of a man, if a man takes care of it. Rich and fertile land that will only be gobbled up."

"Mr. Folsom," she said slowly. "I don't mean to pry, but I'm most curious about your earlier comment of not liking me much."

"Yep!" he said sourly, "I said it. Don't know you really, but got mighty sick of my son talkin' about you. He thinks the sun rises and sets with you. Don't like you, I guess, because of the big notions you put in his head."

"Notions?" she queried cautiously. "Such as?"

"This land deal and his putting it all in my stepbrother's name. Didn't you think he should trust his own father on such a thing?"

"Mr. Folsom," she gasped, "I suggested that he buy the land so he could sell it back to Lord Dunraven and make a profit for himself. I had no knowledge of it being put in Fred Austin's name until just recently. But really, aren't they doing exactly what you said a minute ago? They are taking care of the land, so that it can take care of them."

"Still hurts," he said sullenly.

"Of course it does. But don't you think that I also hurt? I am family to Lord Dunraven and look at the manner in which I am being treated!"

"Different," he snorted. "You've been the man's mistress!"

Dorothy's gasp was so audible that he was forced to turn and stare. Her face was ashen and tears rimmed her eyes.

"If that is what was being said about me," she said on a sob, "then I am most glad to leave that town. How much farther?"

"Couple of miles."

"Good. I shall be most glad to get away and back to a civilization that does not constantly have its mind in a cesspool."

Folsom was quiet for some time. "You really aren't, are you?" he asked simply.

"No," Dorothy said, "I definitely am not!"

He studied her with grave eyes.

"Then why are you letting him chase you away? Lloyd says you are the only one who has been bucking him from grabbing all the land in sight."

"I have no desire to go to jail over a bad loan, Mr. Folsom."

He chuckled. She hadn't thought the man was capable of laughing. "If that be the case, then half of Denver would be crowding the jail to its rafters. Everyone's in the same boat these days, except for a few up on Brown's Bluff. Besides, you're not even an American citizen."

"Mr. Folsom," she said slowly, "exactly why did you agree to take me to Longmont?"

David Folsom saw no reason to keep it a mystery. "Besides the money, Brogan said he would protect me from losing the carting contract. Dunraven wants thousands of board feet of lumber up to his valley by spring. Brogan thought if I got started on it, I would be kinda out of sight and out of mind."

Dorothy was puzzled. "How can you get started on it, making this trip?"

"Simple. All summer trains have been bringing lumber to Longmont. Now the only problem is getting it up to Estes. I hear tell that a few have gotten wagons up there. So I'm going to give it a try after I let you off."

Dorothy's head was in a whirl. Had she been duped by Rufus Brogan for the sole benefit of Lord Dunraven? That possibility grew and grew in her mind as the sun rose as though with a mighty leap. It basked the foothills in brilliant hues and spotlighted Long's Peak like a mastiff's fang. It was inconceivable to her that any one man could own that mountain. It was like God's throne, untouchable by wealth and power. She prayed that the little people going into the region would stand fast against Dunraven's greed.

Theodore Whyte sat smug and confident in Lord Dunraven's study. He had waited until dawn to roust out Rufus Brogan and drag him to the mansion. Whyte knew that Lord Dunraven would be in a foul and ugly mood being taken from his warm bed at such an hour, and that's exactly how Whyte wanted him. But he did not count on how surly his mood would be on that particular morning.

Dunraven had returned to the dinner party in a most joyous mood. He had won back his two thousand six hundred and forty acres on a promise he did not intend to keep. He had beaten Dorothy and it made him radiantly happy. So happy, that he sparkled with so much charm that he captivated the young wife of Harvey S. Carter III. Mr. Carter had rushed east to see if he could salvage any of the Carter family fortune. Lillian Hastings Carter now lay unclothed in Lord Dunraven's canopied bed and the Ear fumed at having to leave her for even a few minutes.

He was in a towering rage by the time Whyte carefully sneered out his first set of accusations.

"I am well aware," he snarled, "that Rufus was to call on Lady Dorothy last evening."

"Perhaps that is true," Whyte said cuttingly, "but were you aware that he took her funds and had David Folsom spirit her out of town, bag and baggage?"

"Rufus?" Dunraven cried. "What is this all about?"

Theo Whyte sat back, ready for his own blood-letting.

Rufus sat unruffled and calm. Under pressure he was learning to emulate the Earl quite well. He had not helped Dorothy without thinking the thing out well in advance and covering in his mind every possibility that might arise. His only surprise was that it was happening quicker than he had anticipated.

"I fail to see Mr. Whyte's concern," he said coolly. "I did not want to disturb you at your dinner party and handled the matter as I thought you would have handled it, sir. You have wanted her out of your hair for some time. She informed me of your visit. You acquired back the land. You had already accomplished my mission for me, it seems. But then she informed me of her plans and desires to return to Ireland. Well, sir, you know the number of times she has changed her mind on that score, so I took it upon myself to help expedite those plans. What faster way was there to get her out of town than send her to Longmont with David?"

There were loopholes a mile wide in the fable, but Dunraven had only been listening to the major points; at the moment he was much more interested in getting back to Lillian.

Whyte saw his victory fire turning to ashes.

"The money?" he roared. "What about the money you took from the bank and gave her?"

"Have you been spying on me?" Rufus asked fervently. "They were, after all, funds from her own bank account. Use common sense, man! What good would just getting her to Longmont do? Trains and boats do not take on passengers without the proper fare."

Whyte started to protest and Dunraven stopped him with a glare. Only one aspect of the whole thing stood out emphatically in his mind. Dorothy had believed him and had left of her own choosing. He was really very pleased with Rufus, and to keep the slate clean, so that no repercussions would be coming from Ireland, he would instruct Rufus to go ahead and pay off the five thousand dollar loan. After all, that was minor. Hadn't he quietly paid Griff Evans fifty thousand dollars for his Fish Creek Ranch holdings? It was the only spot for his hunting lodge and now the lumber would start to roll. He had been very pleased with Rufus's handling of that matter as well. If David Folsom wanted to retain his lucrative contract, the burden was on his shoulders to get Fred Austin to sell back the land. How ironic that he was carting the very woman to Longmont that he blamed for his family problems! Dunraven started to chuckle and then laugh heartily. Without another word to either of them he left the study and laughed his way back up to his bedroom. He didn't intend to leave it all day long. Rufus was capable of handling things—including Theo Whyte.

And Rufus emulated the Earl once again. He

rose laughing and departed the mansion without a word. But his laugh was vicious and mean.

Whyte sat for a long time crushed and defeated. He would just have to learn to play this ruthless game more slyly before striking out at Rufus Brogan again. But strike again he would, sooner or later.

"Home!" Dorothy Goold was thinking. "How many times are circumstances going to keep me from going home."

Folsom sat in a mental gloom. He was unsure what to do.

The station master could give him no positive answer as to when the Denver-Cheyenne train might run. The telegraph lines had been cut, a train derailed east of Cheyenne and a wagon train attacked and burned on the North Platte.

The ramifications of the depression in the country were not lost on the Indians. Once again they saw their lands being squatted upon by the workless force who had been evicted from their homes and mortgaged farms. They, too, were landgrabbers, but without wealth. Their power was only in their numbers. By the thousands they had run away from starvation and right into the arms of a new and different hostility. The still largely unsubdued Indians had been quietly gaining an equalizing force—the white man's fire sticks. The Indians felt they were becoming an island in a lake of whites. They were determined to make the lake turn red with blood.

"All right," Dorothy said suddenly, unexpectedly. "I can't go forward and have no desire to go backward, but I do have land that I can call home."

David Folsom didn't need to be told what land she was talking about, but what other choice did he have but to take her along? His gloom deepened, and then suddenly lifted on a new thought. She might just prove to be an ally and not an enemy. She would never be able to stand the rigors of pioneer life. She did have a strong influence over Lloyd and if she failed . . . He smiled to himself. He would say nothing about Dunraven's threats on this trip. No one would know that she was there until spring, and by then all three of them would have learned something about winter in the Rockies.

13

DOROTHY FOUND the journey vastly different than by horse and mule train. As they entered the canyon, they found themselves flanked on either side by strange-shaped masses of bright red sandstone, outcropping from the surface, and in some places tilted nearly on end. The wagon, oddly enough, seemed to make much better time than the horses had along the banks of the St. Vrain River and in the curves and twists up through the foothills. Then it dawned on her that this was a far different route than before. Here the wagon climbed along grassy slopes, through pine forests, past fantastic masses of rock and across a little creek that she did not recall.

Indian summer had put on its finest dress for her. The aspen and poplars were clustered bouquets of reds and gold and russets. She was awed by the intense natural beauty that seemed to stretch on forever.

Then the wagon trip lost all its joy for the moment. It plunged down two violent descents, causing the leather brake shoe to smoke acridly against the iron rimmed wheels, suggesting ominously that at any moment the wagon would over run the team and careen into the canyon on its own. Then, after a short ascent, they entered a long valley rejoicing in tall, waving grass that had not as yet been nipped by frost.

"We may not be welcome," Folsom grunted, "but we'll camp the night near that sod hut. Dunraven calls the man a squatter, but he's been a trapper here in Muggins Gulch maybe longer than Griff Evans."

"Muggins Gulch," Dorothy laughed. "What an unfitting title. I don't know who it was named after, but I think he should have changed his name before bestowing it upon such a pretty spot."

It was almost a picture. A very pretty mare, hobbled, was feeding; a collie dog barked at them, and among the scrub was a rude sod cabin with smoke coming out of the roof and window. The mud roof was covered wtih lynx, beaver, and other furs laid out to dry, and beaver paws were pinned out on the logs. A deer carcass hung at one end of the cabin, a skinned beaver lay in front of the door, and antlers seemed to be everywhere.

Roused by the growling of the dog, a broad, thick-set man jumped through the door. He was of middle height, with an old cap on his head, and wearing a hunting suit that was nearly falling to pieces. It was a marvel how his clothing hung together, and on him. From the breast pocket of his coat a revolver was quickly drawn.

"Hold it right thar!" he ordered sternly.

Folsom pulled the team to a stop and called back.

"Jim Nugent, we are friends! I am David Folsom and this is Lady Dorothy Goold!"

He started to swear roughly at the growling dog, but with a lady present contented himself with kicking it, and coming toward the wagon he raised his cap.

"Not many call me that. 'Rocky Mountain Jim' or 'Mountain Jim' is more to my liking."

At that angle, Dorothy saw him only in an approaching profile. He was a strikingly handsome man of forty-five. He had large grey-blue eyes, deeply set, with well-marked eyebrows, an aquiline nose, and a very sensuous mouth. His face was clean shaven except for a dense moustache. Without the cap his tawny hair, in long uncared for curls, fell over his collar.

"Pleasure to have you stop. Is there something I might do for you?"

After being shocked by his initial hostility, Lady Dorothy was even more startled at the cultured tone his voice had suddenly taken on.

"Yes," Dorothy found herself saying, "I could certainly use a drink of water."

Rocky Mountain Jim grinned and turned to face her.

"You are not an American. I know from your voice that you are a country-woman of mine. English, right?"

Dorothy was in a momentary state of shock and

knew that she had to answer immediately or embarrass the man. One of his eyes was entirely gone, and the loss made one side of the face repulsive, while the other might have been modeled in marble.

"No, Irish," she stammered.

He scowled until the scarred side of his face had the look of a desperado.

"Lady? Any kin to that Earl fellow who has been here and about of late?"

Dorothy saw no reason to lie. "Lord Dunraven is my second cousin."

He studied her so carefully that David Folsom started to repent having made this stop. Then Mountain Jim grinned.

"That is so hard to believe. You are a lady from head to foot and he's such a little pip-squeak."

"I beg your pardon?"

"Well, just look at me. I lost my eye in an encounter with a grizzly bear, which, after giving me a death hug, tearing me all over, breaking my arm and scratching out my eye, left me for dead. Last summer I came across old Dunraven pinned down by a mountain lioness that was little more than a cub. He had shot her in the belly just before her jump and turned in a panic. She jumped his back and gave him a good bite to the rump. Didn't take much to finish off the little critter, but you would have thought his Lordship had been mauled worse than me. No more than a few scratches to his hindend but he took off for a doctor and civilization as fast as his party could get him down out of here."

Dorothy began to giggle and then laugh. She had all but forgotten what had brought the Earl back to Denver, but she did not have to guess that Lord Dunraven's version was quite different.

She was given her water in a battered tin, which he gracefully apologized over as not being more presentable. For them to camp nearby was unthinkable. He and Folsom would camp nearby and Lady Dorothy was to have his cabin. She thought the out of doors would be much more sanitary, but thought it best not to refuse his offer.

The cabin had been filled with smoke on purpose. He had been smoking a deer carcass for winter use, but was more than willing to share some of it "fresh" for dinner. From the same "smoke-house" he produced succulent ears of multicolored Indian corn and large slabs of a thick-skinned yellow squash.

Even David Folsom had to comment on the delicious dinner presented to them. After he left to unhitch the team and hobble them for the night, Dorothy and Mountain Jim entered into a conversation about the area. As he spoke she forgot about his appearance, for his manner was that of a chivalrous gentleman, his accent refined, and his language easy and elegant.

"I can see Lord Dunraven's desire," he answered her cautiously, "but question his motives. I fear that too many of his 'gentlemen' hunters will wind up shooting each other or else find themselves in the arms of a grizzly or a real mountain lion. Our game is not raised and stocked on the game preserves that I recall as a young man in England. Those were almost tame and these are still wild beasts that have seen very few men—red or white."

"I hate to see the land overrun by men of any color."

"Tell that to my old fried, Griff Evans," he said sourly. "He seems to be doing everything that your cousin commands of him. His old friends might just as well be offal in the barnyard. I hear tell, from this new man, MacGregor, that Griff has even sold out his land."

Dorothy chuckled. "That might have been an error on his part. I've got the three parcels directly north of him."

"Good on you!" Mountain Jim enthused. "Be like me! Muggin's Gulch is mine and they'll have to kill me to get me out of it!"

Folsom arrived back just in time to hear Mountain Jim's declaration.

"That sounds good in theory," he said, wanting to dampen any notion Dorothy may have gained. "But it's a whole new world we are facing. You've got to have proof of ownership."

"Who says I haven't?" he said on a shrug. "Got a written paper from George Hearst, who pastured his cattle in this meadowland gulch about the time Joel Estes and his son came through with a two wheeled cart. Don't know why and don't rightly care, but he used the alias Muggins."

Dorothy took heart. Here was one more man who would not easily give up his land to Lord Dunraven. Now she didn't see the scarred side of his face at all.

But the cabin reminded her of the dinner and his tattered clothing. She was thankful that Folsom had along an extra blanket, for there were none on the pine-bough bed, and the smokey interior nearly choked her. But when she began to feel, or imagined that she felt, all manner of creepy-crawlers traveling up and down her body, she could not stand his bed for an entire night. She stood, wrapped in the blanket, until she could be sure that both men were fast asleep, and then she went to curl up among the scattered antlers.

She awoke warm and comfortable, a heavy bear skin rug having been placed over her sometime during the night. A basin of water and a remarkably clean towel had been placed on the ground near her resting place. From the cabin filtered a rich baritone voice singing an old English ballad. She got up to view a fantasy land. Hoar frost and a rising mist turned the entire gulch to silver. Low hanging clouds made the surrounding mountains appear as flat-topped mesas.

She rose, shivering against the cold, and although Mountain Jim had placed the basin near her but a short time before, she had to break away a thin crusting of ice to get to the water. It was frigid to the touch and made her gasp as she splashed it on her face. But it was remarkably refreshing. She could feel her skin tighten and glow as she rubbed it dry with the towel. She was famished, which surprised her as she was normally never hungry for food.

But David was anxious to get under way and almost rudely accepted only cold tack and biscuits from Mountain Jim to eat upon the way. The mountain-man hardly noticed the rebuff, for he was too busy courteously helping Dorothy up to the wagon.

"I hope you will allow me the pleasure of calling on you."

Dorothy nodded her agreement and David reined the horses forward so suddenly that it nearly whip-lashed her neck. He was seriously silent until they were about a mile up the meadowland.

"They tell me," he said sourly, "that when he's sober, Jim's a perfect gentleman; but when he's had liquor he's the most awful ruffian in Colorado."

Dorothy remained silent. She would reserve her judgment until she knew from her own experience; one way or another. She was through with letting other people make up her mind for her.

The morning sun burnt off the mist like a rising curtain. The wagon rolled to a summit which before starting its 1,500 foot drop, afforded them an awe-inspiring view. Below, in the glory of the rising sun, was the irregular basin, lighted by the bright waters of the rushing Thompson and guarded by the sentinel mountains of fantastic shape and monstrous size. Long's Peak rose above it all in unapproachable grandeur, while the Never Summer Range, with its outlying spurs heavily timbered, came down upon the valley slashed by great canyons lying deep in purple expectancy of the coming light. As they began their ascent the sun rose to turn the rushing river waters blood red, Long's Peak to a burning flame, and bring life to the purple canyons with their painter's splash of fall coloring. Never, in all her life, had Dorothy seen anything to equal that view.

The mountain fever seized her, and, although reluctant to give up all ties with her past, she suddenly knew that she was home. This enchanted region was just as much hers as it was Lord Dunraven's.

Now they switched to a trail that was familiar to her. Sites and names came flooding back. To the right was Mount Olympus—a name she felt was a little too grand for such a minor pile of granite. Then the wagon was out on the smooth sward of the valley. To the right was a swirl of smoke from the Evans ranch—a place she had no desire to visit at the moment—although her heart tugged to ride beyond it and say hello to Jim McLaughlin. Then, traversing a small rise, they came suddenly upon a small lake, close to which was a very trim-looking log cabin with a flat mud roof. Nearby were the beginnings of a barn and corral, and between the buildings a man on horseback was bringing in two cows to be milked. It did not register in Dorothy's mind what she was seeing until a lean, young figure came out the cabin door, shielded his eyes against the sun and let out a whoop that echoed over the valley.

There was no longer any question in her mind, or that of David, who was racing toward them across the pastureland. With the wagon still moving, she jumped down and started to race just as wildly.

This is what she had expected in Ireland. The uplifting feeling of being greeted with unrestrained enthusiasm by someone she loved and admired. Her heart swelled as Lloyd grasped her about the waist and swung her around and around in the air. Their laughter mixed like a musical duet.

The commotion brought Fred on the run from his milking chores. He was about ready to join the merriment when he spotted his step-brother on the wagon and his face fell.

During the last few months of his emancipation from David Folsom, he had indulged in his true inclinations toward self-assurance and resourcefulness. He had dressed casually and comfortably, had let his light brown hair grow longer and now sported a chestnut fringe of whiskers on his chin. Lloyd thought the change made his uncle look devilishly handsome.

David thought it made him look utterly silly and openly said as much. Although he had vowed to hold his tongue upon this trip, within five minutes his old arrogance and dictatorial mannerisms had everyone on edge.

Upon entering the good-sized log cabin he uttered a vulgar word of disgust. He cleared his throat loudly, stamped vigorously on the boarded floor, as if he expected it to immediately collapse, and glared at the rough stone fireplace as though commanding it to fall in a heap.

"Well, now, if this isn't charming!" Dorothy exclaimed, her face glowing with happiness. The round tabletop had been made from a center cut of a log, its legs with natural drift wood; the two rockers had been painted bright colors and a backwoods couch had been covered with a bear skin.

Fred regarded Dorothy with affection. "We are trying to make it into a home."

Home, Dorothy thought. The sweetest word in the world. Now, more than ever, she wanted a home just like this. It may not be the Castle Adare, she admitted, but it was clean, comfortable and weather-tight.

"Mighty small for a home," David criticized. "How can you accommodate all four of us with only one bedroom?"

Fred, falling back under his step-brother's rule, could still remember the amenities of society. "Oh, David," he stammered, his color rising, "we couldn't have Lady Dorothy stay with us. I'll just have to see if she can't visit with the MacGregor or James family, where there are ladies present."

"Very agreeable of you," he said with a quizzical smile. With Dorothy gone he could be more forthright with the two men.

"I hope it is agreeable to Lady Dorothy. How long will your visit be?"

"That I cannot judge, Mr. Austin. I had hoped to hire some help to start my own cabin."

Lloyd rocked the rafters with his joyous hoot. "You can count on me!"

"And there are others who will be helpful," Fred said timidly, not wishing to impose himself too quickly.

"And we have room to store your things until you are ready for them," Lloyd enthused.

"Well," Dorothy smiled, "I seem to be in most capable hands."

David Folsom turned suddenly gallant and helpful. He offered the services of the wagon to Fred and helped unload Dorothy's trunks and crates. She was amazed that she had accumulated so much since coming to Denver. To Lloyd's chagrin his father would not let him drive the wagon or go along. He wanted to reason with the boy privately.

Fred Austin was also glad to have a private moment with Dorothy. They bounced over an ill defined tract toward the Black Canyon for some time before he gathered the courage to speak, and then with quiet determination.

"Well, Lady Dorothy, what brought you to this decision? Remember, I know my step-brother very well. His arrival with you is somewhat of a shock."

Dorothy was silent for a long moment, then very slowly she related all that had been transpiring.

"I have no intention of selling," he said coldly. But he was both puzzled and interested in what his contemptible step-brother might have in mind.

Dorothy let out a gasp as they came over a rise. Below the rock outcropping that looked like perched twin owls a miracle had taken place in a very short time. A few acres of lush fields of grain were being harvested, a figure could be seen working in a vegetable garden less than a hundred feet from a lath and plaster house—with real windows—and there were no less than two barns and a corral.

Fred chuckled softly. "It only shows what a little money and a few hired hands can do. MacGregor not only got himself a pretty wife but a mother-in-law who sold out in Wisconsin and brought her money with her."

"Are they aware of the Earl?"

"Everyone, in one way or another, is aware of him, but MacGregor is a very quiet man who values his privacy and freedom."

The figure raised from its garden work and started toward them. Dorothy could now see that it was a woman. But she amended her thought a moment later. It was a short, cherub-faced girl who came running up to them with a radiant smile.

"Welcome, Mr. Austin," she called gleefully, "I see that you— Oh, excuse me."

"Mrs. MacGregor, this is Dorothy Goold."

Dorothy shot him a smile of gratitude in leaving off the title and jumped down from the wagon.

"I'm happy to meet you," Dorothy said happily.

"I'm Clara," she said just as cheerfully, taking Dorothy's hand and pumping it vigorously. "In the noon sun I thought you might be my mother returning. She has been in Denver shopping and Mr.

MacGregor was going down to the valley tomorrow to fetch her, but my mother is a very strong-willed woman and might just as soon take off with the first wagon or horse coming this way."

"Then I might have saved your husband a trip. Some Indian trouble has caused a temporary shut-down on the Cheyenne-Denver railroad line."

Clara Heeney MacGregor grinned broadly. "Then that shall please them both. My husband hates being taken away from his work and mother is an avid shopper."

"Mrs. MacGregor," Fred asked timidly, "we were wondering if you might be able to put Miss Goold up for awhile? She has claims and my nephew and I will start her cabin right away."

"How marvelous!" Clara enthused. "What fun to have a woman nearer my own age about. I shall have to discuss the matter with Mr. MacGregor, of course, but I have yet to have him say no to me. Take her luggage on up to the house, Mr. Austin. Dorothy and I will walk along after you and get acquainted."

It was the immediate blooming of a friendship. Dorothy soon came to learn why the young woman was such a constant chatter-box. She was starved for conversation. Although there was a love-light in his eyes for his bride, the thin and handsome A.Q. MacGregor was a man of very few words. He nodded his agreement to Clara's request and went back to oversee his three ranch hands.

She did not see him again until dinner time, but around Clara it had seemed but five minutes. The young woman was an accomplished artist and the walls were covered with her paintings. Having made the trip herself, Dorothy marvelled at the furnishings that had been brought all the way from Wisconsin and then up the trail-less way from Longmont. There were lace curtains at every window, carpets on the hardwood floors, splendid brass beds in all three bedrooms, and an indoor pump and sink took up one wall of the sparkling kitchen.

"Mr. MacGregor chides me for using my painter's hands," she chatted on as they cleaned the vegetables she had picked from her garden, "but this is my home now and it should be self-sustaining."

"I love gardening work, as well."

"Then you may help me while you are here. Feeding four hungry men three times a day gets to be quite a chore. Of course, Mr. MacGregor says we won't keep the men on much after the first snowfall."

Dorothy laughed. "I'm afraid I am not much of a cook."

"Then I shall teach you. Mr. MacGregor says that my cooking almost equals my painting. But I think he is much happier with the menu when my mother is at the range."

Dorothy didn't see how the food could have been any better, and she could see that the hired hands seemed to agree. Scrubbed clean of the field dust and dirt they filed up to the back door and presented her with a tin plate and cup. She heaped them until they were almost overflowing and accepted their thanks with a winning smile.

But it was hardly tin service for their own dinner. At first Dorothy thought the lace table cloth, linen napkins, bone china, and Mr. MacGregor's suit were in her honor. His table grace put her straight on that score at once.

"Our Father, we thank you for another beautiful day in your country. Bless this house, and this guest who shares our daily table with us. Amen."

Not another word was said throughout the meal. Nor by A.Q. MacGregor until the dishes were washed up and Clara had entertained them with a couple of songs. She had an excellent soprano voice. Light and bird-like.

"Mr. MacGregor has promised me a piano, as soon as it is feasible to bring one up from the valley."

"Now, Clara," he gently chided, "I said as soon as I found one at the right price."

Dorothy looked at him in some surprise, but not over the comment. His voice had been low and gruff during the prayer, and now it was tinged with a soft highland burr.

"Or which ever comes first?" Clara kidded back.

He rewarded her with a smile that was full of love and softened his face to gentleness. Then, he turned to Dorothy.

"If I am blunt, forgive me, Miss Goold. But it seem a bit unusual for a single woman to come pioneering."

"You are not being blunt, at all, Mr. MacGregor. I'll be most honest. I am Lord Dunraven's second cousin."

MacGregor studied her curiously. "Then you would be the young lady that James McLaughlin speaks so highly of."

Dorothy flushed. "I am grateful to hear that he speaks so of me, Mr. MacGregor."

Alexander MacGregor relaxed back in his chair. Having pinpointed exactly who she was, he felt better about his wife associating with her, even though she was a woman of a higher class than themselves. But he was still curious.

"Your cousin seems to have set quite a goal for himself."

"Honestly speaking, Mr. MacGregor, I've come to look upon his actions as overly ambitious and greedy. You no doubt have been approached to sell your land."

"Not as yet, although McLaughlin has warned me of what is transpiring in Denver."

"That was months ago," replied Dorothy. "It's practically all in his hands now."

"Not my lands," commented MacGregor, lightly.

Dorothy shook her head. "Don't be so sure of that, sir. It is my understanding that they recorded the claims in such a haphazard manner that on some they have two and three filings."

"That is an interesting piece of news, Miss Goold. I have been so busy bringing about this first claim that I have not as yet set boundary lines on the rest. As yet there has been no need. What few families are here are as close knit as one."

"Except for one," Clara said snidely. It was the first time Dorothy had heard her use such a tone and it surprised her.

"Now, Clara," he soothed, "we don't want to give Miss Goold the wrong impression right off the bat."

"Still, Mr. MacGregor," she insisted, "I think Dorothy should be warned about those people and that impossible cowboy they have working for them."

Her insistence seemed to embarrass MacGregor.

"Please, Clara," Dorothy said softly, "your husband need not inform me of anything. I believe you are speaking of Mr. Evans and Mr. Paul Ely."

"My," Clara gasped, "you either learn fast or Mr. Austin informed you of their ways."

"I'm afraid," Dorothy sighed, "that my knowledge of Mr. Ely goes back some time."

"Oh, my," Clara gasped anew, crossing her hands over her breasts. "What a fool I have just made of myself. Your tone tells me that you are in love with the man."

Before Dorothy could react, MacGregor chuckled.

"Forgive my wife, Miss Goold, she's a born romantic."

"There is nothing to forgive," Dorothy whispered. "He is the reason that I came west with my cousin and his wife. But that is over and forgotten."

Her nemesis more than likely, thought Clara, with some grimness. As a woman it greatly troubled her. In her opinion they were greatly ill-suited for each other. She looked at Dorothy with simple and dignified despair.

"Well," she blurted right out, "I'm most glad it is over and forgotten. The man has a tongue that is more suited for hell."

"Clara!" MacGregor warned darkly.

"No, husband, I will have my say on this matter. It was my ears that were offended, as well as your own. Hired hand or no, he has no right to tell you that you can't bring more cattle into this region."

"Clara, he is only repeating what Griff Evans tells him to repeat."

"Excuse me for correcting you, Mr. MacGregor, but I think the situation has been reversed. Lord

Dunraven has bought all the cattle and range, except that of Jim McLaughlin. Mr. Ely is now in charge of them."

MacGregor nodded gravely. "Thank you, Miss Goold. That answers many questions that have been on my mind. Well, we are a farm family and usually tucked in by now. Clara, will you light Miss Goold's way to Mother Heeney's room?"

Like a schoolgirl, Clara was itching to get Dorothy alone.

"Are you sure that it is over?" she whispered.

"No," Dorothy said honestly. "Is any woman sure when her first love is no more?"

"Mine were only puppy love until I met Mr. MacGregor . . . and I wasn't sure even then."

"But you are very sure now?"

"Oh, my heaven's, yes," she giggled. "He has become everything that I always dreamed the man I would marry would be like."

"I never really had such dreams before coming to America, Clara. I just knew that my mother would pick out the proper man to fit into our social and financial world."

"Then it's secret time," Clara giggled again. "I hardly took a second look at Mr. MacGregor upon meeting him. It was my mother who worked behind the scene to bring us together and make me see that he was a man among men. So, we are not too different on that score. Things will work out for you. I am so glad that you are here. Goodnight, my dear."

Dorothy thought all of that conversation would keep her brain buzzing for hours. But she was almost asleep the moment she started sinking into the thick feather-bed mattress. Her last thought was a reassuring one. On this ranch was the strongest man of all to stand up against the Earl. And not once did Paul Ely cross her thoughts.

But Dorothy was very much on Paul Ely's mind that night. He had seen her come riding into the basin with David Folsom and it puzzled him. His puzzlement grew the next day when he saw Folsom ride off without her, apparently in a black rage.

Ely had no use for Fred Austin or Lloyd Folsom, but when he saw them looking about the land on the other side of the lake from the Evan's place—which he now referred to as the Dunraven Ranch—he casually rode over to see what they were about.

He came back more puzzled than ever. They had been most courteous and friendly and short on information. All he had gained was that they were looking for a proper homesite for Dorothy. His mind being what it was, he automatically assumed that she was sharing the two men's cabin. He stewed on the matter for a week and still didn't see a sign of Dorothy. But he saw many others across the lake that week. MacGregor and McLaughlin spread the word and the other men in the valley would come and work when they could be spared from their own chores.

Finally, Paul Ely felt he needed instructions on the matter. He sent a grumbling Griff Evans off for Denver. Because the train was still not running, it took him four days to reach Denver, ten days of waiting for the Earl to return from the sawmill and four days back.

His eyes bulged as he rode down into the basin

with part of the Earl's answer. Not one, but two log cabins had been built across the lake, connected by a breezeway. A corral was up and a small barn almost completed.

"How in the hell did that get built so fast?" he demanded of Ely.

Ely ignored the question and stared at the six men who had ridden in with Evans. He had never seen such an ugly, despicable and heavily-armed group of men in his life.

"Who in the hell are they?"

"Your new range riders—or whatever. Whyte hired them and Dunraven paid them for four months. Letter explains it," he said.

The letter explained little in Paul Ely's estimation. Dunraven was up to his old tricks again. Ely was supposed to woo Dorothy away from the "squatters" so that she couldn't create more trouble, but there were no suggestions as to how this might be brought about. The majority of the letter dealt with David Folsom. If the lumber was being delivered on schedule, which it was, he was to be left quite alone. Dunraven had been unable to find another carter and was stuck with Folsom until spring. No mention was made of what work was expected of the six desperados—four more than Paul could really use effectively. And his instructions as to the settlers was curt: "Do something about it!"

This was as puzzling as the wooing of Dorothy or her need for two log cabins.

The second cabin had come about at the suggestion of Clara MacGregor as she was teaching Dorothy to can the garden vegetables.

"Don't think me rude, Dorothy," she said, "but it might be a long, idle winter for you. You don't sew, knit or quilt. But you do have a gift and a remarkable mind. I have no children, although I want them as soon as God is willing, but three other families do have children of learning age. You've got your books and your ability to pass your knowledge on."

"But where would I teach?"

"Why, right at home," she exclaimed, as though she had given the matter deep thought. "Before the men are finished, I can't see why they can't build you a second structure, a warm fireplace and some little desks."

"But it seems so far away."

It was the first time Dorothy had expressed an opinion that had been growing in her mind since seeing the first logs of her cabin put into place. The Evan's place would be her nearest neighbors and she had seen no one from there since her arrival. She was going to be so far away from Clara, whom she had come to love and admire.

"Nonsense," Clara scolded. "I walked five miles to school in Wisconsin, and I anticipate winter to be much milder here. Shall I put a small word in Mr. MacGregor's ear?"

"Yes, you do that."

Dorothy still wasn't sure, however.

Dorothy didn't know how the time slipped by so quickly. By mid-November it was time for her house-warming. She called it her "Queen Anne mansion," although it was made of big, rough-hewn logs, chinked with mud and lime. The roof had been built of barked young spruce, layered with hay and an outer coating of mud. The sixteen foot living room had a rough stone fireplace and chimney. John Hupp had made sure that the floor boards were as tight and flat as those in the MacGregor house. Mr. James gave up an extra brass bed for her small bedroom as well as making her an eating table. Mr. Ferguson, a "grasshopper escapee" from a farm near Greeley had brought along two cook ranges and polished one to a bright new finish with lamp black. Clara and the other women had secretly made curtains and quilted blankets for her bed. Fred Austin had only had to dig down ten feet to sink her a well for pump water. Lloyd stacked the outside walls of each cabin with enough split pine to supply each fireplace for several winters.

And as if that wasn't enough, throughout that day every family came by with a piece of furniture "that just seemed too crowded in their own cabins," and a jar of this and tin of that to stock her larder. Jim McLaughlin had slaughtered a yearling and smoked half of it to hang in her barn.

Tears brimmed her eyes the entire day and she fought to keep them from overflowing. It was just like home. The tenant farmers helping each other to survive just like one big family. Here was the love that she had been craving without really knowing it. These were her people and not the ones on Brown's Bluff. Now she could really write her mother of something important happening in her small world. Then her mind boggled.

"Clara, something has just dawned on me. How does one post mail from here?"

"Interesting," she mused. "When Mr. MacGregor goes to fetch mother in Longmont I shall raise the point with her. Her father served as a postmaster for a time in Wisconsin and she should know how we can go about having a post office."

Dorothy laughed to herself. Clara MacGregor probably had the answer right in her mind at that very moment, but she always let her husband or mother have first crack at a problem and then amended it to suit her own highly intellectual mind.

To the disgust of some, but to Dorothy's great delight, the next guest upon the scene was Mountain Jim. The disgust vanished when everyone learned that he had bathed before making the four mile ride to her cabin. To lessen their disgust even more he was unusually sober, witty and charming. It took four men to carry in the black, brown and grizzly bear rugs that he had tanned for her floors. Dorothy was too stunned to see the love light that gleamed from his one good eye—but not Clara MacGregor.

"Not that I'm matchmaking, Dorothy Goold, but the hearts that are on fire over you in this room could start the forest afire or another civil war."

"Clara, whatever are you talking about?"

"I wish I had my mother's gift and then I could make you see straight. That shy Jim McLaughlin looks at you as though he's afraid you'll vanish in a puff of smoke, and I'm too much of a lady to tell you what is in James Nugent's good eye. Of course, Lloyd Folsom adores you highly, but he's still a boy. But his uncle? That's the man for you, and mark my words."

"And you just keep your words out of it, Clara MacGregor. I'm in no mind for matrimony."

"It doesn't take mind, just a little prodding."

"Clara, I'm warning you!"

Clara erupted with her musical little giggle and went sailing back to the other guests. Dorothy felt confident that she would say nothing on that score without first consulting Mr. MacGregor or her mother. Lord, how she was coming to love that woman as a dear friend.

And then she slyly took a long look at the four men, for Lloyd could hardly be called a boy any longer. But love? They were all such dear friends, and she had not thought of them as anything else.

But the thought came to her again as she was saying goodbye to each of her guests and thanking them. These four seemed most reluctant to leave her alone, just as she had once been reluctant to be without Paul Ely. Why did the wrong people always have to fall in love with the wrong people at all the wrong times, she couldn't help but wonder. Mountain Jim would have sent her mother right up the wall, as would Lloyd for being too young. And of the other two, although they might be quite acceptable to her mother, Dorothy knew the drawbacks. She could not be a Clara MacGregor—subservient at all times although she was a powerful and highly intellectual woman. She could not do that to herself or to the man.

But then she had to laugh to herself. Of all the men in her life so far Lord Dunraven was the only one to give her mental challenge—and she wouldn't have him on a bet. And as she had told her heart a thousand times, she would not have Paul Ely, either.

Dorothy was still cleaning up the party mess when there was a timid knock at the door. It was still early, although Dorothy was surprised to see that it was already pitch black outside. In the MacGregor house she had risen and retired with the sun, no matter the hour.

"Yes," she said hesitantly, at first not recognizing the small, shawled figure at her door. Then she brightened. "Why, you're Martha Evans. Do come in."

The little woman scurried through the door as though the very devil were on her tail.

"Thank you for remembering me," she panted, as though she had run all the way around the lake. "I didn't want to disturb until your own guests were gone, but I felt a welcome was due you from our side of the lake." From beneath her shawl she produced two glass jars. "This is my own meat relish made from cabbage and dill herb. Enjoy!"

Dorothy felt small and guilty, even though she had done none of the inviting.

"How very sweet and thoughtful of you, Martha. I shall enjoy it. Please sit a spell and have some tea with me. The kettle is almost ready."

Her bird-like eyes measured the door as though it would burst open at any moment and then she smiled weakly. "Reckon I can do that. Ain't got much time to sit and sip a cup without gulpin' it."

That made Dorothy feel even guiltier. She prepared a plate of the left-over cake and cookies and poured the water in a pot to steep.

"Right nice the way you have it fixed up."

"Thank you, Martha, but it's really the work of all the others."

Dorothy wished she had the words back just as soon as they were said. The other women had not been mean or nasty in excluding Martha. They knew her to be a most industrious woman, but with little time to call her own. Five children now and a husband who worked her like a slave and treated her like a squaw gave her hardly time to sleep.

Martha knitted her thick black brows together and stared out the window at the blackness with gloomy anxiety.

"I suppose the other cabin is right nice too."

"It's coming right along. The bookshelves are completed and my books placed. I thought I had tons of them, but they look rather lost in all the shelves that Lloyd Folsom put up. Thank goodness he had enough lumber left to make table-desks and benches."

"Will it be expensive?"

"What?"

Martha gulped out the words. "Your school?"

"Charging has never crossed my mind and how could I charge after all they have done for me?"

"You'd have to be charging us," Martha said, with that disconcerting bluntness of hers. "We ain't done a thing to help you here, although can't recall being asked, either."

"Martha, I think they all realized how busy you are."

"And that Griff wouldn't have helped anyway," murmured Martha, satirically. "Leastways till he got permission from one of his lordships."

Dorothy ignored this. "Well, I can't see charging you if I'm not charging the others. Besides, I'm not a real school teacher and can only give them what knowledge I do have."

"Got more'n me. Didn't have no school out in my country. I was thirteen when Mr. Evans came along. He was a splendid shot, an expert and successful hunter, a bold mountaineer, a good rider, and a generally jolly fellow. For I knew it along came Marymae. She'll be sixteen come Christmas time. The younger four are a ripe age for education, but it's Marymae who worries me. Don't want her life ending up like mine."

"I wasn't aware you had a daughter of that age."

"Others are aware," she said sadly. "Those so-called ranch hands that Mr. Ely has working for him look at her as though they've never seen a girl with budding breasts before. I had Marymae before Mr. Evans would marry me and I'll not have her go through the same."

Dorothy had heard about the ranch hands from Mr. MacGregor and couldn't agree with Martha more. They sounded just like the derelicts and bums who had worked the land fraud and the thought of them disgusted her.

"I don't know when I will start having the children come, but you send Marymae over just any time. As the oldest one, maybe she should have a head start on the others."

Martha brightened. "And I'll be paying for it, what I can scrape together. Thought we'd be better off selling to Lord Dunraven, but poor Griff loves liquor too well for his prosperity. Well, that may all change when he starts paying us for the land and a salary."

Dorothy, though shrewdly doubting that her husband had told her the complete truth about the sale, nevertheless recognized a truth that Martha was not uttering.

"I gather that you would rather not have Mr. Evans know that the children are getting an education from me."

Martha regarded her in brooding and violent

silence. Her face had flushed. Then she averted her eyes.

"I do love my man," she muttered. "Even though he caters to Mr. Ely's every little wish. If Griff weren't dead drunk and Ely off somewhere with his henchmen, I wouldn't have dared come sneaking over here. Griff doesn't realize how wrong and bad this is for the children. It's not fair that they can't associate with any of the other children. They've been alone up here for so long that I thought it was going to be right nice for them to have neighbors and friends. They're lonelier now than before. Ain't good for the boys to associate with them rough men, neither. But Mr. Ely tells the children not to worry, that all these people will be moved out by spring and they will meet a whole lot of new people when Lord Dunraven gets his hunting lodge built. But that will only be the summertime. Winter will be just as lonely as ever." She dropped her eyelids. Dorothy saw the thick hot tears that threatened to run over her cheeks.

The others had given her many material things, but Martha Evans had given her a grain of truth that was far more important. It had miffed her at first that Paul Ely had not even ridden by the MacGregor ranch to say hello. There was no doubt left in her mind now that he was avoiding her because the Earl had learned that she had not returned to Ireland. But the biggest gem of all was Paul Ely's declaration to the children that all the settlers would be gone by spring. She wondered exactly how he proposed to bring that about.

John Hupp heard an odd splashing sound. Although his cabin was near the bank of Fall River, this was not its soothing roar over the bed rocks. As a matter of fact, he couldn't hear its roar at all—just the splashing, like waves against a wharf. He stepped from his bed and right into calf deep water. Just then the cabin tilted and began to move with a rending screech.

"Everybody up!" he shouted at his wife and children. "Get over to the door quickly!"

It seemed an utter impossibility to him that the river could be flooding in November. He had anticipated that such could happen in the spring and so had built his cabin off the ground on three foot pilings. But the flood had torn the cabin away from the pilings and was floating it along like a badly leaking ark. The water was nearly to his knees by the time he had struggled the door open.

Without was nothing but black swirling water. The moonless night was not helping him to ascertain the flood's depth or how distant the bank would now be. His innermost fear he kept to himself. If they were carried to where the river converged with the Thompson, then the force of the two combined would sweep them down into the narrow, rocky canyon and smash them to their deaths.

Out of the gloom he saw the ragged face of a cliff come so perilously close that he shouted anew:

"Brace yourselves!"

The crunching crash was bone jarring. The cabin wheeled about as though trying to free itself and fight for its life. It bounced off the cliff and with the scream of wood tearing at wood lodged firmly between two sturdy pines.

John Hupp waited, his knees nearly turned to jelly. The cliff was but twenty to thirty feet away, but how dangerous was the water and how long would the tree roots stand up against the erosion that had to be taking place at their base?

Cautiously, he stepped out of the door and let himself down into the water. The cabin was making a natural barrier and forcing the more violent current off to the right. His feet hit solid ground when he was only waist high and there was little movement about his bare feet. At any other time he might have made the trip over and back to test the safety of the entire journey, but the fear of the cabin being torn away with his family ruled that out.

"Let me help you down," he shouted to his wife, "and then we'll each carry a child."

Her eyes saucered with fright, she immediately did as instructed. To their thankful surprise, neither the young boy or girl whimpered or cried. They crawled into their parents' outstretched arms and silently snuggled their heads down between their parents' necks and shaking shoulders.

With his free arm about his wife's waist, John Hupp felt his way along one small step at a time. Unseen rocks were bruising and cutting his feet, but he felt none of it—the freezing water had already numbed his legs to stumps and he was sure it had done the same to his wife. He was thankful though that the current was not overpowering.

The cliff was not too high, but rugged with many overhanging outcroppings. He set his son down on a rock ledge and gently commanded:

"Climb!"

Like a little mountain goat the boy scrambled up to the top with his little sister in hot pursuit. It took longer for John to help his wife up to safety, but by the time they had joined their children his eyes had adjusted to the dark night. Mountains and valleys were faintly discernible. He looked back west, toward the solid, towering mass of granite that looked like an old man standing all alone. The river had widened itself from its tree studded base to the opposite rise of mountains. But when he looked down the cliff into the little valley where the rivers converged he was faced with another seeming impossibility. The Thompson River was still flowing at a low level between its four foot banks. It was a total puzzlement to him.

"I know it's going to be hard on our feet, but moving is going to be better than standing here freezing. If we go down this hill, it will only be a mile up Black Canyon Creek to the MacGregor place."

"But what if it's flooded, too, Daddy?" his son asked, a note of fear creeping into his thin young voice for the first time.

John Hupp laughed, as though he had just heard a marvelous new joke. "Then we'll all stand along the bank and wave to A.Q. as he goes floating by. Now, I think we need a song to march us along. Let's do 'D'ye ken John Peel' so that Scotsman will hear us coming and be up to greet us."

He kept them singing and laughing the whole way and never once was a single word said about the battering that their feet took.

By an hour after dawn the river was running normally within its own banks and the meadowland was a marshy lake. There had been no unusual storm during the night and A.Q. and John rode up the river course to determine the flood cause. In the beaver pond valley beyond Deer Mountain the cause was quite obvious—a half dozen of the beaver pond dams had been broken open during the night. No one needed to ask who might do such a thing.

"They might have killed my whole family," Hupp roared. "They're the ones who ought to be run out."

"We have no evidence, John," MacGregor said sadly. "Come on, we'll get a team and logs and see if we can't roll your cabin back to its site."

"Let it stand! It's firmer between the trees than on the pilings. I'll just make that my new site."

"Is it within your boundary lines?"

"Who gives a damn! They flooded me out of my old site, so let them fight me over this new one."

In upcoming days the matter was only whispered about.

Dorothy decided it was time she approached Paul Ely. On the new horse that MacGregor had purchased for her she rode to the area above the Evans ranch where a cabin and bunkhouse had been built.

A few of the filthy, bearded ranch hands sat casually outside the bunkhouse. Paul Ely stood in the door of the cabin watching her approach with curious wonderment.

A muffled scream came from the interior of the bunkhouse just as Dorothy jumped from the side-saddle. The bunkhouse door came flying open and a young girl tried to make her escape. One of the seated ranch hands stuck out a booted foot and the girl cascaded over it and went sprawling in the dirt. With ribald laughter two additional men came from the bunkhouse, grasped her by both arms, lifted her high and swung her back toward the bunkhouse door. No one, not even Paul Ely, made a move to stop them. The girl began to whimper and cry.

Dorothy looked from the scene to Paul Ely. He stood serene and smiling. Her thought were clamoring. She was sick with the knowledge of who the girl might be and what was about to transpire. She ran to Paul.

"You are a filthy beast, Paul," she said. "A foul and filthy minded man. Make them release that girl!"

Her voice was muffled, thick and confused. She struck her clenched fists repeatedly on his chest. He grabbed her wrists firmly, his face alight with malicious mirth.

"She came here of her own accord. Are you jealous because she is going to get what you haven't been getting?"

"She's only a child!" bellowed Dorothy.

"What can I do?" he asked, with honey-sweetness.

"Do? They are your hired hands! If they follow your directions to cause a flood for your evil little plot, then they should follow your directions in letting her go."

The bunkhouse door slammed shut and the girl's screams became muffled again.

"What plot?" he sneered innocently.

Their eyes locked together in a hideous fixity. Then, very slowly, Dorothy smiled. It was as cold and icy as death.

"The game gets a little serious, Paul, when four people are almost killed and you stand idly by and listen to a sixteen year old girl be manhandled by these vultures. I really can't understand you, Paul. I thought I had fallen in love with a decent and honest man. And here you are, all mean and putting other people's lives in jeopardy. You go against me, for something I can't understand. What have I done, except to love you and offer to be your wife? You know very well how things would be, under certain other circumstances—"

Ely was silent. But his glittering light blue eyes were held by Dorothy's in a kind of horrid and frightening appraisal. He smiled internally. How weak every one was, except himself! How stupid was the Earl's order for him to woo her. He knew that she would come running to him sooner or later. How confused and contemptible she was. What they might have accomplished together if she had stayed in the good graces of the Earl and out of his bed. Now he could go ahead with the Earl's plan because he had something that she wanted.

"Things could be the same between us again," he said softly.

"Oh, Paul, don't be blind. How can that be with all that is going on around here?"

"I didn't hire these men and I didn't bring them up here, Dorothy. If you've ever believed me before, believe in that." He hesitated as though on a sigh. Because it was the truth, up to a point, his voice resounded with honesty.

Hearing the tone, she cringed internally, and her vital organs felt squeezed to the suffocation point. How long could she go on believing him?

"I will grant you that, Paul. But even if these are Griff Evans' men, and that is Griff Evans' daughter, does that make you any less of a man to do something about it?"

His eyes did not drop away from her steadfast regard. Their brownness took on a molten golden quality. To his mind her words meant the letting down of the gate once more, and he felt a sensual desire for her like he had never experienced before. Oh, yes, he would woo her, but for his own benefit and not that of the Earl of Dunraven. He could make them both happy, without the other knowing. He felt like playing games with her again.

"Hanson!" he barked. "Tell them to let Marymae go!"

Scowling deeply, an older cowboy reluctantly entered the bunkhouse to carry out the order.

A young ranch hand, hardly older than Marymae herself, immediately filled the door frame and started to shout out his protest. Bootless and pantless he spotted Dorothy and turned a brilliant scarlet. He quickly covered his nudity with his hands and darted back into the shadows.

A second later the frightened girl came charging out, frantically clutching her torn bodice about her breasts. Without seeming to let her eyes stray from the ground she headed directly down through the woods to the Evans ranch.

"Thank you," Dorothy sighed, praying Paul had stopped it in time. From the reaction of the young cowboy she had not seen before, she thought her prayer would be answered.

"Does that put us back on a different footing?" he asked, grinning.

She drew a deep breath into lungs that felt aflame. Could she afford to open the wound anew? Why, with all the men in the world, did her heart have to love this one? If she were clever enough, in the future, she could avoid the mistakes they had male before, but could she trust him?

"I–I suppose it does," she stammered.

Ely laughed, merrily, with a sound of triumph. "This time we don't listen to anyone but ourselves. May I call on you this evening so that we may straighten out all of our differences?"

Dorothy nodded meekly. Now she knew that she was soft, a weakling. She had no steel when it came to this man. Only love. She wished, vehemently, that she had not come there that day. But wouldn't another day like this have come, sooner or later?

"Why don't you come for supper, Paul," she heard herself saying, in a voice she hardly recognized as her own. "It gets dark so early, so you better come around five."

He released her wrists. She had all but forgotten that he had been holding them. She didn't feel the hurt in them. She didn't feel the hurt in her heart. And she hated herself for her lack of control. He guided her back to the horse and lifted her to the side saddle.

"Five, it is."

She was suddenly exhausted and gave the horse its head. She dared not think or logic would command that she immediately cancel the invitation. She had no strength to fight logic.

She still wasn't thinking when she got home. It was warm in the cabin, fresh logs were blazing in the fireplace. A figure raised from the hearth and hurled itself at her, almost knocking them down. Dorothy cradled the frail little form in her arms.

"I–I couldn't go home . . ." Marymae began to wail. "My Maw would wup me."

"Now, now," Dorothy soothed. "I think she would understand."

Dorothy felt her stiffen. "Not when I supposed to have been here all morning."

"I see," Dorothy whispered, quizzically. "Then why did you go there?"

Marymae glanced up, her face streaked with tears, and saw compassion in the face of the woman who had come to her rescue.

"Weren't the first time I been up there," she said truthfully. "I really like lookin' on his pretty face."

Dorothy thought she must mean the young cowboy, for in her opinion he was the only decent looking one of the bunch.

"But . . . but today was the first time anything has happened?"

Marymae rubbed the knuckles of one hand into her eyes and wiped them angrily. "With the others, yes. Mostly, he's just had me use my mouth on him."

Dorothy blanched and was sickened. This was a new revelation to her. But her mind was fertile enough to grasp the meaning.

"I'll take me own two hands and break his head if he lets them touch me again," the girl declared hotly. "Him being such a gentleman and them being such scum."

Dorothy stood trembling, not even hearing the girl's next declaration: "The poor young guy didn't get me good—thanks to ye! He had to wait his turn for those other two old bastards!"

Numbly she patted the girl's shoulders with compassion and pushed her back. The pinched little face reminded her of an organ grinder's monkey that she had seen on the streets of New York. The monkey and the girl were alike in another way, she thought sadly. They each had just been following the instructions of a master without knowing that what they did was only for the master's benefit.

"First things first," Dorothy said, pushing aside her own feelings. 'Take off your dress so that we can sew up the bodice.

Dorothy's hands shook so that she couldn't even thread the needle. Marymae took over and did an excellent job of making the dress look like it had never been torn.

To keep from letting the girl's accusation against the 'gentleman' echo and re-echo in her brain, she tried to talk about Marymae's education. Anything. Anything but Paul Ely!

The girl studied Dorothy thoroughly, seeing the richness of her clothes, the rings on her fingers, the faint scent of her perfume. These things she coveted. She didn't think she would gain them through an education.

Paul Ely had always given her money. That's how she would gain them. He had always treated her, before that morning, with cavalier affection and amusement. She would just have to tell him that she didn't like doing 'that other thing' with the other men. It had hurt too much and she had screamed at them because they had scoffed at paying her anything.

Not a single word that Dorothy uttered entered her head or made an impression. Her arrival at the cabin had been only for the repair of her dress and an alibi in case her mother checked up on her.

"Miss," she whispered shyly, sounding just like

her mother, "please don't let Maw or Paw know about this."

Dorothy frowned. She didn't think she would be able to find the words to tell about it in the first place, but it placed her in a difficult situation. It was almost like letting Paul go scot-free. But, again, first things first.

"I must have your promise in return that you will not see those men again," she said severely.

The thin, plain faced girl beamed thankfully.

"Cross my heart and hope to die, I won't be seeing them again."

But by men, she thought Dorothy only meant the cowboys.

Suddenly, Dorothy wanted to be very much alone.

"Now, you had better scoot. Tell your mother hello."

She intended on telling her mother more than that. Her sly and agile mind was ready to describe the woman and cabin in detail.

Dorothy walked up and down the living room area in a frenzy.

Her mind was now thinking with clear cold logic. To do such a thing to a child was unthinkable, depraved and cowardly. The flicker of love that had momentarily been rekindled had been crushed by an iceberg of disgust. But to openly accuse him? Too many times she had been a victim of his slyness and evil and calculating ways. She felt as though he had plunged another poisoned dagger into her breast. But she wasn't going to bleed, of that she was sure.

With malice in her heart she started to prepare food for supper and think over her wardrobe. It had to be something alluring and sensual. Provocative and yet within the bounds of restraint. She was going to make him bleed—but very, very slowly.

Paul Ely stood in the clear full-moon night. He had been toyed with for hours, but Dorothy had allowed him only to kiss her hand in parting. It was like the hands of time had been turned back to their first meeting. He should charge right back inside, covering her with the kisses that he knew she adored, but he could not; that might ruin everything. If she wanted to start all over again, he was game. After all, the dinner had been excellent and the evening most charming. She was still the most ravishingly beautiful creature he had ever met and tonight she had been witty, charming and nearly drove him out of his mind with a gown that promised everything, but revealed nothing.

"She's no whore!" he whispered to himself. Then his blue eyes narrowed on that thought. He walked slowly to his tethered horse and automatically released the reins and climbed into the saddle. "She's no whore!" he repeated as he nudged the horse into movement. He rode along slowly, letting that thought sink deep into his brain.

"Lady?" he snorted. He had proof positive that even 'ladies' did it. He felt quite confident that the next night would be quite different. She couldn't go without it forever.

But as he rode up to his cabin he realized that his lust not been sated for that night. To win her back, he would have to divorce her from all others. He contemplated who she was closest to in the valley. He went to the bunkhouse door and began to pound vigorously.

That night every split-rail fence that had been constructed on the MacGregor ranch was quietly dismantled and dumped into Black Canyon Creek. By morning the unintentional dam had spread a few inches of water out over the lower fields.

A.Q. MacGregor looked at the fields for some time before he spoke.

"These beaver do strange work," he said quietly. "This is an excellent idea."

"Excellent?" Clara echoed blankly.

"In Wisconsin we can't set a plow to earth until late April. I'll release the dam now, but plug it up again in February. The flooding will unthaw the ground and I can get a good two months jump on plowing. You will not let them know that I am pleased with their prank, Clara."

"Let them know?" Clara gasped. "Mr. MacGregor, I demand an explanation of that statement!"

"Now, Clara, don't get your feathers in a fluff. By law I had to ride over to the Evans ranch last night to inform them that we now have a post office with you as postmistress. I was going to inform Miss Goold of the same, but through the window saw that she was entertaining Mr. Ely for supper. If she is taking up with the likes of him again, I would just suggest caution in what is said around her."

Clara MacGregor was stunned at the news. Dorothy had supplied some, and Clara's quick brain, had supplied the rest of what had transpired between Dorothy and Paul Ely. She couldn't imagine Dorothy ever taking up with him again.

Fred and Lloyd came to help split more rails the next day. They were both gloomy and unsociable. Lloyd had gone to clean the ashes out of Dorothy's fireplace and found that Paul Ely had already accomplished the chore.

The next afternoon Homer and Charlie James came trudging back from school about noon. Seven-year-old Homer put it simply to Clara's question.

"We were the only ones who showed up, so she went off riding with that cowboy."

Over the weekend the Langley's cabin burned to the ground. Clara was ready to cast a finger of suspicion until Jim McLaughlin stopped her.

"Ely wasn't in on it, for he was at Sunday dinner with Miss Dorothy and me. Most miserable meal I've ever ate."

Clara MacGregor bit her tongue. Finally, she could stand it no more and discussed the whole matter with her mother.

The plump, matronly woman listened carefully, and then let out a heartfelt sigh.

"Clara, when a woman is going to make a fool of herself, not even the good Lord above can stop her. Now, mind your own business."

Clara tried, but Dorothy wasn't making it easy for her. Her name was linked with Paul Ely every time Clara turned around.

Horace Langley, before moving his family out, accused her of being a part of the Earl's scheme to get them all out. He saw her dinner for Paul Ely as an alibi and cover-up. Some started to believe him.

Paul Ely thought the man's charges were amusingly funny. It was the man's poor construction of his fireplace flue which had caused the fire, but it was one settler less and if credit had to be given he would take it.

But his conquest of Dorothy seemed to be going nowhere. His presence was making her less and less a part of the settler community, but it wasn't getting him into her bed.

Then, a week before Christmas, when A.Q. MacGregor came back from a shopping trip to Denver, all hell broke loose. He had learned that the James family were 'squatting' on the parcel of land he had taken out in the name of his mother-in-law. When they refused to listen to reason, he began immediately to build her a small cabin a few hundred yards from their own. As a lawyer, A.Q. had looked into the matter very carefully in Denver. If she resided in the cabin but one night a month they could appeal the case all the way to Washington.

"Pettifogging lawyer," Mrs. James wailed. "That woman is jumping our claim. I shall not attend their Christmas party or ever speak to them again."

The fault lay neither with the James' claim or the MacGregor claim, although they were the same It was now very difficult to determine legally what land was available, and not available, since most of it was claimed by Lord Dunraven after a fire in Theo Whyte's office in November. All of the Estes Park Company maps and records were turned to ashes.

It seemed to many, but was never proven, that they all retained a faint odor of kerosene. A duplicate map and records were drawn from the land office files and were immediately challenged by Whyte as being totally inaccurate. Feeling that Whyte's drunken condition had caused the fire in the first place, Dunraven reluctantly took the man east with him to meet Lady Florence for the holidays and turned the entire mess over to Rufus Brogan.

Rufus studied the records like a general preparing for a major battle—friends and foes gaining or losing from the spoils of battle accordingly. Some of the names meant nothing to him, but the James would lose and the MacGregors would win. He would quietly protect Dorothy on her second claims, but would fail, due to oversight of course, to protect her claims on the land on which her home was built. Because the work lasted into the wee hours of the morning the Austin claims were somehow left intact.

But an original fraud was perpetrated once again. Griff Evans had not a shadow of a title on the land he was to sell to Dunraven and there was no motion to obtain it from the government. But like every thing else that was done in that era for a token of regard and esteem the English Company paid under the table for papers to be drawn. But on the papers Rufus reduced the sale price to only $10,000 dollars. He felt that equitable because after all, he had paid an equal amount in 'regard and esteem' to get the new maps drawn and recorded.

But whether it was because of the approaching Christmas season or fear, certain claims went undisturbed so that no 'injustice' could be claimed—even two by an Abner Sprague and Rev. E.J. Lamb that were filed while the map was being revised. To make matters even more legal, but later more confusing, the land office decided to re-survey the area, over three townships, after the first of the year.

It was a pathetic Christmas. Sides were drawn in the 'little land war battle', much to the delight of Paul Ely. Horace Ferguson, as yet, had met with no trouble from the English Company and sided with W.E. James. John Hupp, because of past help, was obliged to see A.Q. MacGregor's point of view. Fred Austin thought they should all be saving their energy for the day they would have to fight the real enemy, but as was normally the case, his voice went unheeded. Griff Evans sat back and chuckled. Others wanted to run MacGregor out of town on a rail.

Dorothy was perplexed. She really didn't want to side with either faction, but MacGregor would be her strongest ally against the Earl.

"My, my," Paul exclaimed admiringly, "that is a gown I've never seen before. You should wear green more often, Dorothy, it makes you look more stunning than usual."

"Why, thank you, sir," Dorothy laughed. "I thought my red coloring and the green dress would be a good color combination for Clara's Christmas eve party."

"For what?" he roared explosively. "You talk like a fool! Don't think that you're going to talk me into to taking you there! What's more—I forbid you to go!"

"I don't think you have that right, Paul," she said firmly.

Paul did not speak. His look was becoming more black and lowering each day, as Dorothy found excuse after excuse to keep him from becoming amorous. He was bleeding, just as she had planned, but he would not be put off forever.

He tried to bluster, sheepishly. "Come now, why do you want to go there? I thought we would be spending our Christmas Eve together."

"I'm sorry, Paul, but you've known about this all along. Everyone has. What with this fight, I'm not sure who might show up or not show up, and I don't want to disappoint Clara."

"Let's be frank," he said. "This is going to put you directly on one side and against the other."

"Nonsense! Now you are talking like a fool. This is Clara's party and not A.Q.'s. Why should women be forced to lose their friends just because the men are squabbling?"

"Well, the least I can do is ride over with you."

"That won't be necessary. I'm meeting Fred and Lloyd at their cabin."

Those damned two! thought Paul, with evil fury. They ruin everything. They treat her so much like a lady I can never get her to see the woman she really is.

He sat in the rocker and stretched his long legs toward the fire. "As your plans seem to be quite set, I will just roast here until your return. I believe in giving presents on Christmas Eve."

"In our home it was always a morning tradition."

He grinned broadly. "You can have it both ways."

Dorothy ignored his true meaning and drew on the rabbitskin coat and fur turban that had been an early Christmas present from Mountain Jim. She put them on slowly, like a sleepwalker, her mind not yet ready to do combat with him.

Actually, she was very proud of the calm manner

she was able to project, when in truth she wanted to scratch his eyes out. She had felt so guilty that afternoon in accepting Martha Evans gift and then having to lie to the woman. Dorothy had seen the girl but the one time, but Martha was under the impression that Marymae had been sneaking over two or three mornings a week. Dorothy knew she should have faced the woman with the truth right then and there, but she wanted Paul to face it first.

"I'm glad you're going to wait for me," she said sweetly. "I, too, have a present for you. I'll try not to be too late."

Paul sat until he heard her horse out of the yard. He sat for five minutes more, rose, stretched and went out to his own horse. His plan was working remarkably well. He would be back long before the party was over—or was broken up—and no one could claim that he had ever left Dorothy's.

Clara opened the door to their knocking and stood there looking at their shadowy figures for a long time before she whispered:

"Oh, Dorothy, how could you do this to—" She stopped on a gasp as A.Q. came up behind her with a kerosene lantern to place on the porch. "Oh, I'm so sorry. For a minute I thought you had. . . . Oh! Come in! My, Lloyd I hardly recognized you dressed up so handsomely."

"Thank you, Mrs. MacGregor," he said, ushering Dorothy in. "And first off I'll make my uncle's apology. He's feeling poorly tonight."

A.Q. snorted, coming in and closing the door. He knew that Fred Austin didn't want to appear like he was taking sides.

Clara flustered. "I hope he hasn't been around

the Hupp children. John came by this afternoon to say they both woke up this morning all broken out with the measles."

"The party keeps dwindling," MacGregor said sourly.

"Now, Mr. MacGregor," she soothed, "you didn't want to have it in the first place, although most of the entertainment will now fall on your shoulders. Take Lloyd on in with the rest of the gentlemen and I'll see to Dorothy's wraps. Mother is still dressing, Dorothy, so we will put your things in my room. If the McCreeys don't show up, we shall be the only three ladies present. The two Jims are already here and a minister came by this afternoon, of all things, and I have invited him back–" She stopped short, as though for once she had run out of words. "I'm sorry for what I almost started to say."

"Look, Clara," Dorothy said, a little hurt, "I know what you were thinking. But I would never impose upon your hospitality by bringing an uninvited guest."

Clara shook her tightly curled head.

"I feel so ashamed," she said. "I've just never seen Lloyd in anything but shirt and trousers and he looked so tall."

Now Dorothy was beginning to feel ashamed She had been so absorbed in her own thought, and furiously mad at Fred's childish refusal to come, that she had not taken note of Lloyd.

"Let's just not say another word on the subject, Clara."

Clara's sigh was gusty with relief on that count but barged right into a topic that even angels would have not dared open.

"I have missed seeing you, since you have taken up so much with Mr. Ely. Mother told me to keep out of the matter, but Dorothy, what some people are saying about you hurts me to the heart of my soul."

She stared at Clara with dawning recognition in her eyes, as though she had been waiting a long time for it to reach this point.

"Are they saying that I am his mistresss?"

"Oh, Dorothy, it's dreadful!"

"No," Dorothy said proudly, "it's wonderful! Clara, you don't know what I'm about and I'd rather not tell you. But I have only to answer to God."

"But, Dorothy dear, it's the gossips on earth you must contend with. That woman, who is illegally on our property, says she is not going to let her boys come under your evil influence."

Dorothy timidly put out her hand and touched the woman's sleeve. She wanted to tell her everything, but dared not.

"Then she is a fool to think such evil," she said. "Clara, I thought I could stay in this area—even though he was here—and not open my heart to him. I weakened."

"But with a minister in the area," she said quickly, "perhaps you can . . . can . . ."

"Marry him?" she said bitterly. "No, Clara, that can never be—now."

Clara was just ready to protest when more guests arrived. She made a mental note to get the whole story from Dorothy before the night was over.

Dorothy took to the Rev. E.J. Lamb immediately. He looked like a Biblical prophet, but talked like a man of the soil.

"This area we call the Little Thompson Mission, but the grasshoppers in the farmland below not only impoverished the country, but lessened this preacher's salary as well. Say what we may about and against filthy lucre, you cannot get clothing, bread, coffee, sugar, and other concomitants without shekels or good credit, and good credit cannot be maintained without cash or land in the background. The pestiferous, hoppery circumstances left me with three dollars' worth of shekels."

"And so you went for the land?"

"When I saw several farmers come back with their pockets lined with gold I knew that God or the devil was afoot in Denver town. Never having feared the devil, I waited for God to give me some word on the matter. Well, as Mrs. Lamb can tell you, when I bring her up here this spring, the angels, like the office workers in the mission conference headquarters, are always misplacing messages. By the time God nudged me in the behind they were no longer buying the land and I could only get a claim some thirty odd miles from here, at the valley below Long's Peak."

Dorothy smiled at him tenderly.

"But how did you file a claim for only three dollars?"

Lamb chuckled until his heavy beard bounced.

"In the wreck of noble lives, something immortal still survives. I think the land office lad was Catholic. I told him I would rather be a preacher than owner of rich lands and bonded wealth. Well, my dear, for three dollars he must have thought that he was putting me far enough away from civilization so that I would not be stealing any good Catholics away from the church."

"But that left you penniless!"

"Hardly! The claim deed gave me sufficient credit to borrow two hundred dollars, with which I shall buy some cows and calves from the Evans ranch and go into the dairy business during the week, and on the weekends see to my throne of power, the pulpit."

Dorothy frowned. She hated to see such a nice man hurt.

"I think you would be better off buying your stock from Mr. MacGregor. Lord Dunraven now owns all of that cattle and more than likely will try to get your land from you, as well."

"Miss Dorothy, land is like a marriage. What God has joined together let no man put asunder. I have pioneered in four territories, and now plan on building my tenth home with my own hands."

"How remarkable."

"Not remarkable, my dear, just the ability of the church to keep giving me new assignments. As soon as I've worn out the ears of one congregation they move me on. Do you mind if I get personal?"

Dorothy looked at him quizzically. "Not at all."

"I love the mystical and sometimes can see things in other people that they will not admit to themselves. It is time for you to forget this love that you bear in your heart, because it saddens you too greatly."

Dorothy never got a chance to even gasp or comment, because just then one of the MacGregor ranch hands came pounding on the door and yelling:

"Fire!"

It was the most dreaded cry in pioneer life. Flood waters would recede, but burned out timberland took a good hundred years to grow back.

Almost as one they clamored outside to determine a course of action. To the west the sky was shimmering with orange heat waves and billowing dark clouds.

"The James' place!" someone yelled.

It was no time for animosities or grudges. Even a simple campfire could ignite a whole forest on a windy night such as that. Everyone started grabbing milking pails from the barn and taking to horse.

The barn structure was a skeleton inferno by the time they came galloping up. It had been given up as hopeless and the James' family were bucketing water onto the roof and sides of the cabin. Charley James's arms were nearly numb from pumping so long at the well.

"That is useless," MacGregor barked. "Form a bucket—"

James cut him short. "If I wanted your advice I'd have asked for it."

The two men glowered at each other and the Rev. Mr. Lamb cleared his throat.

"You with the buckets," he commanded sternly, "start bringing extra water up from the creek. Ladies, find yourself a broom or branch from a pine and start beating out those embers flying east. No use having both ranches timber burned."

"He should burn," James said grimly, "after setting fire to my barn."

"I resent that, sir! I wouldn't put it past you setting your own barn afire so that you could accuse me."

"Hush, you two," Dorothy scolded. "Things might have been different if the land office hadn't double filed you. Now, see to the fire first."

Dorothy knew in her heart that MacGregor would not have had his men set the blaze and then sound the alarm; any more than Mr. James would have burned his own buildings. She had a gnawing suspicion as to its cause.

James, hardly the pioneering type, should have seen that the westerly winds were keeping his cabin from danger. But the winds were taking burning embers and clumps of smoldering hay and carrying them eastward. Once the barn had collapsed in on itself and was under control, the James family was left to watch it while the Christmas Eve party walked back down the canyon, letting their horses trail them, and checking for the least sign of fire every inch of the way.

Rev. Lamb finally caught up with Dorothy.

"Thank you, Miss Dorothy, for being a voice a mite stronger than the preacher. I find myself a little behind times in this apparent battle. Would you care to illuminate me?"

He was not a man of her faith, but at that moment she would have accepted him as The Holy Father sitting in the See of Rome. He was warm, fatherly, and had an ear that listened patiently.

Although she gave him but the highlights, it took the better part of their walk back to relate.

"Well," he said at last, "I don't think in fifty odd years I have had the honor of meeting any one of the titled class. You have demolished one of my youthful air castles. The poor, such as myself, never think of the titled on the field of petty battle. But, God did make them mortal, didn't he?

Well, we shall just handle your cousin as a mortal man, then."

It gave Dorothy such heart that she suddenly found herself pouring out the whole sordid story of herself and Paul Ely. They were now lagging far behind the others.

"Leave them to the fire watch," he said gently, "for the matter at hand is of more importance than the whole world burning about us. Of all sad words of tongue or pen, the saddest are these: 'It might have been'! Dear girl, it may come as a shock to you, but other than Mrs. Lamb, I, too, have known such a love. First love, shall we say. In my daring youth I became intimately acquainted with a young lady of sterling worth, friendship's golden chain bound us together, and soon it ripened into an intense affection and our feelings were one. As we wandered by purling streams, gathering flowers, resting on grassy slopes, enjoying love's sweet dream, we both thought that nothing could or should ever separate us til death. Oh, how pure, holy, and elevating is the passion of sacred affection in the hearts of true honesty and devotion, and the rending corresponding bitter. In short, my dear, I was being duped. She was bearing at the time the child of another youth who was highly unacceptable to her family. I found myself to be the highest candidate on her list, a dubious honor, to be sure. The tragic finale, not necessary to mention, severed the relationship for all time, leaving a shadow over my life.

"I wished to run from family, home and friends. But wiser heads than mine took the matter into their hands and I was soon introduced to the present Mrs. Lamb. As a mortal man I accepted the wisdom of wiser heads and God."

"I think I have been fighting both," Dorothy said hoarsely.

"Oh, no," he chuckled, "I think you have unknowingly been fighting everyone else's battle and calling it your own. You have the true courage of your convictions, but keep neutralizing them. You are striving for the best of your old world and this of the new. I fear that is too radical a change."

Impulsively she asked: "Have you come to love Mrs. Lamb?"

He smiled. "It is better than jewels and gems to have a true and trusty friend and wife. I would not trade her in even if given an opportunity to ascend to Heaven without benefit of death."

Dorothy was silent for several hundred feet of their walk. Then she laughed.

"That boy in the land office was quite correct, you know. Here I am, Irish born and bred, and thus quite Catholic, and yet no priest could make me feel as warm and comfortable as you have done."

He chuckled merrily. "My first convert in the Rocky Mountains." Then he sobered. "Miss Dorothy, I am quite well known for my punning sallies, my humorous flings, and happy illusions of good cheer. But friendship is the mysterious cement of the soul. Call on me whenever you feel you have the need."

"I shall," Dorothy sighed. "I shall sooner than you realize."

An expression of quiet triumph glowed on her face. She was divorced from her mother by thousands of miles, and from her father by death. But here in this unique character was one of nature's noblemen. Not titled by man or birth, but enobled by God.

By the time they returned to the MacGregor ranch the other guests had already departed, except for Lloyd. Clara was quick to explain, due to it being after midnight, that Mr. MacGregor had already retired.

History would record that A.Q. MacGregor was still at work at his diary, which would not be seen by other mortal eyes until nearly a hundred years later:

"Refenced today and finished around as far as James house. . . . James set his barn on fire yesterday (right after midnight)."

It was hard to change a Scotsman's mind once it was made up.

Other minds were seeing what they should have seen in the first place and making quick amends.

"Lloyd," Dorothy gasped, "Just look at you! Oh, you came here looking so dashing and now you are soot from head to foot."

Lloyd had dressed only for her, as he did everything only for her, and had been crushed that she had hardly noticed him. Now, he blossomed anew.

"You don't look much better," he kidded. "Almost like the first day I saw you."

Dorothy looked down at the almost black sleeves of the rabbitskin coat, at her grimy hands, and burst into laughter.

"I'm a mess! Lloyd take me home! Oh, I'm forgetting. Do you have accommodations, Rev. Lamb?"

"He has," Clara said coolly. "A bunk has been prepared for him down with our hired help."

Her equally cool departure comments were lost on Dorothy. She was still floating on a spiritual cloud created by the Rev. Mr. Lamb.

But Clara was seething from a thought planted in her mind by the departing Mrs. McCreery.

"You don't know that woman as well as you think you do, Clara MacGregor. Just look at her! Bring a new man into this valley, age and profession not withstanding, and she is off after them like a bolt. Humph! It will be a cold day in hell when I come to hear him preach!"

The longer they were away, the more the woman's words took meaning in Clara's mind. Now, as Dorothy and Lloyd rode away, laughing and merry, she could not see that she was falling into the same pitfall as her husband and Mr. James. She was automatically branding Dorothy and vowing never to speak to her again. She never gave a second thought to the Rev. Mr. Lamb because he was not of her faith, anyway.

The snowshoes that Jim McLaughlin had given each for Christmas proved cumbersome to carry by horseback, but it was just one more thing for Dorothy and Lloyd to laugh and joke about on the ride home. Lloyd wanted to ride her all the way home, but Dorothy wanted a few moments alone to turn matters over in her mind.

"Dorothy," he said nervously, "may I give you an early Christmas present?"

"If you would like, Lloyd."

He leaned across from his saddle and took her chin in the palm of his hand. Gently he drew their heads together until their lips just barely touched.

"Merry Christmas!" he whispered, wishing to say more, much more.

She gazed at him tenderly, but still not seeing the man that he had become.

"Thank you, Lloyd. That's the nicest present I could have received."

He sat and watched her ride away until she had vanished over the hill. Her words filled his heart to near bursting. He knew that many would laugh at such a thought, but he was now determined to work for the day that she would be his wife.

Another was thinking along the same lines, but in reverse. Paul Ely didn't want Dorothy for his wife, just as his mistress. If gossip accused them of such, then that was the only present he desired for Christmas. Upon returning to the cabin he divested himself of all but stocking, trousers and shirt, rebuilt the fire to a roaring state and prepared a pot of coffee. As the hours slipped away he dozed off in the rocker. The longer she was away, the more successful his plan would be.

When Dorothy reached the cabin, Paul was awake and waiting for her. He did not say a word about the sooty condition of her coat and hands, but sat at the table, where Dorothy joined him for a cup of coffee after washing up. He didn't even try to hide the look of triumph on his face. The smell of smoke about her fully suggested that the wind had taken the burning embers and ruined the party by fire as well. He anticipated the next step to be gunfire between James and MacGregor. He wanted for her to tell him about the evening. But she did not broach any subject. Instead she sat there, daintily sipping her coffee, smiling softly and secretly to herself, as though recalling something amusing. Finally, Paul could stand it no longer.

"What's so damn funny?"

"I was just thinking about a most charming man that I met tonight. A very remarkable man, as a matter of fact."

He glowered. "What the hell? Who is he and what went on between you?"

"Does it matter? I don't feel like talking about it. I just want to sit here and remember."

"Yes," Paul said grimly, "it matters if you have been whoring around again."

"Oh?" Dorothy said, quite without emotion. "Well, since we must talk, I'd better tell you something first."

"Go ahead," he snapped.

"I know all about you and Marymae and the depraved things you have taught her."

Paul sat there, his mouth dropping open foolishly, staring at her as though he couldn't quite see what business it was of hers.

"Now," she said, "we are out in the open, aren't we, Paul? I've always known you only wanted me sexually. You almost brought me to the point of wanting the same. But you how strong I can be, Paul? Even after learning about you and Marymae, I was able to have you around me and still deny you what you desired the most."

"What a sneak you are," said Paul, angrily, "and a fool. It's my right as a man to do as I wish on that score."

"No, Paul, it isn't a right given to man, it is one that he has erroneously taken for himself. Without knowing the full story of who I was with tonight your malevolent mind immediately thought the worst and called me a whore. Society has been remiss in not coming up with a name for male monsters such as yourself."

"I don't have to sit here and take this," cried Paul, flinging himself out of his chair.

"No you don't," said Dorothy, coolly. "As a matter of fact, it saves me the trouble of asking you to leave and never return."

"Leave!" shrilled Paul, with a snorting laugh. "Why, do you know how easy it would be for me to take you into your bed and do with you whatever I desired?"

"Without the benefit of a minister?" she asked, and now her brown eyes gleamed with real mirth.

When she wore such an aspect, even the brash Paul Ely was quelled momentarily. He shrugged. "We are back to that, are we? Why go to all that bother just for a little bit of fun?"

Up to this point Dorothy had maintained great control; now her delicate nostrils flared.

"So that we understand each other quite clearly, no man shall ever again share my bed until he is my lawful husband. That, I have firmly decided, you shall never be—ever! Rape me, if you will, and I shall broadcast it all over the valley."

Ely reared back his head and roared with laughter.

"And what good would that do, they all think you are my mistress as it is!"

In an effort to retrieve the situation, she said coldly: "People believe what they want to believe, be it good or evil. Just as some people want to believe one way or another about tonight's barn burning. Oh, yes, Paul, all that was destroyed was the James's barn. No brush fires. No forest fires. Not even a single MacGregor building singed. Too bad."

"Why tell me this? I was here all evening."

"How nice of you to dress so elegantly for this evening," she said. The apparent change in subject was so sudden that he started. "When I was hanging up my wrap on the peg I couldn't help but notice your blue velvet coat. I recall the first time that I saw you wear it in New York. Of course, that night you hadn't been trouncing through someone's barn. It's a shame the way that straw sticks so stubbornly to velvet, isn't it?"

The mischief was done. Paul's face had become as still and pale as granite. Hatred ran in fiery liquid through his veins. He spoke, and his voice was hard and clear.

"If you want to keep this land you will forget that you saw that coat. If you want to stay alive you will stop associating with all of that rabble. And don't think you can get sneaky about it. I'm going to be here just as often as I have been of late, because no man is going to take my place with you and live."

He stormed out of the cabin in such a rush that he grabbed only the jacket and forgot his boots.

Dorothy sat for just a second and then raced to snatch them up and heave them out the door. She started to shout out a rejoinder, thought better of it, slammed the door and firmly brought down the heavy bolting bar.

She stood for a long moment. She had thought that this moment of revenge would have been sweet. It was like sour bile in her mouth. Nor was it his threats that bothered her. Her animosity was turned inward. She had thought only of herself. She had done nothing to stop him from using Marymae. She had done nothing to stop him from burning down more barns and possibly cabins. She had totally failed.

The Rev. E.J. Lamb saw it quite differently.

During the night, and without warning, God had given them a white Christmas. By morning there was nearly two feet on the ground and it was still falling.

Lamb had wanted to spend this birthday festival walking and meditating upon his land. He had gotten as far as Dorothy's cabin and his horse had begun to flounder.

"Ah, Sister Dorothy," he chirped, merrily, "I am not much of a Christmas present to leave like a foundling at your door."

"You are a most welcome sight. Warm yourself by the fire."

Passing the table that Dorothy had pulled into the center of the living room and had set as formally as possible with what she had, he mentally counted the four place settings.

"My route brought me by the Austin cabin. The uncle and nephew asked if I chanced to stop by here to say they would avail themselves of their new snowshoes to arrive in time for your dinner. But, I feel the intruder."

"Nonsense! There is plenty of food and I really only expect the arrival of Fred and Lloyd."

"Ah, an old tradition kept," he beamed. "My mother, on this day, always set the table for eleven, so that the Christ Child would have a seat if he arrived to bless the ten of us. It was usually my bachelor uncle, Horace, who arrived and occupied the seat. Today I shall be Uncle Horace."

There was no tradition about it. Dorothy had automatically set the place for Paul Ely. At the time of her invitation they had argued about her other invited guests. She had been firm in her resolve to invite whomever she pleased to her own house. Now, after last night, she did not expect Paul to show his face and she was thankful.

Her thankfulness lasted a full five minutes.

Without knocking he came merrily bounding through the door, shaking snow off a fur cap and great bearskin coat.

"I'm as good as my promised word," he started and then stopped short at seeing Rev. Lamb in front of the fireplace. His face mirrored such total shock at seeing the stranger that Dorothy couldn't help but laugh.

"This is the gentleman I told you I met last night," she giggled. "Paul Ely, meet the Rev. Mr. E.J. Lamb. He is up from Berthoud to see to our spiritual and ministerial needs—whichever ones we may have need for."

Paul's Adam's apple jerked in his muscular throat. Slowly he put out his hand.

"Glad to meet you, sir," he choked.

Lamb studied him as he came forward to take his hand, looking exactly like Moses as he watched his people worship the idol Baal.

"Mr. Ely, I feel as though I almost know you, after my discussion with Sister Dorothy last evening."

Paul felt trapped. All of her words of the night before now seemed like a cunning ploy. This was not to be a Christmas dinner, but a wedding feast.

"I-I can't stay," he stammered. "I-I forgot that I promised to take dinner with Griff and Martha today. Nice to meet you. Merry Christmas, Dorothy."

No sooner had the door closed than she began to laugh softly, merrily.

"I do believe," Rev. Lamb smirked, "that he expected to see me pull out a shotgun at any moment."

"I would have turned it on you both, if you had."

"Yes, yes," he mused, "he is certainly quite adverse to matrimony, I feel. A throwback. Exactly like the man who put up castles all over his kingdom so that he could have a convenient wife in each, and thought nothing of selling the castle, with wife, if a travelling knight had the shekels. The serfs snickered behind their liege lord's back and gave us the very apt phrase 'flesh peddler.' You are well to be done with him, Sister Dorothy."

She sighed. "Thanks to your presence. Once you are gone I think he plans to make quite a nuisance of himself."

"The only protection against that is to take unto yourself a husband."

"That is easier said than done," she laughed. "If I wished to adhere to family tradition I could always write mother and have her send over by boat the choice she has probably already made."

"But cannot that proper dignity be done in reverse? Tradition can be kept quite in place if I were to replace your mother and act as a proper marriage broker."

Dorothy smiled with tender appreciation. "A suggestion, Rev. Lamb, that would more than likely be quite acceptable to my family, but greatly lacking in one major commodity—elegible candidates of the opposite gender."

Lamb thought quite differently, but held his silence.

The arrival of Fred and Lloyd put the conversation of candidates to rest, except in the mind of Lamb.

Being an excellent conversationalist he made the dinner party and afternoon a huge success. He was able to bring Fred Austin out of his shy shell like no one had ever done before. Nor was Fred, or anyone else, aware that he was being put through a very sly interrogation.

When E.J. Lamb sunk his teeth into a matter, he didn't let loose until it was settled to his satisfaction. The first candidate to come to his mind, James McLaughlin, had long since been cancelled out. The more he talked with Fred, the more he was ready to pin a blue ribbon upon his chest.

Always one who thought a project started should be finished on the same day, he cunningly took matters into his own hands.

"The Lord might be over blessing us," he said, turning away from the window. "Must be another foot of snow come down since I said grace over that lovely meal. Might I ask the hospitality of the night, Mr. Austin."

"To be sure, sir, but won't your horse founder just as badly going back?"

"I fear you might be quite correct," he said, on a false sigh.

Dorothy's new snowshoes were quite in evidence, but the Rev. Mr. Lamb purposely kept his eyes from roving in their direction.

"What about the schoolhouse?" Lloyd suggested. "The benches can be put together for a bed and the fireplace is quite warming."

"Excellent!" Lamb enthused. "And why not make it a bachelor's quarters for the night. No need for the two of you to founder, as well."

The idea was quickly agreed upon by all. The enjoyment of the afternoon could now be extended into the evening. Extra blankets were found and Fred and Lloyd went to prepare the benches and build a fire. Lamb lingered behind.

"If a man is sound in his faith, possesses land and has great potential in that land, would he not be acceptable to your family?"

"I would certainly think so," she answered, without seeing his meaning.

"Then the battle is more than half over, because this man already has deep admiration and love for you."

"Who?"

"Who?" he echoed. "Woman, are you blind? Fredrick Austin is who!"

Dorothy stared at him.

"Please," she whispered, "I think you are moving just a little too fast. I would just as soon not go into this conversation any further."

Lamb shrugged and nodded a half-hearted consent.

They popped corn, drank hot toddies and laughed and joked. In spite of herself, Dorothy found herself studying Fred Austin intimately. Somehow she had almost looked upon him as being as much of a boy as Lloyd. She had never pictured him as being anyone's husband—let alone hers.

After they had retired early to the school-cabin she lay in her bed thinking. Why would he be any different than what her mother might select for her? she wondered. She didn't know him any more intimately than the boys in the coterie—one of which would have more than likely ended up being her husband. Boys? They would now be men in their early twenties, the same as she. Three years she had been gone. Would any of them still be single and available? Could she learn to love Fred Austin?

"That's ridiculous," she said aloud. "Our women have always learned to love the men that they marry. Their obligation is to bring land into the family to match our—"

She suddenly remembered that her marriage would bring with it a handsome dowry. She wasn't sure of the amount, but knew it would be quite substantial. She fell asleep studying the Lamb proposal from several different angles.

"That's ridiculous," Fred had echoed her words at almost the same time she had uttered them.

"My dear young man, there is nothing at all ridiculous in what I say. In her family marriages are always arranged. Does a tree bear fruit and then leaves? Hardly! A marriage is consummated and is followed by the fruition of love."

"Has—has she asked you to approach me?"

"I am acting on behalf of her mother," Lamb hedged.

"I-I don't know about matters like this and am confused," Fred said, feeling suddenly numb in mind and body, afraid that he was dreaming and would wake to find this had never happened. It had been a silent prayer of his that she would someday marry him, but this had all the appearance of a fantasy.

"Then let me enlighten you," Lamb said, taking his words as an affirmation of acceptance. "It will take time to inform the family of you and win acceptance. That time, in my judgment, is always a logical time for pure and godly courtship. The devil will tempt you greatly, but you must honor her with stout integrity. As she is Irish, she will more than likely bring into the marriage a dowry. You must be quite honest as to your worth and land holdings to assure the family that the dowry is not being cast before swines."

Fred felt his mind and body sink as though he had just been swallowed up by an earthquake. The bubble burst and the dream vanished. If he were to be quite honest, nothing was really his. It all was honestly Lloyd's. He turned away from the man and suffered in silent misery.

Misery certainly did love company that night. Lloyd had lain and listened to the proposal in shocked disbelief. He was the one who loved Dorothey and felt she had a strong affection for him. Why wasn't he the one to be approached, he couldn't help but wonder. Hadn't she let him kiss her and nearly burst his heart with joy? Now it was bursting with a terrible hurt. How could she do this to him? How could Fred do it to him? Couldn't he see the love he had for her? Tears welled up in his eyes and then a hardness came to his heart. The land was his and he would fight for it and for Dorothy. He was tired of being regarded as a child.

As soon as he heard their dual snoring he arose, dressed and returned home through the storm on his snowshoes. He couldn't stand to face any of them in the morning. He feared that he would break into tears in front of his idol—or former idol.

Fred's eyes came open before dawn. He felt that he had not even slept and sensed something was wrong even before he raised up on his elbows. Immediately he knew what an asinine fool he had been. He had not taken into consideration that every word uttered by he and Lamb would have been heard by Lloyd. He was well aware of the boy's deep affection for the woman, but had never considered it of a serious nature. But the absent body spoke a world of words. No day dream in the world was worth putting his relationship with his nephew in such peril. They would each have to learn to live with the facts as they were. He prayed he could make Lloyd see it that way.

When Lamb awoke he saw their departure, which he considered had been at the same hour, quite differently.

"Stout fellows," he said with admiration. "Off already to see after their livestock. Industrious! I do like a man of such determined industry."

And because he believed his theory of their early departure, he was able to make Dorothy believe it as well.

Not being one to outstay his welcome, he trudged away on foot, pulling his horse along behind, around the lake to the Evans' place to purchase a set of snowshoes.

Finding only Martha and Marymae at home in the cabin, he kindly accepted Martha's offer of a warming cup of tea, and saw no reason not to share the news when Martha warmly asked after Dorothy.

Marymae sat silent and smug throughout. An hour later she sold the information to Paul Ely for a handsome reward. That night he got blindly drunk.

The next day Griff Evans ran into Mountain Jim on his trap run. Their friendship had moved onto quagmire shaky ground. To tweek Mountain Jim's nose, Griff informed him of how he had lost his "lady love." To Griff's disgust he didn't even comment. But Jim pondered it the whole day, sharing his thoughts that night when he camped at the McCreery ranch.

His thoughts were twisted by Mrs. McCreery to suit her own notions. The woman was grabbing the first husband that she could—*because she had to.* It didn't take long—snow or no snow—for her thought to be known throughout the valley.

The days cleared and Dorothy thought no one came about because of the heavy and drifting snow. She didn't hear that the Fergusons lost all their chicken to wolves—or so it was made to look. She didn't hear that someone fired on A.Q. MacGregor while he was fencing and he stoutly blamed it on W.E. James. She didn't hear from Fred or Lloyd because they were locked in a silent battle of not believing each other and were unaware that Lamb's story had spread so far afield.

And as the valley had known for centuries, and the settlers were yet to learn, the western storms dropped most of their snow before crossing the continental divide. The worst storms came from the north and east, and always seemed to follow each other a week apart.

It started again on New Year's day and continued without let-up for the next five. It was a silent storm, horribly silent. Just the constant sheets of falling white that closed a person into a very small world. Dorothy began to feel as though she would never see another human being again.

14

SHE HEARD her name being shouted even before the fierce pounding came at the door. With his beard encrusted with ice the man looked like some avenging god.

"Where is my son?" James roared before she had a chance to greet him.

"Which one?" she stammered back.

"Charley! We finally got it out of Homer that he left over an hour ago to walk to your damn school."

His attitude angered her, but she kept her calm for the boy's sake. "I have not seen him, Mr. James, and have had no one at the school since before Christmas. If you will wait, I will prepare myself and help you search."

His red rimmed eyes viewed her with utter contempt.

"Your help would hardly be appreciated, having brought about the situation in the first place."

"I won't even honor such a stupid statement," she said with crisp brittleness, turning toward the coat pegs. When she turned back the door frame was empty.

"I will be reasonable," she told herself firmly. "The man is speaking and acting out of fear for his child. Poor Charley, to want an education so much that he would defy his parents and this weather."

It took her some little time to strap the snowshoes upon her feet and master their unwillingness to make her mobile. Once she learned to lift the paddle shaped toe and gently slide it forward, she was able to stay fairly well atop the snow pack and glide along. She found that, after the first mile, it wasn't bad.

Visibility was the main problem. The day was as gray as the preceding five, the wind was increasing and the temperature continued to plummet, but she was able to pick her way without too much difficulty. Eventually, however, James's snowshoe tracks turned westerly. Ahead of her was a flat unbroken sheet of whiteness.

Then she realized her folly. She was being of little help to Charley by just following his father's search. Reason also suggested that the drifting snow would have completely obliterated Charley's tracks. Again she was reminded of how the known landscape was made unrecognizable by the white mantle.

She urged herself on, but the snowshoes were not to be hurried. She picked her way carefully, cautiously and, it seemed after another hour, with a dimming chance of success.

She began to feel the heavy, insidious cold sliding under her thick rabbit-skin coat. Another wave of the vicious storm was about ready to break. She determined it was time to turn back. And then, even as she was considering, the storm broke. The first blast of wind-driven snow struck with such force that it nearly knocked her over into a snowdrift.

Now the only thing to do was to turn slightly southward and reach the safety of the Austin cabin.

She took a few slides on the shoes and stopped, narrowing her eyes to slits.

Out of the swirling, menacing vortex of flying snow a horse and rider appeared. They hailed each other at the same instant and drew close.

"Which way to the Evans' place?" the rider called down.

Then recognition came for each of them at the same instant.

Pepper Whitfield had vowed never to forget her face. She was the snooty woman who had kept him from getting Marymae, and who he held responsible for keeping Marymae from the cowboys ever since.

Dorothy quickly determined that his company would be better than none at all. "The Austin place is closer," she called against the wind.

Pepper Whitfield silently disagreed. Paul Ely had thought this would be an execellent day for one man to sneak over and burn the Austin barn, but Pepper had been lost for an hour looking for it. He was smart enough, however, not to admit that fact.

"Got to get back," he insisted.

"That's ridiculous!" she protested, not wishing to lose the huge shape of the horse to follow. "Then what about my place?"

He seemed about to burst into laughter, but controlled himself. There was no question in his mind why she was out and about. Ever since Christmas night the cowboys had been stealing her stacked firewood and scattering it so that some morning she would wake up totally without. Paul Ely was determined to freeze her out of the cabin.

Then Pepper shook with lewd and silent laughter, his tongue lapping his cold lips. She was out of the cabin! He could win great favor in Paul Ely's eyes if he was able to keep her out of it.

He jerked on the reins to turn the horse towards her, but the snow was piled high around its flanks and it reared and pawed the air. It began to lose its balance. Pepper stifled the sudden start of panic that flashed in him and hauled on the reins to pull the horse down. The mare shied and then, as he intended, came down and crashed a hoof through the paddle of one of the snowshoes. Thinking itself caught in a trap, the mare snorted, her nostrils flaring and her eyes dilated with fright.

"Of all the stupid things," Dorothy shouted, trying to push the horse back. "Get down and help me free her!"

Pepper hesitated, letting the fright in the horse build. Then he harshly pulled back on the reins again. The bit ate into the horse's mouth and it reared anew from a combination of pain and fright.

The snowshoe was still caught up in the hoof and Dorothy was jerked right off her feet and jolted against the pawing beast. She screamed and the beast brought its weight back down on all fours. It was free of the snowshoe, but Dorothy lay beneath it.

Pepper reined it aside for another charge. She foundered for a few seconds in the soft snow and then regained solid underfooting. Pepper looked back. Dorothy was also foundering, the snowshoes now a burden and one leg oddly twisted beneath her. Even if not hurt, Pepper reasoned, she would have an almost impossible journey on a single snowshoe. He turned the horse and started to plow away.

It took a moment for Dorothy to accept the truth. She shouted at the man and horse to return. Within seconds they were lost in the flying vortex.

She tried valiantly to straighten out her legs and get the snowshoes into a position so that she could rise, and then she stopped. The paddle of the one shoe was completely shattered.

There was only one thing to do—remove the snowshoe. To do that, she had to take off her gloves to unknot the leather thongs and before she finished, the wind and the incredible cold had driven all feeling from her fingers. It communicated itself to her entire body. It seemed to flow up her arms and along her veins like water, while the snow sought out and found every opening and crevice in her clothing.

It hardly seemed like she had the gloves back upon her hands. Using the broken snowshoe as a brace she regained her footing. Her right leg was oddly numb.

No more than three steps told her how useless was the situation. The good snowshoe was more of a hindrance than a help. She steeled her mind to go through the ordeal of bare hands once again. But past experience seemed to make the chore go faster.

She started off again, bent almost double, fighting for each step, and instantly noting another error in judgment. Her right leg was not giving her full support and was nearly collapsing on her. She turned back and was amazed to see that her footprints were vanishing as quickly as she had made them. She lost valuable time in searching out the good snowshoe to use as a supporting crutch.

She turned again into the lashing fury of the

storm. Her full skirt caught the wind like a parachute and made each step an agony of effort. Twice she fell, and struggled only with great difficulty to her feet. The right leg was now completely numb and useless and she had to drag it along.

When she collapsed for the third time, she knew it was useless. The pain in her fingers and right hip was becoming excruciating. She lay, for what seemed an eternity, trying to build up some strength to continue.

She was hardly aware when she pulled herself up again. Her temples were so numb that her brain refused to register the pain and she no longer felt the air sear her lungs with frozen fire. Through it all, one thing alone remained constant on the brain—direction. Her dragging path was as straight as a plow furrow. So straight that she stunned herself into another collapsing by crashing into the split rail fence surrounding the Austin place.

She was so close and yet so far away. Now all awareness left her. Later, she could not recall how long she lay there, although Fred thought it had to be two to three hours. A force that was still functioning within her pulled her to her feet, helped her struggle through the wooden rails, urged her one good leg to drag her across the open area to the barn before it finally could support her no longer and doubled beneath her.

Fred Austin's head came up with a start.

"Something is spooking the horses!"

Lloyd took one look at him and reached for his coat and rifle. Fred didn't wait. He flung out of the cabin hatless, coatless and without a weapon.

In front of the barn door was an odd heap. In those short minutes the snow had already drifted over her. He scraped away the drifted snow and was stunned at his find.

He slapped her hard and got no response.

"What the hell you doing?" Lloyd demanded, running up.

Fred ignored him, gathering her up into his arms and racing back toward the cabin. He dumped her on the hook rug in front of the fireplace and began to shout:

"Get all of our blankets and then build up the fires and put on some hot water."

He started slapping her again until her white face grew scarlet from the blows. She stirred and opened her eyes, but they were glazed and unseeing.

"I hauled out a mattress, too," Lloyd said tonelessly, realization starting to bring a fear to his mind.

"Good! Push it under her when I lift!"

Once she was upon it, Fred began to rip off her outer clothing.

"Fred!" Lloyd gasped, blushing scarlet. "What are you doing?"

"They're holding the cold into her body. They'll all have to come off, because they're wet and frozen through. We'll use your night shirt after we've got her blood circulating. Now, kneel down here and help me."

All of her clothing was discarded. Lloyd hesitated in touching her so intimately, but then noticed that his uncle's administration was not sensuous but life saving. The hands, the arms, the shoulders were being gently but firmly rubbed to bring back color.

"Don't touch the right leg, as yet," Fred warned.

"It looks like it has been broken. Come and knead the left leg and I'll fetch some brandy."

Fred jerked her into a sitting position, while Lloyd rubbed on her foot, calf and thigh. His embarrassment at her nudity was quickly evaporating.

She choked and gagged when he tried to force the brandy down her throat. He pounded her on the back and kept on pouring the liquid into her. It ran out of her mouth and onto her breasts and stomach. Without being told Lloyd went for a wash cloth and towel to clean her up. There was no thrill in touching her breasts through the cloth. He was now as calm and poised as his uncle.

She got some of the brandy, but still didn't respond. Fred slapped her again till her head rocked and the angry red weals stood out on her face. She moaned and opened her eyes again.

"She's awake but not really with us, so let's keep rubbing her."

Slowly all the color started coming back, except for in the right leg and foot. She moaned again and began to relax.

"Now we can get her into a night shirt. You get ready for bed, too."

"Not until I know she is going to be all right," Lloyd protested.

Fred grinned sheepishly. "You'll know. I want you to sleep down beside her and give her your warmth. I figure you've got hotter blood than I do."

Lloyd did as he was told, but with a return of embarrassment.

Fred watched until both of them were sleeping normally, or as normally as he could tell. Throughout the night he kept the fire flinging out heat in waves.

By morning the majority of her body had responded to the warming heat, but Fred was now thankful that she remained in an unconscious state.

"The leg is broken, Lloyd, and I fear her foot in frozen. If we don't set it and get the circulation going, we are in for big trouble."

Lloyd gulped. "What must we do?"

So as not to have two patients on his hands, Fred was gentle and calm with his instructions. Lloyd followed them exactly, a new awareness coming into his mind. He was seeing his uncle in an entirely different light. This was not the shy, bumbling man who cowered at his father's words. He wasn't aware that Fred would know when a leg was broken, let alone how to set it. All Lloyd could see was a horrible looking bruised spot and sickly whiteness of flesh.

Dorothy moaned and clenched her teeth when Fred yanked the bones back into line, but that was her only sign of discomfort. They used two bed planks as splints and wrapped the leg securely into place with torn strips of sheeting.

Then they moved Fred's bed out of his bedroom and placed it near the fireplace. Lloyd was secretly sorry that he would not be required to sleep beside her again.

Day and night he took his turn watching her and stoking the fire. Day and night Fred's fears grew until his face was ashen and haggard. Finally, the tell tale signs told him he could wait no longer to make a decision.

"Three of the toes are frozen, Lloyd. Those little red lines aren't circulation returning, but blood poisoning. If they don't come off gangrene will set in and she could lose her whole foot or leg or die."

Lloyd stood with a strange disoriented sensation, confused and heartsick. Only moments before he had awoken his uncle to tell him that he thought Dorothy seemed a little feverish. Now, he chided himself for not having aroused him sooner. She just couldn't die.

"I can do it alone if you—"

Tears welled in his eyes and he shook his head firmly. Like a robot he sharpened knives, prepared hot water, put the stove poker deep into the coals to heat white hot, and prayed.

But when Fred was ready to start, he could not look. He stood studying her face, memorizing the curve of the cheek and mouth, the way the hair swept back from the temples. Cautiously, he put out a hand and touched her hair. She stirred and he jerked the hand back as if it had been burned. This was not the time for her to come around. Fred had said how thankful they should be that she was unconscious for the operation, because they had nothing to deaden the pain with. He wished to cause her no pain whatsoever.

Then Lloyd realized that he had caused her pain of a different sort. Neither of them had been back to check on her since Christmas. They had left her all alone during the storm. Why had she been coming to their farm? Had she been in need of something? He felt guilty for having brought this all about. He looked up. He could now force himself to watch Fred at work. Fred was saving the life that he had almost lost.

Fred had been quick and exacting about his work. He had already cauterized the left side of the foot, had applied an ample amount of honey to the seared flesh and was lightly bandaging the whole forefoot.

He looked up into admiring and loving eyes.

"I've been a fool," Lloyd whispered. "We both can still love her, but you shall marry her."

Fred nodded sadly. He was not sure he had been in time for anyone to marry her.

At last she was awake enough to take food and start building back her strength. But she recognized no one, nor her surroundings. She became the talk and concern of the valley in a different sense than before.

W.E. James, who had found his wandering son shortly after leaving her cabin, felt great remorse for having brought about the tragedy. Having some practical medical knowledge he offered to take a look at the operated on foot and went away with high praise for Fred Austin. The honey application was allowing the seared skin to heal smooth and scarless. But for her lack of memory he had no ready solution or suggestion.

Griff Evans unkindly said she had a "frozen brain," which greatly angered his wife.

"She needs familiar surroundings," Martha Evans told Fred. "I don't give a hoot what my man says or doesn't say. You get her home, Fred Austin, and my Marymae and I will see to her. Besides, I need Marymae's room. Got an English lady who is willing to pay me eight dollars the week to stay."

Clara MacGregor agreed in principle to the "at home" theory, but felt differently about who should be caring for her. She thought that Lloyd or Fred should move over to the school house and vowed that she and her mother would visit at least three afternoons a week.

Food, almost too much of it, came from everyone. Marymae ate until she was ready to pop, but Dorothy only picked and stared off into space. Her own cabin meant nothing more to her than had the Austin cabin.

The real truth, of course, was known to two others.

As soon as the weather permitted, Paul Ely got Pepper out of the valley for good.

Then, because of the tall protective ring of mountains, the thawing days of February began. Mountain Jim told them to take advantage of it, because the "spring" half of winter was yet to come.

Fields were plowed, fences mended and cattle rounded up from the high country.

Paul Ely's cattle and the fences were in conflict with each other. By night "Ely's Henchmen" would ride hard, tearing down what lay in their way. By day, patiently and doggedly, they were rebuilt. That night the fences would disappear again and the cattle driven right on through. If any man tried to stop them, they were hit with a load of rock salt from a shot gun.

McCreery tried to get James and MacGregor to patch up their differences so that the three of them could join forces against Ely. James was willing, as long as he could stay on the land, but MacGregor stubbornly refused. He wanted James off his property. Each was left to fight alone.

The good weather brought seven new families into the valley. They pitched their tents, put their plows into the grazing land and began to cut the timber for a home and barn.

This invasion Paul Ely could not abide. The grazing cattle were herded back again to the northern sections of the valley and then systematically stampeded through one after another of the tent encampments.

To the utter amazement of all, no one was killed. But the message wasn't wasted. All but one, the fiery little Abner E. Sprague, vanished back down into more civilized territory.

Sprague's determination won the heart of many. To forestall the dangers of tent living, a temporary home was constructed for him and his wife, Minnie, almost overnight. For such a feat to be accomplished, the materials were "borrowed" from the every-increasing supplies just east of the Evans place.

Paul Ely only shrugged at their daring. A slatboard structure would burn much easier than a log cabin.

For those who had helped on the project he struck back with increasing fury. When A.Q. MacGregor complained to the Sheriff in Longmont the man only shrugged. It was out of his jurisdiction and he could only send information up to Fort Collins.

In Denver the territorial authorities still considered the land under the province of the federal government. In his hotel room MacGregor drew up a petition seeking law and order for the area; questioning what was the real difference between the territorial government and the federal governmnt. It caused so much furor that he was given a most illogical answer:

"The Estes Park Company, Ltd., a British owned corporation, being the primary landowners at the present time, are financially responsible for establishing their own security force."

He was not about to let Paul Ely become "the law" of the Estes valley. But his trip was not completely in vain. He returned with an order for the James family to vacate by the middle of April.

Dorothy awoke with a strange but very beautiful face, hovering over her. Her bedroom was awash with bright sunlight and she could hear the chirp of robins.

It all suggested to her nothing short of heaven.

"Who?" she tried to ask, but the word came out a croak. Two months of silence had almost taken away her power of speech.

The woman started. Tears welled up in her beautiful violet eyes. "Praise be," she gasped. "You've come back! This is a blessed day."

Now Dorothy was sure that she was dead. No one outside of England or heaven could possess such a cultured voice.

"I am Isabella Lucy Bird," the woman bubbled, "and I know just what you need. Mrs. Evans . . . Marymae . . . bring in a pot of tea. Our patient is quite awake."

The sight of Martha Evans brought Dorothy back from heaven, but not that of Marymae. The girl had plumped out, and in some of the wrong places.

Martha thought it her duty to make the introductions all anew, which only tended to confuse Dorothy's awakening mind. It filtered through that Isabella was an unusual traveling Englishwoman who was making this a stopping off point in her venture around the world.

But this got entangled with Lloyd's barge into the room, his gaping and silent appraisal of her, and immediate departing charge to spread the news. His horse was gifted with the wings of Mercury, for within the hour the yard began to fill with horses and wagons.

They were bubbling, joyful, thankful—but wisely avoided any mention of her blanket-shrouded legs.

It was finally left up to the stranger among them to put a stop to it all. Isabella could see the draining effect it was having upon her recovery and began to shoo them away.

For a moment Dorothy and Martha Evans were left alone.

"It's like waking up during a nightmare," Dorothy strained to get out, "and not knowing if you are really awake or not."

"While my nightmare is just beginning," Martha blurted out, and then bit her tongue. She had vowed to hold her silence, but had prayed for weeks for Dorothy to come around so that she would have someone to discuss the matter with.

"I noticed," Dorothy sighed.

She was surely now back on earth and would have to face certain truths and condemn herself for coverups and lies.

"Who can't start noticing," Martha began to weep. "She's so closed-mouthed, but I did gain out of her that it had to be that young cowboy, Pepper Whitfield."

At the mention of him Dorothy's blood ran cold and the nightmare came flooding back with vivid clarity. It was still a little unreal the amount of time she had not been a part of the world, but his leering face would remain with her forever.

"So?" she whispered, "what does he say?"

Martha wiped her sleeve across her running nose and scowled, "He'd be standing at the front end of a shotgun, if he hadn't vanished."

Clever, Dorothy thought, all the horrors of earth back around her. Clever, clever Paul Ely. Kill two birds with a single disappearing act. She knew that Pepper was not responsible for getting Marymae with child, but why utter the real truth and ruin Marymae's life by being stuck with one or the other of those worthless older cowboys? And her own accusations against Pepper? The barn door was closed and the culprit gone! Or was he?

"Martha," she said quietly, "don't fret. Paul Ely is responsible for those cowboys. Make him pay for the birthing and care of that child."

"He'll only refuse. He's worse than Lord Dunraven. We ain't seen a single cent on this land since the offer was made."

Earth began to take on a sweet scent again. Dorothy reached out and grasped the woman's hand.

"Just do as I say. Send Marymae to me and I'll give her the words to tell Paul Ely."

Martha started to protest and Dorothy waved the protest aside. Her strength was waning and this above all she wanted to accomplish before it was gone. If she had been brought back for a few moments before she died, she would make sure that she sent Paul Ely to hell first.

Marymae resented the woman returning to the land of the living. The nights she had been left alone to care for her she had been able to dress up in her finest gowns, don her expensive jewelry and entertain Paul Ely without anyone suspecting that he was in the cabin. Once, when he was very drunk, they had even run nude into her bedroom and made passionate love on the floor while she slept numbly above them. It had seemed to arouse Paul like he had never been aroused before, and Marymae had willingly responded. He had come to use all parts of her body and Marymae was not about to give him back to Dorothy now that she was awake.

Dorothy smiled sweetly. "I am well aware that you never came here for school and that you were with Paul Ely all the time. It won't do to accuse Pepper as the father of your child, for I was there, remember? Paul won't claim it either, Marymae, although I somehow think he might be somewhat responsible. So, simply tell Paul that I am awake and that I want you and the child seen to. If not, then I will use every means at my disposal, and then some, to find Pepper Whitfield and bring him back to swear to the truth."

Marymae thought she meant only that Pepper wasn't the father of her child and went away thinking that she had gotten off quite lightly. Paul Ely knew exactly what she meant and went into a black rage. One word from Pepper Whitfield would have them both standing trial for attempted murder. One word out of Marymae might bring Griff Evans to think of him as the father. He was not about to be saddled with the ugly little creature for the rest of his life.

Griff Evans' heart sank. He looked at the fifty-five-year-old, toothless, foolishly grinning cowboy and felt his stomach begin to rumble and churn.

"That's right," Harley Babcock declared again, feeling the hundred dollars in gold in his pocket, "I'm the one who did it and will stand right by what I did to Marymae."

"No," Griff groaned, "just get out! Get out of my sight! I'll see to everything!"

Harley Babcock breathed a sigh of relief. It had happened just as Paul Ely had said it would happen. Besides, Babcock was ready to get out. Fence pulling, barn burning and harrassment was one thing. But he feared the day was coming when the settlers were going to start firing guns back at him. He was not about to get killed for no dollar-a-day and room-and-board.

Griff Evans angered his wife anew, but finally made her see that he was still the boss and would do what he had determined to do. A good woman would be found in Denver for Marymae to live with until the child was born and then it would be placed in an orphanage.

In an odd sort of way Martha Evans blamed Dorothy for her daughter being taken away from her. If Dorothy had not forced the truth out into the open, Marymae would still have been under Martha's protection.

Again, Paul Ely was the only one who escaped someone's wrath. For as Griff Evans took his daughter out of the valley, she turned back and spat in the direction of Dorothy's cabin. Her simple mind suggested to her that she had been duped and that the message had contained a secret code to make Paul come running back to her now that she was awake. Her hate for each of them was like viper's poison.

* * *

Isabella declared that she would stay with Dorothy until she was back on her feet. A statement that she could have nearly bitten her tongue out over. That evening Mountain Jim came to call and brought crutches that he had made. Isabella quietly scolded him and made sure that Dorothy did not see the handsomely contrived contraptions.

More and more Dorothy was hearing of the remarkable job Fred Austin had done in saving her life, but no Fred Austin arrived on the scene to receive thanks.

Mountain Jim was tempted to tell her that he was hiding from praise and in telling her little almost told her too much.

"Your 'doctor' will be around when it's time to change the bandage."

"I couldn't help but notice that," she said on a frown. Then she smiled. "It reminds me of the time that Viscount O'Brien had the gout. What is my ailment?"

Isabella nearly stopped breathing and Mountain Jim pondered if that was to be the moment of truth. He hedged.

"Somehow your leg got broken and you suffered a touch of frostbite."

The "somehow" kept Dorothy from further questioning the frostbite. Her question would only raise questions in return as to what she recalled about the "accident."

Isabella thought it wise to end the conversation right there by a different ruse.

"I think you've had quite enough for one day, young lady. Let me say goodnight to Mountain Jim and then I'll come and tuck you in."

They were gone for some little time. Dorothy lay

back on the pillows and tried not to remember what had happened, but only of the warm friendship that had surrounded her that day. How spendthrift, she thought of Lord Dunraven, that he was overlooking this valuable asset for his valley. Even God put people into his Garden of Eden.

Because women sense such things, Isabella returned with the nervousness of a woman who was secretly in love and had just been delightfully kissed.

Dorothy smiled. "He's an extraordinary man, isn't he?"

Isabella flushed. "The word fits him in more ways than one, I suppose. He does have a gentle, cozy manner . . . and it is a pleasure to listen to his low musical voice with that light Irish brogue."

"Are you in love with him?"

"He is so quick, like a needle," she said, avoiding the question head on. "A thoroughly cultured Irishman."

Dorothy giggled. "Which does make it sound like love."

Isabella took a seat next to the bed and her pretty face pinched into a semblance of its real age. "Dorothy, he is also the most confusing man I have ever met. I fear his black moods when he has been drinking. While you were not with us, he was a guide for the climb up Long's Peak."

Dorothy gasped. "You scaled that mountain?"

Her face turned radiant again. "You might say that Jim, *nolens volens,* dragged me along with patience and skill. Do you know, it is utterly unbelievable, but the mountain is totally flat on top. It's just like God thought it was a little too high at creation and went 'whoosh' with the flat of his hand.

And how close one feels to God in that rarefied air. You are on the top of the world. Giants everywhere rear their splintered crests. Up there, with a single sweep, the eye takes in a distance of three hundred miles—that distance to the west, north, and south being made up of mountains ten, eleven, thirteen and fourteen thousand feet in height. While away to the east, in limitless breadth, stretches the green-gray of the endless Plains. I would not now exchange my memories of that mountain, or the man who introduced me to its perfect beauty, for any other experience in the world."

They were quiet for several seconds. Then Isabella turned and stared at Dorothy with a deep sadness in her violet eyes.

"It was on that trip, in one of his drunk periods, that I believe he told me that he loved me."

"Believe?" Dorothy queried, slightly confused.

"You would have had to have been there, Dorothy, to understand such an odd statement. With the fire lighting up the handsome side of his face, his voice trembled over the words, and tears rolled down his cheek. Was it semi-conscious acting from the drink, I wondered, or was his dark soul really stirred to its depths by my womanhood. For a moment I thought the latter possible, but I put it away as unpardonable vanity in a woman of forty. After our full ascent, and I could bring myself to call him Jim, he explained his emotions satisfactorily and has never shown a trace of it again."

"But he did kiss you tonight, didn't he?"

"What is a kiss to a man, Dorothy?" she laughed. "If he is married, it is an obligation he must perform each morning before leaving the house. If he is unmarried, it is either a prelude of what he next desires, or something he thinks the woman expects of him before saying goodnight. Men are really quite embarrassed about kissing, you know. They show more affection in patting their horse's neck, scratching their dog's head, or raising a stein of beer to a male companion, than they do when they kiss the lips of the woman they love."

"Yes," Dorothy sighed, "I suppose you are quite right, especially in our world of pre-arranged marriage. Love is reserved for the by-product—the children."

"At forty, I sometimes regret having been a headstrong young rebel against such 'forced' marriages. Don't be a fool and end up an old maid who must squander her love on travel and mountains and scenery. They warm the heart, but not the bed. If it were me, I'd snatch up this Fred Austin, while the snatching was good."

"I could turn the tables and tell you to do the same with Mountain Jim."

Isabella sighed profoundly. "One sentence can sum up my feelings on that matter, Dorothy. James Nugent is a man whom any woman might love but who no sane woman would marry."

Dorothy had heard similar words used about Paul Ely and out of experience could not retort.

She awoke to the insistent echo of hammers striking nails and the quiet hum of handsaws being drawn back and forth through lumber. The blind was drawn, the room shadowy, and the sounds a mystery. She exhaled slowly in grateful relief that this day was starting as the last—with memory.

The door opened and Fred Austin crossed to the window and raised the blind. Sunshine flooded the room. Lloyd entered and grinned a wordless greeting. Dorothy pushed herself up on one elbow and smiled back. Fred stood with his back to the window. He looked drawn as if he had been the one ill for so long. She left a surge of contrition. She said tentatively, "Good morning, Fred."

The soft-blue-gray eyes swept from her to Lloyd and back again. He had reversed to the point where he needed Lloyd to back him up and give him courage.

"I'm glad that you are awake. You all right?"

She nodded self-consciously and also looked at Lloyd for support. "Yes, I think so. I understand I owe my life to the two of you."

Lloyd grinned sheepishly and hung his head. "It was really all Fred."

She waited for some response from Fred and when none came, moistened her lips. "I'm afraid there are no words to express my gratitude, Fred."

He made a sound that was half snort and half grunt and strode to the foot of the bed. Without a by-your-leave he threw back the cover and looked at the bandaged foot. Lloyd pulled over the straight back chair and put a wooden box down on it. From it Fred took a pair of scissors and started snipping away the old bandage.

With a slight start of embarrassment she realized that her leg and ankle were exposed to their view. Then she turned crimson with the realization that they would have been the only ones available to remove her clothing on that near fatal night. She pulled the covers to her chin and stared at the ceiling.

"What exactly is wrong with my foot?" she asked softly.

Fred scowled. It was the question he had been dreading and had kept him turning and tossing all night long seeking the proper answer.

"You suffered some frost-bite to the foot, because the broken leg didn't allow it to get proper circulation for some time."

She raised on her elbow again and looked at him. His face was a grim mask. The familiar embarrassment still burned in his eyes. And yet there was something terribly stable about him at this moment, and for the first time she felt a disquieting electricity in his physical presence.

She said gently, "How bad was the frost-bite?"

Fred said, with unusual curtness. "I had to remove three toes."

A million questions flowed through her brain, but her lips and tongue were frozen shut.

Lloyd couldn't restrain himself any further. "He had to do it to save your life!"

Fred frowned. "Lloyd!"

Lloyd looked down, abashed. "Well," he sulked, "she should know about the blood poisoning, and possible gangrene—"

"Indeed she doesn't," he rudely cut him short. "All that is important now is her full recovery. I am not going to rebandage this. Give it a chance to get some fresh air. Lloyd, get Mountain Jim's present and show her how to use them. I'll look at the foot again in a few days."

They went out closing the door before she could utter a word. She didn't want to think about what he said. But how could she avoid it. A part of her was missing. How was it to affect her? Would she be able to walk again? She tried to wiggle her toes, and oddly thought she could feel all five move. Disfigured? That was the next disjointed fragment that filtered across her mind. Well, she just wouldn't look! She just wouldn't look down at that foot ever again! But she would somehow get Paul Ely to look upon it and see how he had maimed her for life!

Lloyd came back in reluctantly with the crutches. She didn't want to look at them, either. They seemed the pronouncement of her worst fears. She would not go about the rest of her life hobbling along on wooden supports.

To avoid discussing them or her condtion, she asked curtly:

"What in the hell is all that echoing racket?"

Lloyd was just as relieved for a different topic, as well.

"A John Cleave arrived last week with quite a work force. They've laid out the hunting lodge and want to get the foundation completed while we still have some good weather. By the size of the layout it's going to be some whopper of a building. Do you want to go out on the porch and see the size of it?"

"I most certainly do not! Why should it be of interest to me?"

"It is what you have been fighting against, isn't it?"

"Was!" she stormed. "What am I supposed to do? Hobble over there on those damn crutches and tear the nails out with my teeth."

Lloyd twisted uncomfortably on the bedside seat. He hadn't counted on her taking this attitude. For the first time ever, she angered him.

"What are you supposed to do? First, consider it a miracle that you are alive! Then stop feeling so damn sorry for yourself."

"Who said I was feeling sorry for myself, Lloyd Folsom?"

"Your tone said it for you," he said impatiently. He laid the crutches against the bed. "No one has said that you are not going to walk again. These are just to keep you from falling until you gain back your own strength. Spring is coming and you've got to get well for your wedding."

"And who said I was getting married?" she demanded.

"Well, darn sakes, it's something . . . I thought . . . Fred loves you and wants to marry you and I think it's a great idea."

"Oh?" she snorted, on a raised eyebrow. "Some idea! Sympathy, I assume. Marry the poor toeless cripple because no other man will now want her!"

"Brother!" he snapped, rising so quickly he knocked over the chair. "It's a damn shame you woke up from that long sleep! I've seen you go through some kind of hell and never whimper or complain. But you're suddenly pitiful. Hell, all you lost was three toes! You didn't lose your beauty! You didn't lose an arm or a leg or your whole life! But you sure as hell seem to have lost your charm and grace and loving ways!"

He slammed out of the door and left it swinging on its leather hinges. Isabella, sitting in the rocker, raised a clenched fist in a signal of "Well done!" She could not help but have heard the raised voices. She considered a little lung clearing a good bit of therapy—and also her non-interference to allow Dorothy to stew in these juices for a while.

It took an hour before she heard the thump of the crutches coming across the wooden floor. She purposely kept her eyes averted from the bedroom door.

"Oh," Dorothy said, "It was so quiet in here that I thought I was quite alone."

"I was just sitting here thinking of my far-off home and when I should depart for it."

"I've been lying in there thinking about how hungry I was getting for breakfast."

Isabella started to rise and then thought better of it. No use stopping a wagon when it was rolling good. "There is mush and coffee on the stove."

Again she avoided looking as the thumps sounded behind her and over to the range.

"Do you know something, Isabella?"

"No, what?"

"It looks like a fist with only the first three fingers closed." She hesitated. "There is only one thing. I'm going to need a little bit of help pouring the coffee until I get used to it."

Isabella jumped up. Help asked for was help given.

"And Isabella," Dorothy said, as she sat down at the table, "I'm going to have to walk, if I am returning to Europe with you."

Isabella Lucy Bird's heart turned over inside of her. It was going to hurt, but she had to apply one more bit of therapy for the patient.

"Then that greatly alters my plans, Dorothy. I had been thinking spring and another climb up the summit. Now, I think it best if I have Jim take me down to Longmont this week."

"But," Dorothy protested, "I shall never be ready by then!"

"Exactly, my dear. Today you don't see it, but you are a part of this glorious region now. I must leave because I am but a stranger and a visitor. I am John the Baptist who must go ahead and sing of its praises. But you I envy. You remain in this clear air where life is so intoxicating. I don't think you really want to leave, do you?"

"No," she answered softly.

"Then I leave this Island Valley of Avalon in your expert care."

15

THE SPRING SURPRISED them all with its mildness. John Cleave did not have to return his workers to Denver and daily the hunting lodge took on the look of no hunting lodge Dorothy had ever seen before. Once the first two floors were framed in, a third was added under the peaked roof with dormer windows. It would boast thirty-three rooms, plumbing facilities, spacious dining room, lobby, library, writing room, sun parlor and kitchens.

But as the air grew heavy with the scent of life's rebirth it was still a shell. Tender green shoots were not the only things nudging their way out of the wet black earth. Although it was only a trickle of what was taking place on the wide plains, two to three families a week were finding their way up into the Island Valley of Avalon.

Now a rare oddity did occur. These were real land squatters—people without title to anything, but just as greedy in their landgrabbing as the Earl himself. But towards them Paul Ely developed a "hands off" policy. He was as silent and unseen as though he were not even in the valley. But his ploy soon became apparent.

His cowboys daily rode the downward trail, greeting the strangers with glad tidings and news of the best land available. The best land, of course, being that of MacGregor, McCreery, Sprague, Ferguson, Hupp, Austin and Goold. More time was spent by the real settlers in chasing off this nuisance element than in seeing to their spring chores.

Early that spring Theodore Whyte made another visit to the valley. Sober and duded up like an English gentleman, he carried about a satchel of hard coin to purchase outright what fear had not achieved. The last vestiges of ice were disappearing from the rivers and lakes, but not from men's hearts. He went away without a single purchase to his credit and left behind a very disgruntled Martha Evans. The hunting lodge and Dunraven cottage were rising on Evans land and she could not get her husband to force money out of Whyte in payment.

Theo Whyte had avoided visiting Dorothy, which amused her. He had purposely done so out of two rumors he had gleaned from Paul Ely. The woman was an invalid and was planning to marry one of the squatters.

Windham Thomas was preparing to leave New York for the west when the wired information reached him. He shrugged indifferently at the news of her incapacitation and fumed with family indignation at the second morsel of news. With righteousness that would have made Rev Lamb look like a fallen angel, he cabled Lady Jane his personal thoughts on such an unseemly match and advised the refusal of dowry and the striking of Dorothy's name from all family records. She, in his opinion, had put herself beyond the bounds of title and family name.

For an invalid, Dorothy was doing remarkably well. Mountain Jim had whittled for her a shoe wedge and wrapped it in doe skin. As she would step on the ball of her right foot, it would give within her boot, just like her natural toes, giving her forward support and allowing her to walk without limping or awkwardness.

Because Fred was shy in his courtship, and because both Jim and Dorothy came to realize how greatly they missed Isabella Bird, their friendship became a very constant thing. Except in the mind of Paul Ely, it was not considered an unnatural relationship.

And when a friendship becomes so rich, it must bear the burden of secrets. Sworn to total silence, Dorothy was able to unburden her heart to Jim about her attack by Pepper Whitfield. And as every priest must admit when he makes his final act of contrition, it is not his own sins that have rounded his shoulders and greyed his hair, but the confessions of others that he has toted through life. Mountain Jim knew that Paul Ely was the real culprit, but his oath bound him from doing anything about it.

But his secret in return seemed hardly any secret. Everyone was becoming well aware of where the squatters were gaining their information about the land. But the wrinkle he added to it greatly intrigued Dorothy.

"Oh, land's sake," Clara sighed with pleasure.

"If this isn't the most welcome sight I have seen all spring."

"Hello," Dorothy called, agilely springing down from her horse.

"Lord of mercy," Clara gasped. "Have you done what I think you have done?" It all ran together as almost a single word.

"I certainly have," Dorothy laughed. "I took a skirt and split it right up the middle and resewed it like a pair of pants. With this foot I find it easier to ride like a man than a lady. Besides, I always thought sidesaddle was the most restrictive, uncomfortable thing that man ever imposed upon woman."

Dorothy was about to add that child bearing was the next, but wisely checked herself. She knew that Clara was beginning to fret about her barren, childless state.

"Don't get your feelings hurt," Dorothy laughed anew, "but I've really come to see your husband."

"Well, really, Dorothy Goold," Clara kidded, good naturedly, "you've already got the heart of every man in the valley in your hand, can't you leave poor little me with Mr. MacGregor?"

"I'll think on it," she kidded back.

"Well think on it over lunch. Mother is cook today and you know that always puts Mr. MacGregor in his finest moods."

"How did you know I wanted him in a good mood?"

"Dorothy Goold," Clara grinned, affectionately taking her arm, "you've got that 'I've come after something important' gleam in your eye."

To her disappointment, A.Q. MacGregor did not

rise to her suggestion. He said, "I will see to keeping people off my land, and let the others do the same."

Georginna Henney downed the last drop of tea in her hand-painted China cup and frowned dramatically. "Alex," she said sweetly, for she was the only one who dared address him so informally, "what about this $300 loan to Bradford D. Bradley we were discussing?"

He gazed at her as though she were beginning to show senile signs. "That was last night at the dinner table, Mother Henney."

"Of that I am quite aware," she said curtly. "I speak of his non-payment of the interest at $9 a month and the fact that his collateral is a Decker Brothers Grand piano. Although it is past time to take the piano as payment of the debt, it would be ruined transporting it from Longmont."

"I fully agree," he said, puzzled.

"Then Miss Goold's suggestion is not only sound but practical, as are most suggestions that originate with intelligent women. I like this idea of a toll road, and her willingness to put up all of her land as collateral until her dowry money is here to purchase it back. If you do not wish to do so, I shall take her paper, and invest $10,000 of my own wealth in the undertaking."

"I–I–" MacGregor stammered.

"I knew you would see the light," Georginna said matter of factly. "Now, Alex, you will leave for Denver in the morning, before Lord Dunraven gets the same idea. His family are not fools, as we can see from the example sitting at our table. The Territorial Legislature must be immediately petitioned to grant–what shall we call it–Oh, yes,

The Estes Park Wagon Road Company, the exclusive right to build and maintain a road from Glen Evans to Estes Park, and collect a toll thereon for the amount of years that it will take to recompense us for the cost of building it. That should keep the squatters out who don't have the price of the toll or papers to prove their claim."

"As you wish, Mother Henney," he said softly.

Dorothy's eyes grew wide with delight. "Oh, I would love to see Cousin Windham's face when he learns that he can't get his hands on the land from Steamboat Rock up to Mountain Jim's claim."

Georginna poured herself a fresh cup of tea and daintily laughed. "My dear child, I personally think it would be far more amusing to see his face when he reads the articles of incorporation that we shall file for such a venture. You, after all, shall have to be listed as one of the officers and stockholders. Wouldn't you agree, Alex?"

He had no choice but to nod his agreement. After all, his mother-in-law was the bankroll behind his success. But he could not have asked for a better partner in business, and for the wife that she had given him he could not be more grateful.

But to be associated with Dorothy left him a little disconcerted.

Because of her quick decision, and A.Q.'s apparent fear not to do as she wished, the Legislature granted the exclusive rights after some negotiations. Georginna had one more chore for him. If Alex were to spend most of his time on the project, then he would be on hand to tell the squatters where there wasn't land.

There were no giant machines to help tame the mountains; even dynamite was scarce. Picks, shovels, large mules and physical exertion were the components that went into the roadway. It meant work for many, with the Estes Park men given first chance. The Island Valley of Avalon became a working valley of women. They plowed and sowed and herded and milked and extended their vegetable gardens into small farms.

Not everyone got in on the work bonanza. MacGregor's memory was long as to who had sided with W.E. James.

Horace Ferguson had helped James build a new home near the foot of Old Man Mountain, but that was neighborly trade off work with no money passing hands. Ferguson was at his wit's end. By an odd fluke he had been able to claim only a forty acre tract which was an island in a sea of Dunraven land. He knew that James was in the same boat. James had wanted a cattle ranch, but his new claim was ill-suited to such a purpose. But he had to do something.

Ferguson was therefore amazed to find him doing nothing but fishing in the Fall River near his new home.

"Bill, are you daft? That wash tub is near to over flowing with trout."

"Still don't seem enough," he said sadly. "Hear tell that fish is going for fifty cents a pound in Denver. Best get these down the canyon to catch the train." Then he hesitated. "Horace, your boy Hunter isn't doing you a lick of good staying down on that grasshopper-eaten farm of yours. Get him up here. You and me will do the hunting and fishing and he can tote it down to the train."

There was nothing Horace loved more than hunting and fishing. Now it was a dawn to dusk business. In three days he had eleven deer and seven hundred and twenty trout—kept fresh in wicker baskets lined with wet grass. Hunter had arrived with the rest of the Ferguson farm equipment and furniture. He had lost one wagon over a fifty foot high precipice, killing about a dozen chickens and turkeys. Enough of the chickens survived for Mrs. Ferguson to start selling fresh eggs locally. Mrs. James wanted to buy some of the chickens for eggs of her own. When Horace took over the chickens he was amazed to learn Bill James had not shot a thing and was starting to build a new cabin.

"Well, Horace," he drawled, in his cultured New York voice, "a lady, a Mrs. Crocker, came by with a sick infant son and begged for a place to stay. Doctor says little Sherwood has to be in the mountains, where it is cool, to save his life. She's willing to pay a nice price to be a guest. House isn't large enough, so I'm building a guest cabin. I'll do my fishing this afternoon."

Although it marred the beginning of the partnership in Horace's mind, he rode off up into Horseshoe Park to uphold his hunting part of the bargain. It turned into a miserable rainy day, with the clouds hanging low onto the mountains and making them look like flat topped mesas. Where he would normally see hundreds of deer and elk, that day he didn't fire his muzzle-loader once.

Disgusted, wet and tired he came down into the middle of the horseshoe-shaped basin. At the far end of a large beaver pond he saw Bill James fishing. He thought his side of the pond would be better for fishing, but luck seemed to be against him again. When he reached in his pocket for the fish line he always carried it was gone. He had hooks in his hat, but what to do for a line? Then he recalled the black hemp thread on which he strung his gun patches. A pole was no problem, for you cut a new one each time you fished.

He had hardly cast his line before a handsome trout snapped at the fly. In less than two hours he brought out three hundred and twenty fish and his arms were just too tired to cast one more time. James had done almost as well.

The ready supply of fish in the dam gave Horace much more time to hunt, as well as Bill James. But the deer and elk meat didn't have to make the long journey to the train. A.Q. MacGregor now had quite a road crew working and was obligated to feed them. He had to eat crow and buy his meat from Ferguson and James. By the middle of July the deer and elk antlers made quite a respectable pile near the James cabin. Then Bill James started building a third cabin.

"What now?"

"I'm out of my bed again, Horace. My wife rented it for the rest of July and August to a Miss Hyde—a friend of Mrs. Crocker. The young lady wants to stay the winter and start a school for my boys."

"Miss Goold has a school."

James sneered. "Not for my boys. Miss Hyde has a certificate making her a *real* teacher."

Ferguson thought it best to avoid the issue any further. "You know, Bill, you keep building and you'll have cabins everywhere."

"You know, Horace, I had no intention of taking in guests, but I think there will be more money in that than raising cattle or catching fish. You and

Hunter can handle it, right? And thanks to your good efforts, I have a name for my ranch."

"Oh?"

"Elkhorn Ranch."

Such determination for survival naturally reached the ears of Lord Dunraven, but did not impress him. If there were to be guests, they would be his and his alone. He began running ads in the Denver newspapers announcing that he had bought Estes Park and warning everybody that he would permit nobody there except as his guests.

Deny something to someone and they automatically want to see what they have been excluded from. A steady stream of the curious filtered up and down from the valley. If there was a bed to be rented, it was snatched up for a night, a week, or as long as it was available while the Plains were suffering from the hottest, driest summer in years.

Work stopped on the hunting lodge so that more and more hastily thrown together cabins could be erected on the Evans place. John Hupp moved his family into a tent and rented out the cabin between the pine trees. In August Bill James started another cabin on his Elkhorn Ranch.

In mid-August a balding, thin, commonly dressed tourist rode his horse around Steamboat Rock and along the St. Vrain. His sharp eyes examined the new road as though he were a government inspector eager to find anything to disapprove of. Coming down off the Pinewood Springs plateau, he stopped at the Little Thompson to let his horse drink before fording. For the first time he smiled with approval and admiration. Along the side of the mountain a shelf road was being built up rock by rock. It would take three miles off the route and eliminate going through the deep gorge that he was in.

Out of the gorge he came upon the road crew camp. For the price of a dollar he could eat roast venison, boiled potatoes, raw carrots and turnips and open-oven biscuits. He thought the food common, but good.

The construction workers were of a different mind. They were sick of venison and wanted some beef or pork. MacGregor was not about to slaughter any of his cattle, refused to do business with Paul Ely, and pork was near impossible to find. Many of the workers were agitating for a strike.

The short, thin man was obviously a gentleman and his opinion sought.

He shrugged. "A strike would do nothing but stop your pay and force him to bring in other workers. The streets of Denver are lined with men looking for work of any nature. Just negotiate and ask him for pork or beef once in awhile."

But he refused to negotiate for them. At the moment the Fourth Earl of Dunraven had no desire to meet A.Q. MacGregor. He was impressed with the road and didn't want the work stopped until it was completed. Then and only then would he use his political power to prove that Dorothy Goold's collateral was a fraud. Why should he be stuck with a half completed road, he reasoned, when he could have a fully completed road at bankruptcy prices?

Lord Dunraven was not impressed with his valley. He wanted his lodge completed and furnished by the next summer. He wanted all of this riff-raff thrown out. He was going to be bringing 'real' ladies and gentlemen from Europe and they would not appreciate having to associate with commoners.

"But that," he roared at Paul Ely and Griff Evans, "is one eyesore I do not want my future guests forced to look upon. Damn that woman! She has ruined my whole view with those two squatty cabins. Wasn't one of you man enough to tell her she is quatting on illegal ground?"

They both were sheepishly silent.

"And what's more," Dunraven blared on, "I want Rocky Mountain Jim bought out, chased out or eliminated. Coming by his hovel is a worse eyesore than what I am now viewing. Griff, go find out what the man's price might be; Paul, tell John Cleave to get his ass back to work on my hunting lodge or there will be a new foreman here before he can gulp. I shall handle this other matter personally."

Dorothy piled an armload of beets onto the horse cart Lloyd had built for her and leaned against one of the wheels which had been retrived from the Ferguson wagon wreck. The sweat rolled off her face in streams and she wiped her forearm across her eyes and then dug into the deep pocket of her 'gardening' dress for a handerchief.

She looked around in satisfaction. Her garden's harvest had been even better than she had expected. All summer, without Griff knowing of it, she had been selling vegetables to Martha to feed her guests and the carpenter crew. Her shelves were crammed full of her canning efforts and, what Martha didn't buy before the crops were all gone, she would sun dry for winter use. It had been a quiet productive summer for the whole valley. She felt a warm pride being a part of it all.

Then her warmth turned to ice water in her veins. She was unaware how long he had been standing staring at her.

"Hello, Cousin Windham," she said coldly.

"My, my, Dorothy, I hardly recognized you. You are so brown and lean and . . ."

She restrained a smile. "And healthy looking for a cripple?"

"I wasn't going . . ."

"Why not, Windham? I'm sure that you have had a most detailed and untruthful report from Paul Ely."

"I haven't had time . . ."

"Don't lie, Windham. At least be man enough not to lie. We Wynham-Quins may be many other things, but we are never liars."

Lord Dunraven flung his hat down on the ground angrily. "How can I even lie, when you won't let me get a word in edgewise?"

Dorothy brushed a stray strand of hair from her face and now allowed herself to smile.

"You may not believe this, Windham, but last week I had to help the MacGregor women herd cattle. One angry bull decided to take an immediate dislike to me. I had to learn not to let him get a word in edgewise, either. He's now happily mating down in Devil's Gulch. Speaking of mating, how is Lady Florence?"

Dunraven flushed scarlet. This was hardly the same creature he had been able to cower at their last meeting. She was not only weathered by nature and the land, she was as rock hard and unmovable as any of the towering mountains.

"She is with child again and desires to return to Ireland for this birth. Her health has been such to keep me away. I really never should have brought her back from New York."

Dorothy shook her head mockingly. "Saints preserve us, why? She is after all only a woman who was told not to bear any more children—or attempt to. Windham, you are a monster. Now get off my land."

Not having expected a violent reaction, she was momentarily stunned as he slapped her soundly across the cheek.

There was a long silence. Finally, Dorothy said, bluntly, "I'm glad *you* did that, Windham. No hired stooges this time to frighten me, attack me with a horse, break my leg and leave me to die in a blizzard. No hired stooges this time to tear down fences, burn down barns, nearly kill people with cattle stampedes. This moment makes the loss of three toes well worth it. You have placed yourself out in the open, dear cousin. All right, fight me! Fight me for this land! I hear you have papers on it, but so do I. Others in this valley have papers on land that you claim. Fight me and I'll gather up every one of them and personally take them to Washington. I, too, if you remember, met President Grant."

She jumped up onto the cart and clucked the horse to move out. She prided herself on delivering her vegetables perfectly fresh. He was a ghost from a past that was rapidly fading from her mind. Snobbish, arrogant, using all manner of other men who would do the work to line their greedy pockets. Her relationship was now with the people of this valley and not with some titled Irish lord.

Rounding Mirror Lake, she determined one other thing. She had been a silly goose to sneak her vegetables over to Martha Evans. It was the law of supply and demand. Clara MacGregor would not supply them vegetables from her abundant garden and the guests and carpenters demanded them. She was the only other major supplier.

Dunraven stood looking after her for a long time. Then he determined to see the manner of life she had been leading in the squatty little cabins, By his standards it was disgusting. Not only did she now look like a tenant farm woman, she was actually living like one. He would not condone a member of the Whyham-Quin family to disgrace the whole clan in this way.

Still, to Dorothy's relief, Griff Evans had gone to see Mountain Jim. Behind the main ranchhouse she helped Martha top and wash the beets in a wooden tub. Neither woman saw the thin white wisp of smoke rise straight up into the motionless air from beyond the lake. They chatted on.

Almost at the same moment, Clara looked up from her hoeing and saw the smoke. It was no fireplace burning on a hot day like that. Smoke, to the pioneering woman that she was becoming, meant fire. Georginna had seen it too, and came barreling down the drive with wagon and team. Clara jumped aboard while it was still on the move. Women or not, they were the only ones in the valley.

Georginna drove the team as though she had been trained by the Overland Express, but even before they rounded Little Prospect Mountain, the entire meadowland sky was being blotted out by white smoke. Women raced toward Fish Creek on horses, mules and wagons.

Dorothy and Martha smelled the smoke before they rushed around the main ranchhouse to see the fire. Both, at first, thought one of the errant tourists had set a shanty cabin afire. But a hissing crackle took their eyes across the lake.

The shock of what she saw tore the air from Dorothy's lungs and left her panting for breath. Both cabins were totally engulfed in smoke and dancing orange flames. She flung herself onto her horse, arms flailing wildly to get him to move.

The horse moved, but she was not aware of it. Her eyes were transfixed on the scene beyond. She watched the fire spread to the trees surrounding the cabins. The orange tongues leapt to the crown of the pines and then roared down them with a blinding flash. Her favorite, a giant blue spruce, went up like a torch, with a sudden, excruciating whoooooooom! of agony, and then continued to burn.

The gathered women could do nothing. The well pump had been within the cabin and the lake was an eighth of a mile away. The air was choked with dust and smoke, and so hot it seared their nostrils as they breathed. All they could do was pray that the sparks would not fly beyond the little grove in which the cabin had been erected.

It was all gone so quickly. Her books, her clothing, her gifted furniture, her hard hours of winter canning—gone. Even her garden was gone—the vegetable tops charred and the juices cooked right out of the roots. Pumpkins and squash lay shattered as though they had exploded from the heat. Total ruin!

And never once did Lord Dunraven or Paul Ely ride over to offer help or question what had happened. Nor did they allow Cleave and his carpenters to come. Because of this Dorothy could not shake off the conviction that the Earl had something to do with the fire. She had been a fool to ride away and leave him there alone.

She only had a hazy idea of the offers of help she declined. Fred and Lloyd were working on the road crew, so the MacGregor women silently escorted her to their cabin.

"Will she be all right?" Clara asked worriedly. "Should we really leave her alone at a time like this, mother?"

"The present moment doesn't worry me," Georginna said, with a heavy sigh. "If this defeats her, then they might take courage to burn down other homes and cabins."

"Surely you don't think—"

"Think?" the woman snapped. "What else can one think? Use the brain God gave you, girl. This is the sixteenth day of August! There were no fires in the fireplace and she was not home to be cooking on the range. Fire doesn't come from nowhere on a clear and bright day like this."

Clara shuddered. The quiet summer had come to an end.

The man leaned over Dorothy, his face ashen white and his scar a raging purple.

"Fire just doesn't come from nowhere!" Mountain Jim bellowed, repeating Georginna's words exactly.

Dorothy didn't answer for a time, then her words didn't make sense to him.

"He can have it."

Then as it soaked in Jim Nugent was aghast.

"Oh, he can have it, can he? Well, he'll not be having Jim Nugent so easily. I told the same to Griff Evans today, I did." Then he laughed. "Might be a good thing if they came and burned me out. Good way to clean out the trash and get a new start."

His levity was not reaching her. She just sat very still and stared straight ahead into nothingness.

Her misery was now his misery. But I am such a heathen next to her, God knows, he thought wryly. But never before had a woman needed a man more to take up her cause, even if he be the man. It was time, he determined, for Paul Ely and Lord Dunraven to pay the piper for their sins.

Lord Dunraven flatly refused to see the man. He hired underlings like Ely and Evans to handle such mad bulls. He pushed Paul out of the door and cowered behind it listening.

"Great God!" Mountain Jim roared. "I ask for the lord and I get his pimp!"

Ely scowled. "I could call you out for such a statement!"

"Then call me out, pimp! pimp! pimp!," Jim chuckled sarcastically. "But you won't, you yellow-bellied coward. You can only send your henchmen to do your dirty work. Sent any lately to ride ladies down in a blizzard? Do you play with matches or is that the lord himself?"

Ely was stunned that the man even had an inkling about Dorothy's 'accident.'

Behind the half-closed door a frightened Griff Evans pleaded quietly with the Earl. "Let me go out. It's only his drunk talk. I can calm him."

Dunraven ignored him as though he were not even there.

Nugent clenched his fists. He was not bringing Dunraven from hiding, or getting Ely to admit anything.

"You know, Ely," he sneered, "it's too bad Evans had only one daughter for you, or do his sons please you just as well?"

Ely blanched white. He was weaponless or would have shot the man on the spot to keep the secret truth from being open knowledge.

Dunraven had to restrain Evans from barging out and attacking both men for such a charge.

"Stay silent," Jim snickered, starting to turn his horse about, "but listen good. If you, or that piss-ant Earl or that polecat Griff Evans tries one more thing against Miss Goold, then I would just as soon shoot any of you than a bear. No, come to think of it, I'd rather let the bear live and shoot you snakes."

Ely came back into the house ashen. He prayed that Evans would take Mountain Jim's words as the raving of a madman. The two men glared at each other silently. Dunraven went to the window and peeked out through the curtains.

Nugent rode away for a few yards and stopped the horse. He had gotten some of the anger off his chest, but hadn't helped Dorothy at all. He had to put things square to Lord Dunraven or he would have accomplished nothing. He turned the horse and started back.

"He's coming back!" Dunraven gasped, terror filling his voice.

Ely blinked foolishly. "He lied! You know he lied! Ask Marymae! Ask the boys if he isn't lying." He rushed forward and grasped Evans' arm.

Griff shook the hand off angrily but Dunraven turned and seized his shoulders and spoke quickly in his ear.

"Evans, Rocky Mountain Jim is coming back. You will not let him shoot Ely down like a dog will you?"

Griff hesitated. Then he shook his head slowly. If any man could reason with Jim, he could. He went to the door, and then he stopped. He turned back and took a double barreled shot gun from the rack. He spat contemptuously at Ely's feet and went out onto the porch.

The sight of the gun broke the last desire Jim had of playing fair. Griff Evans had been his friend for years, but he could not stand a turn-coat. He spurred the horse forward, to catch Evans off guard and disarm him.

Dunraven and Ely burst through the door together, but each would deny later who gave the real command.

"Shoot! Shoot!"

Evans grew confused and fired off one side of the double-barrel without really aiming.

There was a horrifying scream as the horse reared back and then began to fall to its side, mortally wounded.

"Asshole!" Ely bellowed, snatching the gun from

Evans' hands. He fired the second barrel before Jim was able to jump from the falling horse. The blast lifted Jim away from the horse and threw him back ten feet.

"He's not dead!" Dunraven wailed.

Ely drew his revolver and fired four times at the figure on the ground. It never once flinched.

They stood as though totally divorced, one from the other.

In the kitchen Martha Evans had been watching the beet water turn blood red when she heard the shots. Suddenly, she was violently ill to her stomach.

The cabin guests, preparing for dinner, thought it was just someone preparing for a hunt the next day and didn't venture out.

As though nothing unusual had happened, Dunraven turned calmly to Evans.

"Oh, by the way, Griff, I have looked into that matter you raised with me. In my saddle bags are papers making your wife the new postmistress to replace *this* Mrs. MacGregor. She will have to take the papers over there and pick up what is necessary." And just as casually, "And tomorrow you'd best take the long ride down to Fort Collins. Go to a justice of the peace and plead guilty to self defense and file charges against Nugent for assault and battery with intent to kill."

Evans' mind was still numb.

"But he's the one . . . and Jim's dead . . ."

"Don't worry," Dunraven soothed. "We both saw the man charge you with his horse and drawn weapon. You acted to save all three of our lives. So do as I say. I shall see to bail and a lawyer. Now, I think it is time for us to wash up for dinner."

"What about me?" Paul croaked. Realization was dawning that he had just killed a man.

Dunraven put his arm about his shoulders as though he were a bosom companion.

"Well, Paul my boy, I fear I shall now have to stay in Colorado to protect our good friend Griff Evans. I don't think you should even stay for dinner. Because Lady Florence thinks so highly of you, I am putting you in charge of seeing her safely home to Ireland. Need I say that it is to our mutual advantage for you to stay there until I deem it proper for you to return?"

It was obvious he didn't want to stay around and face a murder charge. He went directly to the stable and got his horse, with no mind to waste time going back to his cabin for anything. Lady Florence would just have to re-outfit him. When he rode back through the front yard the Earl and Evans were gone. He averted his eyes from looking at the rest of the scene. That was a grave error. The horse was there, but the body was gone.

I can't even give him back a pair of crutches, Dorothy thought ruefully. All I can do is sit and watch the life drain out of him. It had been so long ago that she had forgotten how she had felt or reacted at the time of her father's death. I will not cry! she told herself, I will not! He deserves my courage now and not my tears.

She heard the horses coming at the gallop and she relaxed. Fred was now here to see to the doctoring. Fred would make Mountain Jim well, just as he had her.

"Thank God you came so quickly. Clara must have flown on the wind."

"We met her part way. How did this happen?"

"He's been able to tell me bits and pieces, but we'll get into that after we've seen to him."

Fred frowned. His face looked so baffled and beaten that she was momentarily confused.

"I'll see to him," he said softly. "You go out and see to your guest."

He turned and went into his bedroom without further explanation. Now, really confused, Dorothy went out onto the porch. The alpine glow still held the crested peaks in pink pastels, but the meadowland valley was basked in shadowy dusk. Three figures stood talking by the four horses. Dorothy did not need to be told which was Clara MacGregor or Lloyd Folsom, but the three figures just didn't. . . .

Then, slowly, she started down off the porch, the beat of her heart starting to thump in the roof of her mouth. The large boned, formidable woman watched her come, holding her breath hard in her throat. Then the tight-held band of silence burst and they were running toward each other, arms outstretched, and Dorothy's tears did come now as she nestled in her mother's arms.

"*Pish tosh!*" Lady Jane growled, thankful to be getting a cup of hot tea into her system. "Windham is only part of my reason for being here, Dorothy. I had a most unexpected but charming visit from Miss Isabella Lucy Bird."

"Isabella came to Ireland?"

Lady Jane sipped at her tea. She was not the manner of woman who could be rushed. Except for her bone structure one could see the woman Dorothy would develop into in her middle years. Handsome of face, with only a hint of the wrinkles that were yet to come. Deep auburn hair with attractive gray bird wings sweeping back from the temples, and the same green eyes that could spark with many emotions.

"And why shouldn't she come to Ireland?" she answered on a near scold. "The woman seems to have been everywhere else in the world. Really a person to envy. You are lucky, Dorothy, to be able to count her as a friend. I believe this gentleman that has been stricken was also a friend of her."

"He was," Dorothy sighed. "He's been a good friend to all of us. Oh, there is so much I want to tell you, that I don't know where to begin."

"Well, for the moment save your breath. Miss Bird is a highly gifted woman with words and descriptions. She was such a staunch advocate for your cause that mother was packing me off on the next boat to see what was afoot in this land."

"Oh," Dorothy gasped, "how rude of me. How is grandmother?"

"About the same as when you left us," Lady Jane said impishly. "She was born a cantankerous and meddlesome woman and shall die as one. I do believe that she has plans, when that day comes, to immediately replace Saint Peter and take over the approval of who may enter heaven. Of course, you and I better not count on passing her muster. She has spent a lifetime tallying up our earthly errors."

Dorothy smiled at her lovingly. Now she realized what it was that she had so missed about home—the constant, good-natured banter between her mother and grandmother. She was glad that her mother had come to take her home. It hadn't been said in so many words, but she sensed it just the same. Any thought of marrying Fred Austin did enter her head at that moment.

Fred Austin and Lloyd finally came out of the bedroom. Fred rubbed his chin ruefully. "For a moment there I thought I'd bitten off more than I could chew. Never saw a man keep so silent while slugs and shot were taken out of him."

Lloyd grunted. "That is no ordinary man."

Dorothy snorted. "Tell that to others," there was an edge of sarcasm in her voice. "He crawled all the way here, just so he could have a witness. Did he tell you anything?"

"Said you'd tell me."

Dorothy rose, rubbing her hands together ruefully. "Lord help me, I'd love to tell the world! He was unarmed and believes Dunraven ordered him shot!"

Fred scowled. "It's not like Jim to ride about without his hunting rifle."

"Well, there it sits in the corner and has sat since he was here this afternoon." The horror that had been building in her heart had to come out. "I–I'm probably responsible for this having happened. Jim has known for some time the truth behind how I got the broken leg in the blizzard. Today Griff Evans was sent to try and buy him out–about the time my home was burning. All I can imagine is that Jim confronted the Earl and Paul Ely with the truth about Pepper Whitfield riding me down while I was on snowshoes."

The room was filled with sudden silence. Neither man thought she had presented reason enough for a murder attempt, but were both a little hurt that she had never confided this truth in them.

It was Lady Jane who studied the three of them

like specimens under a glass. She had been gathering certain impressions about Fred and Lloyd since her hired buggy had arrived at the shelf road workings. The driver had gotten into a violent argument when MacGregor would not let him continue on the unfinished road. The man had charged Lady Jane an outlandish price for the trip and was reluctant to lose any portion of it. Upon learning the identity of the passenger, MacGregor hastily sent for Fred and Lloyd.

Knowing of them from Isabella Bird, Lady Jane was not instantly impressed, even after they borrowed a horse from MacGregor and offered to escort her to her daughter's cabin.

Finding Fred too shy and reserved, and Lloyd too overly eager to please her, she let them know right from the start that she was there to stop the marriage.

Then came the meeting with Clara MacGregor and the double tragic news of the fire and Rocky Mountain Jim's shooting. It did not give Lady Jane a very good first impression of the area.

For the four mile trip back to the valley, the ladies kept apart from the men. Culture and breeding instantly recognized culture and breeding, and Lady Jane was known as a woman who investigated a thing very cautiously and thoroughly.

In Clara she found a woman who gave her straight-forward, clear-cut answers. Even though the answers made her heart grow heavier, she probed right to the core of the matter. She had sent away a little girl and heard a woman being described to her.

And the sighting of her daughter had shocked her. Her hair was unkempt, dirt traces still remained under her fingernails from her morning gardening, and the old cotton gardening dress hung on her like a Dublin street ragpicker. Her face had been drawn from the double tragedy and her eyes red-rimmed after the tearful greeting. But Lady Jane had staunchly determined to hold all such thoughts to herself—at least for that evening.

But now she sat back and studied them all in an entirely different light.

Dorothy broke the silence.

"He said that Griff Evans fired and hit his horse. He thinks that Paul Ely took the shotgun then, but he isn't sure. He just thought that he was seeing his last moment on earth. Shot down, unarmed, by two ruffians and their blood-thirsty commander. It is sickening to think how far that man will go to fill his pockets. And you mark my words, those two will lie and protect Dunraven as they always have. How I hate that murdering bastard!"

"Dorothy!" Lady Jane gasped. "You are speaking of your cousin!"

Dorothy's response was explosive. "You've got a great deal to learn, Mother. This is not a polite little coterie socializing over water-cress sandwiches and tea. Up until today I was fighting him out of personal spite and my own arrogant pride. Stupid pride, if I am to be very honest. And if I am to be honest, I must be shocking. I think Fred and Lloyd deserve to hear the truth, as much as you. I have been trying to hurt the man because he crawled into my tent and took liberties with me by pretending to be the man that I loved. 'Thought I loved' would be a better phrase, because *Lord* Dunraven has done everything within his power to turn Paul against me. Perhaps I should really be thanking our dear cousin, Mother. If my love hadn't been turned to bitter bile, I might now find myself married to a suspected assassin!"

"Great God!" came a bellicose roar from the bedroom. "Don't give up, girl!"

Almost as one they bounded into the bedroom, fearing the worst. Dorothy knelt by the bed and took Jim's amazingly slender hand in her own. He lay staring up at the ceiling.

"That I," he whispered, "an American citizen who has lived on Colorado soil since 1854 must have my life attacked and my liberty stolen. All this for English gold?"

He closed his eyes and a smile came to his thin lips. He squeezed Dorothy's hand tenderly.

"Is he gone?"

Dorothy shook her head. "He's just waiting for my answer."

Lady Jane turned and walked from the room. She didn't have to hear the answer, she had been listening to it for the past several minutes. Never in her life had she ever felt so proud and calm of spirit. She had lost a child, but gained in return something far more valuable.

But there was still a doubt in her mind as to whether Fred Austin was a proper husband. Things being what they were, she determined it was wise to accept Clara's offer to stay at the ranch. There was time enough to see to matters as she wished to see to them.

There was plenty of time for Lady Jane Goold, but not for others. Dorothy's declaration had left Fred doubtful. He felt she had been using him as an unthinking pawn in her spiteful battle against

Ely and the Earl. It hurt. It hurt very deeply. But was he man enough to find the words to discuss the matter openly with her?

He didn't return to the road work, on the excuse of having to see after Rocky Mountain Jim. But with each passing day, he put off talking with Dorothy more and more.

Lord Dunraven, still unaware of Lady Jane's arrival, made sure that Jim Nugent had very little time.

Fred was grateful that Dorothy had gone that morning to pick up Lady Jane. At first he had wanted to refuse the man entrance to the cabin to see the wounded man. But he really had no decision in the matter and Jim took it all stoically.

Fred finished the fresh bandages and straightened up. "There, those ought to hold for the trip." He crossed to the window and looked out while the sheriff slipped a pair of manacles on Jim's wrists.

"I'm sorry, Jim," the man said, "but like I said, the prosecuting attorney has filed with the judge against you for assault and battery with intent to kill."

Jim was silent.

Fred turned back. "What about Evans, Sheriff Black?"

"He's charged the same, but is out on twenty-five hundred dollars bail."

"What will Jim's bail be?"

The old sheriff colored. "Judge says there ain't to be none."

Jim snickered. "The law according to the Dunraven pocketbook, Fred. I am being tried even before a preliminary hearing. How soon is this kangaroo court to take place, Black?"

Now the sheriff was really uncomfortable. "Court only sits once a year up at Fort Collins, Jim. They just finished sitting last month."

"That's ridiculous," Fred flared. "Is he to sit in jail for eleven months?"

"Due to his condition, I'll keep him at my home until he's fully well."

"Now, Fred," Jim chuckled, "you are about to lose a patient, and the sheriff gain one. Let me out of here before Dorothy returns. I don't want her to see this law-abiding citizen being toted off like a criminal."

Dorothy took the news in a manner which Fred never expected. She said nothing. She turned and smiled sweetly at Lady Jane.

"Well, Mother, I think it is time that you paid your respects to Cousin Windham."

"But, Dorothy, your . . . your attire."

Even though others had given her extra of their clothing, she continued to wash out and wear the old gardening dress.

"It is clean, Mother, and all that the man left me of my own. Besides, he has seen me in it before."

Fred was thankful he was not invited to go along. Dorothy was just taking the whole matter a little too calmly.

The first floor of the lodge was completed and the carpenters were framing in the windows of the second floor. Dunraven, who was now causing delay with his constant changing of the plans, saw them coming and almost fled out the back of the building. But, steeling himself, he went to greet them. His face was a trifle pale but he was smiling broadly and the casual observer could never have known the terrible shock it was for him to see Lady Jane in this locale.

"Dear Cousin Jane! What a nice surprise!"

He took her hand and helped her down from Georginna MacGregor's sidesaddle. Dorothy jumped from her mount like a man.

"How are you, Windham?"

"I would be a lot better, Lady Jane, if you would have waited until next season to visit. I have no proper place to entertain you."

"I am hardly here for entertainment, Windham," she said civily. She gazed at the structure with a frown. "I was under the impression you were to build a hunting lodge. This has more the appearance of an English hotel."

Dunraven was thoughtful and then smiled. "You have just given me a marvelous suggestion, Lady Jane. I shall call it the English Hotel."

"Pompous enough, but then that fits you."

A wave of dark color ran over Dunraven's face. His eyes gleamed with sudden savagery.

"I would remind you, madam, that you are not in Ireland. I will not tolerate your condescending ways as long as you stand upon my property."

"Is it your property?" she asked, looking at him coldly and fixedly. "Or must I take into consideration the rumors I hear about you?"

He smiled contemptuously, and with a hateful glance at Dorothy, who stood in calm and rigid silence.

"If you accept only her reports then they are indeed nothing but rumors, madam!"

He flung the words brutally into Lady Jane's face, like stones, for he knew she could be a formidable foe if not immediately blunted.

"My reports, Windham, came mostly from Mr. Moffatt at the bank. I really must say that I don't wholly approve of American banking practices, so I spent a few days in Denver before making this journey. You, above all, can understand my concern in wanting to make sure that my money was in proper hands."

"Don't you mean *my* money?" he reminded her, with a satirical contempt. "For the final payment on the farm land is overdue and I have had to borrow money against it."

"So Mr. Moffatt tells me, Windham."

"He has no right to discuss my affairs with you!" he cried, with sudden savagery. "He has no right to do that at all!"

"What damned nonsense," said Lady Jane, with disgust. "He had every right, because your project becomes more and more of a family matter daily. Your affairs at home are in such a despicable state that the governors of the Bank of Dublin saw fit to have your mother and sisters counsel with me. Are you purposely trying to ruin your family financially?"

He stared at Lady Jane incredulously, and with fury.

"Woman, stay out of affairs that do not concern you and carry that message back to the female members of my family. They will applaud me when my project brings in millions for them to wallow in. Now, if you have nothing more to say, I am quite a busy man."

"Windham," she said softly, "there is so much I could really say about past, present and future. In one respect you are still the lad who chased only the farm girls who were stupid enough to run slower than you. You always were a womanizer, so I won't even waste my breath on that sin. But to purposely cheat and defile a family member is inexcusable, and the shame I feel for the manner in which you have been treating these other good people is unmeasurable. I came here to take Dorothy home, but now feel you are the one who should be taken back in shackles."

Then Dunraven, with one of the sudden and quirky changes of mood characteristics common for him, said in an amused and affectionate voice, "Home and marriage are the best things for Lady Dorothy. With the experience that she has gained here, she will be invaluable in running the tenant farms."

Lady Jane said, calmly, "Yes, I know." Then with wryness she added, "But she is not going home. Her dowry is already banked in Denver."

Dunraven's mouth went livid. "Impossible! I will not have the family dishonored by allowing her to marry one of these commoners."

"That was my thought, too, Windham, all the way across the ocean and this vast continent. It rather hurts my own vanity to have to admit that the man you had shot is the real prince and you are far below even common. Look upon yourself, Windham, when you speak of bringing dishonor upon the family. Now, help me back up. Georginna Henney and I are going into Denver on a shopping spree. And don't be surprised, Windham, when you find that I have had Mr. Moffatt take the charges for our shopping from your account—after all, an eyewitness does hold you accountable for burning Dorothy out."

He helped her into the saddle in an embarrassed

and speechless silence. He dared not ask who the eyewitness might be. He could not look at Dorothy. He bit his lips and clenched and unclenched his hands. He aged years in that moment. Dorothy he might have been able to browbeat down with words and disclaimers. Not so with Lady Jane. He only prayed that his paid judge kept the Rocky Mountain Jim case pending until the woman was back in Ireland.

"What eyewitness?" Dorothy asked, as soon as they were out of earshot.

Lady Jane slowly smiled. "You didn't hear him deny that such might be, did you? As long as he didn't deny it, then your mother hasn't really told a lie."

"Why, you are just as much of a scally-wag as he is."

"I should certainly hope not. He is no man's friend, but his own."

Over the rise they saw the approach of the MacGregor wagon with Lloyd at the reins. He would take the women as far as the road crew camp and then return to work for MacGregor. Georginna knew that she could talk Alex into taking them from there, because she was livid with rage.

That morning Martha Evans had reluctantly gone to the MacGregor ranch to present her Commission as the new Postmaster of Estes Park and demanded the supplies. Clara was stunned and had refused until the mattter could be discussed with Mr. MacGregor. Georginna was going to have Alex discuss it directly wtih the authorities in Denver.

That they at least knew of the matter was a temporary victory for the Earl of Dunraven that day. That night Dunraven gave Griff Evans a bank voucher for $10,000 for his property. That washed away the stinging embarrassment Martha had gone through during the morning. It also sealed forever Griff Evans' lips as to who had fired the shots at Jim Nugent.

But seeing Lloyd made Dorothy recall her mother's statement to Lord Dunraven.

"Mother," she said bluntly, "I'm not even sure I want to go through with this marriage?"

"Who said that you had to? I only said that your dowry money was banked in Denver. I don't even know if a dowry is necessary in America. No matter, it would be your money sooner or later, so you might as well have it sooner. Your grandmother added to it, so use it wisely."

"How much is it?"

"It's a letter of credit for fifty thousand dollars."

Dorothy sat her horse, still and stunned. It far exceeded her expectations . . . and would have to be used very, very wisely.

The news was unexpected and shocking. The long trip to Fort Collins had drained more from Rocky Mountain Jim's system than anyone had expected. On a September morning, a few weeks after his arrival in Fort Collins, the sheriff's wife went in to check on her patient and found him dead. The window was open and there were footprints below in her garden.

Because the man had become a notorious news item, it was quickly reasoned that the footprints were made by the curious coming to catch a glimpse of him through the window.

Because of letters he had written to the *Fort Collins Standard*, the newspaper demanded a post-mortem examination. A coroner's jury was empaneled and came to the verdict that James Nugent "came to death from gunshot wounds at the hands of G. Evans."

The prosecuting attorney thought it time to get an account of the incident from Windham Thomas Whyham-Quin, Fourth Earl of Dunraven. Who would dare question this man's word?

". . . Evans and Jim had a feud, as per usual, about a woman, Evans' daughter."

"Would you assume then that Evans was just trying to protect his daughter's good name?"

Dunraven was not about to assume further on the lie he had just voiced.

"Not having seen it, I can assume nothing. I only heard the duel, which ended in Jim getting all shot up with slugs."

"Duel? Which would mean that Jim was armed."

"All I know, sir, is that Jim was not dead. He made a solemn declaration, as a man who would presently be before his Maker, that he had not begun the scrap and that it was sheer murder."

"This other man, Ely, can he back up your story?"

"I don't see how. He was on his way to escort my wife to Ireland."

"Were there any other witnesses?"

"One of the cowboys."

The well-rehearsed man told his story and disappeared with his pockets well lined.

It was found that there was no case against Griff Evans and he was freed.

But even murder did not gain Dunraven the

land. In his will Rocky Mountain Jim claimed that he had sold his land to Fredrick Folsom Austin during the time that he was caring for his wounds. The claimed $1,000 sales price could not be found, but how does one ask a dead man where he hid his money?

Dunraven's own tactics would be used against him. The quit claim deed would be recorded according to the sales date in Jim's will.

To get away from all the publicity which was resulting from the case, Windham Thomas quickly departed on a hunting trip with Buffalo Bill and Texas Jack. From the Yellowstone area, he headed directly east and to Ireland for the pending birth of his child. Oddly, his departing instructions were but two: get the post office moved and finish my damn hotel!

The tears for James Nugent were few, because he was quickly buried in an unmarked grave almost before the news reached Estes Park.

Dorothy shed no tears, except those in her heart. Something had been taken from her in a far crueler way than even her cabin and school had been. They could always be rebuilt. Who could return this man of friendship to her?

And no court, it seemed, was capable of making any man pay for his death.

"But we can!" she said so suddenly and so loudly that it made Fred start.

"We can do what?"

"Make him pay for Jim's death where it will really hurt him the most. Right in the pocket book. I won't even fight him for my land. You've got land and now Jim's land. I've got some money. First, we'll get David out of the carting business and set him up in the stageline business. We control the toll road, so we can say that will be the only stageline approved to operate on it. The guests for his English Hotel will have to pay our fares or walk. But our guests will ride free."

"What guests?"

"The ones we will have in the hotel we shall build to compete with him!"

"We?" Fred mused.

She felt a sudden pang of pity for the man. He was at times childlike, he was at times naïve, he was too shy and not forceful enough. But he had at times shown great courage, and was no fool. But if he did not see the opening she had presented him with, then she would have to play the dominant role.

"Yes, we, Fred, although in all honesty I have to say from the start that I do not love you. I was against the idea ever since Reverend Lamb presented it to me. But I can learn to love you, given time, just as my mother and grandmother have before me. If the answer is to be affirmative, then I want the service to be quick, short and without fanfare."

Fred accepted the offer with a nod of his head. He was worn out fighting himself silently, tired of endlessly resisting the love of his heart that would not go away. His surrender now, as always, was to her dominating spirit.

The service was quick, short and without fanfare.

16

MARRIAGE was like a thousand springs rolled into one glorious summer. Vastly less experienced than she, despite her own limited encounters, Dorothy had to be the master in this area as well. But Fred had been the man that fate had kept hidden in the shadows of her life until the proper moment. His quiet love placed her on plateaus of sensual passion that divorced her from everything past and made her think only of the future.

This had not been a rocket-bursting thing, but a quiet development over the long winter months. They had argued and fought over the location of the lodge site. She won. They had argued and fought over the naming of it. He won. They had argued and fought with David Folsom over the stageline. Both won.

But each fight ended in a kiss. Kisses new and refreshing and exciting to Dorothy. Under his shy exterior, Fred was a very dynamic man.

And one morning Dorothy noticed that all the reds were much redder, the sky so blue that it nearly hurt her eyes, the robins seemed to trill more brilliantly and the fields of wild flowers seemed more gloriously colored than ever.

Spring! But not just another spring.

She giggled. "If this is love, then I'm a fool to have overlooked it for so long."

But she was paying a price to find her own measure of love. Until she nearly demanded it, Lloyd was refusing to go back to work with his father on the new stageline; and because his love was also a growing thing, Fred allowed her to dominate more and more.

The publicity surrounding the first murder in Estes Park caused new people to visit the area. They were irate at having to pay a toll to use the road and by night would continue to tear down the gates. The collection station was moved to the bridge over the Little Thompson River and the users had the choice of either paying the toll or swimming, or fording the stream with their heavy loads.

The new settlers were still causing a problem for the Estes Park Company over claim-jumping, but it was a new breed of visitors who were causing problems for them all.

"Clara, I think it is highly unfair of Mr. MacGregor to blame me for these happenings."

Clara averted her eyes and fixed them on a point behind Dorothy. "I suppose you know that we lost several acres of good timberland in the Black Canyon because of those hunters' careless campfire? And people seem to think they can pitch their tents anywhere and throw their trash about for us to pick up."

"You are not the only ones suffering that same fate, Clara."

"But we are ranchers and farmers," said Clara, after a moment, with childish resentment and relentlessness. "We are not in the business of catering to tourists. Mr. MacGregor thinks you have opened a very bad can of worms by running that ad in the Denver papers."

"I fail to see the connection," replied Dorothy, impatiently. "It was a modest ad aimed at the people who live on Brown's Bluff. Modest, Clara, because Aspen Inn is still quite modest. We only have rooms to accommodate ten to twelve guests. Bill James has nearly that many cabins built at Elkhorn, but I don't hear Mr. MacGregor sending him a message by you. Nor do I see you going to see your good friends John Hupp or Abner Sprague."

Clara's eyes narrowed to glittering pinpoints. "John Hupp would not have started converting his cabin into a hotel if you had not granted him the right to have it as the stage stop. And it was you who gave Abner and Minnie the idea of building a lodge."

Clara scoffed. "In July, when the English Hotel opens up, then the real ruination of this country as ranch land will really begin."

"You are wrong," Dorothy challenged. "This winter I've come to see that hotel as the key to Dunraven's eventual downfall. The stage will bring in people who will start to question how he gained so much land. Then, he will never be able to gain it all as a private fiefdom."

Clara shook her head sadly. It still wasn't what the MacGregors wanted for the valley. Neither woman was really aware that they had spoken the first words of a new land war—those who wanted to share the health and beauty of the area against those who wanted to keep it closed for ranching, just as staunchly as Dunraven wanted to keep it closed for his own private hunting parties.

Both might have been amazed to know that one of the generals of the upcoming battle was at that very moment meeting peacefully with the enemy.

During the time that Lady Jane had been purchasing a new wardrobe and household articles for her daughter, Georginna Henney had spent her time hounding the land office clerks. Shrewdly, she was able to claim and purchase several individual plots that were scattered throughout the Dunraven domain.

A.Q. MacGregor now quietly pointed them out on the map to Theo Whyte. With those acres added in Lord Dunraven's kingdom would be quite solid, with the exception of Jim McLaughlin's claim, the disputed land of Dorothy's and the Austin property.

Three minor enemies were easier to fight than a formidable foe like MacGregor.

"And what is it you wish for in exchange?"

"This is my present ranch," MacGregor said, slowly and heavily. "This is the McCreery spread. I want everything in between the two, this to the north of them and then south to where the land drops off into what they call Devil's Gulch."

"Do you think me a fool, man? That is three times what you are offering in exchange."

"I did not put a dollar value on the protection that it will afford Lord Dunraven, Mr. Whyte. I shall be like a solid wall on the north side of the valley to keep further settlers and squatters out. Can any other man make such a claim to the Earl?"

With more abruptness than politeness, Theo Whyte quickly concluded the transaction. He felt that he had temporarily removed a rather large thorn from his side. When the time came, and he was sure that it would come, it would be far easier to buy the land back from one man than several.

A.Q. MacGregor shook Whyte's hand and departed the second largest land-owner in the area.

With a stroke of the pen he had doubled the size of his ranch—and without a penny put forth.

Sell the land? A Scotsman never sells his land!

The letter from Lady Jane greatly excited Dorothy. For the gala July opening of the English Hotel, Lord Dunraven had invited everyone in Ireland who was anybody—but with main attention to those in Adare who had scoffed at his project.

Lady Jane, of course, was not invited, but supplied Dorothy with a most complete list of those who had been and were planning to make the journey and attend.

"I'll just have to crash his party," Dorothy giggled.

"Then you will crash it without me," Fred scowled.

"Oh, don't be a stick in the mud! I haven't seen some of these people in nearly five years, Fred. It thrills me to think of their coming here. And what is Cousin Windham going to do, throw me out on my ear in front of all his honored guests? He wouldn't dare! To them I am still Lady Dorothy Goold and will be treated accordingly."

"I think you are making a mistake, Dorothy. Besides, we have all of those schoolteachers coming in that day. What am I supposed to do with eight old-maid schoolteachers that evening?"

"Wear your chastity belt," she kidded. "Now, what am I going to wear that will knock their eyes out?"

The women stared with frank envy at Dorothy's gown of pure buckskin trimmed in bobcat tails, at the smooth plaiting of her sun-streaked copper hair twisted into a crown on her head, at the richness of her skin and the brilliant sparkle of the green eyes.

"But I might as well have come naked," she said to herself.

Friends from childhood were polite in their greeting—overly polite—and then they would quickly dart off on a very lame excuse.

Anticipating that she might make an appearance, Windham Thomas had done his homework well coming across the ocean and continent.

Dorothy had become the outcast, the untouchable for having married below her station. She had been painted as having turned native, and her unusual gown selection was helping to add to the charge.

On purpose, she was the only guest who was not greeted by Lord Dunraven. Only by a chance remark did Dorothy learn that Lady Florence had remained in Ireland because of ill health and the loss of another child. When she was greeted by David Moffatt the banker was quickly steered away from her by a scowling Lord Dunraven.

Rufus Brogan, now head of the firm of Whyham-Quin & Brogan, Land Developers, felt ill-at-ease when she approached him. She was now a married woman and he was squarely under the thumb of the Earl. He didn't even see fit to introduce her to the young Denver socialite that he had recently married. He was on his way up and considered Dorothy on her way down and out. He had once vowed never to love another woman until he could find one to match Dorothy. He now saw his wife as far superior to what Dorothy had become.

"We always seem to meet at gala affairs, don't we?"

Dorothy turned. It was a true moment of *deja vu.* He was even more handsome and dashing and stylishly dressed than she could remember. If only the hands of time could be turned back.

"Hello, Paul," she whispered.

"I am here on orders, but won't act the cur that I am supposed to act. Lord Dunraven would like you to leave before you embarrass him any further."

He reached out and took her arm. She looked at the hand that touched her with severe affront, but did not try to free herself. "It is quite a walk to the front door. I came in as a lady and shall go out as a lady."

Paul chuckled. "You never say die, do you?"

"I was taught never to make a scene, if that is what you mean."

"I've come to learn where a lot of your teaching has come from. This has been quite a time for me in Ireland. Thanks to Lady Florence, these have now become my friends. They should be your friends, as well, Dorothy."

"Very shallow friends," Dorothy muttered.

"They are only listening to the gossip spread by Dunraven."

"And does that gossip include you?"

They were out beyond the glitter and noise, approaching the tethered horses. "Lady Florence wouldn't allow that, you know. Look, Dorothy, she holds nothing against you. Give up this ruffian life and come back with the people you really should be with."

Dorothy wanted to laugh. "Lady Florence held nothing against me? Of all the snobbish, arrogant audacity! You have certainly found your right niche in life, Paul. You can murder for the man and then take his wife to mistress. Of course, I only assume that, knowing you as I do. But forgive me! That is not the way a lady is supposed to think. Well, Paul, I can't give up this ruffian life now. I'm married to it. I am now Mrs. Fred Austin."

He gasped, as if smothering. Then he drew a loud and grating breath. "That's a damn lie. You know that I am the only man for you. Hell, look at the months I waited for you."

She wasn't even going to honor the statement with an answer. She turned and started to untether her horse. The moonlight caught the gleam of the gold band on her finger.

Paul seized the arm and shook her roughly. His vivid lips parted and showed the savage glisten of his teeth. "I don't honor that marriage. You are mine."

He pulled her to him and tried to cover her mouth with his. Dorothy began to turn and twist, but didn't scream out. He was too strong for her, and the flank of the horse was giving her no backward escape. She brought up her knee, in another moment of *deja vu*. In the moment he was bent over in agony, she was upon the horse and fleeing.

Paul's hands clenched into fists. The fire in his eyes was wild and infuriated. He grabbed the first available horse and took off in pursuit.

Dorothy cursed herself for having ridden sidesaddle. She had grown unused to that manner and could not properly grip the horse with her legs to gain more speed. To fall, at the speed she was traveling, would put her in worse peril than having to fight off Paul Ely.

Aspen Inn was dark, except for a night lamp left burning for her. Turning into the gate he was almost abreast of her. When he lunged for her reins, she swerved the horse sharply, nearly making each of them fall from the saddle. The movement gave her a few feet of leeway. In almost a single bound she was out of the saddle and running across the pinewood porch. Her skirt slowed her and just as she began to unlatch the door, a fist caught her at the nape of the neck.

The room swam before her as her head began to drop onto her breast. She felt someone catch her before she fell. She heard Paul say something mean and ugly, but couldn't make out the words.

Then realization started returning as she felt the buckskin being shredded from her body. It was torn straight down from the shoulders so that she lost the use of her arms. Then came her scream. Then came the fist to her jaw. Then came the blackness again.

Then she heard voices. They were hard to locate, and she had to fight out of the well she was in. Time had lost all meaning, but Fred had come upon the scene seconds after her scream, and just as Paul had dumped her on the couch.

The single lamp cast an eerie glow over the two men who stood facing one another in the center of the little lobby.

They were almost of a height; Paul topped Fred by less than two inches. His back was to Dorothy, but she could see Paul clearly. He posed arrogantly.

"That is my final offer," Paul said, as she came fully to her senses. "She leaves with me."

Fred hesitated, glancing around the room as if in search of an answer. The rough-hewn stairway held the nightgown clad bodies of a few frightened women. The man is mad, thought the schoolteachers, glancing at each other in dread concern. They knew not who he was, but for him to want to take away the innkeeper's wife was preposterous.

Dorothy knew that Fred was no match for Paul. She struggled to sit up, fighting to get the buckskin up about her bare breasts. There was only one way to stop them—to put herself physically between them.

Fred saw her rise to her feet. "Get out of here," he said, in a voice he might have used on a dog.

Even then Dorothy knew it was too late to stop them. Paul used the moment of Fred's distraction to hurl himself forward and wrestle him to the floor. Flesh pounded on flesh. There was a difference in the sound, and in the men. Paul's movements were quicker and more violent. His fists smashed with murderous intent.

Dorothy screamed at them, but they were not listening. She darted forward to put herself right into the fray, but one of the wiser school marms shot down the stairs and ringed her wrist. There was the strength of a man in the slender fingers.

Somehow, Fred regained his feet. He leaped back to escape a vicious thrust he was unable to counter. The fist caught him on the shoulder blade. Perspiration streaked his face and ran down his bared throat, soaking his shirt. The blows sent him back, always back. He was moving clumsily now, and was wholly on the defensive. Paul's mouth was set in a humorless white grimace. His eyes were narrowed to slits.

Then the end came. Fred's arm drew back, in a gesture so awkward that even the novice school teachers could see the danger he was in. It left him completely exposed. Paul's fist clipped him soundly on the jaw.

Over Fred's face came a look of childish surprise. His eyes were still open, inquiring, as he started to fall.

And even as he was falling the nightmare started. Paul picked up a straight backed chair and smashed it into his back. Dorothy gave a stifled shriek and fought the restraint of the teacher's hand; and as the restraint was quickly dropped, Paul continued to beat the fallen man about the back and legs with the shattered chair.

Screams now came from a half dozen female throats. Dorothy beat on his broad back with her fists until he suddenly stopped. He flung the chair away with a savage movement that sent it crashing into the fireplace. "The devil take the man who built such a rotten piece of furniture."

His eyes focused on Dorothy, and she shrank away from what she saw in them. His eyes raked her from head to foot with an intolerable amusement.

"You'll come crawling to me before he's able to be a husband to you again."

She raised her hand and struck him across the face. He staggered back a few steps at the blow, but his smile did not alter. He dusted off his hands, as though the matter had been quite trifle.

"If you want to find me, Dorothy, I'll be back at the party," he called to her as he left.

She turned, blindly, without answering. One of the schoolteachers was already examining the unconscious Fred.

"He's not hurt bad," she said, in a voice that

oozed superiority. "Get some men, Mrs. Austin, to carry him to his room."

"There are none," she said numbly. "We shall have to do it."

"What about a doctor?"

"He was the nearest thing we had to a doctor. I'll ride for Bill James if he gets worse."

They were unaware that they were the ones who made him get worse. Six matronly, old maid women —with Dorothy nestling his head—felt strange and out of place grasping his arms and legs and torso. With holds not too secure they jostled him, almost dropped him and were less than gentle in placing him upon his bed.

Dorothy did the best she could in bathing him and making him comfortable, but still he remained unconscious. Twice she debated on going for Bill James, or in the other direction for Lloyd and David Folsom. Twice, she turned back, fearful of leaving him alone.

Because he was on his back she could not see the horrible discoloration to his calves and thighs and the odd twist to his back.

She sat and waited and cursed.

The manner in which Paul Ely removed Dorothy from the party did not amuse Windham Thomas in the least. He expected her to come storming back at any moment, and wanted Paul out of sight and out of mind.

It was hardly how Paul Ely had planned his evening. There were certain 'conquests' he had begun on the ocean voyage that he wanted to advance further. Divorced from circulating at the party made that impossible. Never once did he consider that his lust had brought about the problem. As he was always prone to do, in his mind he made Dorothy the culprit of all of his problems.

In his cabin, above what was now officially Dunraven Ranch, he sat and began to get savagely drunk. Up the hill in the bunkhouse, he could hear that the cowboys were doing the same.

This was a new breed of ranch hands, all personally selected by Lord Dunraven. In his European party were many young ladies of worth. The henchmen type would not do for them to look upon, or help them up into their saddle. He desired young, handsome, virile, muscular men who would reek with Western aura. He got what he wanted and then forgot them.

The young bucks, most of whom were no more Western than the Earl himself, had seen their summer at the English Hotel as being something quite different than sitting in a bunkhouse while a rousing party was going on down the road. They had seen some of the young Irish beauties coming off of the stagecoaches and had mentally started planning some moonlight rides. Their water had been shut off very quickly when they learned they were excluded from the party, even though the Earl did supply them with free liquor at the bunkhouse.

Paul Ely sat drinking alone and listening to their carping echo down to him.

"Bitch it up, boys," he said to himself. "We're all in the same boat."

Then he smiled, poured himself a new drink, and headed up to the bunkhouse. Most had seen him around, but didn't quite know who he was.

"Good evening, lads," he said merrily. "I am Paul Ely, an associate of Lord Dunraven."

His drunken condition and disheveled clothing raised a few eyebrows. "Now, I'm sorry to be late getting up here, but the party is going pretty good, and you can see that some of those titled fillies like to play a little rough.'

This brought a few chuckles and grins.

"But that ain't where the action is. The real party is at the Aspen Inn. Lord Dunraven has brought in for you boys six—maybe even seven—choice little bed mates. Some of you may have to share, but those girls are used to that. Have a good time."

Dorothy automatically assumed that the fierce pounding on the front door was Paul Ely and she was determined not to even answer it. But when it continued, and she heard a woman's scream, she went flying from their living quarters on the run.

She was just in time to see the schoolteacher who had foolishly answered the door going up the stairs four at a time as the lobby filled with ten very drunken cowboys.

"What is the meaning of this?" she demanded.

"Whoooeee!" one howled. "If this be the madame, I'll leave the rest for you studs."

"Like shit, man! I saw that prune in the flannel night gown. That's the madame and this one is up for bartering."

Dorothy could hardly shout over the verbal battle that ensued. The more she shouted, the more she began to see that this was another of Paul Ely's dastardly tricks. But it was hardly funny. The more she tried to reason with them, the more belligerent they became. They had come for women, and women they would get.

Paul Ely had taken away the only male voice in

the house, so Dorothy retreated to the living quarters for the next best thing. But even as she took a rifle from the rack, she could hear the mayhem they were creating on the lobby furniture. If need be they would batter their way to the second floor to sate their lust.

Dorothy could not believe the destruction they had caused in such a short span of time. The lobby was a shambles, but it was eerily quiet.

Cautiously, she went up the stairs, with the rifle cocked to fire. Peering around the corner to the hall, she saw nine of the cowboys staring down confusedly at their unconscious tenth.

Then, as though by a silent signal, eight flannel covered women in their mid-forties barged from the quickly opened doors.

"Save your virginity!" the leader screeched.

It was a battle cry that brought forth umbrellas, fire tongs, bed slats, hat pins, teeth and nails and kicking feet. The cowboys had no more opportunity than to raise protective arms and hands to their handsome faces. With more force than a locomotive pushing a cow from the tracks, they were herded back down the stairs and needed little further inducement to make a hasty departure.

When Dorothy tried to thank them she was rudely cut short.

"You will make departure arrangements for us first thing in the morning," the woman snapped as though Dorothy were personally responsible for it all. "And certainly don't expect to present us with any bill!"

Bill James thought that Fred's condition was far beyond anything that he even wanted to speculate about. Lloyd waned to borrow the MacGregor flat-bed wagon and cart him to a doctor, but Dorothy feared the trip would kill him as surely as it had Rocky Mountain Jim. David Folsom would just have to bring a doctor back with him on the next stage run.

In the upcoming year New York would have Alexander Graham Bell's new toy, the telephone. Estes Park didn't need them. Speculation on the triangle between two men and a woman can outdistance almost the happening of the event itself.

"Of course, she was personally responsible," Lord Dunraven told his guests, as Martha Evans filled the sideboard with breakfast fare. "Didn't I tell you she had turned into a piece of baggage? A married woman, but she's been chasing poor Paul Ely since the moment of his return. That's why I asked him to escort her from our party last evening. I wanted none of her scenes around us, and lord-only-knows, I've seen plenty of her scenes. Poor Paul, having to defend himself against her crazed husband. I'd be crazed too if my wife were running a bawdy house. Nor do I hold my cowboys accountable. Imagine charging such outlandish prices and then they learn the women are older than their own mothers. Really!"

Martha Evans didn't trust Lord Dunraven any farther than she could slide a knife under a snake's belly, nor did she trust the man at her kitchen door, but she did consider A.Q. MacGregor a friend of Dorothy's.

MacGregor's feelings toward Martha Evans or the Earl of Dunraven had not altered, but the farm produce grown by his wife and mother-in-law did bring in quite a handsome little sum from the new hotel.

Never one to gossip, he listened to Martha Evans without a change of expression. Lord Dunraven's words, at that time, did not reach Dorothy. They were recited as fact to the astonished ears of Clara and Georginna. Then they spread outward likes waves on a pond.

Dorothy didn't help matters for herself. She was frightened. She insisted that Lloyd come to help her clean up the mess and move into Aspen Inn. To those who were prone to evil-mindedness, it didn't matter that Lloyd was her nephew by marriage, or that she had lived with Lloyd and Fred after the burning of her cabins. They saw only that she was moving a new man in with her while she had one lying unconscious and the other fuming across the valley.

Lord Dunraven had raised the bawdy house theory and kept it alive by announcing a new rule for the English Hotel: No single female would be granted a room and no gentleman with a lady would be housed unless he could prove without a shadow of a doubt that it was his legal spouse.

Estes Park did not want businesses that catered to those who weren't ladies and gentlemen.

Lloyd and David Folsom were hearing all of this and much more, but kept it all from Dorothy. It was proving next to impossible to get a doctor to make the long trip for a single patient. Theo Whyte was raising hell in Denver over the toll road charter and the granting of only one stage line into Estes Park. But at the same time he was still buying up Estes Park land at a ruinous rate for the Earl. He considered the hotel full, without realizing they were not only non-paying guests but were eating up the food at a rate higher than some of the land had originally cost.

Worthless Estes Park Company, Ltd. checks began to pile up on David Moffat's desk. Thinking he had the authority, Whyte mortgaged the cattle to cover the checks. But this was brought into question because the cattle were in the name of Paul Ely.

As these reports of financial instability leaked out, public indignation grew, both inside and outside the Colorado territory.

As they had learned in the panic of 1873, one giant topples other giants. Dunraven's eastern friends began to act as though they had never heard of him. But the feudal Earl of Estes waved Whyte and Brogan's concerns aside as minor; the subjects of his personal domain had been restless before. Besides, he had a whole new trainload of guests coming in that he had to see after.

17

"CALL YOU SOONER?" Dorothy asked in dismay. "We have been nearly a month trying to get a doctor to come look at him. Every time we have tried to move him, he screams so from the pain that I refused another attempt."

The doctor cast her a look of superior resignation at the stupidity of the layman. He motioned for her to step out of the bedroom with him.

"There are a number of possibilities, my dear woman," said the unctuous doctor. "He may expire if one of those broken ribs has punctured a lung. You asked for a frank opinion; I am giving you that. Then, again, he may survive the crisis. The legs, though badly broken in several spots are mending because of his immobile condition. Therein lies the greatest problem. He is immobile because the back seems to be broken in at least three places. I say seems because I am no magician who can see through the flesh. He was probably better off when he was unconscious. Now that he is awake you will have to keep him rigid at all times. Convalescence will take a long time."

"From your face," she said in a low pent voice, "I understand you are giving him very little hope."

"There is always hope, Mrs. Austin. But our knowledge of broken backs is limited. They heal or they don't. If they do, however, the person is confined to a bed or wheelchair for the rest of their life."

"Oh, no!" she cried weakly. "There must be something that could be done. It isn't fair. He's never harmed a soul, was never guilty of a crime, and you are impotent to help him. Is there no one back east that you might consult on the matter? I am willing and able to pay whatever it might cost."

"It's not a matter of money, Mrs. Austin," he said, with some pity. "How does one pay God for a miracle? Nothing more can be done. You can only keep him quiet and make his life as an invalid a happy one."

Dorothy was silent. Her eyes closed, and there was a sunken appearance about her mouth that gave her the look of an old and exhausted woman full of despair, little hope, self-hatred for being the cause of it all and mostly, a look of over-powering sorrow.

The explosion was muffled and yet fiercely echoed.

Dorothy and the doctor seemed momentarily frozen in place. Lloyd came bounding through the door from the lobby.

"Keep her out!" the doctor shouted.

Dorothy wasn't moving. What she was thinking had to be an impossibility. There was no way that Fred could have reached the rifle she now kept in the bedroom for their protection. There was no way that his immobile body could have moved across the bedroom to the fireplace. It just couldn't be.

An ashen-faced doctor stuck his head out the door. "Son, you'd best go to the stage depot for your father. I'll need some help moving him."

The closing door seemed so final. Lloyd knew there was no great rush. He bent over Dorothy, touching her forehead with his cheek. The act was still so recent that he was still unaware of grief. She was hardly aware that she had been touched. He stepped back and found Dorothy's expression, her passion and misery, far more pathetic than Fred's suicide. Slow tears, each one rounded and unhurried, ran down from her eyes, but there was no contortion or squeezing of her eyelids, no distortion of her face in grief. There was a great dignity, an immeasurable anguish in those tears, but also, very strangely, an immense fortitude and resolution. She would not let Paul Ely go unpunished for this murder. She would fight every inch of the perilous way to bring a measure of justice and equality. She lifted her face in steadfast resolution.

"Get David," she said firmly. "I'll ride over to the Dunraven Ranch."

"Dorothy, this may not be the proper time to confront them."

"What better time?" she said, in a hoarse voice. "John Cleave is the only carpenter around and Fred needs a coffin. Let the building of it speak louder than any words that I might utter."

The message was like thunderclaps from the mountain tops. It echoed up and down the pine covered canyons like the voice of a wrathful God. It was their first shared death. It was a human bond of suffering. Hypocrites forgot that they had been hypocrites. The manner of his death was now overshadowed by the circumstances leading up to it. To grab land with money and power was one thing, but with human life like James Nugent and Fred Austin was quite another. No one dared not attend the graveside services. The Rev. E.J. Lamb's words were a condemnation of those not in attendance:

"Sin's hideous acts indulged in leads man away from all that is good, debases, darkens, and finally damns all who persist in that unhallowed course. Sin indulged in blinds moral sense, hardens conscience, and so destroys the finer feelings of human nature that man becomes a demon, callous to affection, void of sympathy and regard for future consequences. Oh, what crimes and dark deeds are generated by persistent transgression in the broad way that ultimately leads to eternal ruin of body and soul—an awful destiny.

"Man must live with his foulest deeds, but our Fred is gone from the joys and sorrows of this life, leaving us under dark shadows of remembrance of this inhuman, uncalled for tragedy which will linger like a forbidden skeleton on the pages of our memory. We are compelled to say farewell to this loved one. We leave him to God and heaven, until we too are called to that holier garden.

"There are mysterious phases in the drama of life. Let this death not be a terrible victory for others."

The persistent yapping of the little French poodle was greatly irritating Windham Thomas. His guests were in a foul and cantankerous mood because the train was late and now they had to wait for stagecoaches. Funeral or no funeral, he took it as a personal insult that David Folsom and his son couldn't have the transportation there on time. He wished that Theo Whyte would hurry up and wrest the line from them. He was beginning to wish many things, and the approach of Paul Ely made him wish he didn't have to confront the man.

"Lady Florence," he barked, "will you please keep that beast quiet!"

Paul spun about, searching. "I wasn't aware Lady Florence was—"

He stopped short. The overdressed woman holding the dog was hardly *his* Lady Florence Elizabeth.

The Earl flushed. "Paul, may I present Lady Florence Dubbins. Now, come away so that I may speak with you privately before the train departs."

Paul Ely looked at the same woman again quizzically and then he smiled. She was no Lady or lady. He had seen her perform on the stage in Dublin. A performance so shocking that the real Lady Florence had forced him to take her away in the course of the second act. He had little doubt in his mind why she was included with this selection of lords and ladies.

"Paul," Dunraven said curtly, "after the train goes to Denver, you will take it directly back to Cheyenne and east. I've made arrangements for you to sail on the English steamer *Atlantic*."

He paused, expecting an argument that didn't come. Paul Ely had no reason to argue, so waited.

"I'm concerned about Lady Florence . . . ah . . . my wife, that is; and also concerned about you. Of course, the man did shoot himself, but it is bound to raise the ghost of Rocky Mountain Jim. After all, it is a little embarrassing that this man did get Jim's property after his death. With Dorothy a widow, I can bring more pressure on her with you out of the way. Well, have a good trip."

Paul Ely merely nodded. He was regaining what he had not wanted to leave in the first place. In Ireland he was not considered a huge southern barbarian. His name appeared in the pages of the society notes; the Whyham-Quin servants treated him with due respect; he escorted Lady Florence everywhere. He had no qualms about leaving whatsoever.

Rev. Lamb was quite right about the mysterious phases in the drama of life. The English steamer *Atlantic* wrecked off Nova Scotia, sinking with 547 passengers and crew aboard.

The terrible impact of Fred's death did not hit Lloyd until they started to lower the pine coffin into the ground. He went stiff as a board and stared. His father tried to move him away, but he would not budge.

"Lloyd," David snarled, "now snap out of it! That preacher man talked so damn long that we are way late starting for Longmont."

"You had best recruit one of the other drivers," Dorothy said softly. "I'll walk him down to the house. Horace and Hunter Ferguson said they would see to the shovelling after we were gone."

"Damn kid," David spat. "Acts more like it was his own father than his uncle."

"Because that's how he was treated, David," she said, without rancor or bitterness. "He was treated like a man and not a child."

David Folsom opened his mouth and shut it. No use getting into a family argument in front of every busy-body in the valley. He knew his temper and his wife had scolded him to hold it that day of all days. There was time enough to question whether Dorothy had a right to Fred's land or whether it should revert to Lloyd. He roughly motioned for his wife and other children to board the stage. He had to get them down for the train back into Denver or pay a night's lodging for them in Longmont. It annoyed him that they felt obligated to come up for the funeral and deprive him of seats for paying passengers.

Lloyd felt someone take his arm. From far off he heard Dorothy say, "Please. Let me take you home."

Home, she thought, as she guided him down from the pine covered hillside to the Austin cabin. It had been home for the first few months of her marriage. Those had been happy, carefree, loving days. Like strangers, she and Fred had been reborn in those log walls. Each, in their own way, had found the flower of love and passion and gently nurtured it to maturity.

Then why can't I cry, she thought bitterly. I know they were all looking at me and wondering the same. Why can't she weep over the coffin of her husband? Was her love really for another man? After all, look at the months Paul Ely came to her cabin at all hours of the day and night? Fred Austin was just too good for her, if you ask me. The man was a real saint.

The cabin kept her from lingering on such dour thoughts. As a married man, David Folsom was not a good bachelor housekeeper. The living quarters were a shambles, but the open door to Lloyd's room revealed the only remaining suggestion of Fred Austin—it was neat and tidy.

She tossed some stable-smelling clothes off a chair and helped Lloyd to it. Then she kindled a fire in the range and put on the coffee kettle. She knew she shouldn't stay long. Everyone and their brother had brought food by the Aspen Inn and would be there expecting her.

Expecting to see if I am going to cry, she thought bitterly again. Then she looked at Lloyd. No, she didn't owe those people one lick of her time right then. She owed it all right here. This had been her boon companion. This had always been her staunchest ally. He had lost more than anyone else today and needed her to be there wtih him.

Lloyd sensed someone beside him, felt an arm on his shoulders, pressing it. He covered his face with his hands, and broke out into the most terrible sobbing, dry and tearless. Dorothy's heart broke with pity for this desperate and broken young man, who, in his first experience with personal death, had nothing to offer but his agony and desolation of loss.

The impotent rage and torment in Dorothy had been building until she was at her breaking point. She put her cheek down upon the top of Lloyd's curly hair and let the dam burst. She didn't know if she were crying for herself, for Lloyd, for Fred, or for all three combined. Her tears flowed down and began to wet Lloyd's face.

Others might scoff, but he sensed her crushing and frantic remorse. He forgot his own torture and pulled her down into his strong arms in an attempt to calm her.

Their cheeks touched and by almost equal consent moved into a kiss. They clung desperately to each other. Not with passion, but with mutual understanding. They were the last of two sides of a triangle which had shared much. Only they could bend it into a circle for continuation.

Lloyd helped Dorothy to her feet. He looked long into her eyes. His hand was against her cheek, smoothing it. He tried to smile, and his look was unbearably poignant.

"I gave you up to Fred so that you might marry. I now claim you back."

His voice, low and hoarse, came falteringly, feebly. Dorothy listened, her eyes fixed on his face. Then, hesitantly, turned her head and kissed the hand that lay along her cheek. She tried to speak, to form some sort of answer.

"I don't want you to say it," Lloyd said. "I know

that you don't love me except in friendship. But you learned to love Fred. I could read it daily in your face."

She had never heard such a tone from him, nor such words. Strength and power shone in his eyes, and his arms were like bands of steel. She could not look away from him.

"I can never love you more than I did on the first day that I saw you. Nothing can, or ever will, change that."

Dorothy hardly moved, but she seemed to curve towards him, to lay in the circle of his arm. When he began to walk them towards his bedroom door, her body moved without resistance. She closed her mind to the consequences. It felt good to let someone else make the decisions for a change. She was tired of always being a tower of strength. Lloyd had enough strength for both of them. She didn't have to hold Fred up, push Paul away or mentally fight Windham Thomas. For once in her life she was in the arms of a man who would let her relax and be totally a woman.

The fierce thrust of a hob-nailed boot sent the leather-hinged door crashing down to the floor. David Folsom stormed over it like a knight-errant.

"Whore! Slut!" he bellowed. "Your husband is not twenty-four hours in his grave and you find another penis to latch onto!"

Dorothy sat up, startled, pulling the covers up about her bare breasts. Lloyd turned, blinked and yawned.

"Filthy, dirty, bitch!" David ranted on, pacing back and forth at the foot of the bed. "I will ruin you for degrading my son in this way."

Lloyd jumped from bed. His face had a livid moistness over it. But he smiled. He pulled trousers up over his nudity. "Dad, get the hell out of here!"

"Shut up! You cock hound! You don't have to tell me how long you been smelling after this bitch!"

Lloyd looked at him, and his mouth tightened. He could have killed his father on the spot, but he thought subtlety the best answer to deal with him. Then he instantly changed his mind.

"You are hardly a saint," he said, brutally. "Is this any different from the woman you keep secretly in Longmont?"

"A hell of a lot different," he said explosively. "Land is involved here! Not just a change of pace from one woman to the next! She's out to scheme away Fred's land from us!"

There was a sharp silence in the room. Lloyd shook his head slowly and sombrely, as though his father had gone mad. David's face was still congested, and his eyes flashed fire.

But before he could add to the charge, there was a loud cry shattering the sinking violence in the air. Dorothy was on her feet in the center of the bed. She cared not if David Folsom saw that the burnished copper coloring of her hair was everywhere upon her body. She leaned towards him, and her white face was terrible and wild.

"Land!" she cried. "I'm sick and tired over fighting about land! If you want it, take it!"

She jumped from the bed and began to pull on her widow's weeds.

"By damn I shall!" David gloated.

"Like hell!" Lloyd yelled. "It is my land and hers when we are married!"

David glared at his son fiercely. "Until you are of age the land is mine and I will say when you marry!"

Again Lloyd found himself being intimidated by his father's look and declaration. He gulped. The strength he had shown to Dorothy seemed to vanish like a rising morning mist.

Never had she felt so alone and lonely. During the night a new world had opened for her. Never had a man opened such vast vistas of passion for her. Lloyd had been domineering, masterful, exciting. He was strong, masculine, invigorating. She had been slave, student, female to his manliness. She had sipped at his fountain of youth and been refreshed. And now his youth was flaunted in her face like a thrown gauntlet of challenge. It made her Irish blood boil.

Yet she spoke very quietly, and with appalling slow virulence.

"You speak of land, but fail to speak of what has been put upon it. You also fail to speak of my investment in the stage line, for which I have yet to see a dime returned. You paint me as the greedy one. All right, let me start living up to the true colors you desire of me. You can burn Aspen Inn down, for all I care, because I never want to set foot in it again. Touch one inch of the land left by Jim Nugent and I'll drag you through every court in this land. Now, the stageline. You will pay me back in full, within twenty-four hours, or I will take over by default."

Her words brought a profound silence to the room. David gazed at her starkly. He knew he had gone too far, but was too bull-headed to know when to retreat.

"You're just forcing me to sell the land to Dunraven to raise that kind of money," he declared.

"Gluttons do get together with gluttons, sooner or later," she said simply.

"Or maybe you really want me to sell out to MacGregor," he mused.

"That would only make me repeat what I have just said," she intoned, her tone growing colder. "You can tell him that he can buy me out of the toll road whenever he is ready, as well. I'm sick to death of all of you little Lord Dunravens."

Lloyd was then stirred to action. "What will you do, Dorothy?"

She looked at him as she had the night before. He was so much like Fred in looks, but so much more of a man. Her love for him could have grown to the end of eternity. Then her heart hardened.

"Do you care, Lloyd?" she whispered. "Do you really care?"

She turned and slowly walked from the room. No voice stopped her, no voice answered her questions. Everything darkened before her eyes. She felt disembodied. Life seemed such a ferment of the years. Why did some women, like Martha Evans, seem to marry the wrong man and yet stay with him; and she always seemed to be with the wrong man that she couldn't keep.

She raised her head, amazed to find that it was mid-afternoon. The whole area was basked in golden sunlight. Oddly, the words Reverend Lamb uttered to her as he led her to the grave came soaring back:

" 'I shall lift up mine eyes unto the hills, from whence cometh my strength.' "

Yes, she thought, I am changing. David can

change Lloyd back into a little docile boy, but the mountains never change. But Lloyd is right. What will I do now?

"Do you mean to say," Lord Dunraven sneered, his little pig-eyes flashing, "that other guests are complaining about Lady Florence feeding her dog in the dining room?"

The hotel manager was new, having been hired only the week before by Theo Whyte. His salary suggested that he had managed only the finest establishments and he was determined to earn his salary in these rather primitive conditions. He looked unknowingly at Lord Dunraven as though looking upon the dog itself.

"I find your question most unintelligent, sir," he simpered. "Guests at the English Hotel are not accustomed to sharing their meals with canines."

Dunraven glowered. He was extremely tired. He had brought his guests directly from the stage coaches to the dining room for lunch. Breakdowns and a washed-out road had made it a troublesome all-night journey from Longmont. Now he wished nothing more than a bath and a nap.

"We shall discuss the matter of Lady Florence's dog later," he said icily. "Now, have a porter take her luggage to my room."

Charles Lester had seen the man but once before and raised a questioning eye. "Is the lady registered, sir?"

"Listen, you bloody ass, she doesn't need to be registered as long as she is with me!"

Having been the victim all his business life of the pomposity of rich hotel clients, Lester had developed the hide of an alligator and was determined to follow the rules right down to the last dotted 'i.' In his mind there could be no variation on a theme.

"Then, sir," he said tonelessly, "may I have your name to check your registration status?"

Dunraven growled deep in his throat, and Lester had to bend his head to hear the fumbling and hissing words that came through the Earl's shaking lips.

"It shall be the first and last time you hear my name. I am Windham Thomas Whyham-Quin, the fourth Earl of Dunraven and owner of this damn hotel. Now, see to the Lady Florence's luggage and then consider yourself fired."

"That may well be the case, sir, but the rules as stipulated by the Estes Park Company, Ltd. are that no gentleman may have a lady in his room unless she is his lawful wife."

"I didn't mean for that silly damn rule to apply to me!" Dunraven shouted so loudly that it echoed through the English Hotel lobby and started the dog to yapping.

Other guests were beginning to take note of the encounter and snickering. Being personal friends of the Earl they were well aware that he was there sans wife and some even resented his elevating the actress to a titled position. They now looked at Florence Dubbins with sly grins. She appeared to be dissolving. She shrank back, as if lashed. She recognized several "gentlemen" who would have been more than friendly to her—had they not had their wives in tow. She thrust the poodle firmly against her breast, as though it were her shield against such accusations.

Lord Dunraven, in one bound, was past Charles

Lester. He rushed up the stairs as if all hell was at his heels. Only at the top did he pause and motion for Lady Florence to follow him.

Lester moved quickly to block her approach to the stairs and glared up at the Earl.

"Sir, as of this moment you are *persona non grata.* You will vacate your room at once!"

Shrugging, shivering a little, Florence Dubbins raced across the lobby and out onto the porch. She could not stand one more minute of such humiliation.

Lord Dunraven did not answer. He composed his features and marched haughtily back down the stairs. He ignored Charles Lester as though he were not even there.

His anger now was at Florence Dubbins for causing him to chase after her and making it appear that the servant had won out over the master. His anger was also building toward all of his good friends who had stood by snickering and had not stepped forward to make the supercilious little man realize that he *was* the Earl.

He ignored Florence Dubbins as though she were the plague and waved over Griff Evans.

"Have your wife prepare the Dunraven Cottage for me."

"It's full. Everything is full. What happened? Did they rent your room?"

Evans was the last man in the world he wished to indulge with what would become common gossip. He could almost hear the laughter this would cause at his expense. Then he began to laugh, loudly, raucously.

"Get Folsom over here with his stagecoaches," he

ordered, suddenly gleeful. "I don't care if he has to run night and day, but my guests are leaving."

Evans blinked. "But some just arrived with you."

"And they can depart with me."

"But what about the hotel?"

"As far as I am concerned it can perish!"

It was called petty, the callous act of a weakling, a wastrel, a fool. Lord Dunraven never again set foot inside its doors or ever again visited his fiefdom.

Theo Whyte and the Estes Park Company, Ltd. would continue to run the hotel for several more seasons, *sans* titled non-paying guests, but still at a financial loss and great drain on the British corporation. Theo Whyte would continue to operate the Estes Park Cattle Company, but rangeland grass was getting scarcer with so many head of cattle and they were sold off for little more than the mortgage owed upon them. Theo Whyte continued to acquire land for the fiefdom, but the price he had to pay put a further financial burden on the corporation.

Jim McLaughlin saw the decline of the rangeland coming and sold out before he was fenced completely in. Over the strong objections of Lloyd, the Austin land was sold, except for the forty acres upon which the Aspen Inn stood.

Theo Whyte went to court and cunningly won back all the Goold land but two outlying claims. But his day in court was short lived. The Estes Park Company, Ltd. was indicted, along with thirty-two fictitious name filings. Case after case Whyte began to lose and the land put back on the block for reclaiming. Those who got the land were also becoming shrewd and put a stiff resale value upon it. Dunraven, his interest waning, refused to invest further. Theo Whyte ignored the order and mortgaged the hotel with David Moffat. The First National Bank of Denver was not going to accept the mortgage unless the hotel was just as heavily insured and could prove to be profitable. To attract tourists Whyte changed its name to The Estes Park Hotel. Still it lost money and the lost claim cases were beginning to make holes in the fiefdom.

The Earl of Estes, however, was granted one wish. The hotel did perish. A mysterious fire burned it to the ground. The only loser was the insurance company.

A twenty-five-year-old widow was not a rarity in the Colorado territory. But men still outnumbered women by about ten to one and they did not remain widows very long.

Dorothy was a rarity. She was now a woman living within a carefully constructed shell. Losing the land case was just one more bitter blow. She divorced herself from all dealings with A.Q. MacGregor, deeded Aspen Inn to Lloyd Folsom and accepted the stage line investment money from David Folsom without comment.

She was rid of the Earl, but didn't feel victorious. She had fought his dream for so long that she couldn't see that it was slowly becoming her dream. But it was too late. The land was losing its primeval state. Too much publicity was bringing in a new form of landgrabber. Saw mills went up and forests came down.

Because the Hupp Hotel was the stage depot, John Hupp began to sell his land in lots and not acres. A general store, blacksmith shop and livery became the nucleus for the far flung community.

It was not to Dorothy's liking and she crawled off like a wounded animal to heal herself in the only place left to her—her land at the upper end of Horseshoe Park. She called upon John Cleave, who had stayed on to homestead after building the English Hotel, to now build her a home. Here the land was still in its natural state. Chapin, Chiquita and Mount Ypsilon looked down on her protectively.

E.J. Lamb, the only visitor she would allow, outside of the builders, was enchanted with her location.

"One makes errors, my dear; one is engulfed in the grief of death; one runs away from the world. And one believes that in these moments they are the center of the universe. Instead of rising to meet the challenge, so many become bitter and lonely islands. You have so much to offer to the world and so much of God's beauty to share. Don't be selfish."

The lumber wagons continued to roll up the Fall River and into Horseshoe Park until questions began to be raised as to what manner of a house John Cleave was building for the hermit. To the chagrin of all, John Cleave and his workers silently shrugged and rolled the wagons on.

To those newcomers who didn't know her it was an unnatural phenomenon for a young widow woman to be out in the wilderness all by herself. Most were envious because she kept the talented John Cleave so busy that they could not get him for their own construction purposes.

The old timers, who did know her, had learned to hold their tongues. They knew that she never did anything without a good reason. Besides, they were becoming just as disturbed as she.

The land cases were being tried just as diligently in the newspapers as in the courts. Daily headlines blared the latest events in "The Greatest Land Grab Scheme in Territorial History." When an animal is down and wounded it doesn't take long for the vultures to gather. For every honest man who rolled his wagon around Steamboat Rock and onto the toll road, there was also a fast-buck speculator.

That winter everyone soon forgot to question what Dorothy Goold Austin was about and hardly noticed the heavily laden wagons and workmen who came up from Longmont and vanished into Horseshoe Park. There were too many strangers in town to notice them and two words were on everyone's lips. Gold and silver.

Prospectors tents sprang up everywhere and those with legitimate claims once again found themselves fighting to get rid of a new form of squatter. The thirty claims lost by the Estes Park Company, Ltd. were resold ten and twelve times that winter, each time at a higher 'sucker's market' value. Shanty businesses sprang up on each side of the stage depot and for awhile the community boomed.

By early spring every ounce of Central City gold and Leadville silver that the speculators salted upon the claims they wished to sell had been found and carted away—or replaced by the finder to resell the land. Some tried to keep the stories of lost gold mines alive, but the bubble had already burst. It had been a hoax. The tents evaporated almost as quickly as they had sprung up. Some of the businesses stayed, hoping for a different kind of gold.

In that same early spring, Dorothy Goold Austin's secret was revealed. For a time, among the locals at least, it was one of the wonders of the world. Cleave was a painstaking and exacting carpenter. It was indeed a Swiss chalet set in the valley of its own Alps. The window shutters were painted in brightly colored designs, which were mirrored in its own lake. But the real marvel, which everyone came by wagon and horseback to see, was the water-wheel electrical generating system which gave the Horseshoe Chalet illumination, if sometimes a bit flickering. Because the water supply was also at a higher point of gravity, each of the thirty guest rooms had an eastern style pull chain flush box and a galvanized bathtub.

For all its beauty, charm and modern conveniences, most saw the flaw that Dorothy was unable to see.

A.Q. MacGregor was never one to mince words: "It's improper for a woman, widow or not, to run a business by herself. Women just don't possess that much know-how and brain power."

Georginna Henney winked at Dorothy to hold her silence. They each knew differently.

But it upset Dorothy in a way that MacGregor would never have understood. She would have a man with her, if the boy had been strong enough to be a man.

A thousand times she had thought about Lloyd—lost to her forever, dominated as much now by his father as Fred had once been—and the waste of it all made her throat contract anew. She had vowed all winter not to see Lloyd and had staunchly kept her vow. He was the man, he should have come to her. But he was the only one out of her past who had not come to view her secret. Even David Folsom, plush from the wealth the stage line had made him during the false gold boom, had arrogantly come to see a surrey business out to the Chalet from the stage depot. She had swallowed her anger, reminding herself that it was only business, and quietly granted him the contract.

Tomorrow was her opening day, and the curious were keeping her from her work. She put them out of her mind; put MacGregor's words out of her mind. Work had kept her from thinking before, and work would keep her from thinking now. She had hired a staff and they had to be trained. She didn't need anybody. She could do it all alone.

"Rats!" a stout woman exclaimed, as Dorothy sailed through the kitchen. "Mrs. Austin, this box is all saucers and no cups."

"Isn't there another box?"

"Nope. Must still be in town. Most of the kitchen utensils ain't been delivered yet, either."

"I'll get one of the men to go into town."

"They're all working down with Mr. Cleave to finish the barn."

She nodded helplessly. On that point she could agree with Alex MacGregor. She was being pulled a hundred different ways at once. But she could hire a man to help her, she didn't have to marry him. But first things first. She had not been to town in months, but went out to hitch up the surrey and start the seven miles into town.

It infuriated her that she had almost forgotten how to hitch a horse to a wagon. She fumbled with the couplings and a hand came from behind her to help.

She spun. Lloyd was hesitant to look at her, and his handsome face flushed shyly. But when Dorothy saw him, the gloom left her.

"Lloyd!" she cried. "You here! I'm ever so glad you came to see my chalet!"

"And I'm glad to see you," Lloyd said gently. "Here, let me fix that."

"Never mind," she said, on an instant impulse. "I've suddenly decided not to go to town."

"Why?" Lloyd said.

"Because it's now more important to stay here and offer you a job. Come, let me show you around."

"I didn't come for a job," he said sullenly, "nor to see your new toy."

Dorothy studied him closely. The winter had altered him. He, too, had become a hermit to sort out his thoughts. He had closed Aspen Inn and gone to work in one of the saw mills, felling many of the trees that had become her Swiss chalet. He was now magnificently built, with a great new tawny beard and massive curls that fell to his shoulders. He wore a colored shirt, open at the throat, so that Dorothy could see his mighty neck.

Purposely she did not ask his reason for being there and remained silent.

Lloyd stood there looking at her. Never had she appeared so beautiful to him. Then he said, his voice endlessly deep and tender:

"I can't accept Aspen Inn, Dorothy. I couldn't leave, though, without coming to say goodbye."

Dorothy surged forward and buried herself in his arms.

"Lloyd," she whispered. "Oh, Lloyd, you can't leave!"

"I can't stay," he murmured.

"But this is wrong," she cried. "Don't you understand? This is wrong."

"Wrong of me not to come work for you?"

"No, wrong of you not to follow your heart!"

"Oh, hell," Lloyd groaned, "I know what is in my heart. But what will people say?"

"What do I care what people say!" Dorothy said suddenly, fiercely. Then she instantly calmed. "No, I'm wrong. I do care what they say, but for your sake, not mine. You are the one they would make suffer. I love you very much—more than I ought to. And I've been loved more than any woman has any right to by Fred. I'm very grateful for that. Others might say that we defiled his name while he lay in his grave, but I can't believe that Fred would say that. Thank you for coming, Lloyd. Suddenly, all of the ghosts have vanished."

"Then why don't you follow your heart, Dorothy? Will you marry me?"

Dorothy stared at him, her eyes very wide and very green.

"I-I don't know," she said slowly.

"All right," he said, hitching his horse to the surrey. "Get in. You can think about it as we ride into town."

They rode for several miles without speaking, then Dorothy leaned over and took Lloyd's hand.

"You have my heart," she said gently.

Lloyd grinned broadly. "I didn't think it would be otherwise. That's why I told the horse to head directly for the minister's place."

The Earl of Estes had dreamed of a three hundred thousand acre private domain. The majority of what he gained was retained for thirty-three years. Then, when his fame and fortune returned to him in Ireland, he sold it for what he could get and cleared out.

His name and plan had been cursed. But his control of the land for so long was a blessing in disguise. The land was kept as God had created it.

Of his three hundred thousand acre dream, the federal government in 1915 made Rocky Mountain National Park out of two hundred sixty-three thousand, seven hundred and ninety-one acres of the highest and most rugged mountain country. In later years the homestead rights within the national park were negotiated upon so that the area would remain virgin. So today you cannot see where once stood Dorothy and Lloyd's chalet, Minnie and Abner Sprague's Lodge—or Stead Ranch—or Fall River Lodge—or . . .

Only Dorothy's dream—the mountains never change.

The rest of the valley vastly changed.

Before he died at the age of eighty-five the Earl wrote: ". . . But I would love to see again the place I knew so well . . ."

He would recognize only three things—the Dunraven Cottage, the Elkhorn Lodge and the MacGregor Ranch—which is preserved in the original state in which three generations of MacGregors lived upon it.

He would find few recognizable names from his era, not even of his own kin.

Dorothy and Lloyd were granted three daughters and ten grandchildren. None of these generations stayed in the park. Everything changes but the mountains.

TWELFTH IN
THE MAKING OF AMERICA
SERIES

THE RIVER PEOPLE

In the 1800s the Mississippi and the Missouri Rivers were the great roadway that bore men and women westward in search of wealth, glory and a new way of life. The path was turbulent, dangerous, fraught with hazards—often deadly.

The people who traveled on the rivers were diverse: there were lovers, warriors, winners and losers. Among these were two proud and lovely young women, Georgia and Clarissa, and two brave and mysterious men, Eaton and Casey. Their personal destinies were to be profoundly entwined with America's legendary westward thrust on the powerful currents of the great rivers.

BE SURE TO READ *THE RIVER PEOPLE*—
ON SALE NOW FROM DELL/BRYANS